𝔚𝔢 𝔴𝔢𝔯𝔢 𝔫𝔬𝔱

I froze, eyes w...
sense desperately ...wath
through the foggy n...

In that single breat... silence, a sonorous melody lifted across the sky.

The clock tower at the peak of Westminster Abbey sang a lilting warning.

The first and only bell gonged, and the darkness shattered.

I felt it come before it reached me, but I was too slow. A warm body slammed into me, a man's body, impossible to see but heavier than me and broad enough to send me careening into the side of the club.

My shoulder rebounded off the rough brick siding, sending stars of pain shooting through my vision.

I pushed off the wall, blind but determined, ignored the frightful pain in my shoulder. I heard the *clip-clop-clip* of hooves on the cobbled road across the yard.

Someone was coming, and that alone was permission enough for me to give chase.

By Karina Cooper

The St. Croix Chronicles
GILDED
TARNISHED

Dark Mission Novels
SACRIFICE THE WICKED
ALL THINGS WICKED
LURE OF THE WICKED
BLOOD OF THE WICKED

Dark Mission Novellas
NO REST FOR THE WITCHES
BEFORE THE WITCHES

KARINA COOPER

Gilded

THE ST. CROIX CHRONICLES

AVON

An Imprint of HarperCollinsPublishers

AVON BOOKS
An Imprint of HarperCollins*Publishers*
10 East 53rd Street
New York, New York 10022-5299

Copyright © 2013 by Karina Cooper
ISBN 978-0-06-212766-2
www.avonromance.com

First Avon Books mass market printing: January 2013

Avon Trademark Reg. U.S. Pat. Off. and in Other Countries, Marca Registrada, Hecho en U.S.A.
HarperCollins® is a registered trademark of HarperCollins Publishers.

Printed in the U.S.A.

10 9 8 7 6 5 4 3 2 1

In memory of Caleb "Flip" Kors.
Keep on shining, little man.

Acknowledgments

Writing a novel set with a certain amount of historical accuracy is never a one-woman job. The amount of research that goes into a world modeled on our own history is a lengthy, often mazelike endeavor, and I'd be lost without help from the tools of the modern day and the patience of friends and fellow writers.

Where would I be without the internet? I will tell you where I wouldn't be: huddled in a dusty library bent over ancient microfiche, that's for sure. So to you, internet, and those who populate it, I tip my hat. From scanned copies of the *Leeds Mercury* to transcribed articles from gossip columns of the era, you made my research fun, easy, and fascinating.

Maire Claremont and Sarah MacLean: How you keep track of titles, courtesy titles, peerage titles in one's own right and so forth is utterly beyond me. Somehow, between your help and the eagle eye of *Gilded*'s copyeditor, I've managed to keep social faux pas down to a minimum. Bless you with whatever blessings you consider most fine, and add chocolate besides.

Esi: For the hours spent on the phone, working out the details of a story that is as delicate as it is tragic. Thank you for having faith in me; and pushing me when you knew I had it in me to tweak just a *little bit* more.

You darling readers: The St. Croix Chronicles continue to be a fun romp through a re-imagined era, and I must take the time to thank all of you who join Cherry on her many misadventures. You will visit again, won't you?

Yours most faithfully,
Karina Cooper

Chapter One

When I was ten years of age, Monsieur Marceaux's Traveling Circus retained a new magician. Unlike his jolly, rotund predecessor, this man was everything a so-called practitioner of the dark arts should be—tall, lean in build, darkly handsome like a hero out of an overwrought Byronic fantasy, and possessed of a fine sense of showmanship.

His tricks were dangerous things. I was an ambitious child, cloaked under a shroud of opium-induced amnesia, eager to taste all that this life of Gypsy freedom could give me.

By the time Mr. Oliver Ashmore, the executor of my father's estate, found me some three years later, I had been locked inside trunks that were then speared by wicked curved blades, hung suspended from my ankles over pits of fire; shackled, singed, chained, cut by accident and for the titillation to a paying audience, and taught how to escape even the meanest knots. Tight places had long since ceased to bother me. Dark places were my bread and butter.

Aside from my employ, little has changed.

My name is Cherry St. Croix, and I live two rather different lives. In one, I am a collector, a seeker of bounties for coin. In the other, I make my home above London's dreary fog. At twenty years old, I am months away from legally inheriting my late father's estate, and by all accounts, I am considered a well-heeled young miss.

Or would have been, were it not for the tarnishing legacy of my mad father.

They say that my mother, Josephine, came from good stock. Aside from the ill fortune of perishing in a fire, she had been blessed by the favor of Society; a lady whose graces numbered many. I have inherited her green eyes and her hair—a deep shade of auburn red fancied by opera singers and actresses— but very few of her societal charms.

In contrast, I am reminded at every turn that my mother married down. My father had been a middle-class doctor, a scientist touched by a bit of genius—and more than a whisper of insanity, if the tales were to be believed.

I believed them. How could I not? My father was the reason I now stood in this dark place, forced to put my hard-won confidence to the test.

A test I had earlier failed.

This was the thirtieth day of September. I had already stood in this tunnel earlier this month, listening to these very same whispers, with no clue that the man who waited in the dark was the same man all swore perished years ago in the flames of a Scotland estate, my mother beside him.

Every sense I possessed urged me to flee; then and now.

As I could not then, I could not now.

"Zylphia, bring the light," I called, perhaps too loudly. The interior of the Thames Tunnel plucked the words from my lips and carried them on sibilant waves down the dank corridor.

I could only blame the rapid pace of my heart-beat, thudding loudly inside my chest. The sound filled my ears; had since the moment we'd stepped through the twin tunnel entry. Fear stole my breath, but it came like a dream. Shrouded memories plucked at my thoughts until I felt harried from all sides.

I had nearly died here.

But, I reminded myself sternly, the ghosts I sensed in the darkness were merely nonsense. Chilling echoes of coming winter and the dank bite of the river-saturated air. My father was dead, well and truly. I'd seen him killed myself.

The tunnel on either side of me remained empty, and would be until the next train passed through.

Which would be soon enough that we should be quicker.

Years ago, after decades of planning and work, the Thames Tunnel finally saw completion and opened to the public. A marvel of engineering, it burrowed under the River Thames, providing access from Wapping to Rotherhithe. Initially a pedestrian cross-ing and gawker's paradise, the East London Railway Company repurposed it, and now the trains trav-eled through the tunnel at regular intervals.

The dark played host to the occasional vagrants, prostitutes plying their trade, rumored entrances into the mysterious Underground, and—more re-cently—a secret laboratory.

I shuddered, only partially from the chill of the late September air. This far beneath, the dank gloom took on a life of its own. The lanterns kept lit at intervals did little for either the cold or the dark, and I caught myself rubbing my arms through my filched sack coat as my assistant came closer with her own lantern aloft.

"What did you find, *cherie*?"

I found it small comfort that I wasn't alone this time. Zylphia had once been a prostitute for the Midnight Menagerie, yet she now served as my maid—and, of course, fellow conspirator. Called sweets by patrons and Menagerie hands alike, the women taken in by the Menagerie earned their keep in flesh.

Although her skills numbered far beyond that of seduction, Zylphia was doomed to forever look the role. Even in her simple trousers, thick fustian jacket and plain waistcoat, something about her long build and effortless carriage drew the eye. Unlike me, who could often pass for a somewhat rotund street boy in the dark and with distance, there was no world in which anyone could mistake Zylphia's figure for that of a man.

An exotic mulatto, she boasted skin the same color as black tea lightened with a small bit of cream. Her eyes were shockingly blue against her dark skin, legacy of her unknown white father, while her hair was black as the night, coarser than mine but pliable, with enough unusual kink to point to her Negro slave mother. Tonight, like mine, it was pulled up into a severe knot and pinned harshly.

Unlike me, she did nothing to hide the color— black was not uncommon a shade, especially with her obviously dark skin. Which was why I continued to coat lampblack through my own red tresses when I took on the mantle of my collector's role. Far be it from anyone to put two and two together and attach the name of Cherry St. Croix to the black-haired collector drifting about the fog.

Or to the strange goings-on of a few weeks past. Corpses whose organs had been carved away, mad professors, opium dens, deals made with the Midnight Menagerie . . .

And strange symbols carved into tunnel walls.

Exactly the sort of thing one would expect from a madcap adventure tale.

I beckoned with a gloved hand. Zylphia brought the lantern closer to the damp wall. The light flickered, casting the stone into sharp relief.

"Just some etchings, do you think?" But even my maid's tone retained enough doubt to echo my own thoughts.

I crouched, bracing one hand against the cold stone for balance. "It's low enough to remain out of accidental view," I said slowly, eyebrows knotting in concentration. "A marker of some kind."

"You think it points the way to the Underground?"

I shook my head, brushing away a clinging film as the light glistened off the carved edges. "Anyone who wants to find the Underground won't be relying on pictures." My voice bandied back at me even as the dark attempted to swallow it. I waved my free hand in front of my face, as if I could swat the echoes away like buzzing flies. "It's all word of mouth, on pain of . . ." I paused. "Well, there are worse things than death."

"Charming," my friend replied dryly. "Have you ever been?"

"Once." And never again, if I had my way.

"Do you recognize it, then?"

No. It was not something I'd ever seen before. I

studied the grooves carved into the stone, tracing each line with a gloved finger. A complex *E*, the bottom two rungs stretched too far, attached to a smaller *y*. "Eye?" I said aloud, testing it on my tongue. "That makes no sense."

"A name? Initials?"

Neither of which belonged to my father. Abraham St. Croix was a mouthful on any given day, and even his secret alias would begin with a *W*. When I met him, Professor Elijah Woolsey had seemed to be a harmless, rambling man with excellent scientific theories.

How wrong I'd been.

At the time, I hadn't told Zylphia the identity of the mad professor. I didn't intend to now. There were things that defied explanation. One's late father taking to secret laboratories in the Thames Tunnel, eager to supplant your soul with that of your mother's, numbered among them.

"Perhaps it's only a memory carved by a vagrant," I mused.

"Not many vagrants what know their letters," Zylphia pointed out, but needlessly. I knew that. I was just . . . hoping.

This little carving, whatever it meant, was my father's doing. It had to be.

"Search for more." I pointed to the wall. "This height, perhaps. There may be other letters. Perhaps they form a clue, or a word. Directions." *Anything.*

"Right, miss." The lantern bobbed as Zylphia shuffled along the wall. To her credit, she had a keen set of eyes and solid knack for common sense. That she had been assigned to me by the Chinese masters of the Midnight Menagerie still stung, but Zylphia had been as near a thing to a friend I could claim in this identity, and that long before she became my keeper.

As per our agreement, the things she reported of my movements were things that would not cost me anything for the Karakash Veil to know. I worried for her, in this double role. The last time she'd kept a secret from the Veil, I'd found whipping marks upon her back. With that in mind, I retained Zylphia as an in-house maid, and did my best to protect her.

When she allowed it. As stubborn as I, my friend.

I shook my head, leavening a deep sigh. This was not the way I'd hoped to spend my evening. In my expectant fantasies, I'd imagined locating my father's laboratory, stripping it of all useful items, finding the serum he'd concocted in his madness, and then . . .

Well, I hadn't quite thought that far.

In exchange for saving my life from the very same alchemical compound my father had developed, I found myself indebted to the Veil. The price for my freedom?

The Veil demanded the compound—the *móshù*, as they called it—that nearly killed me.

Micajah Hawke, the dark ringmaster of the Menagerie and mouthpiece of the furtive Chinese organization that owned him, swore that he'd had this entire tunnel searched and found nothing.

I would not walk away empty-handed. It was here. I knew it was here.

Unfortunately, my memory is not what it once was. Things in the past, even things more recent of late, often fuzz to a gentle blur. Much as it did when I was younger. I remember bits, and sometimes larger pieces, but try as I might, I could not remember the path taken either in or out of the ruddy laboratory.

My longtime association with the base chemical

in Abraham's serum suggested the opium was to blame. Much of my life is colored by it—and, an unfortunate side effect, swallowed by it.

I pushed at the symbol. Nothing happened. *E* and *y*.

Initials, Zylphia had suggested. Perhaps she wasn't far wrong.

Elijah began with an *E*. And Woolsey ended with a small *y*, at least when handwritten. Perhaps it truly was that uncomplicated?

I braced the whole of my hand over the carving, testing each nook and cranny. When the brick failed to give away, I moved on to others. In a slow, circular pattern, I poked and prodded and gouged my gloved fingers into every edge and divot.

In my choice of work, I had learned to expect even that which seemed preposterous. A hidden catch seemed something out of a Gothic adventure tale; it also seemed rather likely, given my father's predilections.

Click. "Eureka," I murmured.

A bit of brick withdrew beneath my right thumb. "Zylla!"

She came quickly, lantern light bobbing. "What—"

"*Shh.*" Even as I levied the scolding sound, something caught inside the tunnel wall. Scraping, grating together, as if two slabs of stone ground against each other; I listened to an internal mechanism I couldn't picture and counted the seconds.

It took twelve before a seam split along the tunnel wall. Bricks, jagged and sharp, swung outward, causing me to leap into Zylphia and send us both staggering back over the railway lines. My foot caught on a rail spike, tossed me to the cobbled ground. "Oomph!"

I'd fallen many, many times in my life. I had never managed to become gracious about it.

"Are you all right?" My companion caught my arm, helped me back to my graceless feet.

"Delightful," I replied by sardonic rote, but did not stop for niceties. Balance once more firmed, I hurried to the newly formed entrance. Seized the edge of the door, hesitated.

Was I ready for this?

Musty air, oddly sharp and smelling of wet iron, ghosted out from the portal. Though the interior swallowed any hope of clear vision in its murky depths, I didn't need sight to tell me I'd found it.

Something about the smell, maybe, like wet iron or rust. That sharp, acrid smell of the air after a lightning strike. Or perhaps it was the way every fine hair on my skin rose to sudden, nerve-prickling attention.

Without having to be told, Zylphia held the lantern out for me to take. "Is this it, then?"

"It must be," I whispered. There couldn't be so many hidden laboratories in the Thames Tunnel. Of course I was sure. And even if I wasn't, a single step into the dark, yawning vault beyond was enough. Shapes loomed in sudden relief.

My heart leapt into my throat. All at once, I couldn't breathe.

There were the mechanical gurneys laid side by side. There, between them, the tower built to connect the bodies that had once lain on each table.

I had been one, strapped into place by banded metal and injected by the formula he claimed had come from alchemy.

My mother, rotted and gone, had been the other.

Alchemy, that scientific superstition. That myth among otherwise brilliant men.

Just a story, I'd been so sure . . .

My knuckles whitened around the lantern, metal haft biting in my flesh, but I couldn't let go. I couldn't take even one more step. As my heart thudded and my stomach soured from the memory, I looked into the abandoned, cobwebbed interior of my father's grave and could not force myself to move.

Here, I had nearly lost myself. As Abraham St. Croix forced his liquid nightmare into my flesh, I'd dreamed of the ghost of my mother and begged for mercy. To no avail. My father, my own bloody father, had sacrificed his daughter to bring his beloved wife back from the dead, and I had very nearly succumbed.

Here, the man I swore to apprehend for slaughtering Menagerie sweets had saved my life, and in so doing, murdered Mad St. Croix, once and for all.

My knees buckled.

A hand touched my shoulder. "It's still too soon after your ordeal," Zylphia said softly behind me. Understanding. "Shall I go for you?"

She only knew part of the tale: the kidnapping, the drugging. The madness. I'd deliberately left out the bits naming Woolsey as my father, and any such memories that seemed too fantastical to be truth. I did not believe in magic. Science and fact; these were things that a lady could count on.

Magic was the recourse of the unenlightened. And my memories were only the product of opium dreams spun from that ruddy serum.

But the corpse of my father, that would be real.

I stiffened, shaking my head. I had to see. "Zylla, do *not* touch anything."

"Not even if my life depends upon it," she said, matter-of-fact aversion. Anyone who spent any amount of time among the likes of the Menagerie knew better than to muck about with things one didn't understand.

In my case, I knew how dangerous any laboratory could be. I'd grown up among them.

I stepped over pipes I didn't remember, stirred up dust with every footfall. The laboratory was dark, and I didn't dare throw a switch. The last I remembered, electricity had crawled across the metal girders, the rafters, even along the pipes laid out across the floor. The currents traveling across every metal surface in the area must have left at least some remaining charge; I didn't dare risk it.

I remembered my father's laughter. And my mother's eyes.

Only she was dead, wasn't she?

Actually dead.

I passed the first table, copper bindings left hanging loose where I'd picked the lock to get free. The thinner band that had been tightened around my head still dangled, motionless in the quiet tomb. I'd managed to roll off the table, I remembered that. The tube affixed within my arm had torn free; I no longer carried the mark left by it.

Like the first time I'd been drugged by the serum, my wounds had healed quickly.

And then . . . *His* voice. His whisper. *Not just a bounty after all.*

The murdering collector had saved me. Carried me out of the tunnel to vanish after.

I'd woken—not for the first time, but certainly I intended it to be the last—in Micajah Hawke's bed. Unsullied, as far as I could remember, but confused.

I raised the lantern high, flinching when the shadows danced at the outer edges of the golden light. Dust caked the gurney, unmarred after a month of idle abandonment.

But where there should have been more on the second table, there was not.

"Oh, bloody bells."

Somewhere behind me, my maid sighed. "And twice, for that."

"What?"

"You'll want to see this." I didn't. "Best get on with your bit first. What did you find, then?"

It's what I did *not* find. I rounded the table to stand directly in between both. In front of me, an amalgam of metal and wire tubing reached for the dark ceiling. Like spidery fingers, the ends of the tubes vanished into shadow.

But the slot, the groove where a golden cameo the size of my palm had once fit, remained empty.

The collector. He'd taken the cameo and the alchemical serum it held. It had to be him.

"The—" My tongue tangled on the words, and rightfully so. It seemed too gruesome an affair, even for my drug-addled memory. "The body that should be here is gone. And with it, the professor's work."

"Then that makes two for sure. You said the professor was killed here by the dials?"

I turned, stepped over wires and metal girders to where my maid waited. Beside her, a panel of switches and gauges remained grimy and dark.

I brought the lantern, held it over the place where she gestured.

The place where my father had stood last.

Blood dries to an oily brown, like embedded dirt or forgotten paint. Beneath a month's worth of dust, the color stained the floor in unshakeable evidence—I had not imagined everything.

A body had fallen here. Bled out here.

My father, stabbed through the heart.

But everything else was gone. The corpses I expected, the cameo bearing my mother's face, even the odds and ends I vaguely remember scattered upon the desk beyond the panel I stood beside.

Someone had come back for it all. And I suspected who.

I lowered the lantern slowly.

"I'm sorry, *cherie*." Zylphia did not like touching as a rule—legacy from her role as flesh for pay, I was sure—but for the second time that night, she touched my arm. Comfort, even small as it was.

I summoned a smile; it came wearily. "I had hoped, but it seems there are no answers for me tonight. I would have been better served finding a collector's bounty."

"At least you know it happened," Zylphia replied, her eyes earnest, for all they remained shadowed in the dim light provided by the lantern I held. "As you say, even."

I knew what it was she inferred. Unlike everyone else in my household, Zylphia knew of my love for laudanum. Began by the orphanage who relied heavily upon a trick of opium and treacle to keep their charges sedate, continued by Monsieur Marceaux's deliberate bribery, and carried on into my adult life. I used to take it to keep terrible nightmares at bay.

I took it once upon a time to calm my nerves.

I take it now because I must.

Its use had saved my life in this very laboratory. For without its constant supply, I would have succumbed to the serum and died—or worse.

It is a common adage among its heralds, that those who eat it always must eat the more.

I did not *eat* it. Only Turks and savages eat it whole, as if it were a sweet or bit of fruit to savor. Civilized folk here in England distill it, either by liquid or fire. I was not so far gone that I must take it raw on the tongue. Laudanum was my choice of draught.

However imbibed, I owed my life to its use.

"There's nothing here," I said with some asperity.

"But there used to be." My maid observed the laboratory through narrowed eyes, smudged in the lantern light. "Where'd it get off to, then?"

A good question. But not one I had the where-withal to answer. "Needless to simper about it. Come along. We'll be late if we tarry much longer."

"The twelfth bell is not long past." She took the lantern from my unresisting fingers. I frowned at the laboratory, at the empty, skeletal remains. There wasn't even a machine left to show my father's genius. Only the structures that once housed his mysterious electrical components.

As we left the laboratory, pulling the door once more closed behind us, I looked back. In the part of my mind that remained ever dreaming, I fancied I saw a pair of eyes. Watching, always watching. And in the still, musty air, I strained to hear a tuneless whistle in the dark.

Bodies did not simply vanish. This was not the last I'd deal with Mad St. Croix's legacy. Somehow, I knew it even then.

Perhaps it is, as they so often say, truly in the blood.

We exited the tunnel without trial, paused just long enough so that I could place my collecting gear firmly over my eyes.

The fog in London is a vicious thing, made of coal smoke and damp and stench. It sucks at the throat and stings at the eyes, especially for those who do not live among the pea-soup miasma.

I had developed my own pair of protectives for use when I hunted. One lens was tinted yellow, which I had discovered quite by accident to be ideal for peering through the fog bank. The other was plain, a simple circle of glass inset into a bolted metal brace and wrapped in thin leather for comfort.

Unfortunately, a tussle with a rival collector had cracked that lens into four separate pieces, and I lacked the means to repair it. So for now, I had one good lens and one buckled in place by a strip of leather.

The detachable respirator I left in its pouch. It tended to distort my voice, and I needed the freedom to speak with Zylphia, regardless of how often I'd have to clear my itching throat.

She did not carry the same concern. I found that many of the denizens of the lower reaches of London developed an affinity for the scratchy fog. Whether it came from growing used to it or, as I suspected, a certain kind of lung scarring that would be difficult to bear later in life, few were as bothered by the fog as those from above.

Like me.

For this reason, I remained careful not to tip my hand as to my origins.

As Zylphia adjusted her plain, clear goggles over her eyes, she turned to me. "Where do we go from this point, then?"

Unspoken came the obvious: We had no clues.

I shook my head, frowning briefly at the blackened tips of my gloved fingers. The lampblack in my hair tended to smear at the first sign of damp, and it was always damp in London below the drift. I was certain my forehead and cheeks had turned gray and blotched by now.

I did not dare forgo it, just as I did not dare shear the long, thick curls that were my mother's legacy. Caught between both worlds.

"Cherie?"

"I must go look at collection notices," I said abruptly, striding from the tunnel mouth. Just near Wapping, the tunnel didn't fall under the same pervasive fog as the rest of London. The stench of coal mixed with the rotting reek of the river just nearby provided the kind of fragrance that could stand to be scrubbed out of one's nose with a stiff brush and lye.

My maid hurried to catch up with my sudden frenetic pace. "What do you hope to find?"

"Anything." A clue. A sign that I was not the only body on this world who knew what went on in that tunnel. Perhaps a hint that the collector I hunted— the so-named sweet tooth Zylphia and her fellow sweets had hired me to collect—was still out there.

I knew he was. He left me flowers for every successful assassination he answered on the collection board.

He left them for me upon my windowsill, regardless of its height above the ground. Somehow, he knew who I was, and I only knew that he taunted me.

Yet, even as I considered it, it occurred to me that I had not seen flowers for near a fortnight now. Perhaps he'd injured himself on a bounty?

Or he was simply lying in wait. Like a serpent under a slimy rock.

I needed evidence. A trail that would lead me to him.

"We don't have time for a collection—"

"If 'tis easy," I cut in, "we'll risk it." Fishing a small, scratched pocket watch from a tiny pocket inside my collecting corset, I opened the brass facing not to calculate how much time I had left before I would be required home, but when the next train would pass.

Only a few minutes.

"I'll meet you at the West India Dock," I continued after a moment. "I'll have information, if all goes well."

I did not say aloud what we both knew. I would not let noncollectors into the place where all collectors went, and I would not trust Zylphia with the role.

We collectors tend to be a competitive lot. Supportive only when a bounty did not ride on it, and secretive beyond. Zylphia's role was complicated enough without adding the necessity for collection to it. I paid her a fair wage.

The money we acquired for bounties went entirely to easing the sting from my debt to the Veil. And, if there was any left over, to opium from the druggists below.

"If you're sure," she said slowly.

I was.

"Come, then," I told her, and hurried to make the Whitechapel connection.

Chapter Two

A city gripped by fear is an eerie place. Since the first prostitute was murdered in August, all of London below the drift has held its collective breath. Workers tended to their labor, the doxies of Commercial Road plied their trades from the dilapidated corners of haunted Whitechapel to the Limehouse district so named for its lime kilns, yet there seemed over it all a sense of waiting. Of watching.

We passed through the yellow- and black-tinted streets, painted luridly by gas lamps lit at irregular intervals and the damp that infested every cobble and corner. Zylphia said little, and I did not encourage conversation. My mind scattered along paths that held no promise of answers.

I was trapped. There would be no rescue, no saving me from the hole I'd dug unwittingly for myself. The fact of the matter was, I owed the criminal enterprise that ran much of Limehouse's Chinese population. Whether I liked it or not, they did save me from my father's serum.

Or, more precisely, Micajah Hawke saved me.

The methods by which he'd done so haunted me, but in the intervening month, I'd managed to shove those memories into a tiny compartment and had no intentions of inspecting them any closer.

Now, I only recalled the feel of his mouth upon me in the darkest part of the night, and I looked to the laudanum I had not been taking for those.

With my collecting coin cut so short, I could not afford the opium grains I had grown accustomed to. I rationed them dearly; and I keenly felt the loss.

It took careful use to balance my need with my supply.

I needed distractions. I needed, in some unconscious way, to exhaust myself, and I believed Zylphia knew that. This is why she went out with me most nights, despite the lengthy hours she kept by day acting as my housemaid.

The time, almost one o'clock of the morning, would allow for an easy bounty, assuming there would be one to collect. I would split with Zylphia just before we crossed into Limehouse, meet her at the West India Docks with—I hoped—information of that wayward collector and a handful of collections to perpetuate. At least one would need to be for coin, the rest for the Menagerie.

I had hopes that every Menagerie-funded bounty I turned in, but did not get paid for, would chip away at the debt the Veil held over me. I doubted it, but I needed leverage.

Raucous singing pierced the fog, the hoarse laughter of men and women deep in their cups echoing eerily through the darkness. Beyond the alleys we navigated, St. George-in-the-East played host to all manner of folk. The singing I heard told me we were

near the International Workingmen's Educational
Club; a front for immigrant anarchists, as well a favored social center.

I'd been inside once or twice, on the search for the
rare Jew hauled up on the bounty boards.

That put us practically on top of Dutfield's Yard.
"We'll go through here," I murmured, by habit as
well as an overabundance of concern. My voice is
a feminine one, and most footpads see females as
easy sport.

That made individuals foolish and groups more
than dangerous, but it would also waste my time.
Without my respirator, I erred on the side of caution.

Zylphia, no stranger to the dangers of these evening streets, only nodded.

Dutfield's Yard is one of many ways to travel from
back alleys to main streets. A narrow strip of yard
between the club and Berner Street, it had seen my
passage before and would probably do so again.
Few bothered to pay much attention to the comings
and goings of the bodies that traipsed through the
gates. The large gate should have been closed this
late, but rarely was.

The shadows clinging to the interior of the yard
were thick as treacle and deucedly difficult to see
through. Black as pitch, and this even with the
lights from the surrounding tenements struggling
to pierce the pea souper.

I was used to dark places, and I thought nothing
of it as we passed through the four-foot-wide gate
left open to the alley behind us. Already, as my feet
navigated a path I knew by rote, my mind lingered
over the many troubles weighing upon my shoulders.

It was Zylphia who scented the disturbance first.

I felt her stiffen beside me. Then a hand, reaching perhaps for my shoulder but missing in the dark and colliding with my back instead. I grunted a surprised exhale, the sound slipping into the yard and taking wing.

But the echo that came back was not something the dark crafted alone.

A gurgle, strangled as if a breath struggled to escape through mud or worse, and an intake of air. Nearly a growl.

We were not alone.

I froze, eyes wide and painful as every sense desperately tried to carve a swath through the foggy night.

In that single breath of silence, weighted by what seemed an eternity of sudden, crushing fear, a sonorous melody lifted across the sky.

The clock tower at the peak of Westminster Abbey, whose chimes could be heard far as the Menagerie on even the thickest of soot-ridden days, sang a lilting warning.

The first and only bell gonged, one o'clock, and the darkness shattered.

I felt it come before it reached me, but I was too slow. A warm body slammed into me, a man's body, impossible to see but heavier than me and broad enough to send me careening into the side of the club.

My shoulder rebounded off the rough brick siding, sending stars of pain shooting through my vision, and I heard Zylphia cry out as the same figure crashed into her. But this time, I also heard the tangle of feet, a scuffle, a grunted impact with the ground. He hadn't expected two of us; he must have tripped over Zylphia as she floundered.

I pushed off the wall, blind but determined, ignored the frightful pain in my shoulder to run for the same narrow gate we'd only just entered. I heard the *clip-clop-clip* of hooves on the cobbled road across the yard.

Someone was coming, and that alone was permission enough for me to give chase. Whoever manned the pony and cart I heard entering from Berner Street could tend to the body I suspected had made that terrible bubbling sound; I had a footpad to catch.

I don't wholly understand myself at times. I am a collector. By very definition, I have no reason to give chase if I do not have the coin promised.

Yet something about that night—that dark enclosure and the bulk of the man who slammed into me—demanded I chase him. So I obeyed the instinct to follow and sprinted out of the pitch-black yard, through the gate, into the narrow street that was little more than an alley.

Footsteps echoed, splashing through puddles from every direction, but longtime familiarity with the streets of London below allowed me to discern the pattern. I turned right, followed the uneven, heavy tread. Through the yellow lens of my goggles, I picked out a shape—broad, like I'd already deduced, wrapped in a heavy overcoat. Too dark to see more than the silhouette of a man and his hat, but enough.

Nobody ran unless they were guilty of something.

I heard Zylphia's voice behind me, but I ignored her in favor of the chase. Sweat gathered across my shoulders—I came to regret the man's coat I wore over my rigidly plated collecting corset, but I didn't dare pause to shed its weight. My shoulder ached fiercely; I feared I'd twisted the joint or something just as unfortunate, yet I could not stop.

"Halt!" I shouted, my voice rebounding across the narrow cobbles.

He did not. They never did.

As I ran, I became aware that the footsteps grew fainter. But the shouting of voices behind me, somewhere in the direction of the yard I'd left behind, grew louder. Shriller.

Finally, I burst out of the alley onto Commercial Road, my hair clinging to my sweat-damp cheeks and my breath rasping in my lungs. I bent over, gasping, a fierce knot of raw agony stitched in my side, and realized that while I'd plenty of strange looks from the knot of women lounging by the alley mouth beside me, I had no more quarry.

The fog swirled in the street, streaks of gray and white and lamp-lit gold turned filthy by soot.

I sucked in a hard breath, straightened with effort. My ribs burned against my corset; my shoulder throbbed, and I clutched it in my right hand. "A man," I gasped.

One of the women, a dumpling of a thing with a sour face, laughed outright. "Wot's yer type?"

I didn't bother with censure. These were prostitutes; one of many soiled doves working the streets. "Broad, dark overcoat long enough to flap as he ran. Out of breath?"

I received only blank stares for my trouble.

Bloody bells and damn. I turned, peering down the narrow corridor, but I saw nothing. Heard nothing more than the mild din of an uproar farther up the road. And a voice, I realized. Coming closer, shrill and fearful.

"Oh, bother," I muttered.

"Murder!"

The women started, three of them sending up a shriek piercing enough to wake the dead. "Oh, it's 'im!" one cried. " 'E's found ano'ver!"

It seemed that way.

The murderer known through the broadsheets as Leather Apron had already slashed the throats of two women. One in late August, one in early September. The things he'd done to their corpses, to their organs, were the stuff of nightmares.

I could not blame them their fear. Especially since I knew, or at least had been reassured, that there were two such killers in London, and more victims than had been printed in the papers. One, the collector working at the behest of my father. His victims— midnight sweets, all of them—had never made it into public awareness. The Menagerie made sure of that.

The other was this Leather Apron.

Talentless lout, the collector had snarled when pressed for answers. *Eager for attention*. Such derision in the words.

Did I interrupt the very same killer this night?

I watched as the women hurried away across the street, into the well-lit interior of a shop whose upper floors likely provided lodging. Watched still as a man, eyes wild and voice already tearing, sprinted past me. "Murder, murder! Fetch the rozzers!"

With that sort of ruckus, the constables would find him first.

I leaned against the brick facing, forcing myself to breathe, to collect my composure once more, and waited for Zylphia to find me.

I'd taken a right good knock. My shoulder ached clear to my elbow, snaked around my ribs. Whether it was that pain or something triggered by it, my lungs burned. Ached with every breath.

It'd take some time before I'd be able to tell if I'd done myself in, but I wasn't sure if I should risk a bounty as I was.

My companion would have me turn in; I knew it.

She wasn't wrong, either. 'Twas dangerous work I chose, and an injury could so easily compound into something worse. As I waited, I gingerly unfolded my arm, bent it at the elbow. It wasn't until I attempted to raise it at a perpendicular did agony tear through the tender joint.

I hissed in a breath, clapped my bent arm to my chest. The rotter. How could I have been so clumsy?

Zylphia didn't take long to find me. As she approached, I tipped my head and led the way up the street, in the opposite direction of the morbidly curious hurrying to the scene I'd left behind. She was silent as she matched my pace. Only once were we well out of hearing of any constables or curious ears did she offer explanation. "There's a dead twist in Dutfield's Yard."

A woman, then. "And?"

Her gaze, shockingly blue even behind her glass protectives, met mine. "Couldn't tell much else in the black before the cart near ran me down, but—" She held up one hand, the gloved fingers saturated nearly black to the first joint. "There were a lot of blood."

I rubbed at my face, anger curling like a fist in my throat. I had him dead to rights, chased him halfway up Commercial Road, injured myself in my haste, and for what?

Had I just lost the Whitechapel murderer?

* * *

The journey home passed without incident, and the sky ferry manning the West India Docks carried us up from the fog-drenched streets to the clear, chilled night above the drift. My shoulder ached fiercely as I disembarked, worrying me.

How would I hide it?

Captain Abercott of the *Scarlet Philosopher*, a rotting canoe barely worthy of calling itself a sky ferry much less a ship, was no closer to the title than I was to declaring myself a duchess. He was often sotted, and always eager for ready coin. I paid him to take me from upper London to lower, and he rarely asked a word.

Abercott was a thick man, portly yet surprisingly spry for it. He'd lost most of the hair on the top his head, which he made up for by donning a sailor's cap and cultivating a disheveled trimming of stringy fringe around it.

He had taken a strange dislike to my new companion, which gave me a privacy I'd had little of before. Once wary of his quick hands, now I left Abercott to Zylphia to handle.

She settled with the captain rather more quickly than I'd have ever expected, and we moved out of the docks.

Fortunately for my already mildly tarnished reputation, much of London's to-do had long since arrived at the various soirees and gatherings held from one end to the next. Although the best of the Season was all but over, there were those who remained in town come sun or snow, and the best way to remain solvent in fashionable reputation was to be seen.

This was why I chose to remain *un*seen.

Unfortunately for us, half past one of the clock

still left a number of folk about. Many traveled by gondola—no proper gentleman would be caught strolling across the arched bridges connecting each district to the next, and certainly no miss of any distinction—but many of the aether-driven devices had windows, or remained open despite the chill.

It would not do for any gentleman to escort a lady in a closed gondola box, unless they were already wed.

Dirty, damp, coal-smudged and dressed as a man as I was, I did not fit in with the standards above the drift.

"How do we get home?" Zylphia asked me, her voice low. Like myself, she had stripped off her goggles before stepping foot on the ferry. Captain Abercott had a keen eye for business. Which translated to a tendency toward blackmail, when he thought he could get away with it.

I paid him well enough to keep his trap closed, but not so well that greed could overtake what few good senses he retained through drink.

Now, without protectives or respirator, I surveyed London proper with a critical eye.

Decades ago, the Queen's Parliament finally addressed ongoing complaints from the peerage forced to endure the oily smoke and thick fog surrounding the factory districts. Every year, the fog grew in mass, pushing its borders relentlessly. Her Majesty retained, among various other unique habits, a decided view on etiquette and propriety. The end came with a simple declaration: *Rise above it.*

This sparked one of the greatest auctions the civilized world has ever seen, culminating in the efforts of a minor German baron and his son. Baron Irwin Von Ronne went well and truly mad before the first stilts could be completed, but his gifted son completed the plans and construction rather more quickly than expected. The end result was the cleaving of London's well-to-do from its poor, its immigrants and those who couldn't maintain appearances. The accordion girders now held London proper high above the fog bank, leaving canals between districts spanned by walking bridges.

Hackneys had been replaced by gondolas, but much like the drivers below the drift, gondoliers were known to be just as chatty as any fishwife. Zylphia's question wasn't simply an inquiry as to the means of getting home.

She meant how to do so without speculation.

I have been a collector since I was fifteen years of age. I knew London, above and below, as well as I knew my own name. "Stay close," I told her, and set off across the nearest bridge.

This near the docks, we'd like as not get mistaken for laborers. Once we stepped into some of the more posh districts, we'd keep to the back streets and servants' footpaths.

I was very careful. The servants' routes weren't as keenly lit—the better to retain focus on the more attractive byways—and there were few who took to the streets this late. By Society's standards, the evening was well under way. Those who labored would be abed, and those with less *kind* motives would not wait about so far away from the fog that protected them.

A faint blue glow lit the canals, visible as far as the eye could see. It is entirely possible to note the most popular soirees simply by the glow cast off by the aether engines affixed to each gondola. Where the blue sheen was brightest, the more gathered.

My own district tended toward a constant shine, but it did not come from the peerage's gondolas these days.

Within half of the hour, we made it to the safety of my Cheyne Walk home. Set in the bohemian—and rather more unfashionable—district of Chelsea, flanked on both sides by neighbors with a penchant for enormous hedgerows, my home is an elegant thing large enough to hold myself, my chaperone, a maid, butler, housekeeper and one houseboy.

And, upon the rarest of occasions, one demon in human flesh.

Mr. Oliver Ashmore, my mysterious guardian and the executor of my father's estate, spent most of his time abroad. I had only seen him once in my five years as his ward, caught in the throes of one of the worst night terror episodes in memory, and the event had left me terrified of him. Logically, my scientist's mind knew him to be just a man—a seasoned traveler, wealthy enough by Society's standards, but apparently less keen than I to indulge the peerage with his company. I did not know his profession, or if he even had one.

I did know that many of the house's foreign furnishings were in part due to him. He shared the same taste for exotic decor as my father and mother before him. This, at least, was not a trait I disliked.

I simply disliked *him*.

"There are lights in the parlor," Zylphia whispered behind me. We crept along Lord Pennington's carefully manicured hedges, keeping to the shadows as much as we could. I had no fear of discovery from my neighbors. Lord Pennington's mother-in-law, a delightfully wicked woman with a penchant for painting the most extraordinary nudes upon her balcony, kept early hours and would be long abed.

The house on the other side was empty for the rest of the year, to be aired out once more come the next Season.

It made keeping out of sight quite simple—child's play, by this point—and we crossed the small yard easily. Yet what should have been the end of it turned into something much less fortuitous.

I rubbed at my throbbing shoulder, frowning deeply. "Where is the ladder?"

Zylphia made a small inquisitive sound behind me. A lilting note given form with a baffled "Whatever do you mean? I left it out as— Oh, no." That lilt soured.

I knew why. Once, some years ago, I'd smuggled a ladder made of rope into my bedchamber for nights just as this. It allowed me to retire for the night and leave without my staff being the wiser.

It did not occur to me—and perhaps it should have—that I would have to be even more clever, now that my secret had been unfortunately tipped. Someone had been inside my boudoir. Taken the ladder in. Left me stranded without.

I suspected I knew just who.

"Fanny," I muttered dourly.

As if on cue, light seamed around the kitchen entrance. The delicately painted door creaked open.

Bother.

I did not attempt to do anything more than straighten from my criminally inspired repose within the shadows. The jig was decidedly up.

The silhouette framed in the dim light cast by candle was poker straight, unyielding as the ramrods my butler used to clean his unique collection of pistols. The small, pointed chin and elegantly coiffed hair caught in the flicker were pale, but there was no mistaking the edged gleam in eyes I knew were pale as the morning sky and, at the moment, just as cold.

"Inside," came the clipped order, delivered in tones that offered me no chance to explain.

Not that I needed to.

My chaperone, the widow Frances Fortescue, had once been my governess. She'd been with me since my arrival, had seen me at my best and my worst— more often, my worst. She'd stayed on when nannies had fled, and taken me into her own hands when all others swore I'd end up an unfortunate victim of Satan himself.

But until the events of early September, she had never known about my propensity for collector's business, or my routine outings below. Not until the day I'd first run afoul of the alchemical serum Abraham St. Croix had concocted, and lost my mind for a day and night.

I had unwittingly tipped my hand—my father's meddling tipped my hand—and now my chaperone knew what she'd never even had reason to suspect before. Of the many consequences my father's desperate acts of alchemy and betrayal had left me to shoulder, Fanny's knowledge was one of those I regretted most. Now, every foray below had to be carefully timed, and I never would know if she'd check upon me during the night when I should be abed.

She had not quite come to terms with my choice of entertainments, as it were. This without the accompanying knowledge of my steady laudanum intake; I shuddered to think what she would do if that truth came to light.

I hastened to the door, well aware of the lamp-black coating my cheeks and the trousers outlining my legs in stark relief. "Fanny, I—"

Her thin lips tightened, drawing the fragile, lined skin taut over her cheekbones. "I refuse to hear it," she said, cutting my words off in icy reproach. The door closed softly behind us—my proper chaperone was not a woman to give in to fits of violent pique by slamming doors, but she may as well have. I heard the gentle *thud*, felt it all the way to my bones. "Get yourself upstairs and bathed immediately."

I could not argue with such cold tones. Even the glint in her candlelit eyes seemed remote. "Yes, Fanny."

Unappeased by my capitulation, she glared at my maid. "You, girl. Prepare a bath. We will converse about your role in this mischief tomorrow."

I winced at Zylphia's meek "Yes, madam." In trouble again, and on my behalf.

I turned, caught my maid's hand and tucked her behind me. Unlike my diminutive stature, Zylphia had the length of leg and torso to place her nearly a head's height above me. Fanny was also a tall woman, a creature of fashionable length, though as an aged widow she no longer felt the sting of fashion's consequence.

Still, I stood between them, frowning at my chaperone. "Zylphia is not to blame, Fanny."

"She is a girl of her own mind," Fanny told me, neatly cutting through my argument with a well-placed observation. The same type I have been known to make just to spite her. "She will be responsible for her own actions."

"You'll not lay a finger on her," I warned, a fit of anger curling in my chest.

Fanny stared at me over the candle's dancing flame. The light was kinder to her aged features, smoothing lines I knew marred her cheeks. Deep lines had settled into the corners of her eyes, bracketed her mouth, and it startled me to see them.

Had they been there forever? Or was I only recently all too aware of my dear chaperone's aging demeanor?

She sighed softly, the sound keener even than her anger and thrust straight to my heart. "Go on with you, Cherry."

I fled. The weight of Fanny's disapproval settled hard upon my shoulders.

I could not afford the laudanum to ease it.

Chapter Three

The *London Times* is growing lazy," I observed the next day at the breakfast table. I spoke to myself, and to the pages of the newspaper I held in front of me.

There was no need to pretend otherwise. Fanny had not yet forgiven me my evening's excursion and was not currently speaking to me. Guilt stung my conscience. It found a ready home in the dark hole already carved into my chest.

I'd slept eventually, finally giving in to the night's disquiet by taking a small amount of the dwindling laudanum that was all I had stocked, but I did not sleep well. Guilt and anger and frustration conspired to wend through my dreams, leaving me feeling as if I'd spent all of my sleeping hours running through vista after vista. Chasing something.

Chasing someone.

I did not wake refreshed, and this was a startling habit seeded sometime in early September. I once slept the sleep of the dead.

I had not felt the same since my father's conspiracy unfolded beneath my feet.

Zylphia had been reassuring as she dressed me in a gown of peach poplin trimmed in chocolate. The color flattered my hair, turned my cheeks pink. A fine choice.

I felt like summer when all I wanted was to hide away in my bedroom until nightfall.

Nevertheless, I knew Fanny would be hard-pressed to find fault with my appearance. Especially since the fitted jacket helped conceal the mild swelling at my shoulder. The bruising there came in spectacular colors. I would have to be ginger with myself for a time.

The *Times* headlines said nothing of murder; a far cry from the broadsheets printed earlier this month. I wasted no effort on the articles within—I could peruse them at my leisure another time—and turned instead to the Society columns.

The rhythmic and unique cadence of my butler's approach served to ease the heavy weight of silence from the table. *Step-thunk, step-thunk.*

I smiled cheerfully at the man who, with his wife, had run my home with an iron-fisted rule marred only by the subtle indulgences of a childless couple. Booth was a broad-shouldered man, a fine figure impeccably garbed at all times. Unlike most men sixty years at least, he sported a full head of thick, leonine white hair, impressively groomed white sideburns, and a rather surprising collection of firearms from his infantry days in Her Majesty's service.

Not even the ornate brass crutch affixed to his right knee marred the appearance of irreproachable civility. Upon meeting the man who was to run my new house, I had very seriously informed him that he struck me as fine a figure as any gentleman pirate.

He had bowed most seriously, thanked me in his deep, elegantly educated voice, and won my heart forever.

"Tea, miss," he offered, setting a tray before me. On it, I knew there would be toast and boiled eggs, sausages cooked fresh by Mrs. Booth, and jam. I peeked around the papers.

Strawberry. My favorite, and well my housekeeper and cook knew it.

"Thank you," I said, the very model of propriety, just as Fanny offered a regal nod and echo of the same.

Booth withdrew, leaving me and my silent companion to regard one another across the breakfast table.

Fanny considered my interest in the papers a waste of time, and a gentleman's domain, at that. I considered that idea worthless as a rule. I believed in knowing what went on in the world.

But it was not worth arguing anymore, and Fanny had stopped commenting. In turn, I stopped needling, and offered her news from the pages she preferred. I knew the key to Fanny's conversation.

I smiled and dropped my gaze to the paper once more.

The Society columns exasperated me.

Up until a few meager weeks ago, I had happily ignored its existence. Unfortunately for me, this was not to last. While I trusted my staff to keep my secrets, I had no control over anyone else and could not risk the chance of my name serving as grist for the gossip mill. Too many strange things happened last month, too many indications that at least one fiend knew my identity.

I needed to stay aware of the rumors, and do my best to remain out of them.

Unfortunately, this was easier planned than carried out.

For now, I could speak a language Fanny knew well. "Mrs. Bingham's eldest daughter is to be wed," I said aloud, reaching around the paper for my toast.

Fanny's reply came oh-so-politely. "Is that so?"

"A Christmas wedding, it seems. I imagine there'll be snow, don't you?" I kept my tone light and sweet, just the way she had so often demanded of me. A lady was to converse on things that would not strain the mind. Needlework, music, fashion, soirees and marriages; social topics salient to a lady's place in Society.

Bugger that for a lark.

But for this moment, I allowed it. I so wanted to mend this breach between us, and I knew that simply explaining myself would never do. I could not tell my chaperone, who worried for my well-being since I was thirteen years of age, that I continued to travel below the drift because I owed a dangerous criminal enterprise a debt.

Or because the stipend my guardian allotted was not hefty enough to carry the price of the opium I purchased alone.

"Lovely," Fanny said from behind the mask of my paper. "Lord Datchery is a fine match for the family. A second son, already secure. She could have not done better for herself."

So the columns assured me. I skimmed them as quickly as I glanced over the rest, seeking only references to anything that might stand out to me. Or as me.

I did not like Society's speculation as a rule. I have no love for frippery and balls, either, but my role as well-to-do heiress sometimes demanded my tolerance.

I attended when I had no other choice, or to make Fanny happy. And when I did, Almira Louise Compton, the Marchioness Northampton, made certain that I knew the value of my company. To wit, less than nothing. I was a boil on the face of Society, a thorn in her side. She has always been a clever cat and holds considerable power among London's most fashionable peerage.

The evening I met her much vaunted eldest son is the same evening that her family delivered the cut direct—thereby cementing my reputation as worthless.

This kind of terrible blow should have spurned me from every parlor here to the Brick Street Bakers' territory below the drift. And it did, for a time.

Until the marchioness's eldest son, Cornelius Kerrigan Compton, returned me to Society's good graces—and the gossip pages—with an interest in my company that waned as mysteriously as it waxed.

I sometimes wonder if Earl Compton had somehow learned of my evening activities. But surely, he was a man more likely to confront me himself over it.

Whatever the case, he left London within a fortnight, and I stopped receiving the invites to this ball or that soiree. Much to my relief, of course, but also to my chaperone's dismay.

Since the earl's departure, it seemed as if any

temperance once displayed by the marchioness faded. She turned back to her old tricks, and with a vengeance. She and her salon of like-minded bats—called the Ladies of Admirable Mores and Behavior—had once more taken to slandering me in their nasty little columns. Oh so subtly, of course.

The ladies' sermons were cleverly crafted around the expected behaviors of the Society female, artfully arranged in such language that could be mistaken for objective encouragement to the girls I was positive lapped up every edifying word. Yet buried within these lectures, I often found a reference to a faux pas I made, or a bit of strained conversation made under duress at a function where our paths had crossed.

Had it been anyone but a marchioness at the head of that salon, I would have considered the words a threat. Perhaps they were; or could be, if I gave a toss for her much-vaunted company. I did not.

Yet in her language, I suspected that she offered a none-too-veiled suggestion that I—and girls like myself, of which I knew none—was a hairsbreadth away from joining the unfortunate slatterns plying their trade below the drift.

She had said as much before, and to my face. I expected nothing less of her column.

Such remarks did not concern me overly much. To my regret, I knew they hurt Fanny. Not only on my behalf, but her standing among the matriarchs and chaperones in her own social set suffered when she could not go out on invite.

For this reason, I said nothing about LAMB's latest snide suppositions, folding the paper closed. There were days—many days—when I fantasized about the many and varied creative analogies I could make about that den of sheep and their viper-tongued mistress.

Today, I set aside the irritation and the paper that carried it, and turned to my breakfast instead. "It seems all has gone quiet," I said before filling my mouth with toast and sausage.

Fanny, who ate much more delicately than I, sipped at her tea. It gave her the freedom to talk, though I often thought this a rather unfortunate side effect rather than the purpose. "The bulk of the Season is done. Many have retired to their estates. It shall remain quiet, as is usual for the winter."

"A breath of fresh air, then." Or as near as one could achieve in London proper. Murders notwithstanding.

Fanny, lovely in deep purple with her gray hair pulled into a sleek chignon, studied me from across the table. Her eyes were a pretty shade of blue, as expressive as they were pale, and I had many fond memories of the way they crinkled when she slipped a rare laugh or a warm smile.

But her features tended toward stern, and her posture was as unforgiving as the many hours she'd spent forcing mine.

I owed this woman much; yet I could not stop myself from doing what I did best. I was a collector. I took to the streets for coin and adventure, it's simply what I *did*.

Because the alternative—find a husband, marry—robbed me of breath. Of freedom.

For now, I held my tongue and my temper, and said innocently, "What is on our agenda, Fanny?"

"Luncheon with Lady Rutledge," she said. "I would like you to wear the bronze silk."

I wrinkled my nose. The three-piece walking

gown was among my loveliest, admittedly. The color turned my hair into an autumnal sunset, and flattered my fashionably pale skin. That she wanted me to be seen in it spoke of machinations. "Who is attending?"

"Don't make faces, Cherry." I smoothed my features by rote, though it didn't do anything to soften Fanny's stern regard. "As we are talking of Lady Rutledge, I assume it shall be an eclectic collection of characters."

I brightened.

"Do not look so pleased," she added dryly. "I'm not entirely convinced you should be attending such functions."

"Lady Rutledge is—"

My chaperone was nobody's fool. "A pillar of the scientific community, yes, I'm aware. You've said as much time and again." She reached for her teacup once more, taking a delicate sip.

The act gave me just enough time to mutter, "Well, she is."

"Don't mumble." Fanny laid her napkin upon the table by her half-emptied plate. "Whatever her scientific accomplishments, the fact remains that she is the last ally you have in this world, and she could be a powerful one."

"Teddy—"

"*Mr. Helmsley* remains, to my great dismay, a fine friend, but he is not intent on offering for your hand," she cut in smoothly, her shoulders straight as a board. She lifted a finger at me, a gentle admonishment. "Nor does he have the wherewithal to protect you from your own nature. You are bored. There can be no other explanation for why you continue to gallivant—" She hesitated, then dropped her voice several octaves. "*Below.* A family of your own, social engagements, these things will occupy you."

Not in the slightest.

I stared at the food left on my plate—much less than left on Fanny's—and resisted the urge to rub my throbbing shoulder.

"Lady Rutledge will provide you the means," Fanny told me, as sure in her knowledge of the workings of these strange politics as I was in the street gangs that ran below the drift. "However, as the Season is all but finished, there are no other invites to busy yourself with. There are no balls, no soirees."

Just as I liked it. Yet I understood Fanny's concern. I sighed, pushing the last of my eggs about my plate with a delicate silver fork. "I am sorry."

"You are not."

I refrained from smiling, even if there was a wry note to her rebuttal. "What would you have me do? The marchioness is intent on keeping me from my own ambition. This appears to mean all of Society." Save for Lady Rutledge, who seemed quite keen on thumbing her nose at the marchioness.

"If only the earl hadn't left." Fanny sighed.

"Better that he had," I returned, raising my chin as Fanny's eyes narrowed. "I did not fancy him in the slightest." A lie.

A part of me fancied him. The inner thoughts of a girl flattered by the attentions of an earl. Even I, for all my bluster, was not immune to charm.

"You speak of love, Cherry." There was steel in her voice. Strong as the girders that held the city high. "You are nearing one and twenty years of age, this is an ideal time for marriage."

"I do *not* speak of love." Another lie. But a narrow one.

"Then whatever can be the issue?"

"There was no word of a proposal," I protested, pushing away my half-empty teacup with a distracted hand. "He was only making up the insult delivered by his family. Why on earth would you think that he intended to marry me?"

She hadn't seen the kiss, stolen in the exhibit where my father had worn his disguise so well. Or heard the earl's declaration of admiration.

Fat lot of good any of that had done.

These were things men did, weren't they? I knew it better than most, perhaps. Certainly better than the wide-eyed young misses thrown to the cattle market that was the Season. I knew the fallen women who flaunted their wares in the East End. The sweets sold to the highest bidder for an evening's entertainment.

Hadn't I evaded Monsieur Marceaux's auction tables by sheer perseverance?

I'd known, and still I nursed a silent hurt. Lord Compton fled London and could not be bothered to send word to me about it. I shouldn't expect it. What was I but a minor distraction?

Someone he once owed an apology to.

He had delivered. I could expect nothing more.

I wanted nothing more.

"There are signs, my dove," she said with a shrewd glint in her eye. One that suggested her thoughts mirrored mine.

"I am an heiress, Fanny." An old argument. "An independent woman. I shall have no need of a husband when I come of age."

China clinked delicately as my chaperone set her teacup upon its saucer. Each motion came sharp and controlled. I'd upset her. Again. "And what will you do?" she demanded of me. "What do you plan with all of your wealth?"

I rose, shaking out my skirts because it gave me something else to focus my attention on than her sharp gaze. "I will tour the world," I declared. She scoffed, a dismissal. "I will hire a sky ship and travel to America and France. I will fund scientific inquiries and attend lectures."

I would purchase opium in whatever quantity I desired. Fund the finest craftsman to make for me items I could use while I collected.

I would be *free*.

"To what purpose?"

I hesitated, gripping the back of the chair. To what purpose, indeed?

Did I need one?

I shook my head, swiping the fringe of fashionable curls from my forehead with an impatient hand. "I need no purpose," I told her.

Her smile surprised me. "Oh, my dove." She sighed. "One day, you will understand."

I doubted it. Rigorously. "If you'll excuse me," I said instead, picking up my paper with one hand and my gloves with the other, "I've letters to write."

Her mouth thinned, and she once more reached for her tea. "Yes, of course." A retreat, though a tactical one. "Do send Mr. Helmsley my regards."

I fled before the conversation could once more bend around the subject of marriage and duty.

The idea was preposterous. The only reason I was on the verge of independence now came on the coat-tails of tragedy. A woman could inherit only if all other male relatives were no longer living. My father was dead, and I had no uncles, brothers, or cousins to take my inheritance from me.

Common law suggested that should I marry, all my intended wealth—the inheritance protected so carefully by my absent guardian—would belong to my husband. Entirely.

Not an ideal situation for any woman. Yet time after time, women fell to the trap of marriage.

I would not be one. There was nothing marriage could offer me that I could not attain myself.

And so I retired to the sitting room, and its delicate, feminine desk arrayed in one corner. This was my study, because I was not allowed in the actual study. Although it had once been my father's, and retained much of his chosen decor, it was nevertheless Mr. Ashmore's, and Fanny frowned on my presence there.

It was an argument I did not intend to pursue. Much like that of marriage.

I wrote to Teddy first. As one of my dearest friends, the Honorable Theodore Helmsley was a figure I missed terribly when he left Town for his family's rural estate. Although he was the third son of a viscount, his prospects were as slim as mine. If he intended to get on in the world, he would be required to join Her Majesty's service, master a properly respectable trade, or marry well.

Once, he'd considered asking for my hand, but I had little enough to offer him. Wealth, perhaps, and friendship, but I was not keen on marriages of convenience. Or marriages at all, for that matter.

He was my friend, and I was his. Most Wednesdays, we met here in the parlor to talk about the latest science periodicals. We theorized and debated, and I enjoyed my dear friend's company immensely.

Even if I kept the secrets of my collector's life from him.

I was certain he hid his own, for I knew rumor placed him often in the gaming hells below the drift, and frequently among the Menagerie sweets. In a way, I have long suspected that the break from Town was a way for his family to gather their strength for the Season next.

His father, Viscount Armistice Helmsley the Third, was a known hedonist, and encouraged all his sons to be the same. Teddy was a smart lad, brilliant in his own way and possessing a sharp sense of humor, but blood tells.

It *always* tells, doesn't it?

The letter I wrote him said nothing of my current troubles. What could he do from so far away? Besides that, I knew that he received the same papers as I. Just a smidge later. He'd see the columns, know what they meant.

Instead, I included notations from the latest periodicals. I did not expound—we would have much to catch up on when he finally returned—but I informed him in no uncertain terms that his ongoing views on aether as the creator of all life were bollocks.

I included that word, underlined it with a flourish, because I knew it would make him laugh.

When I was done, I signed it, sealed it, and marked it with his family's estate address. Then I turned my attention to the small stack of newspapers Booth left for me.

I did not bother reading them all. Instead, leaving my gloves off to better handle the thin pages, I rifled through each paper quickly and found what I sought in the *Leeds Mercury*. "*Two more women murdered*," I read aloud, frowning at the bold print. HORRIBLE MUTILATION, the headline swore.

A quick read told me what I'd feared.

Two more dead in the East End, but I'd known of only one. It spoke of the woman, identified as Annie Morris, found exactly where we'd left her to chase her killer. Zylphia had proclaimed her dead; the papers confirmed the tale. Yet it seemed that murder was not by itself enough.

The killer—perhaps unfulfilled by my interruption of his work—had found another victim. Another unfortunate character.

How he must have been furious to be so disturbed.

The second victim, this time uninterrupted by the likes of me, was found half of an hour later, throat cut. Body terribly mutilated.

I shivered upon reading the details. With a few grotesque descriptions, I was no longer seated in my elegantly furnished parlor, no longer warm and dry.

Instead, shuddering, it was as if I could smell the pungent damp, feel the choking fog as it slipped through my nose and mouth. I heard the bubbling noise of what I now knew to be a throat cut in the dark.

That was his first stroke; the point where the nub of his disturbed conscience began his signature. The mutilations, the ghastly acts performed upon each body, became his flourish.

Each act an art, each stroke a laugh.

Taunting us?

No. There was a difference between this man and the collector I chased. The latter truly fancied himself an artist; perhaps he even was, and his canvas was the world as he saw it. Brilliant or simply mad; the two so often came hand in hand.

This murderer was nothing so elegant.

Elegant? I shook myself free of the fanciful turn my thoughts had gone, inhaling gratefully the fragrance of the wood in the fire and the aromatic, dark tea Booth continued to bring me.

Whatever this creature was, he was a man, and he would bleed like one.

As he boasted like one.

A rustle of fabric behind me warned me of company. Too harsh a sound for Fanny's silk and velvet day dress, and accompanied by neither the clatter of a tray nor Mrs. Booth's near-constant murmur.

Zylphia, then. "He sent out a letter," I said aloud, glancing up. Clad in a demure day dress, gray relieved by a stark white apron and her head covered by a white cap, Zylphia looked nothing like the sweet she'd once exclusively been.

Or like the assistant she had become.

Her head tilted, cleaning cloths in hand. "The sweet tooth?" Her name for the collector, given he'd been offing sweets at the time.

I shook my head. "Leather Apron. Tend your duties, I'll read it to you."

She wasn't as efficient as her predecessor had been, but even in severe gray and white, she retained a certain grace impossible to ignore.

The Karakash Veil—the mouthpiece, anyway, by which I'd received my orders—had suggested she came not just from mixed stock, but from a *useful heritage*. I didn't know what it meant.

I wondered, sometimes, if the Veil had only upsold her value to ensure my agreement. He needn't have bothered.

"*Dear Boss,*" I read, returning my attention to the paper, "*I keep on hearing the police have caught me, but they won't fix me just yet. I have laughed when they look so clever and talk about being on the right track. That joke about Leather Apron gave me real fits.*"

"Charming bloke, isn't he?"

"I'd say he knows his letters, but there's errors," I said slowly, scanning the rest of the text. Grisly, to be sure. "A dictation, perhaps?"

"Or some minor schooling." Zylphia bent to her task, polishing the grate in front of the fire. "There's some what say this murderer's a lord in disguise."

I smiled briefly, suddenly amused by the dichotomy we presented. Each with a second life, one in Society, one below.

But it faded. "Doubtful. If 'tis true, then he writes very poorly."

"Unless it's a trick."

A fair point. "He goes on. *I saved some of the proper red stuff in a ginger beer bottle over the last job to write with, but it went thick like glue and I can't use it. Red ink is fit enough I hope.* He considers himself charming, anyway." He'd written *ha, ha* after the joke, but I wasn't laughing.

The collector, may his soul rot once I caught up to him, had used blood when he'd written *me* a note. The same letter that warned me he'd kidnapped Betsy Phillips, my last maid and as dear a friend as I'd ever had.

Eager for attention, the collector had sneered. So it seemed. Of them both.

"So who wrote it?" Zylphia demanded, her hands busy polishing but no less intent on me than she was on the chores that kept her busy by day.

I studied the transcribed text, my eyebrows rising. I'd never mastered the art of lifting just one. "Jack," I read.

"What?" My maid scoffed loudly, snapping her polishing cloth into the air in easy dismissal. "Spring-Heeled Jack's nothing more than a legend."

I lowered the paper, mouth twisting into a grim slant. "Not Spring-Heeled Jack," I said softly. "Nothing so fanciful."

"What, then?"

"Jack the Ripper."

My maid fell silent.

The name—false, though it may be—rang like a death knell in my parlor. It was a name that would grip London with fear, I was sure of it.

Jack the Ripper.

Perhaps I'd two murderers to hunt this time.

Suddenly filled with a sense of urgency, I set aside the papers I'd perused and rose to my feet. "I'm off to change," I declared, and left her to tidy behind me.

All I wanted at that very moment was to travel below and begin to retrace the steps I'd taken through Dutfield's Yard. To ask questions of the witnesses, to visit the Menagerie and make inquiries among the sweets.

Unfortunate though they may be, the sweets knew things that most would never let on. Clients talked. I needed to know if they'd heard any word of this Ripper.

If Hawke would even allow me the chance.

Blast. I had no choice in the matter. It was all moot speculation. As I seized my poplin skirts in one hand and hurried up the stairs, passing the large wooden lions carved at the foot, I knew I'd have to wait.

Much as I dreaded social events, I could not pass up an invite from Lady Rutledge. Not if I intended to survive Society's demands long enough to enjoy my own forthcoming independence.

The widow was my only ally of any standing.

Chapter Four

Lady Rutledge was a woman of massive stature. Even with her impressive bosom safely hidden behind a fitted jacket of a particularly eye-watering shade of verdigris—a color that put me in mind of the strange blue-green patina copper could take on—she did not give any impression of delicacy.

Especially since her voice, neither gentle nor demure by any stretch of the word, tended to dominate one's attention. And when one's attention was well and truly acquired, one could not help but notice that her hair was perhaps a shade too dark for a lady of her age, and that her lips a titch too pink. When they twisted into a particularly sardonic slant, one might also notice the beauty mark affixed to the side of her mouth.

I wasn't convinced it entirely natural.

What I did know was that the lady held court in a parlor at least five times as large as mine, with a rug underfoot in the wildly floral pattern that remained all the rage among the posh and polished.

The colors—vibrant reds and purples, accented in gold and brown and green—clashed brilliantly with the bold stripes in verdant emerald and gilt upon the walls. Overstuffed sofas scattered over the space played host to mostly gentlemen, with the occasional lady among them.

As I sipped at my tea, my grip ever so careful on a china cup so thin as to put me in mind of spun sugar, I couldn't help but draw comparisons between this, a Society function, and the Midnight Menagerie below the drift.

Both tended to favor gentlemen. Both put much emphasis on the appearance of a lady.

Of course, unlike a proper well-heeled young miss, a clever woman in the Menagerie might just find her way to a certain kind of freedom.

Or so I hoped.

"I relish the end of Season," Lady Rutledge was saying, perched upon a large, ornate chair as a queen upon her throne. Her skirts, two-toned in a matching verdigris with a ruffled hem of deep purple, were arrayed perfectly. For all her girth, the lady knew exactly how to present.

Around her neck, a gold chain held the matching frames of a pair of delicate spectacles. Once in a while, she lifted them to her face, and more often than not, I found them pointed at me.

I smiled into them, now. Obediently. "As do I, my lady."

"Why?"

A sharp question, and one that left me with the unsettling feeling that I was being tested. I set my cup carefully down upon its matching saucer, the tiny *clink* it made clear as a bell, and barely kept from tilting my head as I did when I thought.

The first time I'd made Lady Rutledge's acquaintance, she called me a rotund bird for the gesture.

Instead, I straightened my shoulders. "I find the endless parade of unmarried girls tedious," I told her, erring on the side of truth rather than prevarication. "I mislike the emphasis on fashion and gossip."

Beside me, a gentleman in a tweed coat blotted at his bristling black mustache with a cloth napkin. "I find the lack of lectures most disheartening."

"I'm sure you do, Mr. Englebrooks." Lady Rutledge's smile was not as apparent at her mouth as it was in her eyes, an intriguing shade of blue most similar to that color the sky turned to as twilight settled in. The fleshy pads of her cheeks turned upward. "Yet did you not meet your very wife during the Season?"

The sound he made, something between a snort and a clearing of the throat, earned raised eyebrows from me, but this was not the sort of thing a lady such as I should comment on.

Nevertheless, I found it amusing.

"And you, Miss Hensworth." Without pausing in her effortless conduction of the orchestra that were her guests, Lady Rutledge turned her attentions to a woman I vaguely recall being introduced as Miss Hortense Hensworth.

I recognized the name. The woman was not one of the peerage's many daughters. Middle-class, perhaps, though I wondered if I were being too kind in the assessment. She spent her time, as I recalled, penning open letters to the universities and the public regarding the rights of women in science and education.

I did not mind the rallying cry of a fellow scientific female, but I took some umbrage at the concept that women posed *better* intellectualists than men. I had met brilliant men. Some I would hold in higher regard than most women of my association. I wasn't positive Miss Hensworth would make friends with her chosen rhetoric.

The name I knew, certainly, though I would be hard-pressed to remember the face.

There was absolutely nothing memorable of the woman at all. Of an average height—which placed her taller than I, at least—and a round, not unpleasant face, she seemed more at ease as a wallflower than the center of social speculation. Her simple dress of blue linen, while perfectly respectable, hovered on the verge of genteel. I detected traces where the hem had been mended more than once, and the shoulders seemed slightly ill-fitting.

Her mousy brown hair, piled upon her head in an artless bun, seemed a victim of circumstance, as it escaped its pins with startling ease. Fringes fell around her cheeks and forehead, which may have been flattering were it not for the simple lifelessness of it. I had never seen a woman as desperately in need of curling paper and tongs as Miss Hensworth.

But then, she had no need of such things. She was, like many of the guests gathered here at Lady Rutledge's behest, of a scientific bent. Some more than others, I suspected, but telling enough in the topics of conversation that drifted across the parlor.

Miss Hensworth's eyes had gone wide, rather pretty in a muted green, and framed by wire spectacles perched crookedly upon her nose. "My lady?"

"The Season, Miss Hensworth, have you been paying attention at all?"

Impatience lashed at the woman, perhaps some years older than I, and I winced on her behalf. "I—

Oh. No, my lady, I pay no attention to the Season," she replied, apologetic enough though the words seemed forced from her pale lips.

Mr. Murdstone Englebrooks leaned over the sofa to offer, "Miss St. Croix, do you read the periodicals?"

"I do," I murmured, though one ear fixed upon Lady Rutledge as she accused the shy lady of lacking spine in social endeavors.

"Penmanship and rhetoric will only get you so far, my dear," she barked, as demanding as a general on the battlefield.

I didn't disagree. I only wondered if Miss Hensworth shone in other pursuits, as well. I resolved to find out. A wallflower had always been my ideal designation among the peerage.

"What of *Angelicus Finch's Gazette*?"

I shook my head, cradling my saucer in my lap. "Not since the late doctor passed on editorial responsibilities. I find it now mostly gossip."

"Do you dislike even scientific gossip, then?" Mr. Englebrooks required, and I studied the inquiring set of his dark eyes with a sudden surge of concern.

Had he inched closer on the brocade sofa?

"I find gossip as a rule tends to muddy the waters," I explained, but cautiously. The rather mixed effect of sharp cologne and aged cigar smoke assaulted my senses. Across the parlor, Lady Rutledge pulled her girth out of her chair, skirts falling in a ripple of color. "It has its uses, but only if one is capable of separating the heart from the . . ." I hesitated.

"From the waste," the lady interjected, with a finality that declared most was simply waste. "Mr. Englebrooks, kindly go bother Lady Tavish with your questions."

And like the emphasis placed on the first portion

of her statement, the word *questions* held a wealth of meaning I wasn't sure I understood.

But he only laughed, an indelicate sound, and rose. "The pleasure was mine, I assure you." He offered me a short bow.

I inclined my head, and wondered if I'd missed something important.

At least below, I thought with some irritation, flirtation was something much more obvious. Even if it often involved an exchange of money.

The sofa creaked as Lady Rutledge sank to its cushion beside me. Her skirts brushed mine, pooling in a flattering overlap of blue-green and bronze. "So you continue to read the periodicals, then," she said, not so much a question as affirmation.

I nodded. "Yes, my lady."

The first time I'd met the woman, I'd claimed "bollocks" to one of her scientific questions. This was the reason I used the word with Teddy in my letter. He remembered, and laughed still when the subject came up between us.

I thought it a terrible blunder, but in some way, it must have earned the lady's attention. This was my second luncheon among her social set.

I met new faces each time. Miss Hensworth, for example. And another girl whose father was a respectable professor at King's College above the drift. What was her name? Dorring. Miss Delphina Dorring. Beautiful girl, all the fashionable rage, but cool as a winter sky.

Miss Dorring now argued with two gentlemen whose names I'd forgotten, but whose manner of dress suggested they walked in highly reputable circles indeed.

•

"I do," I said, aware that the lady studied me through her spectacles once more. "I read the papers, as well."

Lady Rutledge's mouth pinched. "All of them?"

"Many."

"Waste," she told me, and without thinking, I retorted, "Only if one stops with the Society columns."

There, another glimmer. Laughter. I amused her, perhaps. Her eyes glinted as she asked me, "And what did you read today?"

"I read of Jack the Ripper, my lady."

As I expected, the words sent a chill through the room. Conversation halted, but did not stop, and I could not help my head from tilting.

"More waste," she repeated, and flicked the Whitechapel murderer away with a simple wave of her hand. "Did you read anything not promoted by sensationalist rumor?"

My eyes widened as I mulled this over, and I realized she was right. I had not. I'd gone from the gossip columns direct to the Ripper headlines.

Embarrassed, I could offer no rebuttal.

"I see," she intoned, in a way that suggested she did. All too well. "I am interested in your mind, Miss St. Croix. Let us speak on that."

"My mind?" Perhaps not the most intelligent response such a compliment deserved. I shifted on the sofa, aware of closeted scrutiny from the other guests around me. My palms itched. My throat itched, for that matter, and I knew that for what it was.

I could have navigated this social maze so much easier if I'd only a few spare grains of opium. Instead, clutching for dear life at my common sense,

I focused upon keeping myself from social blunder.

I wanted to befriend Lady Rutledge, certainly, but not at the cost of my secrets.

"Yes, yes, your mind." She sighed, dropping the spectacles. "Your mother was a brilliant woman. You've inherited her looks, what of her senses?"

"Her senses?" I set my saucer down upon the tea cart beside the sofa and added, "I don't understand what you mean. I have my father's mind, not my mother's."

Lady Rutledge's darkened eyebrows knitted. Disappointment, perhaps. "Shame." And then, as a movement in blue from the corner of my eye seized my attention, the lady said simply, "I believe you to be mistaken. Play a game with me, Miss St. Croix."

I jerked my head around, Miss Hensworth's position by the mantel forgotten. "What sort of game?"

"A game of deliberation," she replied, and smiled. "Your mother was particularly good at them."

My mother, according to everyone else, was particularly good at everything I was not. The comparison had long since grown wearisome. Especially as my father's intent to kill me went hand in hand with his intent to replace me with his late wife.

"Unless," she added thoughtfully, "you'd rather not." But as kind as the offer was, I recognized it. Refusal would mean social consequence. One of the most brilliant women in the scientific field was extending a challenge.

I could not refuse.

I stiffened, ever so slightly. "What have you in mind?"

"A mystery."

I was aware of the voices nearest dropping to a

murmur. Of the speculation growing around us. Was this common?

Was this what Lady Rutledge did when the Season failed to offer its spectacular array of soirees, lectures and events?

My fingers curled into my palms. "I am listening."

"Of course you are." She rose once more, an effort that suggested as large as she was, she was no delicate woman to suffer under her size. I was, to be honest, a little bit in awe of her. I could so easily imagine the imposing woman leading battles. Commanding men.

Demanding respect.

"A murder mystery," she announced. Conversation ceased entirely. "Our detective will be none other than Miss St. Croix."

"Charming!" Miss Dorring finally deigned to acknowledge me, her lovely, noble features suddenly so much more approachable as she smiled. "I do so love mysteries."

"The subject?" demanded a gentleman whose name I had heard twice and still could not recall.

"Unknown."

"How can a murder victim be unknown?" I demanded.

"Against the rules," crowed Mr. Englebrooks from behind me, and I rose quickly as his hands came down upon the back of the sofa, framing my shoulders. The sheer speed by which I accomplished the distance left a wide-eyed appreciation upon his features, his thick mustache twitching, but Lady Rutledge didn't appear to notice.

She shook a finger at me. "Tut, Miss St. Croix, the rules are as follows. Time is of the utmost importance. The detective may only ask five questions.

The detective may ask only questions whose answers are corroboration or refutation."

"Five? What detective would allow herself to be so bound?" I demanded. "That is impossible."

"Only five," Miss Dorring repeated, quite seriously. "Yet it's not impossible."

"Your own mother succeeded often," Lady Rutledge added with a smile that still dared me to refuse.

My choices were few, then. Accept and succeed, or refuse and risk the social consequences. I was not my mother, but it seemed important that I prove something of myself with her template. "Very well. Does everyone know what you know about the murder?" I asked.

Her eyes glinted. That spark that suggested she knew so much more than she let on. That bit I recognized. "No."

"Then you are the sole personage to whom I should direct my questions to?"

"No."

I was careful. That she said no to everyone else's level of knowledge, and no to *sole personage* suggested others had answers. Just not everyone, and possibly not anyone present.

This game could very well extend beyond the bounds of her parlor.

I could not waste my last three questions cycling through names. Not only were there more faces here than I had questions allotted, I suspect such an easy way would disappoint her.

And, truth be told, myself.

This was interesting. This fed the hole left by the gnawing whisper of need curling inside me. Need for answers. Need for something to occupy me.

Need for one more draught of laudanum, to ease my want for gentle sleep.

To my surprise, even with all eyes upon me, I found myself warming to the game. An inexplicable murder. I turned, smiled upon Miss Hensworth who watched with her brow knitted, and then turned again in a swirl of chocolate skirts to ask, "Is the unfortunate soul a tradesman or laborer?"

"Lovely one," murmured a woman. Not Miss Dorring, who had once more resumed her argument with one of the gentlemen at hand.

"No," Lady Rutledge said. "Caution, Miss St. Croix, that is very nearly two questions."

I smiled. "Neither laborer nor tradesman. Interesting." I almost began to pace a path, the better to think, but caught myself in time. Ladies did not pace.

"Ooh, I'd wager the victim is a lord," said the same voice, and I looked over my shoulder to find an aged woman in a suitable gray dress watching me. Her eyes were heavily lined, her face set into deep grooves, but she smiled upon my scrutiny and suggested, "All the best mysteries involve lords."

Unbidden, my thoughts turned to Lord Compton, and my disguised meeting with him on the stoop of an opium den. How surprised he would have been to learn it was me dressed as a street boy.

How surprised I'd been to see him enter the very same opium den I'd stepped out of.

"Don't they just?" I murmured, and forced myself to cease drumming my fingers into my skirts as I studied the expectant faces around me. I stilled them. "How long—" I caught myself. "Has he been dead for longer than three days?"

"No."

"Is it a crime of passion?"

The lady's beauty mark twitched. "Oh, yes," she said, with much more relish than strictly appropriate.

All right, I could follow this. So a man who was neither tradesman nor laborer. A man murdered due to some high emotion—my bets hedged on love. That often seemed to spark the worst in others.

The victim was also a man who had not been dead long, which—if this were a real murder—would mean that his associates had only just discovered the body. But I had no body with which to proceed.

Clearly, I would need to pinpoint who or what the murdered victim was. Once I had this, I could begin to investigate for clues.

A lord was a dangerous target for a murderer, but given how long until the next Season, it was entirely within the realms of possibility that a murderer could assassinate a lord just as the Season ends. The body may not be found for— No, no. His staff would come looking, of course, and any crime of passion regarding a titled victim would certainly reach all ears.

I couldn't see it. I needed more information, but my five questions were up. "A question as to the rules of the game, if I may?"

"You may," Lady Rutledge allowed.

"How long do I have?"

This time, her mouth twitched into a smile that wasn't entirely nice. Something both amused and edged. "That depends entirely, Miss St. Croix. The longer it takes you to solve, the more will die."

Much like the Ripper's victims. Stacking up by the pound.

"Does this have anything to do with the doxi—" I caught myself, but not in time. A collective gasp went up within the parlor. My cheeks burned. But Lady Rutledge laughed, her bosom heaving with each breath.

"You are beyond your questions, detective," she admonished as she sank once more to her chair. "You have more than enough to begin your hunt. Now, who would care for a drop more tea? Mr. Englebrooks, do be so kind as to fetch Miss St. Croix's cup. She appears to be in quite deep thought."

I couldn't deny it. I had precious little to go on, only a hypothetical murderer and a victim neither a working man nor a craftsman. Where would I go?

"Do you suppose she'll figure it out?" the gentleman asked, not so low that I couldn't hear.

Miss Dorring sighed. "So few do."

I would. I would because every man and woman in this room expected me to fail. I looked up from the full cup placed in my hand and looked not at Lady Rutledge, but at Englebrooks beside her. "Another question as to the rules."

"Ask," the lady allowed.

"Will I find answers any *place* else or is the game locked to your parlor, my lady?"

There. A twitch of Mr. Englebrooks's mustache, a flicker of an eyelash.

I would find clues. Scattered by the scheming lady and her retinue? Or common events likely to trigger questions?

"The game is *always* afoot," Lady Rutledge said, mysterious but for the giveaway of the gentleman she now turned to.

A flounce of pale pink beside me drew my attention to Miss Dorring, who smiled her charming smile at me. "Perhaps you'll get farther than anyone else has."

Faint praise, but I would take it with the grace Fanny drilled into me. "You are most kind. I hope to surprise you all."

Her lashes, beautiful and golden, flickered. Interest? Or disdain? I suspected Miss Dorring might even give Fanny a turn.

As if keen on proving my suspicions, she sat beside me, her smile kind—too kind. "I understand Earl Compton has returned to Town. Has he visited you to declare his intentions yet?"

My fingers tightened on the fragile handle of my cup. Suddenly, all thoughts of murder—real and hypothetical—fled. "I beg your pardon?" was all I could manage, a misstep. It confirmed what she suspected; what all of London suspected.

Mad St. Croix's daughter was no longer quite the earl's interest.

"Oh, that's too bad," she said, every bit the picture of sympathy and intrigue. "I'm sure you'll find a fine enough match in time."

"In time?"

She had no need to explain. I knew the words left dangling between us. Find a husband before my age dictated me quite firmly on the shelf. Before I would be competing with the fresh-faced young misses introduced every Season.

Appalling that even the ladies of this set focused so on marriage. But that was not what gnawed at me.

How long had he been returned? Why had the columns not said?

Had he deliberately failed to visit me? To send word?

Not, I reassured myself as Miss Dorring prattled in my ear, that I cared a whit what one marchioness's son did.

And did not do.

* * *

Booth took me home at the luncheon's end.

With the passage of the horse and carriage—no need for them on London's narrow walkways—the stature of a household came instead on the design of the gondola.

Some were fancy things, hand carved by master craftsmen and gilded to perfection. They boasted up to three pairs of pipes at the tail, from whence a steady stream of blue flickered. Others were subtler in design, dark wood polished to a fine gleam but with none of the excess.

The St. Croix gondola is not the finest of them upon the drift. Commissioned years before I'd ever needed it, gifted to my mother from my father's own coffers. To say my father had not been wealthy is a mild understatement, which placed value on the gift. He'd had it designed by a craftsman, an Italian working as a piano maker far below the drift in Hackney. It lacked the frivolity of many of the peerage's crafts, and boasted only one pan-flute array of pipes along the back, but it retained a covered box and a privacy screen, as well as a clean-air machine for days the fog shifted.

The apparatus by which aether was extracted from the air and used to fuel the device was among the more silent, only a distant hum as Booth guided the gondola along the surface of the fog billowing in the canals. There were those whose rattle could be heard for blocks, and others still even quieter than mine.

But no matter how nice the gondola, the true value came with the skill of the gondolier. Booth was brilliant; not only could he hold a straight line, but he'd mastered the levers lining the driver's seat to such an extent that the bottom of the gondola only just skimmed the fog.

The ride home was quiet as I could like. Or, more accurately, as quiet as Fanny could like, who had stayed at home due to Lady Rutledge's assurances as to my reputation's safe harbor. Silence tended to give me too much time to think.

Too much time thinking ended only in the same thoughts plaguing me from all angles. Earl Compton had returned from his hasty leave of absence, and he had not sent word either before or after.

As Miss Dorring ever so neatly intimated, this could only mean that he had not meant any of the silver-tongued platitudes he'd levied upon me that afternoon in the exhibit.

I had never needed evidence that a man, by his very nature, remained bent only on conquering. War was a telling thing, and so, too, were the auction tables in the worst of the gaming hells below the drift. The Menagerie sold women by the pound, and Monsieur Marceaux was not kind to the girls in his employ.

Those girls, that is, who could not make of themselves something worth selling for alternate demand.

I knew what men wanted.

I should not have been so surprised—or hurt—that Earl Compton was the same.

I must acknowledge how much admiration I hold for you, Miss St. Croix.

My gloved fingertips settled over the softness of my own lower lip. It tingled as I pictured—remembered—the shape of the earl's mouth as it touched mine. The tickle of his neat mustache.

His eyes, so close; their typical reserve lit from within by something I'd felt curl inside me.

One kiss. Only one, and I'd gone calf-eyed for the man. Preposterous.

Micajah Hawke had done so much more than a kiss, but I was not mooning for him. Of course, the things he'd done to me, each memory gilded in a faint pink haze, had been done to save me from the grip of Abraham St. Croix's opium serum. He may have tarnished me some, but he had not spoiled me.

Not that it mattered, either. I would marry no man, so I feared no gossip.

Perhaps, I thought in sudden, manic cheer, I would take a lover when I inherited. That would show him.

That would show them all.

The gondola bumped gently, jarring me out of my introspection with a swiftness that left me inhaling a sharp sound. I tucked a finger beneath the curtain, peered through the narrow seam to see my house-boy hauling a rope along the docking berth of my Cheyne Walk residence.

Levi was a gap-toothed boy of perhaps twelve, thin as an imp and as like a troublemaker as not. He minded himself around my staff, but I had no doubts he didn't bother elsewhere.

I knew what it was to sneak away for some well-earned recreation. Whatever the boy got up to when he thought no one knew, it did me no harm to allow it.

Within moments, he'd tied the gondola, placed the narrow stair beneath the door, and stood back as Booth helped me disembark. I flashed the boy a grin, but did not address him directly. "I shall go in," I told my butler.

"Of course, miss." As I turned away, I heard him add, "Nicely done, Leviticus. See it put away."

"Rightly so, Mr. Booth."

I left them to pull the gondola into the charming carriage house once used to store horses and hurried inside. "I am returned," I called, easily picturing my chaperone's wince as my voice lifted through the house.

My foyer was an impressive thing. Not so much in size as in decor. The walls were patterned in thin stripes of rose and burgundy—my mother's touch, I was sure—while the hardwood floors gleamed in polished cherrywood. It was an outrageous display of affluence, but I admitted to enjoying the red-tinted dark wood beneath my feet. Light streamed through the fan window set above the door, illuminating the lamps affixed to each wall. The wicks were turned down at the moment, but the Westminster clock had sung out a warning that the day would end soon.

Even now, the sky darkened behind the low-hanging bank of wintry clouds.

A wide mirror framed in gilded wood provided guests opportunities to fix hats and overcoats, but I didn't bother with mine. I untied the ribbons curled under my chin and swept my bonnet off my head with a heedless tug. Pins loosened.

"Fanny?" Swinging the bonnet by its ribbons—and jarring its pale cream feathers, like as not—I sauntered through the hall to the parlor, where I suspected Fanny to be.

She was not.

I'd made it no farther than the staircase with its wider base and lion guardians when a rustle at the top caught my attention. I looked up, smiling. "There you are, I—" My smile vanished. "What have you done, Fanny?"

Chapter Five

"C herry St. Croix, what manners." My chaperone came down the stairs, one hand upon the banister, as regal as any queen. But her smile, mirrored by the sparkle in her eyes, spoke of mischief. "Don't swing your hat like that, you'll ruin the bindings."

Something had happened. Something good, I thought, at least for her.

Which meant only one thing. I narrowed my eyes at the hand she held behind her back. "What are you holding?" I demanded, and it was a demand. Neither sweet nor patient.

"A manservant came 'round while you were gone," she told me, deftly tucking whatever it was she held into the folds of her overskirt as she swept around the boldly staring lion beside me.

Who had come? Whose servant?

Lady Rutledge's? I wouldn't put it past the lady to send the next clue straight to my door, but that hardly seemed sporting.

"Come into the parlor."

"I don't want to."

"Stuff and nonsense, Cherry, into the parlor." She tucked her arm in mine and I had no choice. It was either follow her skillful lead or drag my heels like a stubborn child.

Despite my reticence, curiosity plagued me. Was it a letter? A note from the so-called victim's betrothed, demanding a detective's help?

Was it something from Mr. Ashmore? No, unlikely, he'd have used the post, wouldn't he? "It's not from my guardian, is it?"

"No, Mr. Ashmore is currently somewhere near India, as I recall." Fanny's smile didn't fade. It didn't so much as dim as she led me to the settee I favored. "Sit."

"Fanny, really." I sighed. But I sat. "If you've any soul at all, you'll at least let me ring for tea."

She turned, reached for the bellpull and tugged it gently. Somewhere in the kitchen, a faint chime whispered underneath the crackle of charring wood in the fireplace. The room was warm, much warmer than outside, and I was grateful for it. The air retained a sharp bite; warning that winter would be soon upon us.

Within moments, I was perspiring gently, which reminded me that I'd left my coat on. I tugged at the ornate fur collar just as footsteps preceded my housekeeper into the parlor. In her hands, a silver tray.

In her eye, a mirrored sparkle.

Now I knew. "You've the same look as she does," I accused Mrs. Booth, ignoring Fanny's censuring sigh. "Will neither of you confess?"

Mrs. Esther Booth was as much a mother to me as Fanny, perhaps more of the affectionate aunt. She and her husband minded my house well, and I'd never wanted in their care. Though I'd been a terrible creature at the age of thirteen, the Booths had kept everything running as smooth as could be.

But I had no illusions as to the nature of their loyalty. Where I disliked Mr. Oliver Ashmore—and found his behavior exceedingly suspicious—Mrs. Booth doted on the absent man like a mother lacking her firstborn son. I knew they reported on me.

I did not know if they'd ever written to my devil-guardian to inform him of my antics of September last. I had received no letter of censure, and my stipend had not ceased, so I could only assume they had not.

"Let's take your coat, miss," Mrs. Booth told me, not unkindly as she worked it off my shoulders. She took my bonnet as well, though I saw her exchange a querying glance with my chaperone as she did. Ladies commonly wore their hats inside and out.

When Fanny only shook her head, a fraction of dismissal, I rose once more to my feet and pointed an accusatory finger. "Mrs. Frances Fortescue, what devilish mischief have you been up to?"

"Saints above," she said, reproach in the prayer as she reached for tea. She dropped two sugars into the delicate cup—fine with its pale rose pattern and gilt-trimmed edge, but nowhere near as posh as Lady Rutledge's—and passed it to me. "You are less than patient."

"As a rule," I confirmed, removing my gloves before taking the tea. I enjoyed the robust flavor of tea. I found a cup bracing, especially on days when what I really wanted could not be had.

I had not yet grown accustomed to coffee, though many of my acquaintances above and below the drift favored it. Tea was my choice, when a choice was had.

"Are you quite calm, then?" Fanny asked me. A test.

A carrot dangled from a stick.

I was not a circus pony to bite. "Barely," I told her. The anticipation ate at me, clawing at my tolerance with every minute wasted on niceties. "You'd think you held an invite from the Prince." Of course, should His Royal Highness grace my door with an invite, I'd have been rather out of my head, as well.

Her Majesty's eldest son was a known supporter of the arts and sciences. Bending his ear for even an hour would give me wings. Of course, I'd need my inheritance to make any such dreams come true.

No, given that Fanny was firmly seated and her color was otherwise normal, it was not anyone so fine as that asking for me.

That meant only one thing. My gaze narrowed as my grip tightened around my saucer. "You've heard." I didn't need to elaborate.

She offered her hand with, had I not known better, what looked like a flourish. Certainly not. Fanny did not flourish. "This was left for you." Neither confirmation nor denial. Telling in itself.

No wonder she'd hidden it from me. The earl's family crest had been burnt into the narrow box, unmistakable even from a distance: a fierce lion surrounded on three sides by a knight's helm. Starched into holding its shape, a simple gold ribbon wrapped around the narrow width.

My palms itched fiercely. A lump gathered in my throat, one part anger that he thought me so simply bought, and two parts curious excitement.

I wanted to know what was in the box.

I set my saucer down upon the Japanese table within reach. It was, unlike much of the rest of the furnishings, one of the few things Mr. Ashmore himself had acquired. I didn't know how; I wondered, of course, but I would never ask him.

That would involve talking to the man, and I'd sooner slit my throat than invite that demon to my table. Which was his table, for the moment.

I shook my head.

"Open, Cherry."

"I don't want to," I snapped.

Her eyebrow arched, forming lines of age across her forehead. Her smile dimmed. "You don't want to know what it is?"

I did. Very much. But if I opened it, would I then lose the moral ground I fancied I stood upon?

She rose, the pretty purple sheen of her silk skirt offset beautifully by the velvet-patterned overskirt pulled up into an elegant bustle behind her. Zylphia was getting better at the fashionable draping.

"At least open it," she told me, pressing the box into my hands. She squeezed my fingers around it, insistent as well as reassuring. "He may have given you something to wipe all your concerns away."

"Unless it's a pistol, I don't want it," I told her, childishly pleased by her gasped "Cherry!"

I shrugged, and because it cost me nothing, I stripped the ribbon from the box and studied its surface. The wood was perfectly smooth, varnished to a gleaming shine. Where the crest had been branded at the side, the edges only faintly tickled the sensitive pad of my fingertips.

It wasn't large enough for a pistol—and besides, there was a matching set upon the wall of the study, and a handful of Booth's hidden through the house already—but the box seemed heavy. Either the wood was solid, or the item was.

Maybe he'd sent me a box full of opium.

I almost laughed at the ridiculous thought. Smothered it just in time. Fanny would not understand the jest, and I hadn't told anyone about my run-in with the earl outside one of Limehouse's opium dens.

"Come on, then."

"All right, all right," I replied quickly, and slid the very tip of my unfashionably short nails under the hinge. It opened easily, not a creak to be heard. Gold winked in the firelight.

"Oh." I made the sound before I could halt it, as much a gasp of delight as it was disappointment.

So Lord Compton thought me easily bought after all.

But what taste he offered. As Fanny leaned over my shoulder, I carefully withdrew a pair of delicate fog protectives from a velvet bed. The gold rims winked brightly, reflecting back a warm sheen. They would clip directly to the nose. Delicate barriers etched with scrollwork around each socket would protect my eyes from the encroaching fog, providing respite from the sting. The nose piece where it would grip, the frames, the shining clarity of the glass, all of it bespoke care and craftsmanship. French, unless I was mistaken. Much of the craftsmanship coming out of France bore distinctive etchings.

I owned my own set of fog-prevention goggles, of course, but I could never wear them in polite company. In that instant, my memory returned to that place outside Professor Woolsey's exhibit. A time before I knew the man inside was my father. That conversation with an earl had flowed as freely as any conversation between two people could.

Forgive me, but have you no fog protectives?

He'd thought me too poor, perhaps. Or too unfashionable. But he had not pressed. And now, I found he remembered.

Fanny withdrew the card left at the bottom of the box. "*A gift for Miss St. Croix,*" she read, excitement in her voice. "*For our next foray into the scientific realm.*"

I dropped the delicate protectives back into the wooden box, snapped it closed. "I don't want them," I said, and pushed the box into my chaperone's hand.

"What?" Her fingers closed around it by rote, yet before she could push it back to me, I let go. "Cherry, be reasonable."

"Send it back."

Her eyes widened, brow furrowing deeply as lines of stern disapproval bit into her weathered cheeks. "That would humiliate His Lordship," she replied, clutching the box to her bosom as if it were a love letter or a favored pet.

She was right. Refusing a gift, especially from a gentleman, was not only rude, it was all but unheard of.

I turned away, leaving my cup on the knee-high table and did not bother to stoop for them when my gloves tumbled to the floor. "Rightfully so. Send it back. Send it all back."

"We will do no such thing."

"Then *you* wear them," I snapped, and strode from the room. I ignored Fanny's call, knowing that dignity would not allow her to chase me through the house, and fled instead to the dubious sanctuary of my boudoir.

My heart pounded in my chest, an ache echoed in the too-dry texture of my throat. My mouth. I couldn't breathe. Suddenly, it was as if I'd been squeezed around the middle. I needed to stop. I needed to take a moment, take a breath.

I needed a draught.

But there wasn't enough to risk it. Taking some of my precious store of laudanum to calm myself now meant lacking it when I truly needed it. I was all right. I shut the door behind me, leaned against it as I closed my eyes and counted slowly to ten.

I made it until four before my lungs constricted. Six brought a shiver from deep inside, and my hands fisted against my corseted waist. The boning dug into my ribs, forced the air from me in a shuddering breath as my heart threatened to explode out of my chest.

"Eight," I forced through stiff, bloodless lips, "nine . . ."

It took me well past ten, onward to twenty, past simple digits and through all sixty-six of the elements within Mr. Dmitri Mendeleev's organized periodic table. I was well into the recitation of Mr. Edward Horatio's aether-to-oxygen ratio—of which I thought most to be incorrect—before the bands around my chest loosened.

My vision cleared.

I stared at my ceiling, unable to recall how I'd made it to my now-rumpled bed. I'd shed layers of my jacket and bodice, leaving them strewn on the floor, but somehow I'd left my skirt, bustle and petticoats intact. Even my ankle boots. My hair tumbled into my eyes, loosened by whatever antics I'd managed. My corset had been undone, but I was alone.

Grateful, anxious, I drew in a deep breath.

Damn Lord Compton. Without even showing his face—and how dare he?—his very presence in London sent me into a fit of the vapors.

This would never do.

My hands shook as I dragged myself upright. Fingers trembling, I redid my corset laces as best I could, once more dressed, and pinned my hair. At a glance, it would appear as if nothing had gone awry.

I knew better. Cherry St. Croix did *not* lapse into fits of hysteria. I had to get a handle on myself, on the situation.

I needed to collect a bounty that actually paid.

When I was done, I withdrew a large diary from its place upon my writing desk, prepared the quill with its brass nib affixed to one end, and set my mind to something more useful than earls and scoundrels.

Lady Rutledge had set before me a challenge.

A mystery. A murder. One man, neither a tradesman nor a laborer. I had no information on the murderer, either, or even the method by which the victim became such. She knew all there was to know, of course, as the game's mistress, but what kind of detective would I be if I directed all my questions to a single witness?

Murder, I wrote, the nib scratching softly across the fine French parchment. *Lord?* Unlikely, but I left it. Beside it, I added, *Street gang*. There were many claiming the streets below the drift. The Hackney Horribles, the West End Militia, the Black Fish Ferrymen. The one I was most familiar with called themselves the Brick Street Bakers.

Of the many things one could accuse the Bakers of, maintaining a profession was not one.

What other type of man was not a laborer or a tradesman?

Scientist. After a moment, I murmured, "Professors, doctors, philosophers. Sailors? Or is that labor?"

"What's that, *cherie*?"

I looked up from my small writing desk to find Zylphia setting out my collecting garb, her clear eyes on me as she shook out a pair of mended trousers.

I hadn't even heard her come in.

By rote, I reached for the brass watch I'd left discarded beside my diary.

"It's near full dark," Zylphia told me, even as I realized that fact from the worn facings. "I assumed you'd be departing tonight."

Clever girl. "You are correct," I told her, and snapped the watch closed. "Choose the brown woolen, and be sure my knives are sheathed properly." I stared at the words I'd scripted across the pages, only vaguely aware of Zylphia's voice across the lamp-lit room.

What else had been said at the soiree?

Conversation about Mr. Horatio and Dr. Finch. About the horseless carriages that would never make it in London, about a series of patents claimed by a man called Tesla. And, of course, about Lord Compton and his return.

If there were clues in any of it, I was not seeing them.

There was barely a thread to hold them together. Finch was a brilliant man whose work with aether engines revolutionized London. Horatio was an upstart whose claim to scientific infamy involved browbeating the public into sharing his ridiculous theories, even if Teddy tended toward belief in the subject.

The horseless carriages reported in the periodicals would never take hold. Aside from the noise generated by the motors, the energy required for movement would never be as efficient as Dr. Finch's aether engines. It simply lacked logic.

Mr. Nikola Tesla appeared, by all accounts, a disgruntled employee no longer working with America's brilliant Thomas Edison, yet his theories regarding single-speed motors and energy-over-distance transference seemed to hold potential.

Lord Cornelius Kerrigan Compton was merely an earl whose eyes strayed from a prize he likely realized he could never have, thereby breaking any conversational mold.

My fingers drummed on the desk. *Rat-a-tat*. What had I missed?

We spoke of gossip. Of the periodicals, of—

My pen clattered to the disk, ink drops splattering as I jerked upright in sudden comprehension.

"Cherry?"

I waved away her concern. "Have we all the papers today?"

Zylphia paused, her fingers entangled in the laces of my heavily reinforced corset. "Are you asking if we've kept them?" She shrugged, a graceful slide of gray-clad shoulders and white pinafore cap sleeves. "I'll go down and take a look, then. Which do you need?"

"All of today's. Include Mrs. Booth's gossip." I waited with barely concealed impatience as my maid set the corset aside. She left my bedroom, leaving me to study the pile of my collector's garb where she'd left it.

Fanny would have conniptions if she knew.

My bedroom, although not the largest master's bedroom—and that not for lack of trying—was not so much a sanctuary as it was the single room where I could maintain my belongings without Fanny's upturned nose. My books could share a shelf with Mr. Ashmore's in the study, but my chaperone tended toward thinly veiled disgust when she caught me reading some of my more grisly scientific dissertations. It was no longer worth the argument.

Here, with the three-panel vanity mirror, my comfortable bed, the delicately worked writing desk I now paced in front of, I could tend to my own business and leave Fanny to hers.

The instant I inherited my estate, I would claim the study once and for all, but until then, this would suffice.

I widened my pacing to include the whole diameter of the room by the time Zylphia returned, a small stack of papers cradled in the crook of her arm. "One or two have already been torn for kindling," she said by way of greeting, "but I've the rest from the bin."

I took them, spread them over my bed and quickly sorted them in neat rows according to quality of the information within. Gossip and other such useless drivel to the right, actual news to the left. My science periodicals weren't in the pile—I saved them elsewhere specifically so they would not be used for kindling before Teddy and I could meet to discuss them—but I didn't suppose I'd need them.

Murder was not a scientist's preference.

Except for my father, in retrospect.

I frowned. "Where is the *Leeds*?" I answered my own question even before my maid could draw breath. "Likely burnt. No matter, I've read that one already. Now, Zylla, answer me a riddle."

"Oh, grand." I ignored the sarcasm of the reply as she perched at the foot of my bed.

"A man has been murdered."

"A man?" Her eyebrow climbed, an elegant slash of black in her dark tea skin. "Not a West End whore?"

"Them, too," I allowed, but waved it away with a single swipe of my hand. "For now, let us focus on the man."

She nodded. "Fine. Who is he?"

"We don't know," I replied, twitching through three of the six papers. They crinkled noisily. "He is neither a tradesman nor a laborer. Nor is he a lord," I added after a moment's thought. Gossip ran too quick in London to assume all of Society would not know of such a tragedy.

"How was he killed?"

"That is the mystery," I told her, and pulled one set of papers from the rest. "Look through here for any notice of murder. We seek men only, so leave out the Ripper's endeavors."

"Why?" She took it, but over the paper's edge, her eyes met mine in quizzical bemusement. "What is this for?"

I grinned, my lips stretching, pushing as if the skin of my cheeks were too stiff for an easy smile. But I forced it, because I needed to smile. To share my excitement. "A challenge, Zylla."

"By whom?"

"No time to waste," I said over her question, and quickly retrieved my own paper from the lot. It didn't matter which. I did not sit, instead resuming my pacing as I leafed through page after page of Jack the Ripper headlines, notice of impending strikes, editorials written by gentleman I had no interest in unless they were my murderer or his victims.

Behind me, occasionally in front of me as I walked the length of the room like a manic housecat, Zylphia calmly read through her half.

I enjoyed having a literate assistant. I hadn't been

certain when I'd first met Zylphia, painted up like the Whore of Babylon all those seasons past, but—

I dug my fingers into my eyes. Where had that unkind thought come from?

Exhaustion, perhaps. I was feeling out of sorts. That episode, of course that's all it was.

That and my acute awareness of the near-empty jar of laudanum on my bedside table.

I had control of myself. I would simply keep myself busy.

There were always murders aplenty in London below the drift. If the Bakers weren't executing someone in an alley for a cause, footpads were relieving Abram men of their day's earnings, or some wife living in a hovel decided she'd rather be charged and alone than shackled to the now dead man with a knife in whatever extremely unfortunate organ earned the stabbing.

In this case, I found no dead men, but plenty of women. The Ripper's doxies, of course. One woman whose throat had been slashed by her lover, who'd confessed. Another who drowned in the river, mysterious circumstances.

I dropped each paper as I skimmed it, leaving a trail of them from bed to vanity to closet to door.

"Nothing," I muttered, nearly a growl in my frustration. "Nothing, still nothing. Bloody hell and bells, Zylla, what's a lady ought to do to find a dead man about?"

She snorted a laugh, but rustled her gossip rag at me. "Look harder, I'd imagine, or murder her own."

I couldn't imagine myself doing so. I'd never killed a man. Not even for the sometimes ludicrous amount of coin offered to do so on the collection boards.

Unlike my rival, who appeared to prefer assassinations to all other bounties posted.

Which gave me pause. "Do you suppose the murdered victim could be victim of a collection?"

Zylphia sighed. "*Cherie*, I have no idea what you're talking about."

"Nothing, no," I mused, more to myself as I glanced down at the last sheaf in my hands. "I suppose that'd be too—" I stopped. MURDER ON UNIVERSITY GROUNDS.

It really wouldn't be so simple, would it?

"Ah."

"Ah?" My maid glanced at me, but I didn't look away from the small, nearly invisible article buried in the *London Journal*.

"Ah," I repeated, mostly for the reason that my mind was already three steps ahead of my mouth and I knew Zylphia awaited an answer. And then, once I'd read the extremely short article in its entirety, I added, "And here we are. One professor murdered."

"A professor is neither a tradesman nor a laborer."

"Nor a lord." I handed the paper to my maid, picked through the leftover periodicals upon my bed while she read it. "The University College is below, just near the Philosopher's Square."

"Will you be going there tonight?"

Oh, how she knew me. I smiled. "Yes, of course. But first?" I smacked the paper lightly. "I want to see if there was a bounty for this professor."

"How?"

A fair question. I didn't have much recourse. Collection notices were pulled by the collectors who took the work—or removed entirely once complete. Obviously, this one had been complete, were it actually to exist.

Zylphia slid off the bed. "The sweets might know."

A fair point. The midnight sweets, as I'd already considered, heard a lot about life above and below the drift. Maybe they'd hear about death, too.

I stared at my ink-smudged hand for a long moment, considering my options.

I didn't have many.

"We leave after supper, then." Which would be soon enough.

Zylphia left me to help Mrs. Booth prepare the meal. I busied myself collecting the discarded articles and daily gossip rags. I set them in a pile, entertained myself longer with straightening my bed, arranging my perfume bottles, anything but sitting still.

My hands trembled. Excitement, I thought. Nerves. I'd found something to hunt, something so much more than a simple challenge from a Society lady.

What did Lady Rutledge know?

Perhaps nothing. To her, as life could be to so many of the wealthiest denizens above the drift, it was just a game. A challenge. Who could solve the mystery of the murdered professor?

Was this even what Lady Rutledge had meant?

I stilled, my gaze falling to the untidy pile of newspapers and print.

What if the cunning lady's game were simply that? A game. Nonsense drafted on paper. Was I desperately searching for something to occupy me? Something that did not come stored in a bottle, smelling of cinnamon and spice and a faintly bitter edge.

I needed to focus. My hands grew damp.

Perhaps I would beg off from supper. I wasn't all that hungry, anyhow.

Chapter Six

Deep below the drift, not so much hidden as deliberately avoided, there is an abandoned train station. Once upon a time, it had serviced much of the East End's railways, but the rails moved and with them, the station center.

Now, it was one of many fog-ridden buildings lost to time. And, as opportunity must be addressed, claimed by the collectors.

No outside gas lamp light pierced the devil-thick fog as it wafted through the open doors and long shattered windows. I didn't need much. The single working lens of my goggles painted a yellow path through the smoke. It hovered low to the creaking floor as I made my way inside, each stride displacing the pea souper in an eerily muffled echo of my own footsteps.

I did not know who leased the building, if it was owned at all, nor who had decided that the dark, abandoned interior would make for a perfect collection agency. If it was run by a shadowy figure, I had never seen evidence of such. At most, I had come across the occasional collector perusing the wall of notices, but as a rule, I did not often engage with them.

As far as I knew, I was the only woman among them, and if that weren't dangerous a circumstance enough, collectors only supported each other when a bounty was not on the line.

I knew my limits. Just as I often left the assassinations to those who wanted to risk a knife from the hand of one of their own as much as whatever dangers the mark posed, so did I choose to remain outside the collective.

I was never here if a bounty weren't the purpose.

The gas lamps left burning on the east and western walls had always been there. As before, I did not know who tended them. Perhaps other collectors, choosing to refill the basins when the kerosene burned too low. I'd never done so. They flickered now, dim but not impossible to read by.

The far wall, where the brick had long since turned black and pitted, served as the notice board. Bits of paper clung to the surface, some clean-edged and others torn as if pulled from the pages of a greater work. There were voids where bounties had been pulled, claimed by those who pulled them.

It was a safe way to ensure that no other collectors would be on your back.

I scanned them quickly, bypassing many for want of a weighty purse. There weren't more than a dozen tonight. The usual fares, I noted. Money owed, money squandered. Debts accrued a rapid pace below the drift.

Them what held the purse strings didn't take kindly to lost fare. The Menagerie often posted bounties, but I saw none this time. Taken already, perhaps. For all of Hawke's mystery and showmanship, the Menagerie had a reputation for paying well.

When I could get them to pay me, of course.

I frowned at the board, the respirator masking my mouth and nose turning my contemplative sound into something raspy instead.

Something was wrong, here.

I studied the notes again, reached up to rifle a gloved finger through those that overlapped.

As one fluttered in the passage of my hand, I realized what it was I saw. Rather, did not see.

My rival had not been here.

My index finger pinned on a scrap of torn parchment, crinkled about the edges and stained black from the constant coal-laden fog. Written in a careful hand were three simple words and a promise of a purse that might turn most collectors into dreamers.

Jack the Ripper. Demanded dead, and then some.

So a bounty had been placed on him after all.

Yet it wasn't that what bothered me. The paper was dirty, fingered a few times by the smudges across it, but otherwise untouched. Unclaimed. The collector who taunted me often left his chosen bounties upon the wall, but he marked them. A single slice, leaving the two halves parted but still pinned.

The rotter loved his knives. I owned one; the same one he'd used to pin my hair to the ground when Zylphia had rescued me from the Thames Tunnel.

Had he not seen the bounty yet?

Possible. How long since I'd seen his claim? A week, perhaps? A fortnight? Since the flowers had stopped.

I studied the wall, shifting my weight back on my

heels. Only the strangely sibilant whisper of shifting fog reached my ears, emphasized by the occasional flicker of flame from each lamp. I heard no footsteps. No breathing.

A part of me always wondered why it was I dreaded to hear a whistle in the dark. I suspected it had something to do with that collector, and the knives he wielded so casually from the shadows. Much of my relations with the anonymous man remained shrouded in a cloak of opium and alchemical concoctions, which bothered me.

What if it were a clue I failed to recall?

I withdrew from the wall, curious by my rival's absence. I couldn't help it.

If he was not actively collecting, what was he doing?

I hurried from the collection station as a shudder stroked icy fingers down my spine.

The gates to the Midnight Menagerie stood open, welcoming as a devil's bargain on a cold night. My breath mingled with the fog as it tumbled gently just outside the Menagerie's border.

Years ago, longer still than I'd lived in London and shortly before the stilts that raised the city, Vauxhall lost favor with the fashionably elite. While the once-infamous pleasure gardens turned instead to footpads and street doves, rumors of a new decadence began to reach those with coin and time to spare.

The Midnight Menagerie. Circus, private gardens, fairground, events catering to Society affairs or the simpler pleasures of men; anything could be had for a price.

Anything, that is, but subtlety. Neither the Menagerie nor the criminal association that ran it did anything by half measures.

As expected of an enterprise whose specialty often included ownership of one's soul in exchange for earthly delights, the Menagerie's dangerous ringmaster maintained debt that bound me to his precious Karakash Veil. The Chinese organization claimed all magic as its purview and insisted that my father's alchemical work qualified.

Whether I believed in magic or not did not change the fact that I was, in essence, the Menagerie's pet collector. Thank God they hadn't yet demanded that I perform in the circus rings to make good.

I strode through the gates unmolested, stripped off my goggles and respirator. I would not need them inside the grounds. By all reason, the Menagerie should have maintained the same air of stinging fog, decaying fish and acrid chemical stench that filled the rest of the district. It did not. How the caretakers managed to keep the infectious miasma away was a closely guarded secret I had yet to uncover.

I passed the footmen standing watch on the inside. Those, I knew, weren't for the protection of the gardens. No one would dare take on the Veil on their own grounds. Rather, the uniformed men served as a marker of importance, levying just another layer of gilt over the corrupted heart of what was, in essence, little more than a flesh-peddling operation.

But, oh, how dazzling it looked by night.

I stopped on the neatly graveled path, taking in the vista with an unavoidable frisson of admiration. Say what I will of Hawke and his gardens, even I had to admire the effect.

The architect of these grounds had outdone himself. Open fields had been sculpted into a fairy tale by the clever application of pale rock paths through miraculously green grass—somehow, the caretakers managed to grow things beneath the foggy drift—and ornate fountains. Sheltered groves were given an incandescent glow by hundreds of Chinese paper lanterns in every conceivable color. They hung overhead, strung along the paths and cleverly affording shadows by which to entertain one's self, or one's companion, in.

Even as the pooled circles of light offered teasing glimpses of the activities in those same shadows. Everything had its price in the Menagerie, after all.

Various structures dotted the grounds—the private gardens surrounded by tall hedges, the rows of vendor stalls for market events, the ornate façade of buildings that hosted various festivities—but none drew me, and repelled me, so strongly as that of the circus tent lit like a crimson jewel.

I tucked my fog-prevention goggles into a pouch designed to secure them, glowering at the tent as if it could somehow sense my distaste. I didn't need to be inside to know what it would feel like. Cramped, trapped between an eager audience and the thin canvas of the tent above, the heat pulsating like a living heart. *Fear squeezing my throat, my lungs constricting even as that first step over nothing is taken. . .*

Even if I could not recall everything about my time in Monsieur Marceaux's . . . let's call it *employment*, I do nevertheless remember what it was like to stand before a crowd and wonder if the next step taken would be my last.

The skills I learned there, I would not perform.

I turned away from the tent's meandering path, shaking my head hard. The cold air bit at my cheeks, and as I ran my gloved hand over my brow, I realized I'd broken into a sweat.

How close I stood to the crevasse of my past. And yet, I still came. Why?

Certainly not for Hawke.

And not a lie, that one. As the serpent of this earthly Garden of Eden, Micajah Hawke would be inside that tent, smoothly directing the crowd as all ringmasters must. I had no desire to talk to him; a decision with multiple motives. The less I saw of him, the less I would be reminded of my untenable position. And the less opportunity he'd have to remember that though he calls me Miss Black, my hair is red. He should know. He'd seen rather more of me than any other stranger.

I snapped out a word that would have had Fanny turning faint and strode instead for another batch of structures placed deep in the heart of the grounds.

I needed the sweets.

The women of the Menagerie were well cared for. Cleanly, healthy, pampered to a degree. The footmen protected them, and many were slightly more educated than the whores found by the docks.

The payment of such came in flesh—their own. Whether under a man or with a woman, whether by skin or conversation, each sweet fulfilled a role within the gardens that ensured money would continue to be spent. Lures and bait, temptation and more.

I'd bargained with the anonymous Veil to keep myself out of the sweet tents, yet I knew many of the women within and liked most. They tolerated me, even held me up as a type of mascot among them. A woman collector, how exciting.

I strode the path, wiping at my forehead and cheeks as if it would help. I imagined I'd smeared lampblack once more, but it didn't bother me over-much. Being dirty only dissuaded others from looking too close. I didn't expect anyone to place the black-haired collector in red-haired Cherry St. Croix's delicate kid slippers, but care still came easy.

I'd had my fill of unfortunate coincidence. Especially since the rival collector knew where I made my home. He'd said as much, even called me by name.

Zylphia, this collector, Fanny; the list of them what knew my double lives was already too long for my taste.

"Let me go!"

The cry pierced through the lantern light, shrill and more angry than frightened. Feminine, no mistaking. Without stopping to consider, I darted off the path and into the dark, a roundabout route to my destination.

A crack of sound, a sharp cry, and I heard masculine laughter. "Keep 'old, boys," came the raspy, soot-stained voice of a man who'd spent his life at sea rather than study. Not a lordling, then, out for a tussle.

My fingers flexed as I crept closer, skimming a line of hedgerows. To my right, the path remained a golden trail—too obvious an entry point. To my left, buried amid the foliage, I heard the trickle of fountains, or perhaps something more decorative. A pond, a waterfall. I couldn't recall.

"You leave her be!" Another woman, this one husky, as if broken by tears.

My jaw set. Where were Hawke's footmen? Thugs, the lot, but they should have been here.

I crept forward another meter, and found my

answer. A man groaned as my foot came down on a limb, twisted and sent me nearly toppling to the earth.

"You 'ear that?"

"Shut up," snarled the sailor, his voice a lash. I heard muted sobbing, now, and the whisper of women held at bay.

I grinned fiercely in the dark.

This was not my strongest moment, but I can only say now that I had no real care for my well-being. I wanted only something to take the sting from that terrible need in my belly, and this proved the first opportunity. As I crouched over the still figure of the coshed footman, I measured the distance between where I hid, guarded by foliage, and the location of the voices.

"Ca'mon, 'urry up," complained a man, a third one, now. Three to my one, and at least two women.

A sprint, then. If I could break up whatever hold they had on the girls— "Hsst!"

I looked up by instinct, though I couldn't say now why I looked directly up and not over either shoulder. Buried memory, perhaps. A voice carries a distinctive quality when spoken overhead.

Nothing but black.

"Hsst!"

This time, I turned, looked across the narrow confine between my hiding place and the path.

I met dark eyes, near-black in the reflected light of the red lantern nearly concealing him. The boy, his shaggy dark hair hanging into his eyes and his teeth bared in a grin, pointed at me.

I cocked my head.

A child. Perhaps ten, or a well-formed eight. More, I'd bet my last dregs of laudanum that this boy worked at Hawke's circus; if the way he clung to the post was any indication, he was at least one part agile monkey. His grubby bare feet propped around the ornate iron post as if glued in place.

As I raised my eyebrows, a burst of raucous laughter erupted from the gathering I was afraid would not remain tame for much longer. The boy doffed an imaginary cap, scrambled to the very top of the post and darted over nothing.

He did not fall.

Instead, as the lights dipped and swayed, I glimpsed his nimble figure, a faint silhouette colored by the lights, as he sprinted across the lantern line—as smooth as any tightrope walker as I'd ever seen, back the way I'd come and to find, I assumed, help.

The husky-voiced woman shrieked. "You keep your hands off her, you bleeding sodomites!"

"Keep 'er still, damn it."

I heard the unmistakable sound of something weighty against flesh.

"You whore," roared a man, and there was my cue. I leapt over the prostrate form of the useless footman, barreled through the hedge and directly into the broad back of a man in my path. Fortuitous chance. He bellowed like a bull, and all I glimpsed was a frothy pile of blue tulle, blood like a crimson smear against the lace-frosted edge, and a still body upon the ground.

Sweet, golden-haired Talitha, the theatrical "sister" to Jane, who fought in the hands of two other men.

I had no time to take in other details. As I rode the man to the ground, my knees in his back, I reached for the knife slatted into my high-necked collecting corset. It whispered out, obscenely loud in the shocked silence.

The man beneath my weight shifted, shoulders squaring as he braced both hands against the ground. He could easily shake me off. At least until the point of my blade dug into the nape of his neck, impossible to ignore.

He froze. Muscles bulged beneath his shirtsleeves.

"Evening, lads," I said, pleasant for all my heart pounded in my throat and fear conspired to send sizzling waves of energy to my limbs. I forced a smile. It came too easily. "Collector's business. What say you fine gents move along?"

Three of them. Blast it. They circled Jane, the hand of one man curled around her throat, but her wide eyes telegraphed a fury the likes I'd seen before.

Huddled in the dark, two more sweets. I didn't recognize either offhand, one cradled by the other in tactile reassurance, but they were within range. I did not have any cards to play when the game involved a hostage.

One of the three men took a step.

The tip of my blade carved a bloody circle. The sailor beneath me moaned.

"Tsk," I told them, my gaze stern on the stocky fellow who'd moved. "If you'd like your mate back, I suggest all three of you come and collect him." Another smile, all teeth. "Before I do."

"Bitch," the sailor growled beneath me.

"Come for the sweet auctions?" I asked cheerfully, steadfastly ignoring Jane's gaze on me. Ignoring Talitha's still figure half pooled in the dark. Sweat blossomed across my back, but I felt no cold. Instead, I stared into eyes I could not see the color of in the dim light, feeling every muscle in my legs beginning to strain with the effort.

"Get 'er," growled the bald, tattooed man with his hand around Jane's throat. She made a sound like a gurgle, her eyes suddenly much wider as those fingers dug into her neck.

I glanced at the man beneath me. Not the leader, then. Pity. I withdrew the blade, at a slightly sharper angle than strictly necessary. His shoulders jerked beneath my knees. *"Allez, hop!"* I launched backward, pulling my weight into a walkover that surprised everyone but me. It placed distance between us, and with my free hand, I pulled the second knife from the tailored back of the corset.

The blades glinted in the dark. "You want a woman, here I am," I taunted. "Going once . . ." I tossed one knife up. The lantern picked out its keen edge on a thin line of gold. "Going twice."

Two sets of eyes traced it, and I flung the second with unerring precision.

"Sold."

A man's short scream pierced the grounds, echoed by the rattled shock of the two watching sweets. The man I'd already dropped would not move for the moment; not while my blade pinned one hand to the earth.

It was not a wound that would heal lightly, but neither was it a deathblow. A small courtesy he would not thank me for.

Two of the men disengaged from Jane's presence. "All right, little girl," said one, reaching behind him to withdraw a blade that made mine look like children's toys. I swallowed hard, eased my weight to the balls of my feet. "Rumor 'ad it there were a collector bitch." I tended toward hound euphemisms.

Something about a dog collecting bones; I'm sure I didn't know. He grinned. "Can't wait to see what your 'ead costs."

He charged me.

For a brief, yet seemingly eternal moment, silence reigned. That terrible waiting that always precedes a skirmish; that moment when all parties weigh the odds, and stack them where they could.

I'd done no such thing. I had no need. I'd done all my weighing prior and gave no thought to consequence.

Yet the sailor did not reach me.

A crack shattered the taut moment. Before any could react, myself included, a black snake uncoiled from the shadows and wound around the charging fellow's thick neck. It snapped tight, jerked him solidly off his feet, left him clawing and struggling for air as his backside slammed into the ground.

I spun, my last knife held at an angle parallel with my wrist, and ducked the wild swing of a second man. I heard a gasp, a shuddering intake of air, and I didn't know if it was the first bloke or Jane, but I pushed forward with all my strength and jammed my shoulder square into my opponent's stomach.

He retched, as I knew he would, dropping to the ground, hands and knees. He gasped, heaved; a fancy bit of a trick I'd learned from a Baker ages ago.

That crack came again, that terrible hiss of sound, and I realized where it came from.

I turned, blade at the ready, but I had no need.

As Jane flung herself at Talitha's side, the last man—the sailor whose voice I readily picked out—fell to his knees. The whip coiled around his neck, one meaty fist curled around it as if it would help loosen its grasp.

I sucked in air as fast as I could, my hands shaking with strain. With raw fire and energy.

The man's face was red. It only mottled harder as he struggled to breathe.

From the shadows alongside the path, on the other end of the taut length of black, Micajah Hawke stepped into view. Even dressed for his part as ringmaster, he cut the finest figure. His long, powerful legs were encased in slim black trousers, their high waist and tailored fit only serving to showcase the lethality of his lean build. His shirt was also black, but the fitted waistcoat and coattails he wore tonight were a blue so vivid, no sapphire would ever match it.

He must have come direct from the rings, for the whip he carried would fit upon the belt slung around his hips. His straight midnight hair, always so well maintained, was tousled, as if he'd run his fingers through it—or, rather likelier of the intended effect, been caught by a woman who'd done the same.

He did not look at me. He did not have to. Energy turned over into an awareness so sharp, it was all I could do not to gasp. Sweat coated my face, my shoulders. Even the woolen shirt I wore was too hot, but I did not step away.

This was a battle of another sort entirely, and I would not lose.

"Her head," Hawke informed the kneeling, shaking man, "is worth more than your miserable lives will ever see."

Not exactly a compliment.

His fist coiled around the whip, tightening it until he towered over the sailor, the gallows to the man's impromptu noose. The man choked, gasping for it, his skin flushing now to purple.

Hawke had no questions, apparently; I don't believe he asks them often. The rules of the Menagerie are clear. Any man, lord or merely drunk as one, who breaks them does not often see a second chance.

As the man rasped something guttural, choked off by the rawhide about his neck, I turned and bent at the one whose hand I'd pinned. He moaned; I ignored him, wrenching the blade free.

This time, his scream cut off on a crude hope for my imminent demise.

I wiped the blade on his shirt, shaking my head, and tucked both knives into my corset once more. As I did, footsteps pounded the grounds behind me. Within moments of recognizing the sound, a figure in satin—and so little of it that I entertained a bemused uncertainty of where to put my hands—threw herself into my arms.

"Thank God you'd come!" the sweet said tearfully. I recognized her, now that I realized she was nearly as short as I. Lily, often called Black Lily for style, had hair normally as black as mine below the drift, but today she wore a wig of false hair. Red, like mine above. Odd enough to give me pause. "It was terrible, they came demanding time, laid out Peter—"

I was in very real danger of soaking my shoulder with her tears. I patted her mostly bare back awkwardly. "All's right now, Lily," I said, reassuring as I could.

Frankly, I'd been lucky. I wasn't completely ignorant. I looked over her head, frowning at Jane and her prone friend. "Talitha?"

"Out," Jane called, her tear-streaked face still as beautiful as sunshine. "She'll come 'round. Grateful, too."

Four men spilled into the clearing. Within seconds, Hawke ordered them all into action. Only two footmen were needed for the suitably cowed offenders; I noticed they did not head for the gates.

Menagerie justice was something I learned long ago not to inquire about.

Hawke slowly coiled the whip. His eyes, mismatched in a truly unique fashion, met mine. They were dark brown, the kind of rich color earned when a painter has taken layer upon layer of tawny gold and deepened it with shadow. In the middle of his left iris gleamed a brilliant swath of blue, as if the devil himself peered out from a single eye.

"Escort the ladies back," he said, but not to me. The footmen, one already bending to pick up Talitha with more care than I would have credited either, did so. Lily gave me a final squeeze, and hurried after the rest, red hair swaying near to her backside.

The leather creaked in Hawke's gloved hands. Blue gloves, to match the fine waistcoat and jacket. It brought out that blue river of flame in his eye. Warned me as to the level of the ringmaster's fury. "You lack all sense, Miss Black."

I raised my chin, suddenly wishing I'd kept at least one knife out. "All due respect," I replied, sincerely meaning anything but, "if I had not come, those girls would be in worse shape for it."

"Unlikely." He did not move to close the distance between us, which surprised me. And put me even more on edge. Hawke was, for all his outward polish, a brute of a man, prone toward aggression to make his point. "Why are you here?"

Truth, then. "I came to ask the sweets about a possible murder."

"You should know better."

In the daylight, Hawke is a man worth watching. His swarthy skin suggested Gypsy blood somewhere in his parentage, while his black as night hair only furthered the appearance of barely restrained savagery. Sculpted cheekbones, a mouth that might be considered feminine were it not for the face it appeared within, and a build both broad at the shoulder and tapered at the waist conspired to turn heads likely wherever he traveled.

I had plenty of opportunity these past three years to perfect my impression of the man.

By night, however, gilded by the light of half a dozen paper lanterns, he turned into Satan himself. He looked at me now, running that whip through his gloved fingers as if he considered using it upon me in kind.

I shivered. Cold, I'm certain.

I could have played my hand closer to my breast, but in this case, it would serve me nothing. "There's a bounty out for the one calling himself Jack the Ripper. Did you post it?"

"No." A bit of truth. I had no reason to trust all that came from the ringmaster's mouth—his role was to tempt, after all—but most Menagerie postings bore the name. He gave me more without prodding. "Whoever he is, he's never come to my Menagerie. The matter does not concern me or mine." His jaw shifted. "That includes you."

"Much obliged," I replied cheerfully, deliberately smearing on the saccharine gratitude because I knew it grated him. "However, you are wrong. I am not you *or* yours."

His smile, wordless and paired with a raised black eyebrow, did more to unnerve me than any words.

I scrambled for mental purchase. "I didn't come to

ask the girls about that, either. It's about a murdered professor," I told him.

To this, not so much as a flicker of an eyelash. Instead, he turned, strode once more down the path and toward the gleaming tent. I hesitated, a fraction of a second, then hurried to catch him up. "Hawke, it's serious."

"You have an unhealthy obsession with professors, Miss Black."

I winced. He wasn't far incorrect. "This one is different. Professor Isaac MacGillycuddy was found murdered—"

"Two days past, I'm well aware."

The bastard, lovely as he might have been to look at, lacked all sense of manners. He did not hamper his stride to suit my shorter stature, so I quickened my pace. "Slow for a moment, won't you?"

"No."

"Damn you, Hawke."

He stopped, so sudden that I'd ended three paces ahead by the time I turned.

The whip gleamed, sleek and black beneath the violet-tinted light of a Chinese lantern overhead. The same glint of color picked out in his hair, painted lurid designs against his cheek. His eyes flashed, warning.

Always warning.

"What draws you to murder, Miss Black?" A verbal knife, flung unerringly in the dark.

I opened my mouth. No words came.

A muscle ticked in his cheek. "Is there a bounty?"

"That's what I wanted to know." There. Honesty. I could manage that much.

His mouth tightened. "My sweets won't know."

"They might if it's been talked about."

"They do not." Finality. Hawke picked up his long-legged pace once more. "I am not pleased to have been called from the rings to save you, Miss Black. Lost time is debt."

The scorn with which he declared his displeasure slapped me, a bucket of icy water. "You did no such thing," I countered hotly. "I saved them long before you arrived."

He did not reply to that. The circus tent loomed taller and taller, and as we neared it, I heard the melody of lively music, the gasps and cheers of a crowd.

My stomach turned. That sweat I thought had passed returned, a damp, icy bloom down my spine.

How easy it was to remember the steps. A turn of the knee, a bend at the waist, and a knife whistling past my ear. Another dip, a wobble for effect, and an edge sharp as a razor taking a bit of hair.

"Miss Black."

I blinked hard, realized too late that I'd stopped dead on the path, my gaze fixed somewhere beyond Hawke's blue-clad shoulder. He stared at me, features unreadable, even as a lazy half smile shaped his mouth.

I closed mine.

"Every bounty you bring," he said, not ungently for all he closed the distance between us with a step. "Every collection you achieve, every purse you turn away, only serves one purpose."

I found my voice at last, raised my chin to meet his gaze direct over mine. "I'm well aware." I was also keenly aware of his warmth, mere centimeters away. Of the powerful line of his chest, within reach.

I attributed the feelings I experienced to the shared memory of that night in his bed. The night he'd saved me from the serum that conspired to strip my very self away.

He hadn't taken me then. I was not inclined to allow him the opportunity now. But the man had saved my life.

Blast it. Just as he likely had now.

He raised his hand; I did not realize which until I felt the cold length of the whip's handle along my cheek. "You only delay the inevitable," he murmured, a husky warning. "The *móshù*, Miss Black, or it will be you they pay for."

My blood turned instead to ice. I could not hide a shudder, but I raised one hand and pushed his whip away from my face with more strength than I think he expected.

"Never," I swore, and took a step back, earning another lazy smile.

A knowing thing, too intimate by half. "I look forward to your eventual delivery. Whether it comes in a vial, or wearing your skin and little else."

My cheeks flushed. "You cannot put me in the auction rings," I snapped, eager for a fight to warm the sudden chill inside my soul. "The Veil has bartered that away."

The whip uncoiled, a sinuous whisper. "Never fear, Miss Black. I take care of all my pets."

I stared at him, met his challenge as my body vacillated between too hot with fury and too cold with fear. A roar went up from behind the thin red fabric behind him; the battle was lost.

"Return home," he suggested softly.

Pride be damned. I turned tail and fled.

His laughter haunted my every step.

Chapter Seven

Run I may have, but I would not flee home like a beaten dog. Instead, determined more than ever to prove Hawke wrong, I left the Menagerie grounds with my temper high and my common sense middling to low.

I cut straight across London, through Limehouse direct. The fragrant aroma of rotting fish and acrid lime stench the district was so well known for did not lift until I reached the Philosopher's Square.

Before the stilts went up, the square—less a true square and more an asymmetrical collection of structures and courtyards in whatever haphazard format they were originally erected and added to—had been the home of every thinking mind in London. The University of London had claimed it until a fire destroyed much of the territory.

The dean, rather than rebuild entirely, took the opportunity to segregate himself and many of his more affluent students above the drift, leaving the less sociably fashionable below.

Thus were King's College and University College

divided, and thus does it remain. What few enough realize, or care to realize, is that the same affluence that guides King's College still guides the secular and much less posh University College.

Women are, to a certain degree, welcome in the lesser of the two, but there were no scholarships, association, or tolerance of women in King's College. While the faith restrictions had been somewhat lax in this, our age of reason, there were certain lines of the sex that King's College refused to cross.

This was, of course, much to the detriment of the institution, for even those with power and brilliance—those like Lady Rutledge—could not attend. Or ever lecture.

I had never tried. University of any stripe had never appealed to me, and Fanny had always insisted that I'd no use for discourses and studies. Hadn't I come far enough on my own?

Wasn't I already rather skilled at elocution?

I was, certainly, but I chafed at the rift. Any woman who earned her diploma through University College would never be licensed. She could not practice as a doctor, or a barrister or a professor.

The fog filled the square from end to end. Unlike much of the city caught beneath its clinging blanket, the Philosopher's Square was a blot upon the map *almost* respectable enough for visitation. Exhibits often came to the warehouses and facilities scattered across the district, and on some days, even Society gathered for an outing among the scientific minds of the area.

Yet, it was as dangerous by night as the gaming hells and opium dens. I knew of no gang that claimed it their own, which suggested to me it still hovered as neutral ground.

I took care. I hurried to my destination, keeping to the fringes lest I inadvertently stumble on late-night students or professors burning the post-midnight oil.

I did not often have cause to stroll the college grounds. The last time I'd been nearby, it had been on the arm of Earl Compton, and this as a St. Croix. How appalled would he be to find me here, now, wearing the trappings of a collector, and the trousers of a man?

I stifled a smile, though I didn't need to. My respirator kept the worst of the scratch from my throat, and the yellow lens over one eye guided me easily along paths less obvious beneath shifting banks of yellow and black.

What would I do here?

It didn't matter, truly. I would search the dead professor's offices, perhaps find a clue the constabularies missed. Perhaps I would find nothing, and return home all the more clueless as to Lady Rutledge's challenge.

There would be only one way to know for certain.

The University College boasted a fine array of twelve Corinthian columns and a pediment elevated on a plinth by at least nineteen feet. The triangular pediment boasted no ornamentation, but what it lacked in grandeur was more than supported by the large, round dome peeking from behind. Light from the cupola behind the columns shed an eerie flicker as the fog snaked between the dirtied pillars.

This was the main building, the central entry by which pupils and professors alike passed through. The gritty London fog had worn the once-pale stone to smudged gray, and the columns seemed to be suffering with time.

I walked quickly through the guttering lamps affixed to each column, found the doors unbarred. With so many pupils, it should not have surprised me, but I could not help but wonder if such ease of access only hastened Professor MacGillycuddy's demise.

I stepped inside, pulling the door closed behind me, and took a moment to slip the protectives from my face.

All was quiet. Not so much as a murmur of a voice reached me across the vast halls. No footsteps, no echoes. The furnishings were genteel in nature, not fine but neither were they poor. Affixed to the walls, statues carved in exquisite detail loomed over the interior hall. As I passed, I noted Flaxman's *Farnese Hercules*, his rather comically large Michael overpowering a cowardly Satan.

Here in this hall, I was surrounded by more men's flesh than would ever be deemed proper were it actually *in* the flesh, as it were, and I could not help a sudden fit of laughter that I could not muffle behind my gloved hands.

I was no stranger to the concept of conjugation, nor to idea of nudity, but it bemused me, even as it tickled me, that such things cast in stone were wildly more welcome than wrapped in life.

But I did not come to view the art, powerful though it had been reviewed by critics.

Where would I be, then, if I were offices belonging to a professor of naturo-philosophy?

It took me virtually no time to circle back around to the main portico, and even less to locate the study halls of what must be the naturo-philosophers. The door, like the others, was unlocked.

The lights in the hall were kept bright, but only

a distant flicker worked its way through the inky shadows clinging to the open gallery.

Vaguely threatening shapes loomed at me as I peered inside, outlined by what faint ambient light trickled through strangely wide windows. What views must be had on clearer days? Lucky pupils, to be so gifted with the apparatus of the institution.

My footfalls whispered as I crossed the hardwood flooring. No rugs dampened the sound, and I could just imagine the mild cacophony of bright, inquisitive minds filling the hall, seated behind each desk with book and quill—

I hesitated as I passed a long, cylindrical tube. Light danced across it in muted embers, and I reached out before I'd warned myself off. It didn't matter. There would be no traps for me here; only the temptation of an apparatus I could not have.

A telescope, for one. I recognized it, though I'd never looked through my own. A shame, that. There was not enough light, too much fog, to direct it to the window now.

Smiling faintly, I stepped around a large globe hanging from two distended tubes whittled to points. The earth shifted as I brushed past it, but did not fall. A merry shimmer of crystal rang brightly around me as I set glass stars swinging by accidental purchase.

And behind it, a muffled thump.

I froze in a sea of winking light and tinkling glass, unerringly pointed to the front of the hall, and the offices to the right.

Somebody was here. Not a student, for no one would work in the dark. Not, then, a professor.

Or perhaps just so, I cautioned myself, and crept quietly to the first of the doors. I pressed my ear upon it, and heard only a muffled, indistinct sound.

An animal? It certainly couldn't be too far-fetched. Naturo-philosophy covered much of the reasonable world, and animals were as much a part of it as I was.

Perhaps a great deal more free, on the whole.

I sidestepped neatly, pressed my gloved hand to the next door and bent to listen.

This time, I heard a woman's voice. Clipped. Irritated. An argument?

What she said, or to whom she said it, I could not know. I reached for the door latch; it caught, but did not lift.

Well, locked, then. At least something in this university was.

With nothing for it, I raised my hand and knocked. *Rap, rap.* Businesslike.

The voice stilled. I heard nothing, and then, sharply, footsteps. I stepped back as the door latch lifted. "What ungodly hour it is," grumbled the man who eased the portal open. A man? "No, there will be no delay on the tests scheduled for—" A pair of indistinguishable eyes framed by lanky brown hair widened as they pinned on me, in all my hand-tooled finery. "The devil are you?"

"Collector's business," I told him, and watched the color drain from his face. In the kerosene light afforded from the interior of the office, I could see that he was a thin man, made all the more apparent by the clothing that hung on his frame. His cheeks were a bloom of red, as if he could not cease blushing even should he demand it, and his hair was slightly too long for appeal. It was also mildly unkempt, suggesting he ran his fingers through it often.

Or perhaps, I thought as a shadow flitted in the

room beyond his shoulder, I had interrupted that very act, but with someone else's fingers.

"Am I interrupting something?" I asked, more than a little cheeky.

He stepped out of the office entirely, eased the door shut even as more rich color bled into his cheeks. "What do you want?" he demanded.

I raised my eyebrows, hands on my hips. "I am not here to wave a finger under your nose, sir."

"What?" His eyebrows beetled, caught somewhere between confusion and worry. "What's going on, then? Why are you here at . . ." He fumbled for his pocket watch. I let him, and took the time to admire the lovely casing as he opened it with impatient, ink-stained fingers.

The blend of tooled gold and worked copper was virtually unmistakable. The man may have no money now, but he'd once had enough to purchase one of Haldercourt Fussey's finest. I'd long since promised myself that should my trusty little brass watch give out, I'd court the man for a custom piece.

"Past three of the clock," I offered as he squinted at the glass. "That's when we like to come out, didn't you know?" But I smiled to soften the edge, especially when I watched him glance over his shoulder, snapping the timepiece shut. "You may be at ease, Mr. . . . ?"

"Professor," he corrected me. "Professor Johannes Lambkin, newly minted professor of naturophilosophical study."

A mouthful, and a motive. "Newly?"

"Since MacGillycuddy died."

A flicker of disappointment filled me. Was Lady Rutledge's challenge going to be this easy?

Professor kills professor for tenure. How boring.

I frowned suddenly, aware of the words still ringing in my mind like a chime. Boring?

Since when were lives boring?

"Right," I finally said, aware the silence had gone on too long for comfort. I raised both hands. "I'm not here to collect you, Professor. I am seeking MacGillycuddy's murderer."

Lambkin had the courtesy not to laugh outright. "A woman?"

"A collector," I assured him, but I made no move to prove the point. Either he would believe me, or he would not, and I would have to tie him to something sturdy while I bothered his girl in the office.

The next move was his, and fortunately for him, Professor Lambkin was a professor of the mind. He did not question me. "Right, then. Murder. If you ask me, he had it coming."

I tilted my head. "I beg your pardon?"

He smiled, a wry thing that pushed his too-thin cheeks into sharp relief. How a man could be practically blushing with good health and still manage to appear starved was beyond me, but he did. "MacGillycuddy was mean as an Irish bastard," he told me. "I suspected he was one. Never had a kind word, pushed his pupils hard."

"All of them? Did he have no favorites?"

"All of them," he confirmed, tapping the side of his beaklike nose. "But especially the ladies."

That surprised me. "Why the ladies?"

"My suspicion is he didn't have a mother to coddle him."

A bastard, and now a motherless one? It smelled an awful lot of vinegar to me. "If I were to ask you if you killed him, what would you say?"

He snorted outright. "I'd never kill a man with poison."

"Poison?" The word came out before I'd caught myself. That detail had not been in the article.

His eyes gleamed; devilish mischief, for all the morbidity of the subject. "Didn't know that, eh? Shame on your masters."

I stilled. Masters? What kind of woman did he assume me to be?

Aware of his blunder, Lambkin raised both hands. As if by sincerity he could ward away Satan himself. "Now, now, didn't mean nothing by it, miss," he said hastily. "Just a rumor, is all. Dr. Algernon mentioned in passing a day past or so."

"Mentioned what?" I demanded, lowering my voice to that octave that seemed to always cause men larger than I to quail. I watched it take root now, as if it weren't I—shorter, smaller, likely even not as strong—standing before him, but something more dangerous. A man, perhaps.

I would never kill him; I would not even accost him without good reason, but Lambkin needn't know.

I didn't smile, though I wanted to.

"A smell," he said, fast as he could process the words. "Funny sort of smell he said reminded him of a batch of foul stuff once come off a corpse on his laboratory slab. Don't know what, honest!"

I believed him. His shoulders all but twitched in a bid to fall back through the door he protected, his stance practically at right angles to the floor.

"What's your girl know?" I asked, such a quick turn of subject that I watched him blink near for half a minute.

"Girl?" And then, coughing into his open hand, he added much faster, "No girl, certainly not. That would be unseemly and against university law. No fraternization, no, miss."

The rotter fancied himself a real ladies' man, didn't he? Bringing a girl—likely a street dove—to his brand-new office to boast. I didn't have the heart to suggest that most ladies of such negotiable wages would not find a man of science worth any more or less than the coin in his pocket.

Instead, I asked, "Had he any particular students he struggled with? Any arguments? Notices of disciplinary action?"

"No, miss." And then, with a sigh, he admitted, "He was a right bastard, but the pupils respected him for it. To anger him would be to cut one's studies mercilessly short."

"Why?"

He shrugged, a little sheepishly if I was any judge. "Professor MacGillycuddy was also the Master of Admissions."

"What?" I took a step forward in my interest. "For University College?"

His eyes widened, so much that I could see more white than color. "For the University of London," he corrected me. "All of it."

Why hadn't that bit of information been in the article? I understood that all eyes remained fixed on this Ripper, but some professional pride wouldn't go amiss, even in a rag. Blast.

"Thank you for your time, Professor." And then, because I wasn't entirely heartless, I added, "And good fortune on your new position."

"Thank you." He made no move while I stood in front of him, so I departed without another word.

I was halfway across the hall when I heard him open the office door.

At the very least, I wished him a pleasant pastime with his doxy. She'd be no sweet, but if she followed him this far, then she was likely to warm his—well, to ease his burdens for a few hours at least.

I hurried swiftly through the halls, down the stairs once more. What had I learned?

The professor was definitely murdered. But why?

Was it Lambkin? I doubted it. He didn't strike me as a man with the constitution to commit murder. If he ever so much as drew another man's blood, he'd like as not be in tears before the wound clotted.

Then who? Another rival? How many could the naturo-philosopher have?

Certainly not every professor and lecturer in the university. Many would have no reason to kill for a motive of position. Mathematicians would never fill the role of a philosopher of the natural world; certainly the professors of musical study were barred.

Perhaps a better question was who would want to kill the Master of Admissions? And why was a master of the University of London not earning his keep in King's College?

I let myself out into the brisk October air.

Then sucked it in on a hard sound, a bitten off warning, as Zylphia stepped out of the shadows beside me. "You did not come" was her greeting, an accusation interrupted on my gasped, "By all the saints!"

I clutched for my suddenly racing heart.

The slats of my corset allowed me no purchase with which to dig my fingers in, but as I sensed no impending death, I let go. "Don't sneak up on me, Zylla."

Her eyes, strange and vibrant in even the faintest light, were narrowed. "You were to meet me on the edge of Baker."

Was I?

Oh, sod it. Of course I was. That was the bargain we'd made, wasn't it? She would not accompany me to the Menagerie, the better to keep her out of the Veil's immediate awareness, and I would meet with her on the edge of Baker Street territory. My sudden remembrance came on the back of a rude uncivility. I'd forgotten, indeed.

"I am sorry," I said, immediately contrite. "I thought to search the professor's hall after speaking to Hawke, I didn't—"

"Remember?" Zylphia matched my pace as I made my way down the steps, my shoulders hunched against the chill. "Or want company?"

"Come now, you know I wouldn't shed you on purpose." Not entirely the truth, but true enough for this moment. "I truly am sorry."

She frowned.

I could see she was clearly worried about something, so I stopped, faced her in the courtyard, hands on my hips. "What is it?"

When her mouth pursed, then twisted, I dared to touch her arm. It shifted out from under my fingers, smooth as if it were not deliberate at all, but I did not take it to heart. This was just how she was. "I know it isn't easy, having a spy," she began.

Oh, bother. Not this again.

I cut through her words with a sharp, dismissive gesture. "We've been over this, haven't we? You have agreed not to share the details of my identity. That's all I can ask until I retrieve the mo-shoe."

A wince, faint but there. She had long since given

up on my inability to pronounce the word correctly.

"Trust me." I looked up into her face, projecting all the reassurance I could despite my smaller stature. I was curvier than her by a long ways, but she wore her weight elegantly. And she was much taller than I. "You're my friend, Zylla, even before you became my keeper."

"Some keeper." Her smile evened. Rueful, and re-signed. "What did I miss, then?"

Finally! Neutral territory. "The professor was poisoned," I told her, lacking all preamble and relieved for the change of discourse.

Her smile vanished. "By what?"

"By whom," I corrected, "although a what may tell us more. I wonder if I can find what morgue the body was autopsied in."

Her nose wrinkled. "Foul."

"Fascinating," I countered. "There's a new professor in MacGillycuddy's position, yet I don't think he's the type to murder."

"No evidence?"

I kicked at the fog, droplets of mist scattering around my foot like clinging webs. "Intuition, yet no evidence. He's too excited to toss his working girl's skirts than—"

I stopped. Tilted my head.

"Cherie?"

"Did you hear something?" I asked at the same time, turning in front of the university steps. A slow, thoughtful circle. Had *I* heard something, for that matter?

"No," my companion murmured, dropping her voice to near a whisper in case.

I had heard *something*. I was positive.

Or was this my mind once again? Playing tricks

of sight and sound, starved for good sleep and sustenance.

I planted my hands along my corseted waist. "I swear, I—"

Whatever it is I'd meant to say suddenly died on the back of a terrible scream.

Not my own.

I looked up. Zylphia shrieked. I nearly did but for the fact I'd bitten my tongue as a dark shape thudded to the cobbled courtyard at our feet. Grotesque echoes rebounded from all directions; flesh impacting stone, bones cracking. As searing pain lanced from tongue to brain, I blinked back furious tears and gasped.

Professor Johannes Lambkin lay still, a dark figure in a sea of displaced mist curling around his lifeless body. Blood smeared his face, courtesy of a terrible gash across his temple, his cheek. His lip had been all but torn away, hanging now by a thread over his chin, and teeth were missing in a gaping grimace.

I saw no evidence of fists or weapon; he'd landed on his back.

Zylphia, quicker than many would be, dropped to her knees, reached around his throat for signs of life. She held a palm to the man's shredded lips, but his eyes stared wide, and the pallor already claiming his flesh told a tale of blood displaced.

"Dead," she said. "A broken neck, I'd— *Cherie*, wait!"

No time. "Get the bobbies!"

I darted back up the stairs, into the portico, and didn't bother making sure it shut behind me. My footsteps pounded through the halls, up the stairs, following the path I'd taken already.

There was no one to pass me in the corridor. Nothing in the lecture hall but the glass stars, winking in the light spilling from the open office door.

And a window, gaping wide. That explained the absence of broken glass and lacking sound of a struggle.

I hurried to the sill, leaned out of it to gauge the distance.

It would not be a straight fall to where I could just make out the dark blot in the heavy fog. He would have hit the pediment first, rolled one way or another. Bruised and broken, and still alive. He could have impacted the pointed pediment face-first. That would account for the damage.

Which meant he'd flung himself—or been flung—headfirst through the window.

I winced in sympathy, even as the fine hairs on the back of my lampblack-smeared neck prickled in shuddering awareness. The leap was a deadly one, obviously.

But what, or who, had demanded its effort?

The doxy? Certainly not, it would take great strength.

Or surprise.

I straightened from my perch, turned a shade too quickly, as if I expected a looming shape from the darkness of the lecture hall.

There was, of course, nothing. Only the shadows I'd already forged through thrice, now, and the crystal stars. They swung gently, refracting the ambient light in clever facets.

Empty, yet still my heart rattled in my chest.

I hurried to the office. "Is anyone here?" I demanded. "Collector's business, let's see you come out."

No answer. I did not expect one. My suspects, at

this point, were hardly numbered among the many. A single unknown girl, a dollymop without a name.

As I stepped into the office, I glanced over two sets of desks, strewn with papers. A struggle? Or simply an untidy disposition?

I rifled through them, saw nothing of note, and rounded the first desk.

My foot came down on something that rustled.

Surprised, I raised my foot and peered at the crumpled material half pushed underneath the desk.

A skirt?

Why on earth would there be a skirt, and no woman to wear it?

My continued search soon uncovered the rest of the apparel. A single petticoat, a blouse, and the jacket to match the faded green skirt I now held. I raised it to me.

Too narrow to fit my waist. I looked about the floor and saw no underthings beyond the obvious.

Even more curious, I saw no woman, unclothed as she clearly would be, and no evidence that there had been anyone else within. Only a single snifter upon the desk beside me, its contents now a sticky residue.

I dropped the material, left it where it lay. Let the constables make of that what they would.

I sniffed at the glass; brandy. Simple stuff, not the finest, but ostensibly the drink of gentlemen.

Another search of the second desk revealed a handful of papers shoved back into the corner. I had only enough time to glimpse a list of some kind before the first sound of a shrill whistle split the silence. Shoving them into a pouch at my belt, I hurried to make good my escape.

Why would a woman strip off every stitch and kill a man? All right, perhaps a better question would be, why would a woman commit a murder and leave her clothes behind?

The honest truth of that was no woman would. To run naked as a babe through the cold streets of October's grimy London below was simply asking for trouble. The kind of trouble no lone woman, not even myself, could handle alone, much less nude.

An accomplice?

Again, to what purpose? I'd seen no one else.

Was I wrong? Had he been the murderer after all, frightened by my questions? Had he sent his doxy packing without clothing, or had she run when he threw himself from the window?

I met with Zylphia at the edge of the square, and shook my head grimly at her questioning glance. "A mystery upon a mystery," I said, and patted the pouch containing the papers I'd taken. "We have a clue, I hope. Let us return home and peruse it."

Chapter Eight

There was no chance to do so.

Although we made it home in good time, my friend—who would have to take her place among my house staff in less than a blink— lacked the energy and time to sort clues with me. As Zylphia drew my bath, I clipped the article regarding Professor MacGillycuddy's murder from the newspaper, folded it with my own calling card, and insisted Zylphia deliver it immediately to Lady Rutledge's salver.

In my mania, developed of brutal recollection of the scene and many unanswered questions, I was eager to rouse all of London if that would deliver me answers.

I had seen a man fall to his death. My mind replayed the tragedy, over and over, even while I paced the confines of my bedroom in stockinged feet. The dull sound of his flesh and bone connecting with fog-strewn cobbles, the gentle swing of the stars. Back and forth. So at odds with the sharp scream and sudden drop—

Zylphia, much wiser than I in the grips of a mystery, promised to deliver it come a reasonable hour, but insisted I sleep.

Even the word *sleep* leached all vigor from me. Although I sank into bed gratefully enough, lulled into complacency by a warm bath and my maid's soothing hairbrush strokes across my scalp, sleep did not come but in fits and starts. I shivered myself into a slumber replete with nightmarish shapes and remembrances of things long past. I must have woken several times, for I dimly remember seizing with fear and staring wide-eyed and gasping at the darkness of my own bedroom, but I must not have stayed awake for long.

The nightmares lingered, nothing I could paint now but clear enough at the time to haunt every second of the night. Twice I found myself reaching for the decanter of ruby liquid at my bedstead; I know I forced my hands back under the coverlet and gritted my teeth against it.

There remained at least a fortnight before my stipend would once more be allotted. I could not risk being without in case my nightmares grew worse.

Yet my soul demanded a balm. I must have slept through when I reached again for the decanter, because the pain eased in my dreams, and I woke with a start to find Zylphia's hand at my brow. Her eyes narrowed in concern.

Clothed as she always was, somber working dress and white pinafore, I could tell nothing but that it was sometime past the start of the servants' day, and possibly time for breakfast. The smell of sausages filled the house.

My stomach rumbled, hungry as I hadn't been for days.

"What time is it?" My first question, thickly spoken. My mouth tasted as if I'd stuffed it with treacle and forgot to rinse after, my head gummy with sap. The chill I'd experienced all through the night had abated, but I'd curled in on myself and my cramped muscles were not grateful for it.

Her hand, warm and dark, curved around my cheek. "You're feverish."

"I've only just woken, of course I'm not feverish." I batted her hand away, pulled myself from the tangled nest I'd made of the covers and squinted at the windows. The heavy drapes masked much of the day's light; a boon, for my head ached and I truly felt as if I'd been the one to fall from a window to unforgiving cobbles below.

I rubbed at my shoulder, pleased to find only a dull ache beneath my probing fingers.

"*Cherie*, have you any symptoms?"

"No." This came on the forefront of a yawn, and I confessed, "Save perhaps a lingering sleepiness. Time, Zylla."

She studied me for a moment, not quite convinced, one hand on her hip. Then, briskly, "Just nearing noon. I'll fetch your day dress."

She crossed the room, a pleasant rustle of sound and—despite her lack of sleep—effortless vivacity. How she managed, I don't know. Perhaps she was used to keeping long hours. Perhaps the Menagerie had provided excellent training for the life my habits demanded she live now.

"Did you deliver my note?" I demanded, swinging my legs over the edge of the mattress. I winced as my hips popped, one after the other, and flexed my feet gingerly.

I'd slept for my usual allotment, although I could

not place just when I'd dropped off for good. I reached for my watch, frowned when I saw the empty dregs of the decanter on my nightstand.

So I'd taken a draught after all.

Zylphia knelt at the foot of a large trunk, polished to a mahogany gleam and fitted with brass trappings. There were at least four in my bedroom, placed here and there as pretty decoration as well as storage for my various dresses. "I had Levi run it across this morning," she said, elbow-deep in the trunk. "He says he gave it to one of the lady's maids to place in her salver."

"Thank you, Zylla."

She flashed a smile, distracted though it was, and I drew my knees up, tucked them under the billowing length of my nightdress. I clasped my arms around my legs, rested my chin on one knee.

I was tired, 'twas true enough a tale, but I also felt worn. Drained.

It had been years since I'd had a screaming fit in the middle of the night, but I remembered them nonetheless. Not so much what it did to myself— much of the details were lost—but how my night terrors had affected my staff.

I did not like to worry them. And besides that, I was twenty years old. Too old to be suffering screaming fits of hysteria in the dark.

Next time I was below, I resolved to take care of a paying bounty. Certainly I'd have time for a side jaunt. A little extra coin could buy me at least one more night's rest.

Not enough for a full flagon of decent strength, but I'd make do.

My forehead rested upon my knees, and I squeezed my eyes shut. That shiver, that shuddering feeling of terrible fear, clung somewhere inside me. I could just sense it, eager for an excuse to resurface.

Perhaps I was taking all this excitement rather personally.

"I think the plaid today," Zylphia said as she withdrew two pieces of richly hued green, brown and cream fabric. "And perhaps the cream hairnet."

I grimaced. "You never recommend the net. Is my hair beyond help today?"

Blue eyes glinted at me, a sidelong smile. "A touch."

Wonderful. I pulled the long braid of my hair over my shoulder, aware how much of it had escaped in my tossing and turning. Dark red curls hung beside my cheeks, sprung like ruby-tinted coils from the loose plait I examined.

I looked more like a ragamuffin orphan than an heiress of any stripe.

Ah, well. "Let's get it over with, then," I grumbled, less than gracious.

Zylphia worked quickly, but not as effortlessly as her predecessor. I still gave the occasional direction. I didn't mind; Zylphia had been a midnight sweet, not a lady's maid.

She was every bit as brutal with my stays as Betsy had been, however, and I gasped as she heaved on the ties with a surprising amount of strength. "Hell's bells, Zylphia!"

"All done," she assured me, tugging the knot into place. As if assurance would make up for the steel grip around my ribs.

I squeezed my eyes shut. "If I faint," I told her, my voice breathy, "I expect you to misplace the smelling salts for a few hours, at least."

Her chuckle, throaty with genuine amusement, did much to smooth my tired, ruffled feathers.

"Almost there, let's get you presentable. Mrs. Fortescue is already at the table."

Of course she was. "Is there any word of last night's death in the papers?"

"Death?"

"I can't in good conscience declare it a murder," I admitted. *A scream. A thump.* A corpse. Tragic, but not necessarily a murder. "I was there in that room, there was no one else to come or go. I hesitate to say it, but it seems like suicide to me."

"What of the scream?" Zylphia asked me.

"What of it?" I shrugged. "It was his own."

"Would a man who leapt to his death scream in surprise?"

A fair point, yet I waved that away as quickly as I thought over it. "Surprise, no. However, no matter what demons drive a man to leap, I can't imagine a mind would be prepared for the fall. Anyone might scream at such a force."

"I would," Zylphia said, making a grim face. "That's for bloody certain."

"As would I."

"Well, may God rest his soul, now." She shook her head, busied herself with outfitting me in the two-piece dress. The blouse she chose was a starched linen affair, lace at the collar in a modified cravat, the same cream as in the plaid. Not much of it showed beneath the jacket, just a froth. A feminine take on a gentleman's fashion, which I appreciated. Brown ruffles trimmed the skirt's hem, while the petticoat she chose for under was edged in the same cream-colored lace.

It would do. I had no real plans for the day, and did not expect to put on airs for company. To be quite honest, I even felt quite pretty. If a little bit fragile.

By the time I seated myself at the table, my hair had been tamed as much as possible, pinned in soft curls, then trapped beneath a loose cream net accented by shining gold thread. A fringe of red draped over my forehead, wrestled into place by Zylphia's clever tongs. She'd chosen a pretty gold brooch for me, a gift from Fanny some years past, and I at least looked the part of well-rested lady of the house.

Fanny seemed to think no different as she smiled at me over her plate of toast, eggs and fresh fruit.

Breakfast, to my relief, passed without excitement. The paper, once more the *London Times*, held nothing of import as I skimmed over the front page, but I was grateful. My eyeballs ached, and I noticed that my hands trembled. Exhaustion, surely. It caused the paper to crinkle noticeably, so I set it aside.

My uncharacteristic agreeableness to Fanny's chatter did not raise eyebrows, although perhaps it should have raised mine.

Midday found me in the parlor, seated behind the writing desk, poring over a nearly blank page. The professors' untimely deaths would have to wait, at least until I received reply from Lady Rutledge. If, that is, she deigned to reply at all.

Instead, I studied the single page upon which I wrote a capital *E* and a smaller *y*.

It still meant nothing to me. Elijah Woolsey was the name of a fellow he'd claimed to hate; why would my father use the letters to hide his laboratory?

I was in my third turn sketching the ornate initials when Fanny bustled into the parlor, a folded card in one hand. Her eyes positively sparkled with good cheer. "At last!" was her greeting, and all I needed to be wary.

I set my quill down in studied nonchalance, reached instead for the parchment I'd taken from the late professors' shared office. "Is that from Lady Rutledge?" I asked, already sure it was not. "I am awaiting further discourse."

"Better," Fanny replied, waving the card as if it were lined with gold and tipped by diamonds. She held it out, cheeks aglow, smile wide. "You have been cordially invited by Earl Compton—"

"No." Already in the act of accepting the card, I flicked it to the desk's surface with casual disregard.

Her smile dimmed. "Cherry."

"I am not going anywhere with him," I said, with as much urbane disinterest as I could summon. My hands shook; I busied them by sorting through the pages.

A list, on one. The titles of periodicals compiled for a syllabus, unless I was mistaken. Many were respectable titles of philosophy and science; it pleased me to see some of the same I read on the page.

"'Tis only a request for a turn around the Balcony."

A clever renaming of the raised walkways around Hyde Park, as well as a favorite of those on promenade. More often than not, it doubled as a discreet method by which to promote gossip and interest. Or, as the case may be, fictionalize it.

I could think of no good reason for Earl Compton to take me on a turn about the Balcony, save to create speculation. Perhaps he was feuding with his mother, who continued to detest me. Perhaps he had other plans.

I did not care to find out.

She snatched the card up, smoothed it as if its skim across the desk might have bent a corner. "When are you going to forgive him, Cherry?"

I did not look up, though one hand flattened beside my point of study. "There is nothing to *forgive*, Fanny. I do not fancy the earl for marriage, and that is final."

"Oh!" The sound was a flustered exhale as much as a soliloquy on my pigheadedness, I was sure.

I looked up. "Is the estate in disrepair?" I demanded.

Her eyebrows knotted. "What?"

"Are we on poverty's doorstep," I pressed, "or hounded by debtors?"

"No." She glanced at the card briefly, then again to me. "Quite the opposite, I believe."

Exactly. "Then if, as I suspect, Mr. Ashmore is not currently rotting in an East India Trading Company cell, we are fine," I told her, and withdrew a folded bit of parchment from the rest for lack of something better to do with my hands. "There's no cause for me to woo a rich man just—"

"Cherry St. Croix!" Another gasp, and this one sharper. The lines at her eyes deepened, mouth tight with disapproval. "You are doing no such thing."

"On that," I said, "we are agreed upon. There is no call—" I stopped, my mouth half open as the words sizzled to nothing in surprise.

"There is every call," Fanny told me, unaware of my sudden and complete disinterest in the topic at hand. This time, entirely unfeigned.

Ey. The tines on the first letter stretched out farther than it should, the latter character flourished. I skimmed the page quickly as Fanny lectured in the background. What was this? A list of terms, as it were, only lacking in definition or explanation.

There were others. *Ey, DG.* And—I squinted—*ppt* with the first two letters underlined twice. A code, perhaps. Some kind of compressed lettering system that suggested . . . what? I looked up at the ceiling, lips moving. A smuggling ring, perhaps?

No, too obvious. This was London, not some tawdry penny dreadful. Besides, what smuggler worth even a lick would scribe a note in the margins? *King's College, 4th of October.*

A meeting?

Whatever it was, it was not done in the same hand as the notes it was scrawled in. The latter seemed much more aggressive in slant, the lettering thick, as if a heavy hand pressed down hard on the nib.

"Cherry, are you listening to me?"

"Of course," I murmured, leafing through the other four pages quickly. Nothing else looked even remotely the same.

"I shall send word to the earl to expect you, then," I heard, and I jerked my attention fully to my self-satisfied chaperone, and her angelic smile.

"No," I said flatly, and rose. "I am not dancing attendance on any man, Fanny, and that is final!" I flounced from the parlor even as she took a breath to shape a reprimand.

Yet my emphatic departure fell short as Booth's crooked footstep drew up just short enough that I did not plow into his broad chest in high dudgeon. He paused, snow white eyebrows beetling in uncertain regard, before offering a small envelope in one gloved hand.

"This came by boy at the back, miss," he intoned, all pomp and propriety.

I snatched it from him, flashed him a wide smile, and turned toward the light streaming through the open drapes. Fanny, forgotten. Marriage, cast aside. An elegant script across the front bore my name, and the card inside was Lady Rutledge's own; elegant, plain, and smelling faintly of roses. I opened the card stock and skimmed the note. It was simple, lacking in greeting or farewell.

All things are remarked upon, Miss St. Croix, somewhere. You are a smart girl; the answer is likely a yes. What, then, is your question?

Tricky. I'd deliberately left no question with the clipping Levi had delivered, so what was she telling me?

I tapped the card against my hand, my gaze falling through the window and seeing nothing but remembered fog and a dark blot of a broken body.

"Cherry?"

I had many questions, certainly she could not know them all. Was Professor MacGillycuddy my challenge to solve? Was Professor Lambkin's death related?

What did either have to do with my father, who was also a professor?

Nothing, I was sure. My father only posed as a professor, he was in truth a doctor.

As I recall, he'd attended Oxford and Cambridge both, though he'd abandoned the former for the latter. Neither had much to do with King's College. Yet the initials scribed outside my father's secret laboratory now appeared in notes taken from University College, with a scrawl leading me on to King's College.

Did I imagine this?

Why my mind insisted on creating paths between my father and the murdered professors, I didn't know. Only that some part of me despised the mystery my own family had become.

Even as another part of me feared what I'd learn.

You have an unhealthy obsession with professors, Miss Black.

Possibly the wisest observation Hawke had ever made for me.

"Cherry!"

I looked up, the card in my hand bent in a fist. "What? I beg your pardon?"

Fanny's frown promised dire consequences. "Go get your riding habit on, Cherry. You *will* be— For the love of the Almighty," she said on the same breath as I rushed past her.

"I'm going out," I called over my shoulder.

"No, you are not."

I ignored my chaperone's threatening repudiation behind me, but could not ignore Zylphia, who waited at the foot of the stair, one hand upon a lion's carved head.

Her eyebrow nearly reached her hairline, but it was my winter coat she held. "I'll attend her," Zylphia told Fanny; all the words she could convey before I was stepping through my front door.

"Is this more of your collector tomfoolery?" Fanny demanded behind me, but not to me.

I left Zylphia to make excuses, vaguely aware she promised to chaperone me in Fanny's absence, and heard my maid call for Booth.

"No need," I countered over my shoulder. I would take a hired gondola, instead.

The cold slap of October air did nothing to dampen my high spirits. Even the ache I'd thought nestled in my bones seemed now only a memory as I faced the late afternoon sky.

Gray, of course, with low-slung clouds and the promise of icy rain.

Just the perfect day to go searching for clues. And I would start at King's College.

The dean of King's College had neared an age where a once-athletic figure had turned to a certain portliness about the middle. His hair was a nutmeg shade of brown, only dashes of stark salt and pepper at his temples. His eyes were also brown, small in his otherwise distinguished face, and his graying mustache neatly trimmed and well formed. Age left lines at his eyes and mouth, and carved a faint pattern of chronic ailments across his cheeks; a red-patterned web that pointed to a life of chronic excess.

Like much of the college grounds around us, his fashion choices tended toward stark and none-too-subtly prosperous. His brown trousers and matching jacket did not clash so much as provide relief against a waistcoat in muted green. A watch fob glinted, and I wondered briefly what kind of pocket watch the man owned.

Perhaps a Fussey, retrieved from the corpse of a comrade in higher education?

I could only be so lucky.

Dark woods and primarily masculine influences dominated his offices, cornered on all sides by masterworks in marble. Each piece showed to perfection that strength and dignity of the male species.

Without exchanging more than simple pleasantries, I understood my worth in the world of Mr. Wilford Figgins-Coop.

Nevertheless, he gestured me to a perfectly lovely chair in the sitting room of his vast suite of offices. "I have called for refreshments."

"No need," I demurred, raising a gloved hand. "I

hope to avoid taking up too much of your valuable time, sir."

I noticed he neither invited my companion to sit, nor offered her introduction. A terrible faux pas, to be sure.

While ignoring staff would be perfectly acceptable, Zylphia did not give the appearance of maid. Though her dress was the simple gray she always wore, she'd removed her pinafore and replaced her cap with a plain yet jaunty hat pinned to her dark hair. Her coat, like mine, was warm wool, and lined with fur.

It was one of my own, to be sure; I did not mind its borrowing. She was no richly plumed songbird, but certainly respectable enough for propriety to demand an introduction.

I glanced at her over my shoulder, met her gaze briefly and read the same understanding in hers.

A slight? Or a lapse?

It wasn't so long ago that slavery had been abolished entirely by Her Majesty. Dean Figgins-Coop struck me as a traditionalist.

"My companion would enjoy a cup, perhaps," I offered, a sweet test of uncertain waters.

Distaste crossed his features. "Your Negro may beg a cup from the kitchens, if you insist."

It took effort to keep my eyes from widening, and my fist from curling. I was aware of Zylphia standing still as marble behind me, yet no words came to my lips.

I was right, then.

Indignant was not strong enough to define the utter fury that gripped me.

Motion behind me kept my teeth together as

Zylphia sank into an elaborate curtsy. "Massah's too kin'," she said, her husky voice twisted into a parody of an accent I'd never heard before. "Dis guhl na' be wand'rin' 'way from de misseh, neva you min' 'bout ol' Zyl."

If possible, the dean's disgust only heightened at being addressed.

I reached back and clamped a hand around Zylphia's wrist; a sharp warning. "I imagine you're a very busy man, sir. I shan't keep you."

The fine bones of Zylphia's wrist moved under my fingers, and though she'd taken a breath to continue whatever farce she played at, my maid said nothing.

She did not have to. The sting of her pride was my own.

This was not the place to address it, however. Assured that Zylphia would mind herself, I focused intently on the dean.

"Of course," he was already saying. Thoughtfully, he claimed for himself a seat across from mine. His brown tailored coat bulged somewhat with the excesses of his waistline; a fact he did not manage to hide by draping one hand over his belly in what I think he assumed was studied nonchalance. One leg crossed over his knee. "If I may be blunt, what exactly brings Mad St. Croix's daughter to my door? You can't possibly want to apply to my college."

Ah. That would certainly explain why he bothered to meet with me, given his apparent views of women in his domain. "You knew my father, then?"

"Passingly," he replied. His smile was securely in place, but his light brown eyes remained untouched. "We studied briefly together at Oxford. Your father lacked a certain . . ."

I could not help myself. "Religious perseverance?"

I would swear that it was something like pity in his gaze now as he studied me, from the jewel-bright color of my hair to the ruffled hem of my plaid dress. "Quite," was all he said on the subject, and I did not pursue.

Men of science, as my father had clearly been, do not take quite as well to the concept of a higher power that cannot be explained. Faith is lack of proof; but lack of proof defies scientific theory.

The unresolved debate. I did not care for it now. "Dean Figgins-Coop, I am here regarding the murder of Professor MacGillycuddy."

Chapter Nine

ad I slapped him with a soaking cat, I would not have achieved the same expression of shock and dismay. The dean straightened, both feet planted upon the ground. Very real distress colored his tone as he said sharply, "I will have you know, Miss St. Croix, that there is no evidence of murder. Whoever is espousing such rumor is a perjurer, and frankly, I find it utterly beyond the pale."

I tipped my head. "My apologies, sir, but as I am investigating all of my options as an intelligent woman—" There. I did not imagine it; his eyelids flinched with each repetition of the descriptor. "—you may understand why such gossip certainly unnerved me. As King's College does not allow me to apply to its hallowed halls, I must pay close attention to the vagaries of university below."

"There is nothing to be concerned about," he said, with a note of finality that suggested my interview, impromptu as it was, rapidly approached an end. "The entire ordeal is beyond distasteful, and certainly no fit conversation for a lady's sensibilities."

Of course not. A lady could sew a wound shut with needle and thread, but far be it from her to handle a proper discourse on the mysterious death of a stranger.

Zylphia shifted behind me, but she was remarkably skilled at silence and stillness. That she did so now I read as a signal; one I would be wise to take.

I rose, then. "Well, I certainly see that the college is in apt hands," I said briskly.

He rose, as well; a courtesy that likely meant nothing more than propriety's demand. "Does your chaperone know that you are out without proper escort, Miss St. Croix?"

My temple throbbed, yet somehow I managed to sound as if my teeth were not locked together. "Miss—" What? A name. I did not know Zylphia's surname, if ever she had been granted one. "—Communion," I lied, pulling the name from a friend below the drift and ignoring her sharp inhale, "is as proper a companion as necessary."

He did not look convinced. "As you say," he said slowly. Nevertheless, he offered me a leaflet. "You will find the requisite material here, as well as instruction for finalizing your sponsor. You will, of course need a sponsor to facilitate your application. Perhaps your guardian, should he have a mind to indulge you."

"Certainly." I took the offering, passed it to Zylphia without looking at her, and took the opportunity to study my unwilling host. "I've a question," I finally asked, "a curiosity, if *you* would be willing to indulge me?"

He made no secret of checking the watch on his fob. Not, as I'd briefly wondered, the same that once belonged to Lambkin. "If you must."

"I simply need a quill." I said, and brushed past him to his office door.

"Now, see here—"

"Shan't be but a moment!" The door was unlocked, and I swept inside to seize the gilt-feathered quill standing upright upon his fastidiously neat desk. Like the sitting room, there was no sense of femininity here. Only an overwrought sense of entitlement.

I skimmed it quickly, searching for anything out of the ordinary. I found nothing offhand. Tidy, austere yet affluent; everything except rampant with clues.

"Miss St. Croix, I must demand you step outside of the study at once," the dean said stiffly, hovering at the door. As if unwilling to brave the sanctity of his male room while a woman stood within it.

I picked up a paper at random, flipped it over and said cheerily, "Won't be but a lark."

I wondered if Zylphia were laughing at this. She did not follow me; likely, she'd stayed put in case we needed to make a hurried exit. As I recalled, only the dean's assistant hovered within shouting distance.

"You certainly cannot go about behaving this way," the dean said to my back, bluster without barb. Until he added grimly, "Certainly, the Ladies of Admirable Mores and Behavior have the right of it."

My hand jerked.

So he read the Society columns, did he?

Deliberately smoothing my features, I scrawled my memorized *Ey*, included the *DG* and underlined *ppt*, and left the quill dripping upon his desk. I returned to the sitting room and thrust the drawing at him. "Do you know what this is, sir?"

Barely concealed rancor completely stripped any thought of distinguished handsomeness from him as he took the paper from me and scowled at it. His lip curled, cheeks redder. "Gibberish, Miss St. Croix. Exactly the sort of foolishness I expect from a weak mind." He tossed it to the floor.

Well, those gloves had come off, hadn't they? I forced my lips into a smile, as saccharine as I could make it. "Thank you ever so much for indulging me, Dean. I shall waste no time in applying to your college."

"Not my college," he replied, stalking to the door in a pace slightly too hasty for respectful company. "King's College will never allow senseless women within its hallowed lecture halls. If you are quite lucky, you may be allowed below. Good day, Miss St. Croix."

And good riddance.

With little other warning, the door to the dean's offices almost slammed behind me. Only to open a moment later to allow my maid her rigid-faced retreat.

Only once the door had once more closed, this time much quieter, did she raise a hand to her mouth and muffle her laughter. "You should have seen his face when he turned again," she whispered.

"Hush," I hissed, but not without my own amusement. I could just imagine the indignity of it all. Poor Dean Figgins-Coop. Assaulted on all sides by vapid women with no thinking senses.

"Come, we should depart."

"What did you learn?" she asked me, and I shook my head in silent reply. The assistant, a thin youth perhaps a few years my junior, passed us, his gaze wary, his nod respectful.

Perhaps in deference to the fact that his master had actually deigned to see us. Well, me.

Once out of the wide, airy halls of the main building, I took a deep breath. "Zylla, I'm so sorry about—"

"Nonsense." She did not wait for me to finish the thought, or to articulate the anger I still felt at the cut. "Men like him aren't so different from them what come below. I'd wager I could name a sweet or two who knows what he's been up to."

I smiled crookedly. "All right, then." A beat. "What in God's name was that language coming from your lips?"

"Just something picked up along the way," she said with a returned smile. "Now, stay here and out of the wind, I'll get a gondola home."

We had stopped at the end of the college's walkway, and as she moved off along the road, I turned back to study the grounds.

London was cut by a series of canals, it was true, and many of the districts were connected by ornate walking bridges. King's College retained its own spit of stilted foundation, adjoined by open acres of carefully maintained grounds. I huddled into my coat, my breath fogging in the cold air, and wondered what it must be like to undock from a gondola near every day, disembark into this district unto itself, and take the jaunt into a wide, vast world of education.

What days of thinking and postulation. Of practice and theory. The lectures alone might have been worth the dean's contempt.

Gibberish. I wonder if it meant that he'd recognized the symbols. Or if he did not, and hid that ignorance beneath scorn.

I turned away, strolled to the edge of the walkway and gripped the scrollwork railing in both hands. The fog churned at my feet, as if some great disorder caused waves somewhere in the black. Beneath, London below was likely preparing for supper.

Up here, where the sky was just easing to a darker shade and much of Society had only just finished tea, dinner would be only a blink away.

A footstep crunched behind me, as if caught on a bit of grit, a sound I knew better from my hours below than above. I let go of the railing; a mistake. As a hand closed around my arm, I knew all it would take was a solid push to send me tumbling into the black, my scream forgotten on a bloody smear.

I jumped in surprise, spun, and the hand let go. "Forgive me, miss!" I heard, my vision jerking from the surge of blood to my heart and limbs.

It took me a second's breath to recognize the young assistant. "You startled me," I gasped.

The man, a youth with ginger hair and freckled disposition, pressed his hands together, bowing as if to beg his pardon. "Please, I'm sorry, I was only trying to catch you before you departed."

I let out a solid breath, hand to my still-thudding heart. "What is it, then?"

"Your note, miss."

I studied his earnest features in confusion. "My note?" In answer, he handed a folded white square to me, and I recognized the copy I'd shown the dean. "Oh. Thank you."

"No, miss. I mean, you're welcome," he amended, blushing furiously. A trait of a true ginger. Mine was too dark to qualify. "It's just that I've seen it before."

Eureka. "Where?" I demanded, reaching for his arm.

If possible, his cheeks turned even more red, blazed like glowing embers. "In a periodical." Before I could ask which, he offered, "I don't recall the periodical name."

I furrowed my brow. "And so?"

"It's not real popular. You can get it for a penny below." And then, as if aware of what he said, he added quickly, "One made the rounds in the common halls, a lord's son thought he'd bring it in for a laugh. We confiscated it, of course, it's only gibberish. What I mean to say is— That is . . ."

I took pity. "Be at ease, sir," I said gently as I could, even as the demand for answers clawed at me. I needed to know what this was. And why all roads were intersecting at King's College.

"Right, miss." He scrubbed both hands upon his trousers. "The periodical didn't go into much detail, but it mentioned a book. I sort all the lendings, you know." I didn't, but I nodded as if I did. "Professor Lambkin had borrowed the same book. I only remembered when I saw the paper on the floor."

A clue. A happenstance one; just how I preferred them. "What book?"

"Mr. Humphry Ditton's *The New Law of Fluids*."

I blinked at him. "The what?" And then, as I espied the subtle blue glow of an aether engine approaching, I waved it away. "Where would I find a copy?"

"I don't know," the young man admitted, backing away. "A bookshop? A scholar? The only copy I've ever known of was in our library, and now it's not."

"The return date," I guessed. "Was it to be on the fourth of this very month?"

His lips turned into a surprised *O*. "Yes, miss. How did you know?"

I waved that away. *King's College, 4th of October.* The

only reason I could see to scrawl such a reminder on the margin of notes was if those very notes had been taken from the book itself.

The assistant ran an ink-stained hand through his hair, mussing its careful wave. "They haven't even announced his death," he said mournfully. "That's not right, miss. Not right at all."

"No, it isn't, is it?" I smiled, as reassuring as I could despite the cadence of my mind, already galloping far ahead. "I'll find your book, not to worry."

"Luck, miss." He turned, sprinted away in a long, gangly flap of knees and elbows. I watched him, aware of the gondola easing into place at the docking berth behind me, and stifled a laugh as the dean's assistant skidded to a stop just out of the gates and restricted himself to a brisk, efficient stroll.

The gondola bumped the docking berth gently. "Miss?"

I turned, smiled briefly at the gondolier in his uniform of dashing cap and jacket and gloves, and took the proffered help to climb into the box-less boat.

Zylphia raised her eyebrows in inquiry, but said nothing aloud.

Gondoliers, even the finest ones, gossiped. First, we'd have to get home.

And then, I would prepare for another journey below. This time, I'd look for Lambkin's borrowed book.

Ey. How did the initials connect my father and another murdered professor? What did they mean?

The outing took less than two hours, but I returned home to find my staff in an uproar. I no sooner set foot in the entry before Mrs. Booth bore down on me like a mastiff with her eye on a succulent bone.

"What on earth," I began, but got no farther before her hands were at the fastening of my winter coat and she was glaring at Zylphia over my shoulder.

"Quick," she ordered, "fetch the hot water for a bath and use the rosewater."

Clever, nimble-fingered woman that she was, my housekeeper had divested me of my coat even while bustling me upstairs. I caught sight of Booth's tolerant amusement as he limped carefully down the hallway.

And then stopped short as I found every clothing trunk in my bedroom opened wide. All my ball gowns had been arrayed over every available surface.

"What is going on?" I demanded.

Fanny whirled, relief warring with censure and impossible good cheer. "You're returned, wonderful!" She waved a thin hand. "Mrs. Booth, the cerulean, the sunshine or the emerald?"

"I wore the yellow last month," I said dismissively, and stripped my gloves off with impatient fingers. "Fanny, why are all my gowns out?"

"You're right, of course." She tapped her finger along her chin thoughtfully. "The green is too festive for the occasion."

"What occasion?"

"Your bath is near, miss," Mrs. Booth said as I heard the creak of the pulleys designed to haul hot water up from the furnace in the basement. "Quickly, undress."

"Not until I know what is going on," I said stubbornly. Both women exchanged a glance. It was one I knew well; each, a mother to me in her own way, telegraphed the same message.

I wasn't going to like this.

"All right, but hurry, we've limited time," Fanny allowed. She waved me into the bath as Mrs. Booth and Zylphia filled it, and I tolerated the hasty scrubbing I received at both sets of hands.

"Gracious," Mrs. Booth whispered as she swabbed gently around my bruised shoulder. I managed a wan smile.

For her part, Fanny continued to deliberate on choice of gowns. "An invite's come 'round."

"A ball, or else I wouldn't be here," I observed. "Whose?"

"Not just any ball, my dear."

I stiffened, flipping my wet hair from my eyes and inducing a stifled gasp from Mrs. Booth, who received the brunt of spray. "If this has come from the earl—"

"Who like as not will be suffering from your deliberate disregard of his early invite," Fanny cut in sharply, "so mind your manners and be grateful for this opportunity."

I gritted my teeth, said nothing as Zylphia pulled me from the tub and dried me quickly. She fetched the finest of my corsets and underthings.

Fanny tossed aside the yellow gown. "This is an invite to the last fashionable ball of the season, after all."

"Whose?" I asked again.

"The Marquess and Marchioness Northampton."

I opened my mouth, strangled on an exhale as Zylphia jammed her knee into my back and jerked on my corset laces. The word I managed didn't make it past the first vowel. "Wha-*oomph!*"

"Hold on to your bedpost," Zylphia warned.

I obeyed, my astonished gaze on Fanny as she withdrew the only other ball gown worth wearing. I'd never worn the pale lavender, one of those I'd purchased at Madame Troussard's some months ago. "Why in God's name would you have me attend Marchioness Northampton?" I gasped, whooshing out a breath as my stays clamped tightly. "A last-minute invite is practically a cordial request to fail."

"Because," Fanny said as she tucked the cerulean ball gown under one arm and turned to face me with a beatific smile, "this invite came personally delivered by Earl Compton himself. Who, might I add, is looking quite the thing. You and I shall be— *Cherry St. Croix!*"

I winced, rotating the shoulder she gaped at now. "Small accident," I offered meekly enough. "It doesn't hurt."

"It looks *ghastly.*" My chaperone—her dismay reserved for the appearance of the injury, rather than the pain of it, I understood—held up her chosen gown in both hands and studied the fabric that would not drape on the shoulders so much as around them, low on my arms. "Impossible. Mrs. Booth, the lavender."

I had little choice in the rest of the proceedings. Like a field marshal summoning her troops to battle, Fanny directed Mrs. Booth and Zylphia around me, strict efficiency.

In less time than I would have ever imagined possible, I was clad in yards of lilac fabric, draped beautifully at the bustle, narrow at the waist and knees. The embroidered bodice was fitted with a fashionably low décolletage, and the sleeves at each shoulder were comprised of a gauzy tulle draped artfully over the curve of each shoulder. It would hide the bruise, disguised somewhat by careful application of powders.

The same tulle gave added flounce and a certain softness to the bustle, while white gloves reached over each elbow. My slippers were in a dark violet fabric, thin enough that I knew they wouldn't last the evening.

As Mrs. Booth tended to my hair, Zylphia vanished with Fanny. By the time my hair was pulled up into a lavish array of ringlets accented with white feathers—too short notice to collect flowers, thank goodness, for Fanny favored lilies and the fragrance made me sneeze—Zylphia finished with my chaperone.

Lovely and serene in a deeply burgundy gown, her hair more demure than mine yet no less elegant for it, Fanny was the perfect matriarchal complement to my apparent maiden demeanor. I barely kept from rolling my eyes at the farce.

"You look wonderful," Fanny told me, adjusting the dark purple ribbon and pinned ivory cameo at my throat.

"This is absurd," I said, not for the first time. Like all the rest, my protest went ignored, and I found myself wrapped in a white cloak as fashion demanded, tucked into the box of the St. Croix gondola, and well on the way to another evening spent dancing in hell.

"Mrs. Booth performed a miracle," Fanny said happily, snug as you please beside me. False flowers decorated her gray hair alongside her chignon. The lovely amber and blue petals brought out her eyes.

It also drew my attention to the wider streaks of white growing in her hair.

I closed my lips around the words I'd intended to say, looked away.

My chaperone was climbing in age. I could protest

all I liked; I knew it was selfish. These balls, these functions, were Fanny's last years among Society. If my intent, as I'd so often made clear, was to inherit and then take a sojourn around the world, where would that leave her?

Without a charge to shepherd through Society's pitfalls, certainly. Without the opportunity to visit with the other married women and widows that were her social set.

I bit back a sigh.

I had no real hopes for this night—and my stomach clenched in nervous anticipation when I thought of coming face-to-face with the scorned earl once more—but for Fanny, for her lovely, hopeful smile, I would try.

Even if I must graciously eat the coals of the marchioness's disdain to do it.

Chapter Ten

There were days in the off-season when I missed Teddy fiercely. This was one.

Even in early October, the veranda windows in the lavish Northampton home were opened wide to allow the brisk chill to combat the ballroom's sweltering heat. Already a crush, despite the Season being over, the vista before me was little more than an endless swirl of color and chaos; a nonstop din of music delivered by a not unpolished orchestra and the cacophony of conversation, laughter, gossip.

At events such as this, Teddy had been my rock and the one soul from whom I could simply take ease for a time.

With him at his family's estate, I was on my own. I clung instead to a wall away from the homely and tragically shy, for I knew the master of the house would keep a wary eye on them to ensure they danced. I kept one eye out for the man, eager to dodge his Society-dictated meddling.

Fanny, under the guise of fetching refreshment, had vanished amid her gathering of matrons, and

I did not begrudge her the opportunity. She would return soon enough, and insist once more that I make myself more readily available.

I did not wish to. I wished to keep ahold of this wall and do my very best to ensure it remained upright and solid.

It was not a wish I'd see granted.

Fanny threaded her way through a crowd fraught with pale ivory and stunning gold. Blondes were the very height of fashion, and as a rule tended to wear softer, demure colors in the ballroom. Brunettes could wear more bold colors to make up the lack, but my own coloring was neither fashionable nor particularly admired outside of opera and actresses.

Fanny's bold, dark red gown was truly a masterpiece, and I couldn't help my smile as she arrived at my side. Though it wilted a fraction when I noted her lack of refreshment. "Is it a crush around the beverages?" I asked.

"No time," she told me, and laced my hand into the crook of her arm. "Come, my dove, Lady Rutledge is arrived, and I know you'll want to at least greet her."

She was right, on one count, but couldn't the lady come to me?

I didn't dare dig my heels in. I wasn't so infamous as to warrant a single stare from an entire crowd, but I'd noticed a sidelong glance here and there. A whisper hidden behind a gloved hand, a titter of laughter. This followed me as Fanny guided us smoothly through the throng, around the dancers swirling in a spritely gambol taken from the rustic country.

If my cheeks were red, I assured myself, it came solely from the heat.

Lady Rutledge was an impossible creature to miss. Her laugh boomed like a trumpet, and her gown all but glowed like a sapphire jewel amid the sea of frothy pastels and occasional dip of bolder palette. Her hair had been upswept into a crown about her head, into which winked blue jewels I suspected had come from her late husband. She was perhaps the largest woman present, not just of girth but of structure, standing a full head taller than even Fanny.

Her fan waved, a dove gray flutter, as she spoke with the bevy of gentlemen and ladies who surrounded her.

Lady Rutledge, unlike me, navigated the waters of this Society with grace and ease. It surprised me some to think she'd been invited; surprised me further to know she'd accepted. The marchioness and the lady were not friends.

We were nearly across the floor when a giggle from my left drew my attention. "There she is."

A whisper, or almost such. There is a certain truth to the saying that a whispered confidence in a crowded room will garner attention quicker than a normally spoken tone. It was a fact I'd long since learned to take advantage of.

My gaze swept over a knot of women of middling age. The youngest, Lady Sarah Elizabeth Persimmon, had only just come out this Season, and rumor suggested the dark-haired beauty's father had only to choose from three excellent suitors to make a match.

The eldest was not Lady Northampton, but the marchioness clearly ruled this roost. Before I could warn Fanny, the gaggle of seven women flowed around us in a net of silk, perfume and tulle.

My nose itched.

"Miss St. Croix."

I dropped immediately into a curtsy, because that is what Society demanded of a lady faced by a marchioness. Fanny did the same. "My lady," I murmured as I rose.

Lady Northampton, Almira Louise Compton was, as ever, a statuesque beauty. Once upon a time, her hair had been fair and her skin unmarred by age; rumor suggested she and my mother had been considered the great beauties of the Season.

She was among the fortunate. Time only lent her a stately air, dignified and no less striking for the appearance of fine lines and the faded tones to her upswept chignon. She wore a gown of ice green, a color that matched the steely glint in her eye as she looked down her aristocratic nose at me.

She wore no jewelry but for the band at her wedding finger, and needed none to declare her reign over this ballroom.

I was, in a word, outmatched.

"I am surprised to find you here," she said, her ivory lace fan churning the air in lazy sweeps near her face. A gasp to my left did not come from the ladies who surrounded me. I flushed.

It was as close as declaration of unwelcome as one could tender without delivering a cut direct.

Fanny stiffened beside me.

I forced a smile, even as my heart pounded in my ears. I had done this dance before, and come out the stronger for it.

Of course, Teddy had been at my arm to see me through it, and it had taken the lady's eldest son to undo the harm, but such a debacle would not be repeated. "I was delighted to receive an invite from the Northampton family," I said sweetly, and watched the barb land square between her eyes. They narrowed a fraction.

So she hadn't known her son had sent the invite.

Brilliant. Now I stood in the middle of a family affair.

It seemed to me as if conversation ebbed around us. The Ladies of Admirable Mores and Behavior clustered tightly, a veritable wall between me and freedom.

Wolves in lambs' clothing, the lot of them.

I did not look around. Such a display of fear would only reveal weakness.

"Miss St. Croix," piped up Lady Sarah Elizabeth Persimmon, her husky voice similar to Zylphia's but polished to perfection. My gaze turned to her, a nod of acknowledgment. "Your gown is very lovely."

I blinked. "Thank you—"

"Of course, such a color belongs to one of Lady Northampton's stature and coloring," she continued, her gaze sliding over my hair, my dress, "but you are very brave for daring it."

Fanny's grip tightened on my arm.

I almost winced. "Thank you," was all I repeated, contrary to the acid building in my throat. The heat battered at me, made all the worse by the leering gargoyles of the marchioness's sycophantic salon. "May I say that your hair is particularly fetching tonight?"

Her smile, cool as glass, suggested she had no need of compliments from the likes of me. Her father, an earl in his own right, had seen to that.

"Oh, Lady Sarah Elizabeth's handmaid is quite skilled," chirped Mrs. Douglas, one of the marchioness's elder following. She wore widow's colors still, despite her husband being dead these seven years past. In deference to the Queen's own depth of mourning, perhaps.

Or because no other colors than dour grays and somber blacks suited her heavy-jowled demeanor. I had my suspicions. If she were truly in as deep a mourning as her black silk and organza suggested, she would not be at this event.

"You really ought to consider sending your maid to learn from hers," added Mrs. Douglas with a vicious smile. "I'm sure the lady's maid shan't be *too* busy for the likes of yours."

That was two insults on the back of a subtle first.

My smile was beginning to hurt.

Lady Northampton remained, in the thick of it all, as elegant and cool as a statue, untouched by all but the most gracious of charm. Cold and lovely as the Snow Queen of fairy tale.

My knees were beginning to ache. I deliberately softened them as I fanned my face with my own beribboned lace fan. "If you'll excuse us, my ladies, I was just—"

"Come, Miss St. Croix," laughed Lady Sarah Elizabeth. "Certainly, you've nothing of import to do *here*. I daresay your usual sort of people aren't in attendance."

I froze, my eyes pinned on the elegantly shaped black eyebrows raised ever so knowingly above laughing blue eyes.

What did she mean by that? My sorts of people?

What did she know?

Beside me, Fanny took a step forward, her mouth set into a grim slant. "Now you see here, young lady," she began.

"Look! Is that Mad St. Croix's daughter?"

The whisper, once more as out of place as a discordant note in a symphony, jarred a surge of anxiety down my spine. "It's all right, Fanny," I murmured, my cheeks blood-red now. With anger or heat, I couldn't be sure.

"It's not," Fanny said worriedly, but she was clearly torn. Righteous indignation was no shield against the vicious undercurrent of a salon already out for my blood.

Snap. The marchioness's fan closed with a distinctive sound that I swore echoed across the full ballroom. But it wasn't anger in her eyes as they levied first on Fanny, then on me.

It was satisfaction.

"Oh, my," Lady Sarah Elizabeth drawled, raising her fan, half unfurled to hide her shock. "It seems the columns are quite right about you. Is *all* your house so unruly?"

My fist clenched against my skirt. My vision trembled with a sudden surge of rage; unlocked as if it had only slumbered beneath the thinnest of veils. "How dare—"

"Miss St. Croix, there you are!" Lady Rutledge's delight filled the void beyond the biting question, and I watched the marchioness's gaze flit from smug satisfaction to sheer venom.

Blue filled one end of my sight. I curtsied as proper, Fanny echoing the gesture, and managed, "Lady Rutledge."

The woman smiled at me, the fleshy pads of her cheeks raised high and pure mischief sparking in her gaze, now painted bluer by the shade of her gown. That impishness, so out of expectation for a woman of her stature and girth, turned to the marchioness. "Almira, always a delight. I should have known I'd find you cornering our Miss St. Croix for yourself. A treasure, is she not?"

Five sets of eyes pinned on me in mute surprise. One, pale green jade, hardened. "Euphemia," the marchioness murmured in chilly acknowledgment.

Lady Sarah Elizabeth covered her lips as she tittered a lyrical note of dismissive humor. "Surely, you jest, my lady. Why, she is barely cognizant of what patience these tolerant souls must invoke in her presence."

My teeth clenched. Yet before I could spit the sharp rejoinder fully formed on my tongue, Lady Rutledge laced her arm through my one free elbow and looked down at Lady Sarah Elizabeth from her much taller stature. "I am very well acquainted with your mother, Peashoot. I suggest you keep a civil tongue in your head before she decides you're a year too soon for marriage."

The lady paled.

"Oh, dear me!" Lady Rutledge raised her fan to her mouth, in direct mimicry of the lady before her, and laughed in abashed apology. "Did I let slip your pet name? Forgive me, my dear, it is rather darling, isn't it?"

"Peashoot?" repeated a man's voice from somewhere in the *certainly not eavesdropping* crowd beyond us.

The milk-white glow of the lady's cheeks filled with sudden color.

"Now," Lady Rutledge continued jovially, "please forgive my terrible manners, for I simply must claim Miss St. Croix and her chaperone. Ta!"

With little chance for thought or farewell, I found myself tugged through the throng of idle speculation, Fanny at my side both red-faced and gasping.

I did not realize until we stopped that she held back laughter, not anger. "Did you see her expression?"

Lady Rutledge smiled upon my dear friend with graciously mirrored amusement. "Mrs. Fortescue, you are an admirable champion, but I know you must be eager to visit with your friends."

"Now, wait just a moment," I interjected, but to no avail.

Lady Rutledge spoke over me as if I did not exist. "Would you proffer to leave your charge in my care? I shall take excellent care of her."

Fanny pressed my hand between hers, her eyes bright, and nodded to the lady. "Thank you, my lady."

Lady Rutledge watched my chaperone move to the cluster of more somberly gowned matrons at the far end of the ballroom before turning her smile upon me. "That was bracing. Stand up straight, girl, you look like you've lost a battle."

"I did not come here for warfare," I pointed out irritably.

Her laughter earned curious eyes. "Then you have come to the wrong soiree. All such matters are a battle, Miss St. Croix, the question is what weapons are you willing to bring to bear?"

"I've no weapons at my disposal," I said, "only uncertain allies."

"Good. You learn quickly." She patted her unnaturally dark hair into place, one gloved finger easing a sapphire into a more tenable hold. She scanned the crowd as she did. "I have championed you tonight. That will mean something."

I was uncomfortably aware of that. And of what felt uneasily like a debt forming between us.

"Ah!" She laid a large hand on my shoulder, preventing me from turning, and winked at me. "And here, your latest weapon in what I expect shall become an extremely effective arsenal, indeed."

"What?" But I received no answer, only a widened smile, a sweep of blue fabric pooling to the floor as Lady Rutledge eased into a curtsy that placed her head roughly level with mine.

I was aware of a sudden vacuum of silence behind me. Though music played, and conversation contin-

ued, it was as if there were a wall between this unlikely moment and the rest of the ballroom.

I turned slowly.

Steel green eyes met mine. And twinkled. "Miss
St. Croix," Earl Compton said, the greeting of my
name like something whispered, something sweet
and warm in his educated tenor.

I fancied he'd have a lovely singing voice.

Lady Rutledge sighed behind me. "Manners, girl."

"Oh." A vapid syllable, one I desperately attempted
to hide as I curtsied. When I rose again, my stomach left the place it normally occupied and surged
upward instead. Into my chest, where my heart beat
like a drum gone manic and wild. "M-my lord."

He bowed smartly. "My lady," he said to Lady
Rutledge, who waved her fan like a flirtatious girl
half her age. "Might I beg a dance of your charge?"

"By all means," she trilled, ridiculous in her mature
voice. I stared at her blankly. "Go on, then. And close
your mouth," she added, tapping my wrist with her fan.

Face burning, lungs constricted, I glanced guiltily
at the earl I'd been avoiding since his return—at the
earl who had avoided me since his departure—and
could not for the life of me remember what to do next.

His hand, held steadily, palm upraised, did not
waver. "I shall return you safe to your chaperone,"
he said, not unkindly. "You have my word."

"Oh, for the love of all," Lady Rutledge sighed, and
turned in a whirl of petticoats and sapphire blue.
Her elbow jabbed into my wounded shoulder, an accident to any who might call the bluff; I sucked in a
breath, staggered a step and found my hand firmly
clasped in that of Cornelius Kerrigan Compton.

The eldest son of my rigorously avowed arch-
nemesis.

Chapter Eleven

Among the studies Fanny did not approve of, I had also been tutored in all the ones she did. Fortunately—and I had never been so grateful as now for it—I knew the dances of Society.

Earl Compton led me to the floor, and it was as if the crowd parted like magic. Whispers followed us, many speculative. Some unkind.

He did not deign to acknowledge them, and so I kept my head high, yet I was sure I blushed from forehead to navel by the time he guided me into step.

Thank God we had no immediate opportunity to converse. We broke into groups of four couples. The ladies circled each other, hands together in the center like a pinwheel, as the men walked clockwise in the opposite direction around us. I vainly attempted to collect my thoughts, to gather the scattered remains of my intellect from wherever dark corner it hid, but as we broke apart, glided hand over hand from partner to partner, I met his gaze from across the circle and forgot even why I'd avoided him.

Of course, it came back to me as our hands clasped in the dance, and we turned as a pair into the steps.

The man was a snake. Not nearly as obvious about it as Micajah Hawke, but just as oily. Why else would he visit opium dens in the dead of night? To say nothing of his departure while I'd been "ill," recovering from my foray with my father's alchemical concoction.

"You had me concerned," he said by way of greeting. His voice washed over me again; a power within its own right, I decided. What was it about the Eton polish that brought to mind pleasant days of discourse? Of company kept and intelligent conversation pursued.

"Did I?" The question came archly.

His mouth, framed beneath a neatly clipped mustache the same color as his artfully styled sandy hair, twitched. A faint flick at the corners; as near to a smile as I expected from him while gossips watched.

"Rather. I was not sure to ever see you again, were it left to your choice. I imagine you are upset," he said carefully. His posture as he guided me from turn to turn was perfectly aligned; I had merely learned the steps, he executed them flawlessly. So well, in fact, that my occasional misstep went all but unnoticed with his own masterful reinforcement.

"Why would I be upset, my lord?" I asked sweetly. "You are a grown man—" A faint flinch about the eyes, tipped with lashes darker at the base than at the length. "—and you owe nothing to me."

"That is not entirely correct."

"Which?" I turned, arm outstretched, and allowed him to promenade me as the other couples moved in step. When we came together again, his hand solid at my waist, I added, "Are you not a grown man or do you consider yourself answerable to any common girl of your acquaintance?"

A touch of censure shaped his handsome features. "That is hardly fair, Miss St. Croix."

I looked away, focusing my gaze instead on the fine fit of his formal attire. His black trousers, black tailcoat and white shirt were, as ever, beyond fashionable. No one would ever find fault with the way he wore formal attire on the dance floor. His bow tie was white, impeccably starched, his gloves also white.

I'd always considered him attractive. With a fine bloodline like his, he bore the features of aristocracy well. His nose was, like his mother's, noble, his jaw etched with a fine grain. Any artist of stone or paint— Lord Pennington's mother-in-law included—would have been pleased to retain the earl as a subject.

As silence enfolded us, the dance drew to a close. He bowed, I curtsied. Requirements of the event complete.

But rather than return me to the arm of my chaperone—either chaperone, for that matter—he once more took my hand as music soared.

I could all but feel the nearly palpable clamor of a collective indrawn breath.

We were being watched. *And how.*

This, a waltz, afforded me no chance to demur, and plenty of opportunity to glance at the crowd beyond the dance floor. Eyes raked over me, over the earl, some in surprise and many in envy or dismay.

When I lifted my gaze to the earl's, they remained on me. My throat dried. "My lord?"

"I have precious little opportunity to make clear my intentions," he said, his voice a low, almost too intimate pitch. My breath caught somewhere in my stays. "You are rather difficult to invite out, and somewhat headstrong when you believe you are wronged."

"Am I?" A squeak, caught on a gasp as he whirled me expertly through the graceful waltz.

"Wronged?" No sign of mockery in him as I stared up at him. "I believe so. I owe you another apology, Miss St. Croix."

It was quite possible that I would faint on that floor. My heart kicked inside my chest, my breath came in shallow pants. I struggled to maintain composure, even as the color of dozens of gowns swirled by me in a bleeding rainbow.

But I *was* stubborn. "Why?"

The hand at my waist tightened. Possession? Or support, I wondered as we stepped into another lovely turn. The music painted the ballroom in a sudden shimmering net of lyrical notes.

"A family matter demanded my attention," he explained, a small frown touching the corner of his mouth now. "I would be humbly grateful if you did not share such confidences beyond this dance."

I found myself nodding, even as I wondered if such *family matters* included his younger brother, Piers Everard Compton, or were something to do with the opium the earl partook of.

I could not ask. It would be rude, and none of my concern, besides.

"You said you had no opportunity to state your intentions," I said, frowning in thought. "What intentions, my lord, could you have with a mad doctor's daughter?"

The strains of the waltz flittered through my words, and this time, I would swear the smile that almost shaped his mouth gleamed like something warm and beckoning inside the ever so rigid confines of propriety.

I could fall into eyes of jade.

Fall, and like as not return scarred for the landing.

"I shall call upon you soon," he told me.

My eyes widened. Call upon me?

Intentions?

Impossible.

"Then," he continued as his fingers gripped mine with care, "I shall send a letter to your guardian. Mr. Ashmore is not expected to return in the near future, am I correct?"

"My lord," I stuttered, and was forced to take a breath, straining against the unyielding band of my corset. Stars winked in the corners of my eyes; a sea of color, light and motion. "My lord," I repeated, much more firmly, "certainly there must be at least a dozen females more suited to your needs."

"Likely," he replied, as quick and smooth a rejoinder as expected of the clever earl, "yet none half so engaging."

"But I am not well liked by—" I hesitated, quickly amended it to, "That is, much of Society sees me as not worth the effort. Other ladies are of your station, my lord."

This time, he smiled. A quick, endearing thing that flashed a touch of even white teeth. "A little polish, Miss St. Croix, and there could be no fault found."

What? Polish? I only just kept myself from frowning, but before I could inquire as to his meaning, the music died away, and the earl's fingers tightened briefly on mine. "Would that I could claim another dance," he said.

A third dance was as a scandal not easily repaired, and as good a declaration of engagement besides.

Before I had any thought as to the repercussions, I jerked my hand from his. Smoothed the faux pas quickly by gathering my skirts and delivering a polite curtsy. "You are kind," I said, if not smoothly, then at least with enough emphasis to mend the startled raise of his eyebrows. "Although I am quite positive you jest. Surely, you've no desire to tempt the gossip mill this night." At least, no more than he already had by claiming the two dances.

He, ever the gentleman, inclined his upper body in a bow. Gracious, though that damnable smile lurked at his lips. "Very wise. I approve, of course. I shall return you to your chaperone," he told me, "as promised."

Much better that he did. I followed his lead as he tucked my hand through his arm and guided me back to where Fanny waited with Lady Rutledge, holding her own colorful court.

"I give her back to your safekeeping," he said to my beaming chaperone. "Mrs. Fortescue, are you and Miss St. Croix available for a luncheon tomorrow?"

Her eyes widened, practically saucers of delight. "We shall be ever so pleased," she gushed, ignoring my frantic, emphatic stares.

I restrained a sigh.

He turned to me, pressed my palm fervently with his gloved fingers; my heart lurched. Pleasure?

In some part. It was . . . pleasant to have such ardent interest, even if only for a moment.

"The pleasure of the dance, Miss St. Croix, was certainly mine."

"My lord," I replied carefully, and watched the

set of his lean shoulders vanish once more into the throng.

"Oh, my dove," Fanny cooed. "Luncheon!" She said the word as if the word *marriage* had somehow been redefined by the fine minds at Oxford and categorized under the letter *L*.

Oh, I repeated silently, closing my eyes. *Bollocks.*

I could not make my escape fast enough. Scandal and gossip would follow if I left too soon, but I could only tolerate a handful of hours spent dodging the marchioness's venom, the earl's studied interest and my own chaperone's unwavering delight before folding in upon myself like a house of bent cards.

We left early because I insisted upon a headache; not entirely a false line. My head throbbed steadily in counter to my own heartbeat, a constant thrum of pressure beneath my severely pinned hair. I wanted nothing more than to tear the mass of pins out and rub my scalp in peace.

I closed my eyes in the gondola. I must have appeared as pinched as I felt, for Fanny made nonsensical sounds of sympathy, patted my hand and left me in relative peace.

She like as not suspected me overwhelmed with the earl's attentions. She was wrong.

Yet I could not flee my own thoughts as neatly.

Intentions. What nerve! What gall to assume that such attentions from Compton were to be at all received, much less with any certainty of approval. I had made my position clear, over and over again until I was blue in the face. What use did I have for marriage?

Such an institution would see me shackled to a

husband and stripped of all freedoms. My fortunes, my desires, my very name to be bound forever to a man who would look no farther than his own puffed-up sense of duty.

I refused to be the lesser half of a set. A functioning prop to serve tea and smile while the barbs of Society continued to arrow for my heart.

I leaned my head back against the seat, the muted hum of the aether engine whispering softly in the silence. Now and again, Fanny hummed a tune under her breath, the way she was wont to do when things were well.

It occurred to me then that I hadn't heard her humming since before my ill-fated venture to investigate the man who would reveal himself to be my mad father.

My fingers clenched in the folds of my skirt.

The same night I'd first tasted those much-vaunted pleasures of the flesh. Not entirely by choice, no, but necessity had provided the opportunity, and I could not rid myself of its memory now.

A marriage bed could achieve that much, at least.

My mouth quirked; a wry thing. I knew as well as any other woman trapped below the drift how little a marriage bed was needed for such a thing. Yet Compton had kissed me once.

The feelings that strangely passionate moment had engendered were not unlike that which Hawke created in me to combat the effects of the serum. Neither had been wholly unpleasant. Neither had been necessarily by my own desire, yet . . .

Yet Compton had needed no drug.

Was it me, then? Was I somehow offering the wrong sort of . . . signals? Clues?

Was such a thing even possible?

Nonsense. I could see nothing of myself that would suggest to a man that I only awaited their strong arm and kind word.

Perhaps it was I that was being cruel. Leading the earl on because I had not found the strength to place my slipper squarely down upon the ballroom floor and deny him his intentions.

Yes. That seemed much more likely. I would have to be bolder from here on.

"In we go, love," Fanny said quietly, and I jarred to sudden wakefulness to find the door opening and Booth's white-gloved hand extended.

Fanny made no argument when I begged off to bed. Zylphia had been given the night to herself, as such events always run into the wee hours of the morning. I did not expect to find her nearby, so shed my own clothing, stripped off the tight vise of my corset and took the time to unpin my hair and give my head a thorough rub.

It helped, but only a little. My breath came as if through a tunnel, leaving me with a faintly light-headed feeling.

Perhaps I was coming down with an ailment. A touch of the ague?

I certainly had no time for such things.

In truth—contrary to the uncertain ailment squeezing the breath from me—my heart pounded as if I were giving chase, excitement flowing through my veins.

I was in high spirits, eager for a run; a mad dash into the unknown. The kind of feeling I associated with the day after a fact-collecting sortie into an opium den.

Quickly, I pulled my collecting garb from the trunk I hid it in, stepped into the thick woolen trousers and cotton shirt, cinched my own corset and fastened its high neck collar around my throat. Made of thin slats of the finest metal I could acquire, it had protected me from many a stray blow and the occasional blade.

I'd designed it to be close-fitting but not overly snug, straight in form enough to give pause from a distance—though only a blind man would be fooled up close as to the nature of my sex.

I added warm woolen stockings, thick workman's boots and wrapped the blackened length of my braid about my head. Finally, placing a street boy's cap over it all, I glanced at myself in the mirror and nodded. In the fog, it would do.

I seized a worn sack coat, pulled it on and hurried out my window.

It wasn't so late that I could afford to be careless. Making my way to the West India Docks took precision and planning. To get out of Chelsea, I stepped in the shadow of more than a few parties crossing the footpaths with lanterns aloft and spirit-laden cheer apparent.

Once upon a time, the district had been the home of fashionable sorts like my mother. Intellectuals and philosophers, even artists of true talent and possibility. Now, much of the night was spent among bohemian wastrels carousing and spouting poetry about art and love and other such dreams.

I liked it. It kept much of Society's worst gossips away; save when said gossips were wastrels themselves.

By the time I made it to the docks, my small brass watch warned me of Big Ben's coming chime. A quarter of an hour would put the bells at one of the clock. Plenty of time to tend to my business, and late enough below that only vagrants and the nighttime dwellers would be about.

I was forced to wait five minutes while my chosen ferryman returned to the dock above.

"You again," was his greeting as I traversed the plank.

I said nothing; I didn't have to. We'd long since finalized our arrangement, and he quickly set to work stacking more coal into the furnace. I watched as he did. The sky ferry was a rather simple piece of engineering, for all its purpose was complex. Coal in the fire heated the mechanisms by which steam would power the aether engine. The aether engine would draw the appropriate supply of aether from the steam, and voilà.

A simpler and yet more unstable version of the engines that powered Her Majesty's Navy's sky ships, and even less powerful than the gondolas in London above.

It took an inordinate amount of time for the shuddering ferry to reach the ground; time I spent clutching the rail and briefly wondering how many trips I would make before the old girl simply shook itself to pieces.

The fog swallowed us within moments.

I left Abercott his coin on my seat, hurried off the ferry and into the choking soup, holding my breath for as long as I could before forced to inhale. The fog immediately stung my nose and throat. I swallowed a sudden coughing fit, lest it draw attention from the dock men huddling around a furnace inside the warehouse I hesitated beside. Quickly, I pulled my goggles into place, fastened the respirator into the rivets under each eye and behind my ears and took a grateful, cleansing breath.

So attired, I hurried away from the usually busier lanes of the docks and to my destination.

I was not accosted. This, while a relief, was not a surprise. London, whether above or below, had cultivated a certain understanding with collectors. While I'd been led to understand that my presence as a woman collector was something only speculated upon, I did know that only certain sorts of people had the means and reason to wear equipment such as I displayed.

Many collectors were inventors of a sort, or knew someone who fulfilled the role. I had seen nets cast from uniquely developed pistols, goggles which provided a certain kind of magnification, even weapon holsters specially designed to allow for the maximum amount of reach with minimum time and effort.

We were, by necessity, a creative lot. As I spent much of my time hunting bounties more to do with debt than with actual danger, I did not need as many such things as others did. I designed my own items—my corset, my goggles and respirator.

The end result was that I was easily recognized as, or at least assumed to be, a collector, and only a fool messes about with such.

Above the drift, collectors were considered very different creatures indeed. I knew of a few gentlemen who dabbled with the role—I called them Society collectors with a sneer—but they were considered only *fashionably* dangerous. None knew of me.

The unspoken code of the night below the drift was this: When accosting a mark, the safest way was to do so from the shadows. A cosh, a quick struggle, and the mark's money and valuables would be there for the taking.

When accosting a collector, the safest way to do so was in a very large gang, or not at all.

I suspected even Jack the Ripper would leave a collector alone, taste for street doxies notwithstanding.

And so I found myself once more climbing the steps to the University College, sometime after the Westminster clock rang out its one o'clock warning.

Nothing had changed, although I hadn't expected much. The cupola remained lit behind the columns, providing not so much light as atmosphere reminiscent of ancient Greek temples. The fog was eerily thick tonight, muting everything down to a reflected glow. My yellow lens provided a clearer path, but only just.

I could all but taste the choking edge of coal smoke in the pea souper tonight. The factories must be working double-time.

I stepped through the front door—once more unlocked, as if two professors had not suffered a sudden and unexpected loss of life within these very halls—and made my way to the offices MacGillycuddy had shared with the unfortunate Lambkin. I stripped the goggles and respirator from my face, tucked them away.

The door opened to my questing push, and light spilled into the lecture hall.

Here, there had been changes. A new professor, I imagined. Gone were the winking stars of crystal. The desks were fewer in number, but arranged in a circle, which I found odd. The window Lambkin had tumbled from was now closed, and in the faint lamplight from behind me, I could pick out the shape of a large, knobbed telescope beside it. Peering up, I noticed, though I wondered what it could possibly see through the miasma.

A book remained on each desk. I peered at its gilt lettering as I passed the closest. *Complete Works of Galileo*.

Only mildly scandalous. If I recalled my lessons correctly, the Holy See had authorized the printing in 1741, thereby removing all dichotomy between faith and science.

Or, well, in theory. Such divides still persisted, but as University College remained a secular school, I approved of the choice of reading material. I patted the book, but felt no need to leaf through it. Mr. Ashmore retained a copy in his library; I'd read it many times over.

I passed through the hall, tested the door leading to the office of the late professors, and for once, found something locked.

Not that it truly mattered. I'd long ago learned how to take a lock apart, and picking one was as easy a puzzle as setting one's mind to it.

I retrieved a long, thin bit of metal from my tool belt—a gift from Ishmael Communion, a friend as well as one of the Bakers' most accomplished dubbers—and withdrew a pin from my hair.

A dub, of course, is a master key such as what he gave me. Ishmael has large hands—he is a very large man—but the things he can do with a lock would surprise even the master dubbers of the black art of lock-picking.

I was not nearly as accomplished as he, but within a few minutes of cautious application, the tumblers gave way. The door creaked open.

I grinned, exultant. A few more moments of searching located the lantern kept on an iron hook by the door, and I struck a match from the packet on a small shelf next to it. The wick caught quickly. Firelight filtered over the strangely tidy office.

So the new professor had made his home here, as well.

Both desks were wiped clean, papers organized into neat stacks and clipped in place. I leafed through them, found a set bearing promising symbols different from that of other formulae and folded them in half. I tucked them into my corset for later study. A bookshelf behind one desk now featured the spines of treatises and dissertations, bound and printed in gilded lettering. I brightened. Perhaps the book I searched for was here? I reached for one, read its title and replaced it quickly.

I could spend hours among books, and frequently did. I had not the time now. Thank heavens for the tidy new professor. I found the book I sought after only a moment's searching.

Mr. Humphry Ditton's dissertation.

I withdrew the tome, opened it reverently and with great care.

The New Law of Fluids, proclaimed the title page in bold, Gothic lettering. I quickly muffled a laugh. *Or,* it went on, *a Discourse concerning the Ascent of Liquids in exact Geometrical Figures, between two nearly contiguous Surfaces.*

It continued like this for six more lines, but I only shook my head and closed the book with a muted snort. Men. Even in the sixteenth century, they could go on and on.

Yet in the onslaught of verbiage, I realized what I held in my hands, and I did not like the sudden and unmistakable comparison.

This, written in 1729 by Mr. Ditton, was a text on alchemical solutions.

Which meant the letters I'd taken to be initials weren't. They were alchemical notations of some kind. My father's laboratory, the notes I'd found in this very room, all conspired to paint a picture of alchemical study.

Fools' study, I thought, but I'd seen it in the flesh, as it were. My flesh. I had been the victim of my father's own experiments.

What, then, was I to assume as motive for the professors' deaths now? The dean of King's College had considered the alchemical symbols gibberish; did he know what it was I'd drawn?

Or did this mean that I was investigating a deeper madness? One that fell too easily along similar lines as my own insane father's legacy.

I didn't know. What I knew at that moment was that this book was what I'd come for.

It was time to return home to study it. I turned away from the shelf, tucking the tome under my arm.

Thud.

I froze, certain I heard a footstep outside the door.

A policeman patrolling the college grounds? A student come for some forgotten item, or the professor himself?

What would I say?

Collector's business masked many sins to the common folk, of course, but the business was not a legal one. I could not justify theft to a constable.

Perhaps it was the murderer returned to the scene of his crime.

I was not prepared to tangle with a bobby, or to be caught unawares by something worse.

The latch lifted.

Chapter Twelve

I sprinted for the door I'd seen at the far end of the office, leaving the lamp burning on the desk with a silent curse. This entry led to a narrow closet stacked with forgotten tools of the trade. Chalk and cloths to wipe the boards with, rulers, odds and ends I suspected were meant to maintain the apparatuses in the hall. There were other books I could not take the time to read, and I set my stolen book atop them quietly.

There was no room to turn, much less reach for my blades hidden upon my person.

Which all conspired to mean that there was precious little room for me at all. The shelves climbed up farther than even a man could reach, but I squeezed inside and shut the door as I heard the office door creak a warning. Darkness filled the tiny space. I could feel the door pressing against my bosom, trapping me against the shelves at my back, yet I could see nothing. Only smell the musty air of a storage space and hear the faint step of my unwanted guest.

I held my breath.

There, a whisper of sound. Papers, I thought. Rifled through. I'd only just made that sound myself. And another footstep, a quiet one. Either the person was light of frame, or attempting to be as discreet as possible.

I heard a muted thump—a drawer, perhaps—and a low mutter. A curse? Or simply talking to one's self. I could not distinguish further characteristics from my cramped hiding place, though I strained to do so.

As I struggled to breathe quiet as possible, another footfall thumped gently, and with startled dread, I realized the intruder was coming straight for me.

Bloody bells and damn! I looked side to side, looked down at my feet and saw shadows flit through the seam of light. I had no choice. I was not ready to be caught by a possible murderer, and could not reach my weapons even as flexible as I was.

Setting my jaw, I braced my hands against both sides of the closet, sucked in a breath and stiffened my arms. I leapt straight up. *Allez, hop!* My arms caught my weight, screamed in protest, yet I held it as I braced my feet on either side.

Once splayed, I moved cautiously, only as fast as I dared. The occasional creak of straining wood seemed masked by my fellow trespasser as I scurried up the closet interior like a spider. My limbs strained by the time my feet cleared the door jamb; my arms shook dangerously as I locked in the awkward split of my legs, each foot braced against the closet's interior and my knees bent due to the narrow confines.

This weakened the strength of my locked hold, and sweat bloomed across my shoulders and forehead.

Yet I'd moved just quickly enough. The closet door opened, allowing in a blast of light that I felt only pointed the way to me, hovering a mere few feet above. I gritted my teeth, elbows shaking with the effort as I peered down between my splayed legs.

The narrow tunnel showed me nothing. Only the vague impression of a silhouette beyond the closet.

But my nostrils flared as the sensitive interior of my nose began to itch fiercely. With mounting horror, I recognized the onset of an ardent need to sneeze. Of course, that could have been anything in the closet; my passing likely stirred up more than dust.

My nose twitched, throat beginning to itch with the same need. I sucked in a breath.

A hand appeared, barely a shape in the suddenly blinding corona of the lantern held within it. The light speared through my head, skewering the dark vision I'd grown accustomed to. Blinking as my nose prickled uncontrollably, my limbs shook and my eyes watered, I was certain this would be the end. All my mysterious trespasser would have to do would be look up.

Yet, I realized as no hue and cry took place, it did not happen. I blinked fast, my vision clearing on an arm clad in simple, inelegant brown fustian. I heard the mild thud of books falling sideways; felt the repercussions of it in the shelves digging into my back. I didn't dare move.

Every second became a nightmare. A dull ache centered behind my knee, matched by the mirrored pulse of my still-tender shoulder. I was reaching an age where such contortions and feats of strength no longer came as easily as they once did, and I feared any second of losing my grip upon the wooden walls.

If the sneeze building inside my nose did not give me away first. I bit my lips hard together, stretching my face in vain attempt to soothe the tickle.

My eyes burned with it. Yet still the light shone, and still the figure poked and searched. Until finally—finally!—the light withdrew. The door shut, and I heard the footsteps recede.

Just in time.

The sneeze tore through my chest, captured between my teeth and sending fireworks of pain through my nose. I winced, froze as much as my shuddering arms and legs would allow, but heard nothing.

That was it, then. If the explosive release only just trapped behind my nose hadn't earned me a demand to come out, I had to be alone.

I made my way down the narrow closet, wincing with each scrape of shelf from backside to nape, and finally reached the floor with a grateful sigh. Gingerly, I pushed open the door, blinking to find the lamp once more where I'd left it.

Another sneeze seized me, and this time I muffled it in my hands. I wiped at my watering eyes, grimacing. That had been a close thing.

I turned, reached for where I'd left *The New Law of Fluids* and found only tilted books beside a pushed aside bookend.

I bit back a rude word.

My thieved tome was gone.

But it couldn't have gotten far. I darted out of the office, scanned the empty lecture hall, the still-closed window. Hurriedly, I sprinted out of the naturo-philosophy wing, eyes sharp for any sign of motion; ears straining to hear even the faintest step that wasn't my own.

Nothing.

I spilled from the University College entry, dragging the back of one arm over my nose—not nearly so itchy now that I'd left the room—and glowered at the fog painted in sickly yellow from the lit cupola.

As I pounded one fist into my open hand, my skin prickled. Warning, sharp and clear as a bell. Alarmed, I turned; only I saw nothing, heard nothing from the silent edifice of the college's Corinthian columns.

Yet as I kicked at the fog and muttered a handful of terse uncivilities, I could not shake the sensation of being watched. Measured.

And possibly, I thought angrily as I stalked away from the grounds with only a handful of notes to show for it, found entirely lacking.

My options were dwindling, and I had only my fool idiocy to blame for it. As my high energy and simmering irritation fueled my stride into the Philosopher's Square, I considered what choices I had left.

Things I knew: Whoever was in that office wanted that book. And, potentially, the notes I'd stolen beforehand. Why?

An alchemist? What for? What did this book tell the reader, aside from what I assumed to be a collection of inane and illogical recipes for gold making and immortality shaping?

Whatever that book held, it was worth the lives of at least two professors.

Or was I reaching for a solution too pat?

Was MacGillycuddy involved in this charade or was he simply a victim of circumstance?

Was Professor Johannes Lambkin a suicide at all?

Dear me, this particular train had gone off the rails

rather spectacularly. I strode through the Square, turning up the collar of my sack coat against the damp. The cold bit deeply, though the air was not as frozen as could be expected above the drift that protected it somewhat.

I could be grateful for small favors.

I was nearing the center of the Square—a place dominated by a courtyard long since left to molder— when the idea struck me from nowhere at all.

Where would I find a copy? I'd asked.

The dean's assistant had shrugged. *A bookshop? A scholar?*

I stopped mid-step, turned abruptly and picked my way to the west.

I knew a man. A bookseller. I'd once run a bounty for him—timeworn books, stolen by a filching cove with more debt than sense. The old shopkeeper had been pleasant enough when I'd returned his belongings.

This had been, oh, what? A year ago? No, longer. Summertime. I remembered the putrid smell of the River Thames reaching all the way across the city.

If he hadn't closed shop, then I'd find him just on the edge of the Square. It was late, but this was a crisis.

And I was impatient.

I found the neat row of shops, side by side with nary a crack between them. The road in front of each had once been a sweetly maintained lane with gas lamps lining the way for students and professors and scholars and more. I imagined it had been a bustling place, filled with shopkeepers taking delight in their wares; of purchases made by the ounce and the pound, by the flagon and the stack. Books, quills, charts, odds and ends.

Now, in the dark and the damp, it looked a dreary place to be. The night tore any warmth from the row of derelict edifices, leaving them rather reminiscent of skeletal teeth in a lurid grimace.

Not the kind of place I'd expect to find a bookshop, but perhaps that was part of its charm.

The door I required was the third from the left, marked by a single lantern hanging from an iron post. The brave little flame within it struggled mightily from its iron confines—a beacon to my yellow-tinged sight, but sadly weaker than the fog it guttered in.

Only the faded stains of rusted numbers remained over the lintel. Yet it wasn't the bright windows in the first floor that told me my quarry was in reach, but the light flickering from behind drawn shades in the story above.

Mr. Augustine Pettigrew never went to his bed with a lantern still on. The risk this posed to his precious books far outweighed the comfort of a light in the dark, and as I recalled, he'd only ever had the one fireproof brazier.

I glanced over my shoulder as I approached the shop's front door. No sign hung where chains used to offer one; the row of storefronts had fallen on difficult times, obviously. The street in either direction was silent, only visible for a few feet when the fog shifted.

Yet I still squinted at shapes in the mist. The fine hairs on my neck and arms had not settled during my chilled jaunt across the square, and I could not help but think it was not all the wet October air.

Of course, paranoia would only serve me well as long as I did not let it overcome my sensibilities.

Shaking off the ghosts in the smoke, I hammered

on Mr. Pettigrew's door. The sound echoed like a drumbeat, tossed this way and that before vanishing into the hungry dark. I waited.

Too much noise, and I'd earn the attention of others in the row. Not my intent.

It was a full minute before I heard a shuffled step inside, counted in my own heartbeat as I half turned and kept a wary eye on the roiling coal-laden cloud behind me. Iron caught, clanged faintly as a latch was lifted, and the door opened a scant few inches. Light spilled from the crack, incandescent and near blinding after my nighttime foray. "It's a late night for guests," whispered a frail voice.

I turned back, my smile hidden behind my respirator. "Mr. Pettigrew? Collector's business, sir."

The light shifted, lowered, and I could just make out the bulbous edge of a nose near pressed to the gaping door. One eye, once green and now turned milky with age, searched me. A grunt, a sigh. "Best you come in from the damp, then," he said, turning away from the door and leaving it to swing slowly wide in his wake.

I stepped in, and it was as if I'd found a miracle in the cold depths of London below.

Mr. Pettigrew's establishment, once called something unrecalled but now only referred to as, "old Gus's shop," among those enlightened enough to know of it at all, was a haven of sorts. Shelves lined the full of the downstairs, books filling each near to overflowing and some stacked upon others where there was room. New bindings, old bindings, some no more than sheaves of paper wrapped in cloth. Comfortable armchairs, worn near to the stuffing, beckoned a weary soul to take ease by the brazier.

The warmth did not only keep out the drafts, it

kept the room inside toasty and dry for the books. The last I'd come by, it'd been warm enough and cozy for a cup with the old man.

Mr. Pettigrew did not age as well as the books he loved. Nearly stooped double, he was frail of build, with long, thin arms and a rail-slight chest that occasionally gave over to a wheezing cough. He wore a faded purple dressing gown—which didn't scandalize me at all, despite Society's claims to the contrary—and a nightcap perched atop his mottled, sparsely furred head.

He shuffled to one of the chairs slowly, his gait hampered by his years. "Close the door, then," he called, his voice a thin memory of the robust man he must have been once.

I obeyed, locking out the creeping damp, and stripped the protectives from my face. "I apologize for the lateness of my visit," I said politely, because Mr. Pettigrew was a kind man.

A shrewd one, even in his advanced age, but nevertheless kind.

A gnarled, heavily veined hand waved at me, then plucked the folded nightcap from his head. "Come, girl, sit. Tell me what you're searching this time. Not for me, I hope?"

"No, Mr. Pettigrew, I am not here for you," I reassured him. I approached the armchair across from him, its upholstery a rich, lovely shade of red reminiscent of Fanny's ball gown. The wood was scarred and scuffed, its arms bearing witness to many a comfortable visit.

Beside it, shedding heat as I sank to the chair in grateful reprieve, the brazier shone spotless and brassy. Small by design, yet fitted with bolted copper and brass pipes, the stovelike mechanism took coal through its grinning grate and pumped the excess smoke up through the pipe in the ceiling and out. The grate was bolted in place, not a single ember could fall from within, and the heavy piece proof against accidental falling or knocking over.

It was a fine bit of engineering, certainly.

I held my hands to the warmth, but my gaze remained fixed on my host. "Are you well?"

His eyes vanished behind a web of crinkled lines as he grinned a yellow-toothed grin. Amusement, snapping as brilliantly as the fire within the brazier. "I am old, girl. That I still live is a matter of courtesy from the Almighty."

"Come now, you aren't so old as to be digging your own grave just yet," I countered lightly, unable to keep my smile from tugging at my lips.

His long, spindly hands folded over his patched dressing gown. "We are both so much older than we used to be," he said, cryptic and discerning all at once.

And not wrong. I inclined my head. "I am delighted to find you well."

"And awake, no doubt."

"I apologize—"

One finger rose from his entwined hands. "You speak like a toff and behave like a collector. Pick one, girl, or you'll forget which is what." It was on the tip of my tongue to apologize yet again, but I sealed my lips as his faded, rheumy eyes crinkled once more. "As for me, not a worry. I sleep less and less as the days go by. I'd offer you tea, but I know you won't take it, and I don't drink it much no more."

Nothing would mark me as obviously from London high as the way I took my tea. Fanny had done an excellent service in my training.

"No," I agreed. "Mr. Pettigrew—"

"Gus, then," he corrected me with a dry, whispery laugh. "That's what they call me when they come by now and again. 'Checkin' up on ol' Gus,'" he mimicked.

"Gus, then." It cost me nothing to use his name, and the old man likely didn't get as much company as he liked. I shifted on my chair, eyes flitting to the shelves. "I search for a book."

"Ah." A parched sound. "Which, exactly?"

"Mr. Humphry Ditton's *The New Law of Fluids*. Do you know of it?"

Mr. Pettigrew rested his head back on the chair, the thin cords of his throat and sharp Adam's apple thrust into stark relief beneath his wrinkled, fragile skin. "Early seventeen hundreds, unless I am mistaken. Not the entirety of the title, either."

I twitched a grin. "You are correct. I can't remember all of it."

"The New Law of Fluids," he whispered slowly, *"or, a Discourse concerning the Ascent of Liquids in exact Geometrical Figures, between two nearly contiguous Surfaces."* He shook his head, rasped a chuckle. "It has been a long time since I've seen a copy."

My face fell. "Oh. So you don't have it?"

"No, girl, I'm afraid not." His gaze remained on me, not to the shelves I'd have expected if he were telling a lie. The firelight turned the watery depths of his eyes to something glinting and unreadable, but his frail frame remained at ease, fingers linked, slippered feet crossed.

I read no falsehood here, and my heart sank. "Well, it was worth finding out for certain. I apologize for taking your time."

I placed both hands upon the arms of my chair to

rise, but he lifted his head and asked baldly, "What are you after, then?"

I hesitated.

His smile faded, and he leaned forward carefully, his bald pate cherry red in the light. But the eyes beneath his still-bushy white eyebrows did not drop from mine. "You're on business, then," he rasped. "Fine, fine. I don't have that book, but I have many. Tell me your need and I'll direct you to a book just as good, if not a counter argument to the contents."

I reached into my coat, withdrew the sheaf of papers I'd stolen. "I am not sure exactly what it is I'm looking for," I confessed, abashed at his raised eyebrows. "Whatever is in Mr. Ditton's book directly correlates with the information on these pages."

"Ah. Let me see." He patted his pockets with trembling fingers for a long moment, searching for the spectacles he finally found in a stitched pocket. He placed them over his nose, beckoned impatiently.

I rose, crossed the narrow divide and offered the sheaf to him.

"My glass," he said as he took them. "Fetch it."

Glass? I looked about me, found no snifters or any sign of such drinking. Then, on the narrow counter that doubled as desk and shop cashier's station, I saw a large magnifying glass.

Spectacles and a glass. The poor man.

I collected it, running my gloved fingers along its use-polished haft. A lovely piece, solid brass around the perfectly maintained glass.

I returned it to Mr. Pettigrew's searching grasp and waited, shifting from foot to foot in my sudden impatience.

He took his time; perhaps it was his faded sight, perhaps instead the complex symbols drawn on

each page. The handwriting was the same as the notation in the notes I'd left back home, neat enough
but cramped, and strung together as if full words
were too much trouble to take the time to write out.

After a few agonizingly long minutes, I understood that I would not get an immediate answer. I
left Mr. Pettigrew's side to walk instead along the
shelves, allowing my fingers to trail over the books
within.

It was, I could admit, a guilty pleasure to be surrounded by so many books. Mr. Ashmore's study—
once my father's—was fine enough. I'd spent many
an hour hidden beneath the large desk, reading the
things Fanny hadn't yet given up on forbidding me
from.

I loved books, even as I loved the similar way
opium had of transporting a mind elsewhere. Both
habits had formed from a desire to escape; my advanced age at the time of learning my letters meant
simply that I devoured more books when I'd finally
realized what magical things I'd missed in reading.

Papers rustled softly as Mr. Pettigrew shuffled
through them at a snail's pace. Finally, as I wandered
back to the chair and braced one hand upon it—
quietly lifting one leg to ease the ache within—he
looked up, mouth set in a slanted, thoughtful line.
"This," he said on a sibilant note I translated as deep
in thought, "will take some time, my dear. Complex.
Not impossible, but certainly complex."

"What is it?" I asked.

He set down the magnifying glass. It thumped
gently. "Before I answer a question much deeper
than you know, I must ask you one." He did not wait
for my agreement, raising the papers like proof at a
trial. "What is it you seek from this?"

"The author," I said, not bothering to think too hard on the subject. It was true. "And if the author is a murdered man, then I seek his murderer."

"Hmm." The sound became a long exhale. Mr. Pettigrew lowered the papers, his gaze returning to it in the vacant way of a man no longer seeing what was in front of him. Then, suddenly, he nodded. "Very well. Come back in three days' time. I should have something to show you then."

Three days. That was a lifetime in the scope of an investigation such as this, but I had precious little else to go on.

"Very well," I allowed, though I didn't like it. "Now, what is it? Is it a formula?"

"Clever girl." He rose on unsteady limbs, his faded purple dressing gown swishing about his ankles. But he gripped the papers with a surety, an interest, that had seemed less focused when I'd first come in. "Perhaps. I can't know just from looking, but it seems to me that you have in your possession a working theory."

"On what?" I asked, bemused. "I don't recognize those symbols from existing scientific elements."

"No, you wouldn't," he murmured, shuffling by me. Distracted, I realized. I couldn't hide my smile this time, rueful, though it was. I recognized that level of distraction.

I often did the same.

"This is alchemical theory," Mr. Pettigrew said.

My smile faded. "Alchemy. You're sure?"

"Oh, yes. Quite." He set the papers on the counter, then turned, one hand flat upon them. His weathered, skull-like face split into a grin. "Come, I'll show you."

Curious, I approached his side as he spread the

papers on the surface of his worn desk. "This," he pointed out, tapping a triangle with its point down, "is water."

"Just water?"

"The symbol by itself, yes," he explained, "but look at this beside it." Another symbol, three circles arranged in another triangle, with a fourth in the center. "Aether."

"What?" I scowled at the unfamiliar figures. "That is not. Aether is characterized by the periodic table, not by random etchings."

His chuckle, reminiscent of the papers he shuffled, was amused. "It is to alchemists, girl. You must recognize the language of those you search for if you hope to find them."

Bloody bells. I refrained from sneering outright, but I also raised a finger as an idea struck. "Sir, do the letters *E* and *y* mean anything to you?"

His brow folded. "Show me." He gestured to the quill and blotter at his desk.

I took it, turned the paper already there over and sketched the *Ey* as I remembered it. And then, because I couldn't not, I added *DG* and *ppt* with its double underline. "This," I said as I placed it in his hand.

"My glass," he said again.

However did Mr. Pettigrew manage without another soul? I crossed the small shop, bypassed the brazier and fetched his magnifying glass.

This time, as I put it in his hand, he patted mine in absentminded thanks. After a long moment, he said, "The first is not an *E*. It is an *F*. This symbol represents fusion."

My knees buckled. My heart surged into my throat, and I seized the edge of the desk for balance as I stared at his earnest, studious face. "Fusion," I repeated, my mouth suddenly dry. An "*F*" and a "*u*", with ornate tines to confuse the eye.

He did not look at me. "It has many applications, notable most by what elements surround it."

Fu. Fusion.

As in the ghost of Josephine St. Croix and the living shell of my body?

As in the combining of the living and the dead?

Or was this just another one of my father's terrible jests?

I swallowed hard. "Do you know the others?" I asked, working to force my voice into a semblance of normality.

"Digestion," he said after another moment, "and I'm not as certain on the last. I recall seeing it, but not as an element. A notation, much like digestion. A rule? Ah." He rubbed the bridge of his bumped nose. "Not to worry. I'll find your answers. Three days, girl."

I frowned. "Digestion? As in, it must be eaten?"

"Not always so literally," the old man replied, suddenly eager to warm to his subject. The heart of a scholar would always lend itself to lectures. "While that could be one aspect, it could also be the process by which one element overtakes another, or draws it in. Imagine a parasite, if you will—"

I raised my hands, a gesture of tacit retreat. "I understand," I said hastily, before he truly lost the thread of the conversation to whimsical hypotheses leading him away from the point. "When you find out what this actually means, you will know which form of digestion it points to?"

"Three days," he repeated. "And the sooner for it if I return to work."

I sighed. "I shall be back on the third." Sensing the dismissal for what it was, I fished out my protectives. I did not have to look up; the man had stooped from age and years hunched over books, his thin frame bent to my height. "Be careful, then," I said seriously. "There's a great deal of mystery here."

"That, there is," he said, and patted my shoulder with an awkward, affectionate hand. "Do be safe."

I never made such promises. With a smile, I affixed my goggles and breather in place and left Augustine Pettigrew's strange and lovely little bookshop behind.

Three bloody days of twiddling my thumbs.

I had come below with questions; mysteries compiled within mysteries.

The answers I'd received—alchemy, fusion, digestion—only served to bring me more questions.

Why was I suddenly surrounded by elements of alchemy?

And how did this all fit with Lady Rutledge's challenge?

I had much to mull on as I returned above.

Captain Abercott was well into his cups by the time I returned to his docking berth; I'd swear he guided the ferry by sheer habit, now. He eyed me from his station at the levers where a wheel now stood as useless decoration, but said nothing I could make out.

It wasn't until I jerked my chin high, startling myself awake, did I realize I'd nodded sometime between mutters. The fog had drifted to my knees, placing us only a few minutes away from docking.

I knuckled my eyes, oddly gritty, as if I'd gotten too much chalk in them.

The unease that had shadowed me since my near

discovery was gone. Now, I felt empty. Drained. I left the docks by my usual route, and was nearly home when the Westminster bells tolled out the four o'clock warning.

Just in time.

I could barely bother myself with keeping to the shadows. I stumbled across the hedgerows, heedless of the rustle and snap of twigs around me. Dragging myself up the rope ladder took much more effort than I expected. My limbs felt filled with lead, aching already from the unexpected struggles of the night.

Perhaps I was getting too heavy.

Monsieur Marceaux kept his performing charges on a strict, often hungry regimen. Meals were structured, the hours were long and we worked hard. We had to perform well, and there were delicate considerations of weight and balance to maintain. But on the other side of that grimy coin, only his performers received regular meals.

I remember often being hungry.

My window was still ajar, and I crawled inside with muttered words even I couldn't translate; curses or complaints. With suddenly bone-tired fingers, I pulled and yanked at my clothing, managed somehow to strip down to my underclothes, shook out what I could of my pins, and crawled into bed.

The instant my sooty brow touched the soft linen, I fell to sleep.

But it was not kind. I dreamed that I ran, that I passed league after league, aware that something I could not see remained just behind me. I ran harder, sweating, gasping, until my legs gave and I fell to the same cobbled street I'd been running on forever.

Sweat dripped to the stone, splattered over my fingers, and I saw it was red. Red like the blood of a street girl's throat as the knife slashed it through.

I tried to scream; I must have, for I woke in dark with fear like a drum pounding in my chest and sweat cooling on my skin. My throat ached, closed off as if I strangled on my own voice.

Had I made a sound?

Every part of me felt ill, from the tips of my throbbing toes to the ends of my hair.

I turned, buried my face in a pillow and clutched it hard enough to burn against the taut skin of my knuckles. Tremors assailed me, tore through my body until I was forced to clench my teeth, lest I bite through my own cheek.

Everything hurt. Everything clamored.

I'd gone to sleep and woken in hell and I hadn't the faintest how to stop it without the laudanum I no longer had.

This, I was to learn later, was only the beginning of a nightmare that would worsen with time. I had no conception then that the ailment I suffered through wasn't a case of night terrors.

But for now, as I lay curled in my soot- and sweat-streaked bedclothes, I rocked myself into a mindless sort of oblivion where my shuddering breaths and muffled gasps were stolen by the feathers in my pillow and time ceased to matter. How long I sweated, twitching and restlessly swaying, I don't know. Somehow, unconsciousness stole through my aching head and I must have slept again.

If I dreamed a second time, I did not remember.

Chapter Thirteen

Dear me, what terrible calamity brings you to the table so early?"

I looked up from the *London Times*, pasting a smile upon my lips as Fanny swept into the room. For the first time in as long as I could remember, I'd come to the breakfast table first.

The surprise she'd initially greeted me with faded to worry as she took her seat, lovely in charcoal trimmed with dandelion yellow. "Are you feeling quite the thing?"

"I simply rose early," I said, reassuringly enough despite the near-lie. "I did not sleep terribly well."

"And how," she agreed, nodding with utter propriety at Booth as he laid out a tray before her. Her usual fare, as she preferred it. Fanny's breakfast did not often change, though the fruits in her jam would with the season. "My poor dear, were you terribly upset by those awful creatures?"

"Thank you, Booth," I murmured as he set before me another small pot of tea. My second of the morning. He bowed, turned and made his slow, dignified way back to the kitchens where his wife labored. *Step-thunk. Step-thunk.*

When the spasmodic reverberation of his step faded, I looked back at my paper and said through it, "Certainly not. I simply wasn't feeling well."

"As you say." But the tone of my chaperone's voice did not suggest that she believed me.

Perhaps rightfully so. Those *awful creatures* had followed me home.

Among the Society columns in today's edition of the *Times*, found earlier after Zylphia had performed a minor miracle and turned me to rights early this morning, the latest *on dit* from the Ladies of Admirable Mores and Behavior waited for me. It was not kind. My name was not attached—such things may be too crass, even for the salon—but I had no doubts that today's moral came at my expense.

> *To imagine such boldness in the demeanor of a young lady is to wonder at the education that surely has gone missing in her household. Would that such a young, impressionable girl's mother had the presence of mind to refrain from abandoning her child to the improper and ofttimes vulgar fancies of nannies and simple governesses.*

The passage, read for what seemed the hundredth time, no longer caused red streaks across my sight.

> *In truth our hypothetical lady of example may have no choice in her own behaviors. Remember that her mother stooped so far as to wed a common tradesman; an act so far beyond the pale, that one may only reach an assumption that such poor de-*

cisions must run truer in the blood than previously credited. Truth, gentle young misses, is rarely so kind when one comes from a lengthy line of ill choices. Remember that all young ladies of decent breeding must choose that which benefits her father, and if she is wed, then her husband; for those choices will then fall to your daughters to suffer.

And this, I thought in sightless anger, was deemed the polite form of bullying.

I did not know who penned this one. As ever, anything that came from the marchioness's salon fell under the overarching designation of LAMB's communal title. I could easily imagine Lady Sarah Elizabeth's smug smile as she counseled, *Mothers! Mind the gentlemen with whom your daughters consort, for those persons of hedonistic predispositions or affinities to the unnatural will only lead your cherished daughters astray.*

Teddy and my father, all in one fell swoop. It was no secret among Society that the Viscount Armistice Helmsley the Third had a wild taste for hedonism, and encouraged all three of his sons to follow suit.

Though Teddy was the third son and thus quite safe from Season matchmakers, his reputation would continue to suffer as long as he befriended me.

"—and I believe you should wear the rose gown for today's luncheon."

I blinked, forcing my attention away from the small print in front of me, and lowered the paper to frown questioningly at my chaperone. "I beg your pardon?"

"Don't scowl so," she admonished, and paused to take a sip from her cup. I waited, deliberately—with effort—smoothing the lines my features had settled into. "You do recall Lord Compton's invite, do you not?"

I stuffed a bit of bread crust into my mouth and said around it, "Hardly an invite."

Her pale brows drew together in censure. "Cherry."

Grimacing, I dutifully swallowed my fare before adding, "He practically forced my attendance. I don't—"

"You don't want to go, yes, yes." She sighed, a dry sound of exasperation. "Let's not have this argument today, my dear. You'll wear the rose, you'll charm the earl, and everything will go perfectly."

"Fanny." I stopped at her raised eyebrow, took a breath, and tried again in gentler tones. "I do not want to marry Lord Compton. I do not want to marry at all! Why must you insist on placing me in this untenable situation?"

But she did not react with anger as I'd expected, or with dismissal. Instead, setting her china delicately upon its saucer, she looked me in the eye—her own oddly misty—and said with utter frankness, "Because I watched you while you danced, Cherry, and I have never seen you look so happy."

I stared at her.

Her thin, lined mouth pulled at a corner; a smile tinged with sorrow and with delight all at once. "He engenders something in you, my dove. You may not admit it yourself, but these old eyes have seen enough of the world to know what it means when a woman moves so gracefully with a man in the ballroom."

Heat suffused my cheeks. "He is an excellent dancer," I pointed out. "Of course we move well, he was covering my graceless steps."

"You may choose to ignore what you know already," Fanny said, her smile widening as if I'd only just proven her point. "We are still going."

This time, I was quick enough to raise my paper before I made a face. "Into the lion's den," I muttered.

"Don't mumble."

I stuck my tongue out at the print, made a show of shaking the paper into shape, turning pages as loudly as possible, before my eye fell upon a column placed amid the rest.

The Scientific Mind, I read in small, nearly overwhelmed letters, *as Evidenced by a woman whose Mind is better suited to Science than the Induced Boredom of the home.*

All right. I would take back my snide commentary of last night's adventures. Perhaps it wasn't only men who would go on and on. I read the letter slowly, taking my time to absorb the piece written to the masses in supplication for understanding.

I had known of the women's movement—I thought the highly rational tea gowns of the Aesthetic reform a brilliant invention and had long petitioned Fanny to allow me to wear them, albeit in vain—and I followed the periodicals written by Dr. Elizabeth Garrett Anderson with *great* interest.

She was the only licensed female physician in Britain. According to this letter, which I already suspected was not penned by the good doctor for it referenced her direct, this made Dr. Anderson the only doctor worth consulting.

A woman's mind is by definition a mind suited to searching for the unknown. Centuries of subjection by the male of the species has left us with only one task—to raise the young of the men who choose us.

*But by that very definition, do we not exercise an
aptitude for creative and logical endeavors?*

It went on like this for some time, until I realized
that what I was reading was not a letter regarding
merely suffrage in science. I read a call to arms.
A demand for intelligent women to stand united
behind the banner unwittingly thrust over the path
of the author's heroine, Dr. Anderson.

I whistled soundlessly, pursing my lips and pretending the note so I would not disturb my chaperone's welcome silence.

*University College has gone so far as to claim a "lower-
ing of standards,"* the author continued, and I could
all but see the scorn dripping from the words.

*Brilliant women determined to partake of an edu-
cation that a majority of male students simply idle
through are now placed not on a pedestal, but upon
a stoop; the meanest of urchins who may scrap together the tuition will be welcomed more honestly
and with greater warmth than a woman whose intellect cowers that of the professor's, yet who will
never progress beyond that of assistant or helpmeet.*

Raising my eyebrows, I searched again for the
author and nearly laughed aloud when I saw it. *Miss
Hortense Hensworth.*

So the wallflower had thorns, after all.

Good girl, I thought. *Give them the very devil.*

The contents of Miss Hensworth's letter still brought
a muted chuckle to my lips as Zylphia prepared me
for the dreaded luncheon. I mulled it over while my
maid worked her magic; it wasn't until she plucked

a delicate perfume glass from my fingers that I realized it was the fourth time she'd done so.

Her eyes met mine as she tilted my face up. "What's bothering you, *cherie*?"

"You mean besides this luncheon?" I asked flippantly.

Her brow furrowed, lovely black eyebrows meeting in her tea-dark skin. "I mean besides that, yes. Your bed looked as if you'd rolled in soot on your way home, and you never sleep without removing the black from your hair."

True. On both counts. I affected a shrug, unsure how to explain my night. "You were out last night. I was too tired to draw a bath myself."

"Are you even capable?" Her wry smile smoothed the sting. "The very fact I was already out suggests you should not have been."

I frowned from beneath the thick fall of red she draped over my face. "I am a collector, Zylla, and have been since before you came. Remember that."

"Don't use that tone with me," she shot back. "I'm not truly your maid and you and I both know it. Whatever you're up to, it's getting more dangerous by the day." My head wrenched as she pulled hard on a handful, twisting it into place.

I couldn't argue that. I'd filled her in on the details this morning, and she'd obviously had time to work up a good head of steam. "There was nothing to worry about," I assured her, for the moment choosing to ignore the veiled threat of her employ. Or lack thereof. "Simply a book, that was then stolen from me."

"With that Ripper about? It's a fool what steps below, and a twist alone besides. I don't like it," Zylphia insisted, scraping my hair back so she could fashion it into an ornate selection of gleaming twists. Each pin jammed into the thick mass was a line of pressure, nearly pain, in my scalp.

It wasn't because she pressed too hard. That strange fragility that had haunted my night clung to me still. I sighed and squared my shoulders; covered completely in the lovely rose linen day dress. Deeply rich wine detailed the fabric, accented at the three-quarter sleeves, décolletage and hem with a frothy spill of cream-colored lace.

It turned my hair to sunlit ruby, flattered my pale complexion. Exactly why Fanny demanded its use, I was sure. Even I could admit what lovely things the dusky rose did for my coloring.

Zylphia pinned a fashionably jaunty hat in place, designed primarily to match the dress and tease the eye with a spill of wine-colored roses and the speckled plumage of some poor feathered creature. Its silky ribbons tied at my nape in a darling bow, accentuating the beautiful coiled mass of Zylphia's handiwork. "There," she announced. "Go charm your earl, *cherie*."

I frowned. "Why?"

"Because the alternative is not what you think it is," she said, with such seriousness that even I hesitated in glib retort.

What was there in her shockingly blue eyes that I did not yet know how to read? A warning?

A regret?

She looked away, collecting my warm outer garb. "I'll be stepping below for some work," she said, a complete change of topic not even one of Communion's Abram men could miss. "In a few days."

"What kind of work?" I demanded, gaze sharp on her determinedly nonchalant features.

"Personal work," she said, and smiled. "Fret not, I won't be gone long." Before I could press her, she left the room.

She was right on at least one matter. She wasn't truly a maid at all. I had little control of her, if she chose a headstrong path.

I studied myself critically in the vanity mirror. "Perfectly done." I sighed. "Fanny will be pleased."

And so she was. She fussed and fretted as Booth guided the St. Croix gondola along the now-familiar passages between Chelsea and the much finer Northampton estate. I found myself twisting one foot in restless counter to the agitation clamoring underneath my too-sensitive skin.

I did not want to be in this gondola. I did not want to face the marchioness in her den, and I most certainly did not want to put up with the hours and hours of scrutiny I would be walking into.

Fanny braced one hand on my knee. "Stop your fidgeting," she warned. "Ladies do not fidget."

This lady did. Not that I laid much claim to the title. Ladies did not sneak off in the dead of night to hunt men for bounty, either.

When Booth disembarked, my stomach had turned itself into a shriveled thing, coiled tightly around the rapidly disintegrating strength of my spine. My gloved hand shook as I placed it in my butler's.

His eyes twinkled at me from his so-stoic features, proud nose and impressive white sideburns all serving to give him quite the distinguished air. With the whole of the Northampton home gracing the late afternoon skyline behind him, he looked as at home as I'd always imagined a man of his caliber should.

Booth was a true butler, a gentleman's gentleman.

How long had he wasted his talents with me?

His fingers squeezed mine for a heartbeat before letting me go, turning to offer the same steadying courtesy for my chaperone.

I took a deep breath, somewhat soothed by the kindness.

If Booth—darling, steady, kind Booth—thought me worth his attention, then the least I could do would be to see this through.

What could the marchioness say when the invite had come from her own son?

So armed with such shallow reasoning, Fanny and I stepped into the Northampton entryway and pulled the bell that did not ring as sweetly as the mechanism my father had installed in my own home. Instead, a simple bell chimed.

Within moments, a staid man less old than Booth but every inch the groomed butler in black and white opened the door. "Miss St. Croix," Fanny offered, card in hand, "and Mrs. Fortescue, her companion."

The butler took the card, bowed formally. "You are expected," he said, not so much looking at us as over us and down his long nose all at the same time. A true trait of the elite, I thought, restraining an inappropriate giggle. To have a nose so long that a man could look down it and across it with one glare.

The estate, seen usually by evening, was truly something to behold. The foyer was magnificent, a large staircase winding up the far side and the floor gleaming with polish and care. The art upon the elegantly papered walls was heavy with gilt frames and bold colors; men and women I did not recognize looked down upon us as we passed through the halls.

Family, I suspected. There was something to the eyes, the set of the mouth.

"Today's function," the butler said as he led us, "will be in the largest music parlor."

The *largest*? Were there more?

Why? I couldn't fathom a need for more than one music room, unless there were more than one musically inclined members of a household whose tastes would not complement.

I had no chance to ask. The butler stepped through a set of lovely doors patterned with lattice and gilt, cleared his throat and intoned, "Miss St. Croix and Mrs. Fortescue." With no more than that, we stepped inside to find too many eyes pinned on us.

On me.

This was it. If I did not perform well here, I would never lay claim to a place in this Society.

A tempting consequence.

One that did not allow me much time to consider as Earl Compton disengaged from a small knot of gentlemen. His mother, I noticed, made no move to rise from her place at the center of a circle of chairs and settees. She held court with her salon, as expected, but also with a few others I recognized.

Lady Rutledge was not in attendance.

"Miss St. Croix," the earl said by way of greeting, bowing gallantly. "Mrs. Fortescue, I am delighted to see you in good health."

My chaperone colored, but her eyes sparkled in pale diamond blue as she curtsied in returned greeting. "My lord, you're too kind."

"Nonsense." The earl's gaze, kind in eyes that mirrored his mother's in all but intent, reflected a smile that only hinted at his mouth. "'Tis always a pleasure to invite two more fetching ladies to one of my mother's luncheons."

Not quite a lie of convenience, or of motive. I discerned nothing but simple truth in the words, flattery though it was.

I glanced at my chaperone.

Her day dress was among some of the more somber in a muted shade of navy blue, but its trim of crimson gave it a lovely splash of color. She was quite fashionable, I realized in surprise. I had not noticed just how much so until her smile widened upon seeing two other matrons of her circle. She stood out, like a subtle lantern in the fog.

"There's no need to dance attendance on me," I said suddenly, smiling as demurely as I knew how when her gaze sharpened on me. "Go greet your dear friends, I shall be safe."

"Indeed," murmured the earl as Fanny made her farewells. His gaze remained fixed on me, and was it my imagination that they seemed filled with a warmth of approval? "There is no place more safe than here, I daresay."

Oh, I wasn't so sure of that. I was keenly aware of the marchioness's catlike glare from her position in the center of the room.

This would be a long, long event.

But as the earl led me to the knot of women surrounding his mother, I could not help but raise my chin.

"Mother," the earl said, when the babble of inane female conversation faded. Beside her, Lady Sarah Elizabeth—resplendent in peacock blue trimmed in green—smiled in abject warning. A viper's smile. "I present Miss St. Croix."

The marchioness did not rise. "Lovely to have you," she said, her mouth shaped into a smile but her cool tones anything but welcoming.

I dropped into a curtsy. "Your Ladyship," I returned, pleased and relieved when the tremor hammering at my chest did not find its way to my voice. "You have my thanks for the invitation."

Those cold eyes, so like her son's, flicked to him. "Indeed." She raised an elegant, gloved hand. "Sarah Elizabeth, make room for our guest."

If the marchioness had taken a dagger and plunged it in Lady Sarah Elizabeth's back, she could not have caused more damage. The hatred I saw beneath the younger lady's calculating smile chilled me to the bone.

My stomach, already twisted beyond all reason, pitched. I swallowed hard as the lady rose to her feet, smoothing the skirts that needed no such thing, and gestured to the seat. "Please," she chirped, every inch the gracious hostess, for all it was not her parlor.

To refuse would be rude. To look at the earl now would be tantamount to declaring my surrender. I forced my smile to remain, to brighten, as I took my place beside the marchioness.

It was akin to sitting beside an ice box in the dead of winter.

"You may fraternize with your friends, Cornelius," the marchioness said dismissively. "I shall borrow Miss St. Croix for a time."

"Of course, Mother," the earl said, giving me a small nod as if I'd done something right. A short bow, a sketch of a formality, and he added, "I shall return to claim her for a turn around the parlor."

"Of course," the marchioness murmured, repeating his own capitulation but with none of his sincerity.

My hands in my lap, I studied the faces now ringing me. Lady Sarah Elizabeth standing at my left, causing the skin between my shoulders to itch. The marchioness, perched just so on the settee beside me, this time wearing a day gown of a beautiful shade of pale blue. Cut for a matron, it nevertheless flattered her still youthful figure, and outlined every way that she was still the finest shape of fashion.

I felt stuffed and plump between both women. Likely, I thought miserably, on purpose.

Mrs. Douglas was in attendance, wearing black poplin once more, trimmed with white. I saw Miss Cordelia Clarkspur, a barrister's eldest daughter and—abashed that I remembered this from the periodicals—engaged to Lord Trefawney, a viscount of Teddy's acquaintance.

As I recalled, Miss Clarkspur had turned down two suitors prior to landing the viscount.

She studied me without sympathy or interest, as if I were merely a passing thing soon to be forgotten. She was not as lovely as Lady Sarah Elizabeth, but she had a good face and a pleasingly shaped bosom. Things I knew a man would look for in a wife, even if he would be considered crass to admit it.

Of the six gentlemen in the room, I recognized only the Marquess Northampton and the aforementioned Lord Trefawney, dapper in his paisley waistcoat and dark brown coat tailored to near perfection. He cut a fine figure with the earl, his friend, beside him. They looked, to my cynical eye, like a pair of tomcats idling on a fence, taking in the females clustered for their attention.

Unfair, perhaps, but every time I looked upon Earl Compton, I could not help the way I noticed the fit of his gray frock coat, tapered at the waist, and the length of his striped trousers. His waistcoat was a vivid pattern of Oriental design, brilliant blue silk embroidered by gold and green. He was a fine figure all by himself, to be quite honest, and I noticed.

Of course, with the kind of social warfare he'd been waging on me since we first met on that ballroom floor only last month, it was no wonder I noticed such things.

My fists clenched into my skirt, ruffling the rose fabric.

"What say you, Miss St. Croix?"

I startled, suddenly aware that I'd become the attention of the pit of viperous women I'd promptly ignored. "I beg your pardon?"

Lady Sarah Elizabeth did nothing to hide her scorn as she laughed a lilting sound. "Oh, dear, have we lost the poor bird?"

"We speak of manners," Miss Clarkspur said, not unkindly. Not particularly friendly, of course, but she at least added, "Most particularly, those that dictate the conversation between a gentleman and a lady."

My brow began to furrow; I forced it smooth. "Oh?" Feigning interest might get the conversation moved along at a pace that would allow me to make my escape. "What exactly is the question at stake?"

The marchioness's mouth compressed. "I am given to understand that you do not attend these functions much."

The group fell silent, and color burned clear to my ears at the unbridled censure. "N-no, my lady," I said, suddenly furious to hear the stumble from my own lips. My throat closed.

My breath vanished, and I could not speak even if I wanted to.

Where? It became a word that stretched like a net across the sudden void where my mind had been.

Where? Where could I escape to? Where would I find peace?

Where could I find laudanum to ease this ache?

Where could I get money to purchase more grains of opium for the tincture and soothe my terribly fractured nerves?

"Tea, Miss St. Croix?" This from Miss Clarkspur, and I realized she held a delicate cup and saucer, filled with steaming black liquid. "How do you take it?"

I stiffened my spine, forced myself to swallow down the knot in my throat. "Two sugars, please," I managed, blinking away a film over my suddenly blurred vision. "Thank you ever so kindly."

Beside me, the marchioness sipped at her own cup. "Propriety insists that conversation between the sexes should at all times remain distant. I am in agreement. There is no call to share, for example, similar interests in matters that belong strictly to a gentleman's domain."

I gritted my teeth as I accepted Miss Clarkspur's proffered cup and saucer.

It must have been a thinly veiled reference to the first conversation I'd ever claimed with the earl. We spoke of the periodicals, and the HMS *Ophelia*, anything I could seize upon to keep my foot from entering my mouth instead.

Regardless of intent, I would not let it stand. "I disagree," I said, and could not have managed a more resounding silence if I'd reached over and slapped her.

Where did the words come from?

I took the cup in hand, made as if to lift it, but put it down quickly as I realized that my hand shook too badly to hide the tremor in the liquid.

This wouldn't do. I needed control of my own limbs.

"Oh?" This from Lady Sarah Elizabeth, likely sensing blood in the air.

I glanced once at the earl; froze when I inadvertently met his gaze direct from across the brightly lit parlor. The corners of his mouth turned up.

"If men require discourse of a deeper nature," Mrs. Douglas assured me gravely, "it is with men they will meet. Women are better served providing alternate forms of conversation, lest she find herself thrown over for company of a more agreeable sort."

"What, like a mistress?" I asked, as much to my own shock as theirs.

Gasps ringed the parlor, and even the low murmur and laughter of Fanny's older matrons fell silent.

"Miss St. Croix," gasped Mrs. Douglas.

Two sets of pale eyes, fog-lit green, studied me.

I don't know where the words came from; or perhaps I knew exactly then what it was I did. Suddenly, it was as if a net had torn inside my mind, a deep well of pressure giving way within my skin. I watched myself as I smiled brightly, even as a part of myself gesticulated wildly in dismay at my own temerity. *I could not stop myself.* "Many is a woman kept by a gentleman because she is intelligent and lively, besides. It seems to me, then," I continued, unable to keep myself from raising my voice louder than strictly proper, "that a woman may be as intelligent as she wishes, so long as she performs in the marriage bed while she does so."

Silence fell like a death knell upon us. I bit my lip, forcing back a surge of hysterical laughter as Mrs. Douglas's pallid skin turned ember bright.

The marchioness did not smile.

Chapter Fourteen

M y nerves stretched to the breaking point. As I lifted the teacup to my lips, I looked down to find the tea sloshing within the delicate china. Too late, I realized my error. Too late, I lost the struggle with my own body; my hand seized, and the dark liquid splashed over the rim.

If my words hadn't been enough to achieve the unintended effect, this would be the end of it.

A lady did not, under any circumstances, spill her tea.

Yet here I was, seated beside the Marchioness Northampton, with the dark, wet stain spreading over my bodice and dripping down my décolletage.

To my endless consternation, sudden, angry tears filled my eyes.

What the devil was wrong with me?

I heard a rustle, Fanny's voice, and then the rich, educated tenor of Earl Compton. "Mother," he said, in the tone of one who is preparing an excuse, "ladies, if you will forgive the intrusion, I would escort Miss St. Croix in a turn about the parlor."

"By all means," murmured the marchioness, who knew what her son had not said.

There would be precious little I could do—except perhaps make good on a mistress's role—to seal my fate on the outside of his world.

She was pleased. Quite obviously so.

I took a deep breath as the earl took the saucer from my gloved hands, set it upon the tea cart and offered his arm.

I took it, because anything was better than remaining among that nest of vipers. Including a final reason for the earl to understand the mistake he made in me. Now was his last chance.

"Let her go," I heard from one of Fanny's friends. A sad advisement; one that suggested the matron had seen her share of social faux pas and knew the weight of those I'd made.

What possessed me?

If the earl heard the same damning whispers I did, he was too much a gentleman to acknowledge them. Instead, with my gloved hand in his elbow and the tea stain cooling on my bodice, he led me along the far wall, passing the wide windows with their beautifully dressed crimson draperies.

He said nothing. A glance up at him revealed only the façade I'd grown used to seeing. His handsome, aristocratic features were in stern lines, his mouth set beneath his sandy-colored mustache. His hair, as it ever was, was perfectly groomed, swept to the side and displaying that hint of curl in the waves.

The silence stretched between us. I grew increasingly aware of the stain on my chest, and the words he was not saying. Would he end his ill-fated infatuation with me?

Did I want him to?

Of course I did. What hope could a man whose mother loathed his choice of partner have, in the end?

I was too much for him to handle. I recognized this.

Finally, I could tolerate it no longer. "I am not accustomed to such fine company." I did not stress the word; it was not his fault that his mother was such a cat.

"Such things may be learned," came his response, quiet yet lacking in the recrimination I expected.

"Learned," I repeated, drawing the word out.

"Tutors," he replied, "and those with the patience to instruct." He glanced down at me. "I would be pleased, myself."

What manner of game was this?

"You confuse me, my lord," I blurted, my voice low to keep from prying ears. Conversation had resumed behind us, yet I knew if I looked I would find eyes pinned to where we walked.

"I am a simple man," he replied, inflection steady. His eyes met mine. "I am not so complicated."

"You require a simple woman," I pointed out.

His laughter surprised me. Quiet, even restrained, yet I read its warmth in those eyes, so different at times from the woman who birthed him. "I require," he retorted, "a lady who thinks before she exclaims the first thing that comes to her not unintelligent head."

I winced. "You won't find that here."

"You lie," he assured me, "if I may be so bold as to accuse a lady of such."

"Why, sir," I replied lightly, for all his words caused an unhealthy knot in my chest, "you dare accuse me of falsehoods? Shall I fetch my second?"

He said nothing for a moment, and I wondered if

I'd gone too far. Again. Then, quietly, he said, "Miss St. Croix, if ever there was a woman to duel a man, I would wager on you."

And with that, the knot in my chest turned into a weight. And from the weight sprang a sudden inability to speak—guilt, uncertainty, and, yes, even curiosity—as the earl matched my shorter stride in a way that suggested he did so deliberately.

Propriety colored his every move; so why, then, did he defy it by undoing the cut direct of his mother? Why did he continue to hound me?

It would not stand.

I shook my head, at last. "You should not say such things," I whispered. "Mrs. Douglas assures me that all conversation between a lady and a gentleman should be distant." We passed molding after molding, each panel in the music room framed by the ornate stuff and glittering faintly gold.

More draperies filled the walls—it kept the sound of the room ideal for music, I knew—and the occasional statue on a pedestal broke the isolated lines. Greek in nature, various Muses. It surprised me.

"Perhaps." Compton raised his eyebrows, a shade darker than his hair. "And what of the weather, Miss St. Croix?" he continued. "Rather chilly for an October."

The clever man. He'd timed this just so; such an innocuous conversation as we once more passed the guests.

Or was it coincidence? A natural progression of my chastisement.

"Certainly, although I understand it's not as wet as some years past." I glimpsed Lord Trefawney's unadulterated amusement as he bent to say something I couldn't hear to his fiancée.

The marchioness did not look nearly so pleased.

"You don't truly wish to speak of the weather," the earl continued as we passed the group entirely.

I looked up at him in surprise. "No?"

"No. You wish to discuss other things, such as aether engines and"—a flicker of distaste crossed his features—"the correlation of electricity and the human body."

My surprise turned over into something much less clear. Slightly more warming. "You remembered."

"There are many things I remember of that outing, Miss St. Croix." The silken note in those simple words completed what the topic had started, and I shivered despite the warmth of the room.

I looked away from the earl's searching gaze. "A kiss does not cement compatibility," I said flatly. "You require a proper wife."

"A proper wife is a woman blessed by the sanction of marriage," replied the earl, whose unending font of rejoinders and semantics was rapidly leaving me with no room in my shrinking corner.

"A proper wife is one who smiles and sews and makes delightful conversation. She does not spill her tea, or stumble in the ballroom." *Or take opium for her nightmares.*

I had so many more secrets than he would ever know.

Though I made as if to remove my hand from his arm, his flattened over my fingers. Trapped me against the warmth at the bend of his elbow.

My gaze lifted to his.

A single corner of his mouth tilted up; a near-smile I found so much more evocative than his others. His eyes all but glowed as he looked down on me. A shared warmth caused my lips to tingle in memory.

He'd looked just like this when he'd kissed me.

He would not dare here. No matter how pleasant a kiss had passed between us, it was not enough.

"A proper wife," he murmured, low and more than a shade too intimately, "is a woman who may converse with Society on all the topics required of her. She may charm the gentlemen into agreeing with her husband's politics, or engage the ladies in shared dialogue of fashion and social requests."

My jaw tightened. I did not make the conscious decision, but suddenly stopped, withdrawing my hand forcefully.

He was quicker than I, stopped at the same time and faced me as if we only shared a conversation that did not leave anger pulsing through my veins.

He did not know me at all.

I opened my mouth.

His gaze twinkled. "A proper wife, Miss St. Croix, will then discourse with her husband on whatever topics capture her fancy, from whatever periodicals she has delivered to his door. She will engage in intellectual debate with him at her leisure, debate the merits of aether or electricity, ponder the weight of Her Majesty's flagship, *and* perform in the marriage bed while she does so."

The bottom dropped out from under my stomach. Whatever words I'd intended—brilliant, scalding things designed to strip the skin from his aristocratically self-entitled bones—came instead on a squeak. Surprise. Shock, more like.

"Think on it," he said, once more offering his arm.

I stared at it. That perfect arm clad in spotless gray, gloved hand held just so.

"I offer you more than just a name, Miss St. Croix," he said gently. "I offer you shelter, kindness,

and support. All I ask is that you fit the demands
expected of a future marchioness."

I swallowed, hard enough that his eyes tracked
the motion at my throat. And then they skimmed
lower. Tracing the stain at my lace décolletage, burning a path along my skin.

This time, I recognized the slow uncurling of
heat low in my belly. I found him quite attractive,
certainly. I could not argue that. I was a daughter
of science and a creature of experience, or at least
knowledge. I understood that I found him attractive, just as a part of me felt drawn to handsome
men with character.

His eyes lifted once more to mine. The stern angles
of his face set in earnest lines. "I offer you a place,
Miss St. Croix."

Yes. But the price was far too high.

I did not sleep that night.

My skin seemed made of parchment as I lay in
my bed, staring blankly into the dark recesses of my
bedroom. Everything pressed upon me, until I was
sure my chest would cave and my skin would tear
and whatever it was trapped inside my flesh would
escape. Free, finally free.

The canopy over my head became a tomb, and
sometime in the darkest hours, I fled the dubious
sanctuary of my boudoir.

Mrs. Booth found me first. I paced Mr. Ashmore's
study, my dressing gown swirling in a froth of linen
and ribbon about my ankles. I don't know how many
times I traversed that single path—from the heavy,
polished wood desk in strong masculine lines to
the window set into the far wall, masked by heavy
drapes of striped slate and blue; back to the desk, my

feet dragging on the vivid Oriental carpet, and then to the bookshelves that lined the opposite wall.

Back and forth, around and again, my stride short and harried. I must have walked it for hours as my mind turned and turned within the confines of my aching skull.

So much need in one small form.

Had I any laudanum in the house, I'd have taken it all, but there had been no injuries or ailments of late—and my stipend was all spent on my last batch. Fanny did not keep it near, for the very same reason that I wanted it.

I needed to sleep, blast it. I needed time to dream, to work through these manic thoughts swirling in my wild and unshackled brain.

If my housekeeper said anything to me, I did not realize. She was gone almost before I even recognized her presence.

What was I missing?

Answers. I needed answers.

The mystery of the murdered professors. What a terrible crime; and yet as thrilling a chase as I could expect, short of literally chasing the murderer through London below.

That would come. Once I knew what and who I searched for.

Jack the Ripper?

No, decidedly not. I turned at the window, the faintest seam of light gathering beneath the drapes. My hair swayed at my waist, a tangled plait whose curls had wildly escaped in my tossing and turning.

The Ripper didn't care for common murder. One had been poisoned, the other fallen from a great height.

Were they both murders?

My thoughts flashed to the narrow closet, and the stolen book.

Yes. I would wager both were killed in the name of this mystery. Killed, or persuaded to die. It became the same thing, after a point.

Why?

Back to the desk, my feet carrying me without command.

Alchemy. "Bloody stuff," I muttered, striding past the desk and to the shelves. My eyes raked over the books—polished, dusted, gleaming like teeth in neat rows—but I saw another book in the surging place that was my memory.

Why?

That was the question, was it not? "Why," I repeated, muttering the word. And again. Over and over, with every footstep. "Why? Why? Why?"

"Cherry St. Croix."

I spun, snapping my fingers as my nightgown hem flared gently. "Wrong question!" I crowed, and hurried for the desk. Fanny's presence only dimly registered—her shocked dismay, Mrs. Booth's silent concern behind her. Ignoring them both, I snatched up the quill I'd used to doodle nothing at all on several of Ashmore's finer parchments and scribbled out the symbols I remembered from the papers I'd left with Mr. Pettigrew.

"I am asking the wrong questions," I said from between my clenched teeth. My heart hammered; too hard, too fast. I bent over the parchment, forgoing the chair to stoop over the desk like a vulture eyeing a carcass. "It's not about *why* alchemy is involved, it's *what.* What the formula is purported to *do.*"

"Cherry, my dove," Fanny said gently; the tone of one approaching a madman, hands extended.

One touched my shoulder. I shrugged her away and drew like a thing possessed. A triangle, three circles, *DG* and the newly recognized *Fu*. Not an *E*, not a *y. Fusion.* "Cherry, it's time to come away for a bit."

I looked up, my eyes wild. I'm sure I looked like the devil himself had possessed me, my hair a ruby corona about my face, smudges of exhaustion beneath my reddened eyes. "Why?" I demanded.

My chaperone, clad already for the day in subdued violet and cream, raised her eyebrows as if she intended to answer.

I sliced a hand through the air, braced the other with the dripping quill against Ashmore's desk. *My desk.* "Why would you kill a professor?"

"Madam, I've her tea ready."

I glowered at Zylphia, fresh as a daisy in spring and regarding me with the same outward concern as the rest of my staff. Traitor.

I was not mad. *I was not!*

I pushed up from the desk, flinging my hands in wild impatience. "Why would you murder a professor?" I demanded again. "The answer is there. The truth is so close, I can feel it."

I watched Fanny and Mrs. Booth exchange a glance. It was a careful thing, a worried and determined thing.

Snorting my contempt, nearly a growl in my parched throat, I threw the steel-nibbed quill to the desk—splattering ink in indigo drops guaranteed to stain the dark wood if I did not wipe it away.

I didn't bother. "One kills for obvious reasons," I continued flatly, circling through fact after fact in my head. "But a body does not change *how* he kills." A beat; a snap of my fingers. "Unless opportunity provides the motive. But no, that is too random, not suited for two men of the same profession."

Why kill professors?

"To retain knowledge," I said aloud, turning for the window without conscious awareness I'd done so. I shook a handful of parchment as if for emphasis. "To keep one's secrets at bay. For money, or prestige, or power. Bloody bells and damn, there's too many reasons to kill a man," I added, an indignant afterthought.

It was as if I remained trapped inside the walking shell of my body. Watching it turn and pace and frenetically dart from one perch to the next like a manic butterfly.

I had never until that moment looked so much like my father; I would not recognize this until much, much later. Maybe if I had seen it then, I would have frightened myself into decorum.

Instead, as I crossed the study on my bare, aching feet, Fanny caught my arm. "Stop," she said firmly.

I almost didn't. Indeed, Fanny stumbled once as I careened on my reckless trajectory. But I did stop when her grip tightened; stopped and turned and studied her with very real surprise to find her there, holding on to me, her gaze fierce and mouth in a thin, worried line.

"Yes?" I prompted.

Her features softened to something very like fatigue. "Oh, Cherry." Such a sad, soft note I'd never heard from her before. Her grip eased, she cupped my cheek in one long, thin hand. "Take a moment, my dear."

I shook my head, although the part of me exhausted and trembling allowed her to lead me to the overstuffed armchair by the fireplace. There was no fire stocked in it. I hadn't realized until I sat how cold the study was. "I have no time to breathe, I must solve a mystery."

Another exchange of glances. Zylphia handed my chaperone the steaming cup of tea she held, but her gaze met mine and narrowed. Censure? Or a warning?

My shoulders slumped.

"Take this, there's a love," Fanny crooned softly, like a mother easing the fears of a lost child. She smoothed back my hair from my face. "What can we do to help?"

Help? I blinked. Help! As if I needed it; as if I were floundering in the dark like one of the Ripper's own . . . One of . . .

The papers. Of course. Lady Rutledge was not a woman who thrived on what-ifs and pretending. It would be in the papers. Didn't she herself ask me if I read them?

A clue.

Was it so simple?

"Brilliant," I breathed. I reached up, caught Fanny by the hand. "We will make a collector of you yet," I continued in fervent regard. "Zylla, the newspapers."

"Today's?" she asked, bless her soul, not arguing.

"For the past fortnight. All of them! Levi will take you." I tried to stand, wavered, flinched when the hot tea rimmed the cup I held and splashed to my fingers.

Fanny rescued the cup and my fingers. "All right, Cherry," she continued in the same gentle tones. As fine a mother as I'd ever known. "Rest for a spell, and then we'll get you dressed." I sat, more because I'd lost all the steam I'd built by night than because I was listening.

As Mrs. Booth, tsking loud enough to hear her clucking from two rooms down, made her way to the kitchens, I looked up at Fanny and frowned. "You look tired," I told her.

Her smile did not quite reach her pale eyes. She tucked stray curls behind one of my ears and said simply, "Don't you worry your pretty head for me, my dove. It's time you allowed others to care for you, instead."

Was it?

Well . . . perhaps . . . For a little while.

I reclaimed the teacup she placed in my trembling palms and inhaled gratefully the fragrant brew.

Just this once.

Chapter Fifteen

I slept for a few hours, although I don't recall drifting off. When I awoke in the chair with my neck stiff, the house was very quiet.

Zylphia dressed me in my bronzed chocolate poplin, but she did not speak much when it became clear I was distracted.

I felt drained. As if I'd spent days soaring on the crest of an energy so vibrant—the kind of golden wave I often attributed to my forays into an opium den—and now paid the cost.

But I had not had so much as a drop for two days, now.

It weighed on me.

It . . . *gnawed* at me.

"I'll be helping Mrs. Booth today in the kitchens," Zylphia said lightly, tucking the last pin into my hair. "You don't go getting yourself into any trouble, you hear? You gave us all quite a scare."

"I seem to be developing that habit," I admitted wryly. "I'm sorry, Zylla. I'm just so close."

"Close or not, won't do any of us a lick of good if

you run yourself into a fit." Her hand flattened over the top of my head, very dark against my auburn locks. She met my gaze in the mirror, terribly serious for all her levity. "I won't be telling Cage it was a mystery what done you in."

Point well taken. The last thing I wanted was Micajah Hawke in my business, above or below the drift. "I'll stay cozy and warm," I promised. "There's too much to study to allow me time to gallivant about."

She grinned, most cheeky. "As if that would ever stop you, *cherie.*"

I left my bedroom feeling somewhat more the thing; properly dressed and with a bit of tea in me. I hadn't eaten. I wasn't hungry. The mere thought of food sent a tremor from the very depths of my stomach to the back of my throat.

It wasn't food I wanted.

I found Fanny in the parlor, a stack of periodicals and papers beside her. Booth had wheeled in a tea cart, and my insides roiled uncomfortably at the array of treats Mrs. Booth had put together to tempt my appetite.

I had no appetite. I was busy, after all, there were other things than food on my mind.

This reasoning would serve me well for a small amount of time.

"I've been searching through these papers for a clue," Fanny announced, surprising me to the point of openmouthed regard. The paper in her hands— the *Leeds Mercury*, I noted—rustled as she raised her eyes above the print and narrowed them. "Close your mouth, Cherry."

I did.

"Pour a cup, and enlighten me as to what exactly I

should be looking for," she continued, artlessly commanding as I sank to the settee and blindly obeyed.

It wasn't until I dropped two sugars into my tea and had the saucer in hand did I manage to put two thoughts together. "If you can take the gossip columns," I said slowly, "I will read the news that fall under the headlines."

"For what?"

A good question. But I was sure that Lady Rutledge would not issue this challenge if there were no clues to be had. *All things are remarked upon, Miss St. Croix, somewhere.*

This began with a brief article in the newspaper. It was not too far a stretch, to my searching mind, to think I would be able to trace the connections I could all but sense through the same.

"Anything that stands out from the normal gossip," was the best I could give.

"Hmm." The low hum was not encouraging, but for a time, we lapsed into a companionable silence, broken only by the occasional snippet of shared information.

" 'The visit to London of the great Houlier, the celebrated Paris detective, has caused quite a stir in Scotland Yard,' " Fanny read aloud.

"No, too big and too . . ." I flicked my paper. "Unrelated. Detective Houlier won't care much for anything beyond the Ripper, I'm sure."

Again, a companionable silence fell over the parlor. I combed through article after article, many about the terrifying Whitechapel murders and others about politics in Her Majesty's Parliament, various reforms, the latest on the travails with the Irish Home Rule—I admit to being more than a little impressed with the now infamous three-hour speech given by the disgraced Mr. Gladstone some years ago—and various carry-ons reported below the drift.

I found once more the article regaling readers with the death of Professor MacGillycuddy—poison was not once mentioned—and set that aside.

"Ah."

I glanced up, my head full of so many useless facts, it took me a moment to place the sound. "Yes?"

Fanny studied her paper, now folded for easier reading, and glanced at me through her spectacles. "There was a scene at the Athenaeum Club nearly a fortnight ago."

"The Athenaeum," I repeated slowly. A fine establishment, and one of very few gentlemen's clubs in London that had converted to electrical lights. A remarkable feat in and of itself. I'd often dreamed of stepping foot within, yet the membership was limited to a mere thousand, and the waiting list long.

And, of course, while the charter welcomed all who were of distinguished renown in literature, science or the arts, it would never, ever allow a woman. No matter how wealthy, well-bred or brilliant.

I grimaced. "What set them on their ear, then?"

"An unwanted guest," Fanny replied, her gaze once more flicking at me, but over her spectacles this time. "It seems a woman was found wearing the guise of a man. In fact, a member's very suit."

I stared at her for a long, unblinking moment.

Fanny raised her chin, looking down at the paper as if even her spectacles were no longer quite so helpful. "I see the names of the gentlemen involved with evicting her from the premises."

"Either MacGillycuddy or Lambkin?"

"Neither."

I chewed on my lip for a moment, lost in thought.

A woman braving the depths of a club known particularly for its patronage of science and the arts.

A link? I tossed aside the articles I skimmed in favor of one I remember viewing some days ago. Was it over a week, now? "Does it say what she was there to accomplish?"

"No," Fanny said after a moment's reading. "Cause trouble, I'd wager." I ignored her scorn, hastily rifling through the now jumbled pages.

"Why was the woman there?" I repeated to myself. "To what purpose? Thievery? Espionage? An illicit tryst?"

"Cherry, really." She sighed. "Although it seems the gentlemen of the club have been much more arduous about checking the identity of its patrons since."

"They would, wouldn't they?" I muttered. I'd often considered pulling the same prank on the Athenaeum. Or the Gresham, or even the Travellers' Club, who retained the most distinguished personages from across the globe. Whoever this woman was, she beat me to that race. Soundly.

Of course, as far as I knew, I retained the distinction of remaining the only female collector. I would take that win.

Although, I certainly would like to meet the woman who'd been so bold. "A name, then? Of her?"

"Ah . . ." Fanny frowned at the small printing. "Yes. A Miss Hensworth. She has been delivered a citation."

"Eureka!" The word snapped out of me, a triumphant cry emphasizing the sudden flash of illumination Fanny's delivery achieved.

Miss Hensworth. Of *course.*

"Good gracious, Cherry," sighed my chaperone as I shook a folded newspaper in triumph. "What does this have to do with your . . ." She paused delicately. "Your *mystery*?"

I flipped to the requisite page, muttering to myself until the now-familiar header caught my eye. "A letter," I explained, though it wasn't much of an answer to my exasperated companion.

"What letter? Cherry, slow down and clarify."

I could barely endure to remain seated. I took a deep breath, skimmed the words once more, and laughed outright. "Oh, Miss Hensworth, you are so clever," I crowed. There her name was, once more affixed with fiery bravado to the words that demanded the Master of Admissions permit women to study the same courses that allowed men to be licensed by the boards of medicine. " '*Allow this,*' " I read aloud, " '*or be removed from a post that continues to be mired in the stench of male hubris and fear.*' "

"Oh, my."

"Indeed." I chuckled, waving the paper now over my head. "This is a declaration of war, by our very own Miss Hortense Hensworth."

Fanny stared at me blankly. "Who is she, dear?"

Oh, of course. I lowered my evidence, set it aside for research purposes later. "A suffragette, it appears. One who all but demanded Professor MacGillycuddy's head on a platter, if not by name."

Fanny frowned, looking between her gossip columns and my small stack of articles. "It's not enough, Cherry."

"What?"

"It's not enough," she repeated firmly. "There is no evidence to mark her as the murderer, much less the villain you wish to paint her as. Good heavens, you would vilify her for speaking her mind and doing what you would do, indecorous though it might be."

Had I? An outspoken woman, suddenly painted by own hand as cause for concern?

Damn and blast, she was right.

Our innocent wallflower could be just that.

I needed more. Was either professor a member of the Athenaeum? How would I go about finding out? "There must be something else," I said, more to myself than to her. I reached for the next paper, leafed through them at a rapid pace. Silence fell for another hour, broken only by Booth's limping step as he replaced our now cold tea with fresh.

I found nothing. Only another letter, same as the others but lacking in threat, names or link to the murdered men.

I leaned back in my chair, crossing my ankles under my skirt as a man often did, and stared at the ceiling in blank thought.

Perhaps I'd leapt to this conclusion. Miss Hensworth certainly had a mind of her own; I could respect this easily. But was she a murderer?

I couldn't see it. Quiet, genteel Miss Hensworth, hardly the face I'd draw when confronted with such impassioned words of suffrage, or the derring-do required of a woman in a man's garb.

A coincidence?

The word stuck in my throat and would not make it fully formed beyond my skepticism. *Coincidence* was not a thing I believed in.

"Here are the facts," I said aloud, uncaring if Fanny heard me or not. "One, Miss Hensworth demands Professor MacGillycuddy's capitulation on the twenty-fourth of September. Two, she is forcibly removed from the premises of a gentlemen's club.

Three, said professor is murdered shortly thereafter, ostensibly by poison."

"Goodness me."

I laced my fingers together, tucked them under my chin as I stared at the light played over the pale ceiling. "Four, Professor Lambkin takes his own life, some days after his colleague. Or he is dispatched, like his predecessor, by someone else."

"Why someone else?"

"Entirely different method," I explained, patient for all I'd mentally moved past this detail. "Murderers tend to follow a pattern, a method by which they are most comfortable. Women often select poison, but when pushed, we choose to go for a knife rather than, say, a garrote or simple strangulation as a man would. Pistols, by the majority, are also a man's domain."

"Oh, for goodness' sake." Fanny huffed, rising in a rustled fall of silk and linen. She set her paper down in a neat pile, so at odds with my chaotic nest, and glowered at me. "Why on earth would you be mired in such a sordid affair as this?"

I did not straighten from my lackadaisical sprawl. "Lady Rutledge set the challenge."

"Really." Another sigh, and back ramrod straight, she crossed to the tea cart and poured another cup. Yet she paused before setting the pot down once more. "Perhaps," she said slowly, "you aren't looking at it with the right set of eyes."

Now, I straightened. "I beg your pardon, Fanny?"

When she turned, her mouth was set in a pursed line that suggested she was deep in thought. "Perhaps," she continued in the same contemplative tone, "you should look less at the professors, and more at . . ."

"At?"

"Well." She gave herself a small shake, her smile rueful. "This is hardly my forte, you understand, but you should look at something else. You're not looking past the professors."

Past the professors? What the devil did that mean? Of course the professors were key, if I could learn why they died—

I froze, suddenly stiff as the thought flared like a beacon.

Alchemy.

Whether the notes had been Lambkin's or MacGillycuddy's, it did not matter. They referenced some kind of alchemical study, a formula or series of them. To what end?

Perhaps the professors weren't the key.

"That means the formulae are," I said suddenly, and leapt to my feet. I whooped loud enough to wake the dead, grabbed Fanny and spun her madly in a circle before planting a kiss on her cheek. "You are brilliant," I swore, and hurried for the hall.

"Wait, where are you going?"

"To fetch the key!" I called, plucking my winter coat from the stand by the door.

I'd given Mr. Pettigrew the very motive I'd been searching for. All I needed was to know what it was, and I would track down the killers from there.

It wasn't about the individuals, God rest their souls. It was about science. Intent! *Results.*

"But, Cherry, you can't—"

I closed the door on Fanny's near-panicked hue and cry, turned and hurried for the main thoroughfare, where I would be able to hire a gondola for the duration.

Mr. Pettigrew would have my answers. I would

visit earlier than his three days, but given the circumstances, he would understand.

The gondolier I fetched at the main thoroughfare
looked at me as if I'd lost my mind, but at promise
of double his usual fare when he returned me to my
home, he closed his mouth and depressed the lever
that widened the spigot in the small aether engine
at the tail.

I was so close to the heart of this mystery, I could
all but taste it on my tongue.

Alchemy.

Not the first time such mysteries had ever driven
a St. Croix to recklessness.

I was halfway to my destination before I realized I'd
never been to Mr. Pettigrew's without my collector's
disguise.

Much too late, now. I would have to brazen my
way through; and if necessary, swear the old man
into secrecy.

As the gondolier lowered us into the fog, I remembered with longing my fog-prevention goggles. As
my eyes began to water and sting, I found myself
considering even the delicate French protectives
Compton had gifted me.

Once more, I'd gone off on a wild fit, and I would
feel this sting for a while.

I instructed the gondolier to drop me at the main
concourse just outside the West India Docks, and
bade him return to my home for his fee.

"Are you sure, miss?" he asked, scanning the
thick, daylight-swallowing fog roiling about us.

"I'm sure."

"Daft," he muttered when he thought I could not
hear. I only smiled, waited until the shape of his

gondola faded into the smoke, and hailed a hackney.

The looks I received weren't as pointed as I'd expected. The last time I'd come below without my collector's garb, I'd been wearing something much more somber. Today, my poplin would draw attention, but not nearly as much as if I were wearing one of my more delicate day dresses.

Yet I would not risk traveling through the districts below the drift garbed as I was. Certainly, I would not be the only woman going about my business, but I did look more like a toff now than I ever had in my own company.

I would prove an irresistible mark from some of the more unfriendly gangs, and could not stop to beg help from Ishmael Communion on the way.

He did not know my identity, either, and I preferred to keep it this way.

It took me too long to fetch a hackney, and longer still to convince him to take my fare. I had no coin upon me, and I swore he'd fetch his coin once he delivered me safely to Mr. Pettigrew.

Finally, he relented. "Get in, then," he growled, jerking a thumb to the carriage. His horse, long since accustomed to the stench of the coal-laden miasma, nickered softly.

Within the hour, I disembarked, bade the large driver to remain waiting, and hurried across the damp cobbles to the third shop in the row. By day, a faint ambient light colored all things.

I could see where I stepped well enough, and the fog even took on a lighter hue in these early hours. Deceptively friendly, if one had no sense of trouble below the drift.

For my part, I sensed nothing. The fog dampened everything—sight, sound. Even the rustle of my

shimmery poplin was swallowed into the smoke.
Waving at the fog in front of my face, I reached Mr.
Pettigrew's door and knocked loudly.

There was no reply. I knocked again, coughing
against the near-constant sting in my throat and
echoed by the horse's restless hoof falls on cobble.

It was day. Not that one could tell by looking, but
it was decidedly working hours.

Where was the old man?

I looked back, squinted my burning eyes to barely
pick out the huddled shape of my hired hackney. I
couldn't very well go back and suggest he go without his fare.

I sighed, reached for the door and found it un-
latched.

The first sense of unease skittered through me.

Now I sensed trouble. Why did I continue to follow
my impulses and end up weaponless for it?

The shift in my stance was as unconscious as it
was telling. Weight to the balls of my feet, odd
enough in my skirts and delicate boots, I pushed
open the door.

A wave of familiar warmth washed over me.

"Mr. Pettigrew?" I called, seeing nothing but the
one corner of his bookshop outlined to me.

Nothing moved, not a voice or a sound.

Frowning, I stepped inside, shut the door behind
me to keep the damp away from the books I knew
he considered precious. My footsteps creaked along
the wood floor, lacking carpeting that might collect
damp. Wood floors and the occasional small rug for
creature comfort; these were the things Mr. Pettigrew preferred.

At first glance, all seemed exactly as it should be.
The shelves were orderly, not a book out of place,

the brazier glowing merrily and giving off its dry, welcome heat.

And then I noticed the paper on the floor.

Mr. Pettigrew would not approve.

Nor, I realized as my gaze trailed to the work desk beside the stray parchment, would he care.

The man was dead.

"Oh, bollocks," I said quietly, because it was all I could think to say as sympathy welled in a great tide and my heart twisted to think I might be responsible. Rubbing the back of my neck in abject misery, I forced myself to approach the slumped figure of old Mr. Pettigrew. My gaze darted from one side of the shop to the other, but there was nowhere for anyone to hide; I was alone.

Alone but for a body.

He had been attacked at his work table, that much was clear. His frail frame, wrapped in his beloved dressing gown, had fallen forward, forehead against the worn wood. Blood, thick and very red, matted the back of his head. A terrible cavity where there should have been none showed me bits of stained white bone.

I swallowed hard as a shudder wrenched through me.

Poor, dear Mr. Pettigrew.

As I circled his still form, I noted the crimson smears on the papers beneath his flattened face. His nose was bent crooked, as if he'd come in contact with the table too hard and too fast. His milky eyes were wide open.

Fixed, I realized in mounting curiosity and horror, upon a hole in the table.

There were no splinters, no sharp grooves as there would be if something had driven through the solid oak. Beside his outstretched hand, weathered palm turned up, a broken bit of glass glinted, but there was nothing to indicate what could have caused such damage.

Or why beside it, lined perfectly with the missing bit of table, was half a book.

"Why sever a book?" I asked of myself, unable to imagine such a reason. If all the murderer had wanted to do was make it unreadable, there was a brazier at full light just behind me.

Full light. . .

I spun, bracing myself with a gloved hand to the table, and stared at the shining brazier. Of course. It had been fed recently. I looked down at Mr. Pettigrew's corpse, bent until I was eye-level with the terrible, gaping wound in his skull.

The blood was only just beginning to congeal, possibly slowed by the unseemly warmth of the room.

I flexed my fingers, steeling myself as I lifted my hand from the table and stripped off one glove.

If Mr. Pettigrew had been killed recently, his body would still be warm. I gritted my teeth and forced myself to touch his cheek. His throat, where I knew to find a heartbeat, if there would be any. There was none. I did not expect one.

Yet it was not the stiff resistance of a body caught in *rigor mortis*, either. The warmth of the room wasn't enough to keep a corpse at this temperature, added to the as yet uncongealed color of his blood and the strange dampness on the table—I frowned at my fingers, pulled on my glove but saw nothing staining it—and that meant he was dead within moments of my arrival.

Mere moments.

Elation—energy, anger, a surge of righteous

justice—filled me as I spun, once more scouring the shop.

Perhaps upstairs?

I left poor Mr. Pettigrew where he was, promising to send someone to care for him when I could, and took three steps to the small stairs inset into the far corner.

Creak.

It was all the warning I received, for I saw nothing at all before a great weight leapt into my back and sent me tumbling to the floor.

Chapter Sixteen

My knees collided with the floor much harder than I expected, sending pain licking all the way to my back.

A figure wrapped in a concealing cowl leapt over me in a fine display of adroitness, and sprinted in a flapping wake of black for the back door.

I leapt to my feet, the thrill of the chase surging through my veins like molten metal; only to fail to remember that I did not wear trousers this time, and my skirts would not allow for easy maneuverability. One foot came down on my hem, my ankle twisted and I stumbled into Mr. Pettigrew's chair, rocking him to the ground with a terrible thud. Silently apologizing—*no time!*—I seized my skirt in one hand, wrenched it over my ankles and hurried pell-mell for that back door as it slammed shut.

I would not lose this time!

"Stop," I called as I burst out of the door, just in time to catch a shape flapping from my right. The small alley was little more than a delivery corridor for those who brought goods to the shops, and only marginally maintained, at that. Dreading every step, I sprinted off the stoop, into the choking fog as my opponent's footsteps slapped like echoes on the uneven cobbles.

I was not used to running in these shoes with the delicate heels, but I could not let this travesty go unanswered. Mr. Pettigrew deserved justice!

And I deserved answers.

Setting my jaw, my lungs already burning from the smoke I inhaled with every labored breath, I lowered my head, caught my skirt higher, and ran faster. Harder. Lanterns valiantly opposing the fog flickered as I passed, guttered in my wake; shapes loomed in leering silhouette from the swirling bank of mist and smoke. Here a cart, abandoned for the day, there a bit of wall crumbled from rot.

And still my quarry teased me, too far ahead to see more than the shape of the cloak that concealed him.

"Watch yerself," snarled a man, whose poor chance had him stepping out of a door just as I passed it. I did not stop, though it nearly meant his introduction to the unforgiving ground.

We were headed for populated ground, I realized, as more figures stepped from the fog. I hurried by two children, head to toe covered in black, beaten down by the demands of a factory workday. A small knot of men flowed around the figure in surprise, only to catch me as they turned to study the runner.

"Out of my way," I demanded, using my sharp elbows to carve a path through the suddenly swearing laborers. A hand caught in my bustle; fabric tore. I did not stop.

Ahead of me, the figure leapt a small collection of barrels; I heard a woman's cry, another's scream, and the figure whirled, stumbled and pushed abruptly to the right.

I rounded the pile instead. "Apologies," I tossed at the woman staring openmouthed from her sprawled position on the ground.

"Lunatic!" she shouted back. To me or my fleeing opponent, I did not know.

We passed greater crowds, men and women headed home for supper, children darting through the smoke. We'd left the Philosopher's Square, that much was clear, and my lungs were seizing within the grip of my corset. The distance between us grew.

I would not lose him. I would not!

Lowering my head, aware that my hairpins had long given up the fight, I summoned what strength and endurance I had left, ignored the pain in my ankle and burning in my side, and poured every last ounce of effort into my run.

Six feet.

The distance closed.

Four.

"You . . . won't . . ." I couldn't finish the warning.

The cowled head turned; I saw only black in my watering vision. I heard a sound, low and unrecognizable as word or curse, and the figure wrenched to the side.

Down an alley, footsteps pounding, splashing in the collected puddles.

Groaning, I caught myself on the corner before I bypassed it entirely, wrenched myself around and darted after the fleeing figure.

Only to turn a bend in the maze of back alleys and come face-to-face with a knot of men loitering around the bend.

We all froze as one.

In the sudden, shocked silence of real surprise, I recognized two things—one, I'd stepped into the territory of the Black Fish Ferrymen; and two, a discarded cloak drifted to the ground not eight paces away.

My ghost had gotten away.

I clutched at my side, my breath a labored pant in the foul alley air.

"Well, well," drawled a man whose stature was short as mine, yet whose width would fit three of me in a line. His teeth were blackened, his eye mirroring the color from a bruise that suggested he was no stranger to a brawl.

Three of his mates flanked him, two remained behind, watching with avid interest.

I raised my chin. "Co—" *No!* I was not a collector in this guise. "Pardon me, gentlemen," I said with a smile, as polite and charming as the very devil on holiday. "I appear to have gotten turned about. Did anyone see a figure fleeing through here?"

"Figure, eh?" This from another man, tall and lean like a blade. Holding one, I noted, flush to his wrist.

The Black Fish Ferrymen had a reputation. One well deserved. I kept clear of their territory, unless I had a specific goal.

In this case, I was too well dressed for Cat's Crossing—that was the rooftop avenues, utilized mostly by children and cats and those too foolish to be afraid of heights.

And I had not paid attention to the territory signs in my haste.

I took a step backward, my skirts rustling. Every eye in every lean, predatory face settled on my hips.

"No one else but us," drawled the short one, a lackadaisical tone flush with innuendo. The very

way he studied me, as if I were a possession simply
waiting for his claiming, sent a shudder of revul-
sion up my icy spine. "Stay a while, luv." And then,
before I could demur, he added in obvious command, "Cooley."

The thin one was Cooley, then. His gap-toothed
smile turned up, and he slunk forward.

Hands closed over my upper arms, and I shrieked
in surprise. "Got 'er, boss," announced a man I had
not heard behind me. Like a bloody cat, he'd cut me
off from the back and held to my arms so tight, I
could feel the bone aching in complaint.

"You must be Cooley, then," I corrected myself
aloud, forcing my voice to be even, though my gaze
didn't leave the thin one approaching with a lanky
stride.

The leader, three men with him. Two behind, one
at my back.

Seven Ferrymen.

Not even on a good day could I account for more
than four.

My heart hammered at my throat. I kept my
chin high as a glint of a tarnished blade winked in
Lanky's dirty hand.

A grunt from behind confirmed it.

Stupid. Stupid me, I should have known my quarry
would know these streets. I'd gotten careless. Again!

And now I would have the fight of my life.

"What say you and I—"

Whatever the leader intended to say stopped
short as a high, lilting whistle pierced the alley. He
turned, squinting—I noted with distant amusement
the balding spot just beneath the rim of his frayed
cap.

"Check it, lads," he said darkly. "If it's another

foray by them Bakers, give 'em somethin' t'smile about."

Three of the men turned and faded into the fog, swallowed by the yellow-tinted haze.

"Gang trouble?" I asked sweetly.

"Shut yer mouth."

Lanky stopped in front of me. The fingers at my arms squeezed. I would bruise there, I was sure of it.

"Pretty bit of dollymop like you," continued the short, balding man with vicious glee, "oughter have 'erself a nice time, doncher think?"

Lanky didn't touch me. He didn't have to. His leer said it all, his watering eyes like reptilian glass in his sunken sockets.

This wasn't the first such offer I'd received below the drift, but it was the first outside of my guise as collector.

A lady should not walk about on her own. This was exactly why.

Another whistle came at us from the growing dark. I watched the leader's eyebrows snap over his tiny eyes. "Who goes there?" he demanded, turning again to stare into the blank wall of smoke.

"Ghosts?" I asked cheekily.

I should not have. He snapped, "Dicker," and the man I privately called Lanky casually lifted one hand and backhanded me.

I saw stars.

The Ferrymen, I reminded myself, had earned their reputation.

Blinking hard, I missed the cue that sent the last filthy man into the fog to seek the ghostly whistler.

"She a spy, boss?" asked Cooley behind me, from a direction that suggested he was somewhat taller than his companions. Not as large as Ishmael Communion, but bigger than I.

"She's a toff," scoffed his boss, and flicked his fingers in dismissal.

A knife whizzed from the dark, scant inches from his hand. The leader jumped three feet back, swearing most foul as the blade sank into the wooden frame of a boarded door.

I would get no clearer opportunity.

As all the men scanned the fog, most swearing, I drove one elbow back as hard as I could, grinning fiercely when I heard Cooley's breath exhale on a pained *whoosh*.

"*Allez, hop!*" I huffed, digging my feet into Lanky's knee, his groin, walking up his chest so quickly that only his surprised instinct to push back kept me aloft. Cooley didn't know what to do with me, all the more obvious as I flipped over his head in a froth of concealing skirts. He flailed, wrenching his grip open, and I landed awkwardly behind him, stumbling as the fabric of my skirt caught and tore. "I so would love to stay," I said lightly, but hastily as the leader opened his mouth. "Simply must get on, so sorry!"

I turned, sprinted back the way I'd come as the leader screamed, "The fog! They're in the fog, y'addle-minded twits!"

I made it halfway down the alley when a slight figure stepped out of a door and beckoned. A child? With his cap pulled low and his features smudged in black, I could discern nothing but the impatient hand.

Yet what were my options?

I darted into the doorway he once more vanished into. The door closed, leaving the room in pitch black.

I sucked in a breath, bent over myself with my hands on my knees, and tried not to catalogue in all the ways my body ached.

"Shh," scolded a whispering voice. A hand gripped my arm. "This way."

"I can't see," I protested.

"Keep your voice down," said the young whisper, and a small hand slipped into mine. "Just walk with me."

My eyes strained to make out something, any-thing in the dark, but all I could sense was the pres-sure of unending night. Certain I would run into something—bark my shin, fall down a hole, collide with a wall—I walked gingerly as I dared while the small hand pulled.

It felt like forever, my breath loud in my ears, the musty fragrance of disuse thick in my nose. Even-tually, we stopped. "You're two hops from a bobby shack, marm," whispered the urchin. "Best not get caught this side of the Ferrymen again."

To hear myself called a marm in that achingly young voice made me cringe. I was a long way from a frumpy old school mistress; and while I flirted with the future stigma of spinster, I was hardly there yet.

Yet this boy had saved me. And not for the first time, unless I missed my guess.

He let go of my hand, and I heard the screech of metal against rusted metal. A seam of light ap-peared before me, cracked into enough to pick out the boy's low cap and patched jacket. His trousers were torn at the knees, his boots likely fraught with holes.

But his eyes, dark and expressive in his soot-covered face, gleamed up at me with clear mischief.

I saw now the fringe of his brown hair, long enough to tangle in his lashes. My fingers itched to brush it away. And haul him in for a bath, while I was at it.

"You're from the Menagerie," I accused, and an accusation it certainly was.

His eyes crinkled; delighted, I think, that I recognized him. "Yes, marm."

"Did Hawke send you?" And then, because I couldn't help my own curiosity, "Are you a circus performer?"

He first shook his head, then nodded, pressed his body against the crack of the open door and peered outside. He rose near on his tiptoes to do it. Over his head, I recognized little enough but the ever present cloud of smoke-ridden fog.

The gas lamps were being lit, about this time. Slowly, the pea souper would earn its moniker. Above the drift, there were a handful of daylight hours left, but not here.

"Why are you here?" I hissed at his back. "Are you sent?"

He shrugged, as much an answer as I could expect from a boy his age. "Cross the street here, and make like a line for the bobbies. The Ferrymen'll see you, maybe, but I'll keep 'em spinning."

"Why?"

This time, his teeth—a pale gleam in the little sliver of light—flashed over his shoulder at me. "Wait a bit," he counseled, streetwise in the same way a rat knows his sewer, "and then take tail. Run fast."

With that, he pulled open the heavy door and slipped outside.

"Wait!"

He paused, his posture bent at the knees, rounded at the shoulders. I recognized it; it was the demeanor of every urchin who had ever made his home in the dangerous streets of London below.

It was the stance of a clever child who'd learned early that if given a chance, an adult would rather take the opportunity to get the boot in than offer a hand.

My heart twinged. I saw myself in him.

Myself, and something much less tragic. "What's your name, lad?"

Again, that smile. A flash, an impish line. "Flip, marm," he offered, doffing that threadbare cap of his, and scampered into the growing dark.

I watched him until he faded, perhaps three seconds. The fog provided excellent cover. Unfortunately, without my protectives, I was as good as blind. Worse, still, than them what lived here every day, for they developed a tolerance to the sting.

I waited for as long as I dared, slipped out of the heavy door, and pulled it shut behind me. Gathering my skirts, I looked first one way, then the other, and saw nothing but empty cobble and the muted shine of struggling lamps.

Make a line for the bobbies, he'd said.

I could not risk walking through Ferrymen territory while they remained on guard. My choices had just dropped to one.

Berating myself soundly, I stepped onto the street, took a deep, stinging breath and sprinted for the police station.

I have a terrible habit.

When I am not lying outright, I am sharing too much information. In my guilt, I asked the rather surprised constable on duty to tend to Mr. Pettigrew—he had no kin that I was aware of it, and I could not bear the thought of his body rotting amid his beloved books.

Such a request only garnered interest, and before I knew, I was answering question after question, fired at me from a grizzled detective whose lined features suggested he'd seen as much of the streets as I.

Yet I could not be as truthful with him as I wished.

I maintained my innocence in the subject: I'd gone to fetch books for my collection, found his body, was coming to fetch the police when the Black Fish Ferrymen had intervened. The raw, red mark on my cheek gave credence to my tale.

I said nothing of the killer in the black cloak, or the same discarded bit of fabric tossed in the alley. What would I say? That I, a young lady of Society, chased a fiend into the fog? Only to lose him when he vanished like a ghost.

Implausible, at the least.

Yet the constable—a Mr. Harrington Brisco, Esquire—had instincts that I could only admire. Even as I fended them off with every tool in my arsenal.

Not until I, Cherry St. Croix, broke into exhausted, bitter tears did the constable cease his questioning, and allow me to send word to Fanny for fetching.

For the next half hour, Mr. Brisco was the very model of conciliatory courtesy. He bade me keep the handkerchief he'd awkwardly pressed into my hand, fetched me a cup of coffee from the station stores, which I pretended to sip. I did not like the taste as a rule. And he allowed me to sit in his small office, in relative peace from the prying eyes of the other policemen tromping in and out of the station proper.

Exhausted by my day—by every aspect of my life, if I could be so dramatic to admit—I could barely summon the strength to do more than stare at my small brass pocket watch while the minutes ticked.

Finally, when I could stand the small, cramped interior of the station no longer, the door to Mr. Brisco's tiny office opened. "Miss St. Croix," came the man's gravelly baritone, "your escort is arrived."

Gods of all things kind and fortunate bless Booth.

I rose, aware of what a frightful mess I looked. My hair had shed over half its pins, now hanging in a tumbled twist of curls to my waist. Dirt and soot smudged my fingers—I'd stripped my gloves and held them in one tight hand—and I could only imagine what my face looked like after crying so bitterly.

Exhausted to the very depths of my bones, I nodded my thanks to the discomfited yet inherently kind Mr. Brisco, squared my shoulders and strode through the station.

Three policemen stopped to stare. At least until Mr. Brisco cleared his throat most tellingly.

"Be more careful, Miss St. Croix," he warned me as he opened the station door for me.

"I shall," I lied, and stepped outside.

Only to freeze, every limb rooted as an open carriage bearing the Northampton crest greeted my astonished eyes.

A driver in livery sat at the reins, facing forward in strict propriety. But the man who waited beside the carriage was one my heart thudded to see; even as it plummeted to a gloomy death in the pit of my soul.

"My lord," I gasped.

The earl offered a gloved hand, his eyes unreadable behind the lenses of his clipped protectives, but his gaze fell on Mr. Brisco beside me. "My thanks, Constable."

"Of course, m-my lord," stuttered the man, who was clearly unused to dealing with lords and their sons. He bowed, an awkward thing, and took his leave of what I was sure was his private version of hell.

A wayward Society miss caught in a murder mystery, while the Earl Compton flies down like a guardian angel to pluck his only witness from the constable's grasp.

I almost smiled, but the hard line I saw between Compton's eyebrows stilled the urge. I took his hand, wincing when I remembered that mine was still bare. "I suppose my chaperone requested your aid?" I asked, sounding every inch a sulking girl.

The earl helped me aloft, waited until I found my seat before stepping up behind me. The set of his mouth was firm. "You gave Mrs. Fortescue a fright," he returned, as much a reprimand as an explanation.

My shoulders rounded. As the earl settled to the padded seat across from me, the driver flicked a whip, clicked once and the horse whickered softly and plodded into motion. I was keenly aware of the silence between us, and the eyes staring blatantly at the earl's open carriage.

Unconsciously, I lifted a hand to my cheek.

Compton caught it, pressed a clean, mono-grammed handkerchief into my palm. His fingers were strong, firm enough to brook no argument of verbal or physical design, but it wasn't that what caught me.

It was, instead, the way his mouth set in an uneven slant. Angry, of course I could see that, but con-cerned. Relieved, even, as his gloved fingers pressed fervently into my palm. My hand closed over the of-fering, even as I shivered.

"I apologize for the open carriage," he said stiffly. "You understand the necessity."

Of course. Propriety demanded open carriages when the sexes mingled, especially with lack of a chaperone. Yet that very lack might be enough to doom this to the scandal rags, regardless. I could not summon the will to care.

Truthfully, the air was rather cold on my cheeks and nose, but I would rather suffer than complain.

I did not have to do either. The earl lifted a large fur from the floor, and as the carriage plodded along the streets lined with flickering lamps, he pulled it over my shoulders. Unlike me, he'd come dressed for the weather, with his greatcoat pulled up over his ears.

I'd graduated, then, from forgetting small details to even how to take care of myself. Shame bit deeply; my cheeks flushed as his fingers pulled the fur tightly around my throat.

I did not know what to say. Here was an earl, come to rescue me. I sighed, my breath fogging somewhat against the chill damp. "Thank you," I whispered.

Compton's hands dropped. The carriage was not so large that we had room to sprawl, and I was aware of the driver's back behind him, but his gaze remained steady on me through his glass lenses.

"Why," he finally said, drawing the word out in stiff demand, "were you at the scene of a ghastly crime, Miss St. Croix?"

So the constables had passed details. Of course. I looked away, at my hands, clenched around his handkerchief, and remembered I'd meant to clean my face. I did so now. "I wanted books," I said. Not quite a lie. Not wholly the truth, either.

"That is all?"

Not in the slightest. I lied with ease. "I truly just

wanted books. Mr. Pettigrew has . . ." I paused. "*Had* a fascinating collection."

He blew out a breath, and I realized how tightly he'd held himself. All that lordly reserve had hidden more than I suspected. His jaw set, and he reached up with two fingers to remove the fog protectives from his nose.

Without the glass in the way, I was suddenly viscerally aware of how sharp his eyes were; how clear and acute.

What did he see?

My throat dried, already near to parched from the fog and my tears and the ailment festering deep in a secret part of me.

"When we are wed," he said, leaning forward so that I would not mistake his words, "you will have staff." I blinked. "Anything your heart desires, Miss St. Croix. You will never have to do anything so foolish as this again."

I would have anything? My smile, I fear, was sad. I couldn't be sure, but I know that he saw it. "I desire freedom, my lord."

But whatever he read in my features, it did not dissuade him. As the carriage bumped gently over the cobbled street, he clasped his hands between his knees and said most reasonably, "What greater freedom than a countess?"

I opened my mouth, but no word came.

He was serious.

I licked my lower lip; warmed as his gaze fell to the motion. Followed it with cool appraisal. Yet when those pale eyes met mine again, I realized I was wrong.

He was not so cool that he could hide the flicker of warmth within.

He had kissed me once. I remembered it vividly; it had been my first real kiss. Yet it would take more than a simple meeting of the lips to change my mind. "You presume acceptance when I've offered none," I told him, drawing pride around me like a shroud—what little I could claim, at the moment.

"Is it your inheritance?" he asked, more shrewd than I'd given him credit. "You will lose nothing. It shall be entrusted and invested securely, and over time, it shall double. Perhaps even more."

"Why?"

"I am a very wealthy man in my own right, and will be the more so upon my own inheritance. I've no need of your fortunes, Miss St. Croix. Even without the investments, you will have access to a generous allowance. Spend it on a mountain of books, for all I care."

"No." I clutched the fur around me tightly, grateful now as warmth began to trickle back into my flesh. "Surely there are a dozen females far more suited. Perhaps less interesting, as you maintain," I admitted, referring his previous answer on the subject, "but far less trouble." Or scandal.

"You are only as much trouble as you take upon yourself," he told me, as if he had it all figured out. Perhaps he did; he wasn't wrong. "As my wife, you will have no need for such adventures as you've taken here. Anything you require will be provided, and you will be more than busy seeing to your new life." A pointed pause. "Which will not be even a little boring, I assure you."

"So all I must do is change?" I asked, my eyes narrowing.

And then I saw it. A tilt at the corners of his mouth, that damned smile that didn't quite shape his soft lips, but I read it clear as day in his eyes. "We are suited," he said simply. "All you require is polish." And, as a faint blush stained his cheeks, he added, "I am fond of you, Miss St. Croix, and I believe that you could grow fond of me."

Certainly marriages had been built on worse. Yet I could say nothing, staring at his handsome face, chapped by the cold and no less appealing for it. Women across all of London would give their eye-teeth to sit where I now sat.

Offered the world by an earl, soon to be a marquess.

The horse whickered uncertainly. "Whoa," soothed the driver, and I looked beyond the earl to see the horse's ears turning this way and that.

What did I want, then? Freedom? From what? As a countess, one day a marchioness, I could be as ec-centric as I wanted. Who would say?

Entertain the world by day, and I would be free to pursue whatever intelligent interests I wanted with his support.

All I needed was to fill the role of hostess. Of wife.

Fanny would have a constant home, care for the rest of her life. Booth could remain in the Chelsea home, live out his years with Mrs. Booth at hand. And Zylphia . . .

Zylphia had spent so long beneath men who lived the life I wanted to give her. She would live as my maid in surroundings she had only ever seen from the outside.

This was the logical thing to do. The choice that would make my family, the people who loved me, happiest.

But what about me? What would I give up?

My freedom, for one. Actual freedom, free of the marriage laws, the demands, and the thumb of a husband who would only see me change to suit *him* to be happy.

My fingers tightened on the fur. "Lord Compton, I must— Oh!" The horse shied suddenly, clipping a few paces to the side and jerking the carriage.

In a sudden flash, I acted. I could not even say now what caused me to do so, but blindly obeying my instinct had saved me many times; my fog-sense was keen enough by practice. I sensed trouble. I threw off the fur, seized the earl's collar in both hands and wrenched hard as I possibly could, just as the horse reared, twisting with a loud, screaming whinny of warning.

The carriage tilted.

Surprise filled the earl's face, promptly followed by as determined a scowl as I'd ever seen. In one smooth motion, his arms banded around me. He twisted. All oxygen fled my lungs as we collided with the street below—his back to the unyielding street, my body to his.

The horse shimmied and danced in unruly anxiety; the driver wrestled with the reins, calling sharply for the pedestrians about us to move out of the way. The carriage wobbled wildly.

The earl had shifted us so that he took the brunt of the fall. I was not so delicate as to shatter on cobblestones, but it would have hurt tremendously nevertheless, and he . . .

What common man did that?

Gasping for air, I pushed up to see his face. "Cornelius!"

Pain etched a line beside his mouth, between his eyebrows, but his chest expanded beneath my hands as he took a deep breath.

There in the muck of the street, the gas lamps guttering all around us and the horse shying nervously as its ears flicked this way and that, one of Compton's gloved hands slid into my hair. Cupped the back of my head and held me when I would have wriggled away.

Someone, something, had spooked that horse. Deliberately, no less, for I saw no sign of accident. There'd been nothing. Only the horse's own senses.

And mine.

Yet I could say nothing of this; how would I explain the instincts finely honed after years in this very fog? The surprisingly hard shape of the man sprawled beneath me caught me unawares, one of my legs tangled between his and his palm warm at the back of my skull.

The driver exclaimed urgently to see if we were well, but the earl ignored him. "You called me by name," he said, soft, but no less resolute for the gentleness.

"You have an exceptionally stubborn dedication, my lord," I assured him, attempting for chastisement but falling instead to uncertainty and concern. "Are you hurt?"

"I will be the more so if you deny me." The grip at the back of my head tightened. "Say you'll have me, Miss St. Croix."

A crowd was gathering. Demanding answers, yelling. In my peripheral, a large longshoreman grabbed the horse's reins, but the beast was placid now.

I stared into fog-green eyes framed by heavy-lidded sandy lashes, felt his heart pounding solid and warm beneath my hand.

His mouth was only a breath away; it would be so simple to lean down and press mine to it.

Was that an answer? Could it ever be?

Marriages have been made on less.

Mine would not be one made. "My lord—"

"Think on it," he said over me. Under me, for that matter. "I shall ask again."

A firm hand wrapped around my upper arm, the polished shoes of the carriage driver at the edge of my vision. I frowned down at Compton's determined stare. "My answer will not change."

"I will not hear it," he told me, nodding with a glance to his footman, "until it does."

Stubborn. Inexcusably so!

"My lady," the driver said by way of warning, and I found myself partially lifted by the one, partially supported by the other man whose body had protected my own.

Stubborn, indeed, but kind. Demanding. Wealthy, of course, titled. He claimed to be fond of me.

I shook out my skirts, studying the throng around us as several of the stronger dockworkers righted the carriage with much shouting.

Was the danger I'd sensed among them? The person who somehow spooked the horse must be close. He'd want to see the damage, wouldn't he?

The fur once more settled around my shoulders. "These roads are terrible," he commented.

Of course. The roads. As if that were all. He watched the men work, and I inspected his profile and barely kept from sighing.

Just my luck that I would be saddled with the one man in all of England who would not be put off by a lady's refusal of his hand.

A put-off proposal would not do it, but I'd wager all of my inheritance that if he knew that I chased a murderer in the fog, his indignation would be fierce, indeed.

One gloved hand settled over his own shoulder. I detected a subtle wince.

"My lord, you're hurt."

"Nonsense," he countered, with a tone that declared that was the end of it. Whether he was or was not, I would not get an honest answer. I suspected more than his service in Her Majesty's Navy kept his upper lip stiff. Pride came part and parcel with the Northampton legacy. "Let us get you home, Miss St. Croix. Mrs. Fortescue will not thank me for tarrying too long in your company without a chaperone."

Oh, yes, she would. I bit my tongue and allowed the earl to help me alight.

From my higher vantage point, I scoured the chattering folk now turning away; curious event witnessed, now all must return to their daily routines, their goals. None stared too long. None lingered, save for the few beggars and Abram men hoping for a scrap or two.

Who, or what, had spooked the horse so badly?

Chapter Seventeen

As if some secret announcement had been made, as if the gossips had learned that I was once more solidly in Earl Compton's favor, social invites began arriving by the following day. I greeted this new development with a facial tic I acquired on the spot.

Fanny all but waltzed through the house, humming in a rusty but perfectly acceptable key. More often than not, I caught her humming Mendelssohn's Wedding March. I gritted my teeth and said nothing.

I would not keep shouting my denial to deaf ears.

To make matters worse, Mrs. Booth became her conspirator and enabler. I had never seen either so cheerful. Often, I came upon them in the kitchens— where Fanny rarely ventured—or in the parlor, head to head studying this fashion periodical or that catalogue of silk ribbon and gilded fluff.

I drifted out of view before either could see me, silent as a ghost, contemplative as a nun.

Hungry for something beyond food or drink.

I passed Booth as he walked from the door to the

parlor, a small stack of carefully organized cards in his gloved hands. His smile was indulgent, his gray eyes snapping with good health and nature.

He said nothing to me; I did nothing to engage him. Booth was too proper a butler to invoke casual conversation with the lady of the house.

And I had nothing to say.

I rested one hand atop a lion's head for balance, circled the silent, watchful beast with an affectionate, distracted pat and took the stairs quietly. My plaid skirt rustled; the only noise to combat the girlish laughter and delight drifting from the parlor.

Zylphia was just coming from Fanny's room, her arms loaded with pale linen bedsheets. The look she gave me over her burden wasn't cheerful or excited. It was probing.

And all too knowing. "You look peaked," she said flatly. She dropped the bedsheets into a basket, pushed them down with a strong hand. "Are you taking any of that laudanum at night?"

I looked away. "There is none left."

"Are you sleeping?" Because Zylphia was not the type to fritter away an afternoon gazing at fashion plates, I followed her downstairs.

"Not entirely." An honest answer, for all it revealed nothing. "There is much going on, Zylla, it's difficult to ascertain my sleeping habits."

"Hm." A noncommittal sound as she balanced the basket upon her pinafore-tied hip. "Have you considered a bit of Ashmore's brandy—"

"Good heavens, no," I denied hastily. "I'd never developed the taste for it, and I've been assured Mr. Ashmore's private stock is beyond my reach." But I lowered my voice, because we neared the parlor, and Fanny would not approve. "May I help?"

Zylphia snorted outright. "You, doing housework? That one would have my head," she replied, nodding to the parlor. Whether she meant my chaperone or my housekeeper, it didn't matter.

She was right.

I needed something to do. I was tired of idly sitting, listening to the cheerful harmony of my door chimes as caller after caller depressed the mechanism just to leave a calling card.

Propriety stated that I would have to go through them, decide who I would call upon in turn and who I would simply send 'round a note.

I couldn't give a fig for any of it.

I felt trapped in my own house.

And I was, to a certain degree. Fanny would not allow me to go below; not while so many eyes were suddenly trained on me.

I kicked at my skirt hem in silent, childish protest. "What are they so gleeful about, anyhow?"

Zylphia's sky eyes, filled with sympathy, flicked at me. "I'm not to say, but . . ."

I frowned at her when she trailed off. "Zylphia." A warning.

"Shh." She glanced at the parlor entry, then whispered, "Your earl sent a letter of intent."

"The devil he did," I gasped.

She nodded, blue eyes steady. "Mrs. Booth was talking it about it to Mr. Booth this morning. Have you considered, *cherie*?"

"Considered what?" I considered many things. Escape by my bedroom window, fleeing to the eastern desert savages where I understood women of pale skin and vivid coloring like myself were prized harem jewels, even so far as briefly considering asking the Menagerie for sanctuary. Of course, the fact that the Menagerie seemed a far more bitter pill to swallow than a harem's life amused me, but I still considered it.

I discarded all of them. Fanny would only be upset, I'd likely balk under any man determined to keep me a possession—as gossip rumored all such desert princes demanded of their kept harem women—and I would rather die than give Micajah Hawke the satisfaction.

"I mean," she was already asking as my thoughts drifted, "have you considered what would come of your *other* life if you are wed?"

"Of course I have," I snapped. The retort escaped before I realized another figure now filled the parlor entry in the corner of my vision. I started guiltily; too late.

"That life," Fanny said determinedly, closing the distance between us and cupping my cheek in one hand, "will be over, and soon." Her gaze fell on Zylphia, haughty as only Society could be to a servant. "And I'll thank *you* to get back to your duties."

"Yes, madam," Zylphia murmured, bobbing a partially formed curtsy. But the lingering question in her vivid eyes haunted me as she vanished into the kitchens, making for the washing tubs in the basement below.

My fingers twitched. It weighed on me, how much I wanted a draught to soothe my fraying nerves.

Fanny patted my arm and said cheerfully, "Fret not, my dove. All will proceed smoothly, you'll see. Nerves are expected."

"Expected of what?" I demanded.

My chaperone would not engage me. Fuming, I

watched her as she walked away, as determinedly ignorant of my attempted unrest as a satisfied cat upon her own territory.

If she ever suffered a drastic change in her lot, Fanny would make a disastrous fortune-teller. Her words of comfort turned instead to a taunt that came on a harmonic warning.

It was only just after teatime. Seated in the parlor, Fanny knitted quietly in her favored armchair, the fire sparking brightly beside her. She'd complained of chill, and I knew we'd the house funds to maintain a steady supply of coal for the burning, so I kept the flame stoked for her.

The tea cart was only just cleared away and a book cradled in my hands when the mellifluous chime of my doorbell sang sweetly. I didn't start; a credit I gave to the mildly entertaining book I idly read. It had been at least two hours since any caller, but I'd already developed the knack for ignoring the sound.

A shame, for I loved that doorbell. According to Fanny, my father designed the system—a complex pulley to trigger a set of carefully balanced gears and strikers against a row of delicate bells inset in the attic—and had it installed to please my mother.

They say she smiled each time a caller came, for there were days when the pretty melody would not be heard at all.

My mother had lost much favor when she married Abraham St. Croix.

I envied her, sometimes. Silence, I was learning, was becoming an extremely valuable commodity.

Step-thunk, step-thunk. Booth's uneven footsteps traveled down the hall. I turned another page, a silly bit of Gothic fluff from my own collection, and did not look up as he passed through the door.

He cleared his throat. "Her Ladyship," he intoned, not a single syllable out of place, "the Marchioness Northampton."

Fanny's gasp emphasized the sudden energy in both of us as we both surged to our feet. The book tumbled from my hands, fell open to the carpet in a flutter of pages. "My lady," I said, propriety at least hammered that far within me, "welcome to my home."

The marchioness did not look impressed. Neither in the cursory glance she gave my not inelegant parlor, nor in the following scrutiny leveled upon me.

I couldn't entirely blame her. Lady Northampton was a fashionable, graceful creature, no matter where she chose to go. Whether in taffeta and silk in a ballroom or, like now, wearing sage green linen trimmed and patterned by lovely darker green velvet, her winter coat firmly in place and a matching top hat perched jauntily upon her upswept hair, she looked the very picture of Society at its finest.

A right thing, for the Marchioness Northampton had always been looked to in fashionable decree.

Her gaze through the dark green netting draped from the brim of her riding hat was not kind. Nor did it allow me even a shred of uncertainty as to her thoughts on her son's proposal.

Suddenly, I felt myself to be a very small, insignificant thing indeed.

"I will take up precious little of your"—her gaze dropped to the book upon the floor, contempt clear within—"obviously valuable time, Miss St. Croix."

Dry mouthed, I nudged the book under my settee with one foot, even as I gestured to my now-vacant seat with a—dear heaven, I only just noticed—bare hand.

"Please, take your leisure, my lady," I managed, the very picture of polite, save my forgotten gloves. I must have taken them off for tea and left them draped somewhere. In this room? Where? If they were left in sight, that would only take the prize, wouldn't it?

"Would you care for a cup, my lady?" asked Fanny, setting her knitting down in her also abandoned chair. Her expression was oddly set; one part uncertainty, one part determination. Every bit the very picture of model civility.

"No," the marchioness said, flicking that icy stare to my chaperone. "You may leave us, Mrs. Fortescue."

There was no argument to be brooked in that clear dismissal.

When Fanny looked at me, one gloved hand curled in her rust-colored skirt, I nodded slightly. This would be worth hearing, I was sure, even as my stomach clenched in nervous anticipation.

I thought I knew the subject she would broach.

Her son must have made clear his intent to his lady mother, as well as my own chaperone. With a proposal extended, the fate of her family now rested on me. No gentleman could back out of an engagement without terrible scandal to the lady involved, and I knew enough of the earl that I was sure he'd never do so, even if he did come to his senses.

Was that why his lady mother was here? To convince me to turn him down?

Did she know I already had?

The marchioness circled the settee, inspecting it with obvious disdain before sitting. As Fanny took her leave—I would wager my next few grains of opium that she would not go far, and rather expected Mrs. Booth to do the same—I took the seat

beside the marchioness, smoothing my green plaid
skirt. Today, I'd paired it with a simple brown silk
blouse and matching linen jacket. I thought I looked
fetching this morning.

Now, I was positive I looked more the dowdy
spinster beside the marchioness's fresh glow.

"I shall make short work of my intent," Lady
Northampton said, studying me with abject dislike. She was too polite to ever say so, but I knew
the signs. Had always known them. "I am prepared
to sign over to you a moderate sum, Miss St. Croix."

And just like that, I was shocked into stillness. I
stared at her, searched her perfectly arranged expression for any clue that she jested, yet saw only
the same iron-clad determination that so shaped her
son's features.

When my silence did not give her what she expected, her eyes narrowed.

I found my voice. "My estate," I said quietly, when
all I wanted to do was find that bloody Gothic book
and fling it at her, "is in excellent health, my lady.
Money is the very *least* of my concerns."

"I see." The entire frigid north seemed weighted
in her voice. Her chin rose, back ramrod straight.
"What will it take? Name your price, I am capable of
affording a princely sum."

Crass. And she knew it, the marchioness did. Yet
she persevered. As mounting anger overcame my
shock, my hands laced tightly in my lap and I could
not tell if the heat in my cheeks came from fury or
from the fireplace. "What is the result of this *princely
sum*?" I inquired tightly.

There, a flicker of satisfaction. And of outright con-
descension. She expected me to take her offer, the
money-grubbing *unfortunate* soul that I was. "You

will inform my son that you will not, nor will you ever, marry him. Today," she clarified flatly, "now, via letter that you shall give to me."

I swallowed hard. My fingers trembled, I locked them tightly together. Mirroring her rigid pose—because anything less would reveal the turmoil juddering through me—I met her eye to eye and asked without art or malice, "Why do you hate me so?"

She blinked those so-familiar eyes. Once. Surprise?

Her nose turned up. "Breeding always tells, Miss St. Croix."

My mother.

Lady Rutledge had once informed me that the marchioness retained no love for Josephine St. Croix.

And yet again, I found myself painted with my mother's colors.

My jaw set. A surge of anger—of hurt, if I were to be honest—replaced my fear. "I see." Clearly, whatever malice she carried for my mother now fell to me.

I would have no part of it.

Or, rather, I would do my part well. "I must disagree," I replied, rising. The words came from me without conscious approval; I also made no effort to halt them, for the venom sprung full-formed in my heart.

"Oh?"

I stepped back, as clear a dismissal as I could suggest in posturing alone, and explained evenly, "Your son is kind and honorable. He is, as you well know, the very model of civility." I smiled. It was mostly teeth, I know. "In short, Your Ladyship, he is nothing like you."

Had I slapped her outright, I would never achieve

the same expression. Shock, I read, as if I were the first to refuse to be cowed. Or perhaps she had not expected spirit from a St. Croix. Foolish woman.

She would get that and more.

"I am very busy, and although I had not delivered a formal acceptance to your son," I continued, deliberately turning the knife I'd delivered, "I believe I shall pen one up immediately." The skin of her eyelids tightened, a marked flinch. "I understand that you may wish to withdraw your financial support. Not to worry," I continued, with a gay bravado that I did not feel, "my estate is perfectly capable of handling matters. Good day, my lady."

The Marchioness Northampton weighed me for a long, silent moment, all but bristling with fury. I half expected her eyes to turn slitted like a snake's as she finally rose, smoothed out her coat, and sailed past me. The breeze of her departure was as frigid as the woman herself.

I heard Booth's step out in the foyer—he'd waited like a good man—but I did not relax until I heard the front door close.

I sagged suddenly, clutching the table set in the center of the parlor and rattling the salver with its pile of cards.

Fanny's skirts whispered behind me. "Oh, dear," she said quietly, making no attempt to disguise that she had listened. Likely through the far door. "You have made an enemy of that one."

An enemy too well-bred to return my insult direct. I would feel this one later.

"Perhaps," I said, looking up and pushing my wilting figure from the supporting table. I raised my chin a notch. "But I will not allow her to bully me any longer."

Fanny said nothing.

She did not need to. I knew exactly what kind of feud I'd only just cemented as my own.

I made my excuses and walked sedately out of the parlor, up the stairs and into my bedroom. I shut the door with trembling hands.

My knees gave before I reached the bed. I sank to the floor, every particle of my body vibrating with mounting hysteria. As I reached for the decanter upon my nightstand and uncapped its topper, it rattled against the rim of the flask—a crystalline chime that sheared through my nerves.

The edge touched my lips before I recalled that there was nothing left.

A pit opened wide inside myself; fear, anger, frustration. Need. I feared it would devour me whole.

The decanter fell to my lap, my fingers clenched tight enough around it that the edges pressed into my flesh.

I shuddered. For the first time, the only time I'd ever managed to be as forthright as I relished in my collector's role, I'd faced down the Marchioness Northampton. I could not be bought.

Not, at least, by the likes of her.

It was something. I wasn't sure what, even then, but it was *something*.

Chapter Eighteen

The next three days turned into a blur I couldn't remember even if I wanted to. Soiree after soiree, luncheons in pretty rooms with faux picnic atmosphere, teas and of course, the fittings. They all stacked atop one another, obligation after obligation.

On the sixth of October, one of the better known gossip rags caught wind of the marriage dance vainly enacted by Earl Compton. The impertinent paper printed the details—many made up, near as I could ascertain—and was then mirrored by other newspapers in town, resulting in even more cards. Letters of interest, sycophants who smelled fresh blood and were eager to be the Judas goat to my would-be titled lamb.

Maybe some were well-meaning. Some perhaps genuinely cared to meet the woman who had cracked the earl's shell, or so the papers claimed—after all, he'd resisted the trap of matrimony for so long.

I couldn't even begin to guess. All I knew was

that time passed in a series of small productions—events where I playacted the part of a Society miss, smiled and curtsied and did everything in my power to avoid the topic of marriage until I could return home. And then I acted that of the dutiful charge. Though I was genuinely happy to see my chaperone walking about in a state of near-constant bliss, it wore on me. Tore at my nerves until I could not sleep more than an hour, maybe two at best.

I had no time for mysteries. None for trips below—and no clues to make them for. There were no new articles, not even letters of suffrage from Miss Hensworth to amuse me. Even the Ripper had gone quiet; and there's a sad state of affairs, when I must turn to a murderer to provide for me an escape.

I sent Zylphia into the fog to learn the outcome of Mr. Pettigrew's investigation, but she returned empty-handed. There were no clues, no evidence at all.

All I had was the knowledge of Miss Hensworth's previous letter referencing the master of admissions and her removal from the Athenaeum. It was a frail link, yet on a thready hope, I quietly sent Levi with my card, asking Miss Hensworth to meet.

When Levi returned, he admitted to finding no sign of the lady.

"Did you leave my card?" I asked.

"In the post box, miss," he swore earnestly. "Just like you asked."

"Was it full?"

He scratched the top of his head, beneath his cap. "Now that you mention, miss, no."

Good. That meant she was still about, somewhere. Once I located her, I would have answers.

Three dead. Even if this weren't part of Lady Rut-

ledge's game, that bit of wisdom had certainly applied: The longer I waited, the more would die.

On the fourth day, the invite I'd been dreading
most delivered Fanny and myself to the Northampton estate. The dinner invite came complete with the
combined efforts of my chaperone and the damnable persistence of an earl. The weather had taken a
nasty turn, pouring down rain by the bucketful. It
hammered against the window, coloring the conversation at the long, filled table with a sonorous drone
that worked its way into my skin and dragged like
iron nails.

On edge as I was, it took every ounce of concentration to make artless conversation with my table
companions on either side.

The earl was one.

Shortly before the last course ended, he bent his
head to mine and whispered, "Make your escape in
half of an hour. I've something to show you."

My eyebrows very nearly winged their way right
off my brow. "Truly?"

When he raised his eyebrows in subtle reinforcement, I nodded to show I understood, and turned
back to the table to find his younger brother, Lord
Piers Everard Compton, watching me.

A mystery, this young man. Perhaps my age, perhaps a shade older, he nevertheless had developed
quite a reputation as an inveterate gambler and rake.
The gossip columnists loved him; as, I was quite
sure, did the ladies above and below the drift. I knew
for a fact he was no stranger to the midnight sweets.

The younger Lord Compton was handsome
enough for it, with the family golden hair a shade
darker than his brother's, and cut shorter as fashion
strictly demanded. His sideburns were impressive,

shaping his lean jaw and barbered to perfection. He lacked the icy polish of his eldest brother, yet utilized a certain urbane air that reminded me sometimes of him.

But unlike the elder, the younger maintained a dissolute demeanor that usually involved a rakish smile, at least when directed at me. There was nothing subtle about his wink.

I barely caught myself before I pulled a teasing face in return. I was not unaccustomed to the games men played—a girl did not grow up in the circles I had without learning a thing or two about holding one's own weight among them—but I would not dare risk accusations of flirtations with the earl's own brother.

Dinner finally closed. After the requisite parting of the sexes—women to the parlor, and gentlemen to the study for brandy and cigars; I would have given my eyeteeth to be included among the latter—I was all but climbing from my skin with curiosity.

And with that prickling, barbed anxiety pressing outward from my skin.

After dinner, there was the musical selection. This was much less painful than the ladies' gathering. Fanny did her best by me, but I felt frozen out by the marchioness and her salon, even as they deliberately included me into their circle.

There was inclusion, I thought, and then there was that point where one realized one wasn't a part of a group, so much as held as an example by them.

And not a flattering one.

The chance finally came for me to make my escape. It came, to my surprise, on the arm of my Lord Compton's younger brother. "Have you seen the courtyard from the windows?" he asked, bending slightly so that his voice would not overpower that of the rather talented Lady Sarah Elizabeth.

Beautiful *and* the voice of a songbird. If I were ever required to stand in a parlor and sing, I would shoot myself with Ashmore's dueling pistols first. I could play marginally on a small sampling of instruments, but I had nothing near my mother's reputed talent.

"No, my lord," I said, eager to escape this festering knot of cold study and judgment.

"Excuse us, won't you, Mother?" continued the charming young lord. "I would like to give Miss St. Croix a glimpse of your pride and joy." And then, a grin, that cheeky rotter. "Your other pride and joy, that is, for she has already met Cornelius."

Bloody hell, I thought slowly as the marchioness inclined her head. For although I was used to the frigid wall she insisted be erected between us, I would never have expected to see that glint of affection as she looked upon her youngest son.

Even . . . even amusement?

Lady Northampton turned to Mrs. Douglas, effectively dismissing me from her mind and company.

I leapt at the chance. Familial affection or not, clearly, I was not included in that attendance sheet. "Thank you, my lord," I murmured.

"Please. If I am any judge, we are to be family, soon," came his all too easy rejoinder. His eyes, colored more by his father than mother, were that muddled mix between brown and green. More brown, I suspected, than the other. They also retained a disconcerting habit of twinkling, as if all the world were a jest. "You may call me Piers."

We would *not*. Yet I was tired of the constant pressure I kept myself under. "Very well, Piers," I replied, surprising him, I think.

His smile widened with it. "I won't be so bold as to call you by your given name just yet," he returned lightly, his gloved hand patting mine on his arm. "Formalities being what they are, and I am given to understand that you have yet to accept my brother's proposal."

"Correct."

We strolled along the music hall wall, the by-now familiar patterns of gilt and red drapery passing at a moderate pace. "Good for you," he said, rather cryptic at his approval. But his head dipped as he murmured wickedly, "Although I might slip your Christian name once and again just to watch my brother's mustache twitch."

It did, didn't it? I muffled a chuckle, swallowing it as we passed a pair of matrons whose disapproving frowns were as much a part of the societal charade as anything else. I smiled at them—a demure thing. Fanny would be proud.

Yet when we reached the far doors, Lord Piers did not stop.

"My lord, where are you taking me?"

"A surprise," came the inscrutable reply.

I looked up at him, much taller than I, even a hair's taller than his brother. "You are mischievous by design, not by nature," I accused, rather baldly.

His step did not falter as he led me to the foyer, and then up the great staircase. But his laughter fell easy and without artifice from his lips. "Perhaps you are correct."

"And if I am?"

"Then my brother has a rare prize, indeed," came the unexpected compliment. And the grating assumption.

He paused at a large, oaken door, its carved surface blackened as if burned in place. There were no real images, just a pattern.

"Here," he offered.

"What is here?"

"Open the door and see, busybody." But there was no sting in Lord Piers's words, only an indulgence that continued to surprise me. What had I done to earn such sympathies from the marchioness's own sons?

Yet there was a challenge in the lord's eyes, the folded arms held loosely across his chest. He leaned against the doorjamb beside me, and I tilted my head.

"Very well." Challenge accepted. I gripped the latch with a gloved hand, and pushed gently.

It opened easily, without so much as a creak. Light filtered into the hall, painting my striped skirt in a splash of white and peacock blue luminosity.

And when I stepped inside, my breath escaped me on a rush. "Oh!"

I could not help myself. I rushed into the room, one hand tangled in my skirt and holding the fabric away from my hurried tread. I saw nothing at all, paid attention to nothing, but the walls.

Shelves upon shelves of books. Hundreds of them, maybe more. Every wall filled to the brim with bookcases, every last surface. Only the mantel was free, and that for a hazard, I'd wager.

Daylight, what little of it could break through the rain sliding over the tall, wide windows, painted the library in pale gray. Lamps hanging from the ceiling flickered and countered with a warm golden glow that gilded everything it touched.

I spun, my gaze darting from one wall to the next.

I had gone to heaven, and it was a place mad with books.

"I do believe this was well planned, brother."
Piers's voice seized my attention, and I turned again
in a swirl of poplin and lace. My eyes were wide,
I know, and my heart pounding as I followed the
young lord's gaze to the man who'd waited patiently
by the large desk while I gawked and envied.

The smile I saw on Lord Compton's lips stole my
breath. Genuine warmth. Doubt, the kind of endearing hesitancy found in a man courting, and affection he had not earned.

My gaze flicked to the books once more.

Maybe not earned, I admitted silently, but he was
close enough to forgive the presumption.

"It seems so," he said, much more seriously than
his brother. Piers had followed me in, but leaned
now against the shelf just by the door, while the earl
waited patiently, one hand resting upon the desk I
could so easily picture him seated behind.

The library, doubling as a study, was very masculine in many ways, but I could see touches of femininity in the trim chosen, the striped fabric of the
upholstery, even the flowers placed at each window.

The marchioness kept an excellent house.

My throat closed. Nerves. So many new uncer-
tainties.

"I . . ." I tried again. "My lord, this is wonderful."

"My brother was quite sure you'd think so," Piers
volunteered.

But my gaze remained fixed on the man who'd assured me that all I required was a little polish to be
his. A little refinement.

And in exchange, I would have this. A library
large enough to put my father's and Ashmore's collections to shame. A man, a husband, who understood on some level what this meant to me.

I approached the earl, and realized suddenly that while the brothers shared many similarities of form and feature, the earl did not share Piers's easy confidence. His shoulders were tight, jaw set as if prepared for . . . a blow? Rejection, perhaps. "You appear to like your books very much," he offered stiffly.

I smiled, sank into as deep a curtsy as I knew. "You are well remembered, my lord."

When I rose again, it was to find him staring at me. Not in the way of a man who saw what he did not expect, but one who saw something I wasn't sure I could live up to.

A conviction, perhaps. A knowledge in his eyes that I would be everything he expected and more.

The tremors began low in my body. But when they reached my hands, they were not pleasant, or kind. I tucked my fingers into my skirts as Piers cleared his throat behind us. "Before I lose you both to each other's eyes," he said dryly, "I've a gift of my own, Miss St. Croix."

A gift? I tilted my head, my gaze flicking between both men as Piers rounded me to stand beside his brother. In his hands, a thin book, no more than a journal. The leather was tooled beautifully, but worn.

The earl's stance shifted. "My brother, always sticking his nose where it doesn't belong," he added, with the affectionate if reserved air of an elder sibling, "found this in here. He insisted it be given."

It was clear that though there were rumors of argument and ill-temper between the sons, they were affectionate, as well. A sort of . . . bond I wasn't sure I understood. I had no siblings, after all.

"My brother is not particularly convinced this will

matter," Piers said jovially, "which allows me the indulgence of being all the more determined to give it. I expect it to intrigue as much as it did myself."

"Just give it to her," the earl muttered, his expression so tense that I did laugh, and muffled the sound behind my gloved fingertips when he stiffened.

"You are terribly apprehensive," I accused lightly. "Should I be wary that this gift will bite?"

Piers offered the book, his barbered chops gleaming as they tilted somewhat with his smile. I took it carefully. "My brother is always apprehensive, Miss St. Croix. And proper, and cautious, and—"

"Not likely to fritter away his money on habits and ill-fated hobbies," interjected the earl ominously.

The smile died from Piers's expression. Turned, instead, to a rueful slant, and that twinkle. "Consider yourself warned," he whispered, and turned. "Cornelius. Don't keep her long, or the gossips will talk."

"Don't you dare leave—"

I stared after Piers, left holding the proffered tome as my reputation's chaperone left me alone with the man who insisted that I require in him a husband.

Lord Compton did not swear, but he stiffened even more and thrust his fingers through his hair. "That ill-behaved child." He turned to me, his jaw tight. "We must depart immediately, before anyone comes looking."

Why? Why did I find this adorable, rather than the vexation it should have been? Perhaps because my reputation wasn't as valuable to me as it seemed to others.

I caught his arm as he half turned.

He stilled.

Suddenly, the tableau in the library was not the

kind that should have been allowed. Would not have, if Piers had not wandered off so suddenly.

We stood surrounded by a sea of books, two separate beings bound only by my gloved fingers upon the sleeve of his dinner jacket.

Yet the very undercurrent this mild touch sparked seemed to crackle like lightning. Like the promise of energy, that warning hum as a mechanical device charged.

Again, I remembered that I did not find him deplorable. Without the promise of matrimonial chains, I found him quite likable, indeed.

He did not look at me. He did not have to. I did not know what he looked at instead, but I know what I saw. A fine man, an upstanding man, worried for my reputation even as he arranged this illicit meeting to show me that he listened. That he heard me.

Slowly, his hand covered mine on his arm. Warm. Strong. "You wanted books," he said quietly.

"I did."

"I wanted to show you that you would not be without."

My fingers ached against the book I held to my bosom. "All I require is polish, is that not so?" I couldn't help myself.

Now, he looked at me. Turned so that he faced me direct. A soldier, I thought, an admiral facing one of his own. He'd done well for himself in Her Majesty's Navy. I could not recall what rank he'd served under, but I know he'd been admired for it.

"You are wild," he said, his tone even but not sharp. "You travel alone where you should not—"

"Like the Philosopher's Square?" I interrupted, gratified to see him blanch. Seizing the opportunity, I pressed, "Rumor often places you below the drift, my lord. Why should you be free to wander such places and I cannot?"

Pure disdain colored his features; turned him into the near mirror of the marchioness. Yet as I glared, suddenly filled with the frustration of too many secrets, too much wanting, I realized his was not disdain for *me*.

A trick his lady mother had not refined.

"You will be a countess," he told me, unbending now. Yet, he did not let my hand go. "A countess has no call for traveling to such dangerous and ill-reputed streets."

"What if I want things?" I demanded. "Books, materials only found in the shops there?"

"What manner of things cannot be found along the shops catering to King's College?" he asked shrewdly.

I did not answer, setting my jaw in obvious obstinacy.

He met my unyielding glare with his own implacable regard. "Then I will have them fetched for you," he replied, a thread of heat in his voice now. His eyes. Anger? Or frustration.

"Why do *you* go?" I would not give in. I could not admit that I had run into him myself outside that opium den last month, but I needed to know.

Did he share my taste for the stuff or not?

He looked down at me, mouth set into a thin, disapproving line. Finally, he let go of my hand. Allowed me to pull it back, wrap around the book whose cover lacked a title. "There are . . . secrets to this household," he said after a long moment. "My brother has . . ." A pause, and I saw the fight in his eyes.

His brother.

The inveterate gambler, and . . . opium user?

"I often must go after him before he spends too long among the degenerates below," he confessed quietly. "When he falls prey to his own weakness too often, he is exiled to one of our rural estates, allowed to dry."

Forced to remain sober, I'd wager.

The thought sent a frisson of fear through me. To never have laudanum again? Would that be the price of any proposal tendered?

The earl caught my hand, pressed my palm fervently in all that was allowed between us. "Promise me that you will not go below again," he said, not so much a question as a command. One I recognized, and bristled under, yet . . . Yet I contemplated it. "I know you are a woman of your word, Miss St. Croix, a rare thing. Say it, say you'll have me and all that I offer, and I shall do everything in my power to make you happy."

I bit my lip.

Books. A home. A *place*. These are things Fanny had always told me I needed. I had ignored her. I had a home, didn't I?

But . . . what kind of home was it? Not really mine. Even once I inherited it, what did I plan to do?

Leave.

Here, I had a future, didn't I? To wake up secure, warm. Cared for.

To know that my family, my staff, was safe.

All I needed was to refrain from going below. To leave the life of a collector; a life often fraught with danger and discomfort.

I could avoid the Veil for certain. Couldn't I?

Somehow, I wasn't so positive that the Veil would forget my debt so easily.

"I . . . I need time to consider," I whispered. It was not a no. Not this time.

Was he wearing me down, or was I really looking at the life laid out before me?

He bowed, formal. Stiff. "I understand. Your parents left you alone too early." I blinked. "I know you will make the right decision. You *will* learn to trust me." He let go of my hand. "I shall send a maidservant to escort you back to the music hall." He stepped around me, stopped halfway to the door and turned. "I hope you enjoy my brother's gift, Miss St. Croix. And . . . and mine."

With that, he was gone, and I was left staring blankly at the book between my palms.

Trust him. In many ways, I believe I did.

Absently, I opened the book, searching for a title page.

Instead, I found a handwritten note within. In lovely, elegant script so much more polished than mine, I read, *For my dearest Almira. Love, your Josephine.*

What?

No . . .

What?

I could not even begin to make sense of it.

My mother. The marchioness. Gossip had always claimed them enemies. Why, the marchioness *hated* me. She loathed me!

What on earth could possibly link such foes?

Trembling, I leafed through the pages of the handwritten journal I found a collection of symbols that took the remaining breath from me.

A triangle. Three circles, a fourth in the middle.

Alchemy.

How? Why? This made no sense!

I spun for the door, but stopped before I took even a step.

What would I say? Who would I ask?

Who knew that my mother was as involved in the so-called art as my father became?

My father.

When I'd met him in Woolsey's guise, he'd called Josephine *the best of us*. Us.

"My lady?" A maid, barely a blur in my racing mind.

Not the university, as I'd thought then.

A society of some kind. A salon that included women. It had to be. A club? A meeting place. Something! The marchioness had been part of it, then?

"I can escort you, if you're ready," said the hesitant maid, and I strode for the door, beating down a wild rush of exhilaration—of hurt and anger and outrage at this revelation. I could not follow any clues now. I had to return to the soiree, listen to the skin-peeling melodies of my peers, and force myself to be patient.

But I would find a moment. And when I did, I knew who to ask.

Lady Rutledge had already known.

I was convinced of it.

Chapter Nineteen

It seemed an eternity before I was allowed to escape to the uncertain sanctity of my own home. When I did, I found more than simply peace and quiet.

I found my crystal flagon filled with a fourth of jewel-bright ruby liquid. A card had been propped against it, one of my own. Zylphia's distinctive hand scrawled a note across it: *Take in moderation, as needed.*

The gesture, thoughtful even as it seemed something I should be ashamed over, made me smile.

I read late into the night. Much of the pages made no sense to me, but I could not stop. These were my mother's words. My mother's handwriting. I had never been so close to her as when I held that book.

Studied its writings.

Much of it was, near as I could fathom, simple speculation. Much of it was philosophical—an interesting series of theoretical and moral conjecture, flavored heavily by the concept that all things were bound by aether.

A theory often passed among scientific circles as

the intelligent hypothesis. Yet the dates upon these entries came earlier than most.

Had my mother shared these theories?

Had she been among these intelligent minds when postulating them?

And if so, why in the name of all things holy did she dedicate this journal to the marchioness? Her enemy?

I fell asleep with a draught of laudanum that night, cradling the book.

For the first time in many days, I awoke feeling not as if I'd been beaten, but with an energy that I'd been lacking for too long. Although the return of my morning headache signaled a need for care, I nevertheless was awake when Zylphia tapped upon my door.

"I'm to remind you of Lady Rutledge's masquerade," came her greeting. "Fanny was extremely intent upon it."

Lady Rutledge's masquerade came once a year, always the talk of the Town and often the reason much of Society remained in London later than the Season. The lady did not leave London like much of the elite, and did not much mind those who did.

Yet I considered it a play, a subtle indication of how much power Lady Rutledge truly wielded.

Unlike most soirees, hers was not closed to those who were not titled or landed. In truth, the yearly event was often filled to the brim with the most ornate creatures—men and women masked and bedecked in outlandish garb, each invited out of some unknown formula. None knew exactly how she comprised her guest list, or what qualifications she demanded. In many cases, the location would vary. This year, she held the lavish event in King's College.

The dean was all too happy to offer the college grounds for the last great event of the year. He was nobody's fool, and he knew quite well whose families his pupils came from. Society demanded much of a man in his position, and so the college retained grounds for soirees, balls, events to keep him circulating among the elite.

A clever business.

I had, in the past, received invites. I had never gone, sure that I would be out of place—a creature to point at and whisper over. Mad St. Croix's daughter. Yet when the summons came last month, shortly after being introduced to the lady herself, I'd decided to hedge my bets entirely and go.

Fanny wasn't convinced; she didn't like events that turned into a crush, and this one would be that and more. At the time of the invite's receipt, I wasn't positive of the intent behind my going.

I knew now that I would seize the opportunity to speak to Lady Rutledge and the dean about my suspicions. Or, rather, perhaps only to the lady and allow her the trial of maneuvering the dean.

Professors were dying. If I were Miss Hensworth, and in fact murdering those who stood in my way as my theory suggested, I would target the dean next.

She was a smart woman. I was sure she'd do the same.

Still, of all the events I'd been invited to, this one piqued my interest. Lady Rutledge's set seemed geared more toward intelligent thinking and scientific interest than the frankly useless claptrap spouted off by most of London's elite.

Zylphia rolled my hair into three elegant knots and pinned them in place. It was fetching enough, and would do until we prepared for the masquerade.

"Cage sends his regards," she said offhandedly as she cinched my corset tight.

My breath whooshed out. "Oomph! Charming," I managed. "I assume . . . gracious, Zylla . . . you did not tell him of my engagement?"

"Of course not." She tied off the stays, tugged them hard to be sure they'd hold. "If anyone knows your identity, I haven't said a word about it."

"Thank you." I took a testing breath, winced. "You're meaner than Betsy was."

Amusement flashed in her eyes. It sobered, as did her expression. "What will you do about your mysterious murderer, then?"

I turned, then, perched upon my vanity seat as she fetched my rose day dress. The stain had been removed, thanks to Mrs. Booth's expert hand. "I don't know," I said honestly, rubbing at my waist idly. The brocade corset was rough against my palm. "I believe the strongest candidate is, in fact, Miss Hensworth."

"Why?"

A fair question. "At least one professor was directly standing in her way," I pointed out thoughtfully. "Professor MacGillycuddy allowed no women into King's College. Lambkin took on the role, yet it's possible that he believed the same. To that end, he, too, must go."

Zylphia nodded, but cautiously. "It's speculative."

"Of course. But let me pose you this," I said, eagerly warming to my subject as she helped me step into my skirt. "Say you have dispatched two men, only to find the real obstacle is another entirely. What would you do?"

She didn't take long to consider. "Having killed two, I would feel a third is rather easy pickings."

"My thoughts exactly."

"But it's still speculative," she told me. I knew it, but what else had I to go on? "What of the earl?"

I blinked. "What of the earl?"

"Marriage is a different world, you know."

"Do you speak from experience?" I asked, but she only smiled—a quiet thing, something weightier than I had ever seen upon her lush, exotic features— and said instead, "If you marry this earl, you cannot continue as you are."

This caught me, even more than the presumption of my interest in marriage. "As I am?"

"Your laudanum," she clarified, buttoning me into the gown.

"No one will care that I drink it for my night terrors," I scoffed.

"Not that." As Zylphia smoothed my dress, ensuring she did not meet my eyes in the mirror. "I mean the rest of the time."

I stilled.

How did she know? I'd done for years without Betsy catching on.

"I have seen many a good soul lose themselves to the smoke," she said, awkward now, yet no less sincere for it. "I would not see you go the same way."

Lose myself? I wouldn't. It wasn't so bad as that. At least I wasn't eating it by the cube, as the Turks were known for. "You worry too much," I said, forcing cheer. I caught her hand and added with a grin, "Besides, I'll have you to help me, won't I?"

"Will you?" Zylphia removed her hand from mine, yet not unkindly. "Go on, then, breakfast is waiting for you."

I obeyed, rubbing the back of my neck as I did so. Doubt weighed upon me.

Why was it that part of my house was so blissful and happy about the hope of marriage, yet the part from below the drift remained so skeptical?

Why did both parts of me feel the same?

I found both the *London Times* and the *Leeds Mercury* waiting for me at the table. Fanny, as well, though she only gave me a brilliant smile and chirped, "Good morning, my dove."

"Good morning, Fanny," I replied dutifully. "You look well."

"Just wonderful. Are you quite prepared for Lady Rutledge's masquerade?"

If the many, many hours of fittings I'd endured meant anything, I was. I said as much, only in much more polite terms, and picked up my paper as Booth filled my plate with his wife's handiwork. "Thank you, Booth."

"Of course, miss."

ANOTHER WHITECHAPEL MURDER.

The headline seized my attention. I stiffened, excitement and dismay curling through me, warring for supremacy over the other. Another murder.

Not the sort I was looking for, mind, but gruesome and tragic all the same.

I read the article in the *Times*, and found my appetite wholly diminished by the end. "Jack the Ripper has struck again," I said, frowning. "That makes the seventh murder in the area."

The details in this one were gruesome indeed. The victim, Mary Kelly, had been brutalized terribly after her throat had been slashed. A messy, ghastly end. The article spared no ink for the tale, and I did not share the details. Not with my chaperone, who would like as not faint.

"Dreadful," Fanny said sadly, shivering in shared

sympathy for the departed. "Just terrible. I do wish the constables would capture that beastly person."

"As do I," I murmured, surprised somewhat to find such ready conversation on the subject. Fanny often did not share my love of the morning papers.

Perhaps the subject of Jack the Ripper had finally infiltrated even the most delicate sensibilities. The murders were real and very present. If the amount of ink given to the news was any indication, the doxies' plight seemed to resound much more strongly than the fateful deaths of two professors.

"It's a wonder he hasn't been caught yet," she continued, her frail fingers curling around her teacup. I set the paper down, head tilting as I studied her somber expression. "With as many police as I'm sure must patrol those streets."

"Not as many as you'd think," I said before I thought, and watched her flinch at the pointed reminder of my habits. "Still," I hastened to add, "I imagine it's only a matter of time. This so-called Ripper can't possibly get away with this any longer."

Perhaps I would see about a bounty myself.

Promise me, the earl had demanded, and I shook my head hard.

Fanny sighed. "One might wonder if this monster were invisible to the searching eye, the way he carries on."

"Fanciful," I replied with dry amusement. "Why, I—" *Invisible.* I froze, words only half formed on my lips.

"Cherry?"

I saw Fanny, saw her thin gray eyebrows knot and lines form between them. Saw the way she stared at me in mingled surprise and concern.

Yet I didn't linger there. *Invisible.*

An empty dress. A figure cowled and then gone.

Why didn't I think of this before? I'd spent all bloody night reading my mother's blasted journal. Notations had been scarce, only enough to illustrate this point or that hypothesis, but I'd seen the same symbols.

What had my mother's journal included? Of course: *ppt*, a notation for preparation.

My brain turned over and over, gears spinning in place, working, smoking with the effort.

"Prepare the formula," I murmured, and if what I recalled of the notations was correct, it involved a process of distillation. Aether, water, fire, a Star of David. The star . . . Mr. Pettigrew had made clear that such symbols no longer meant what religion and order had assured.

The star . . . meant . . .

I bolted upright, upset the table and caused the china to clink merrily. Both papers slid to the floor. "Imbibition," I said, suddenly and without further preface. "Zylphia!" My voice rose, loud enough to send Fanny into fits of indignation.

"Cherry St. Croix, we do not—"

I waved her into silence. "Zylphia," I called again, rounding the table. "Get down here this instant!"

"Is all well, miss?" Booth's baritone echoed from the far entry, his eyebrows mirroring the shape of my chaperone's. Worry. I engendered a lot of worry in my staff, I realized.

I waved at him, not so much dismissal as an indication for patience, and caught the edge of the entry as Zylphia's step pattered down the stairs. As her white-capped head cleared the rail, I pitched my voice to carry. "Zylla, have you my gloves from the day I visited Mr. Pettigrew?"

Her eyes rounded, wild blue flowers in the dark frame of her skin. She seized the railing, bent over it to talk to me directly. "Er, which . . . ?"

"The last," I said impatiently. "When he was murdered. Have you laundered them?"

"No," she replied, and then looked beyond me and hastily added, "miss."

I had no time for it. "Good, fetch them."

"They're in the rag bin," she explained, and hurried down the steps. "They were quite ruined."

"Hurry," I urged, and turned back to the breakfast table to find Fanny watching me with unconcealed displeasure.

I couldn't take the time to argue with her. "I promise this will soon be over," I said instead.

This seemed to mollify her. At least a little. "Once you are wed," she told me, quite firmly, "all this will stop."

"I will not—" I bit my tongue, ceasing the careless cruelty of my distraction, and was spared the need by Zylphia's return through the same door Booth and his wife now looked in on.

Her expression as she sidled past my butler was perplexed. "Ah, Cherry?"

I ignored Fanny's sharp intake of scandalized breath, and the echoed sound I heard from beyond a pained-looked Booth. "Quick, give them here." I beckoned impatiently.

"Of course, it's just that . . . Well, see for yourself." She pulled two scraps of white bands from behind her back. As if someone had taken the palms and a portion of the fingers and cut them directly out.

"What on earth?" Fanny demanded, and raised a lecturing finger to my maid. "Young lady, if this is how you launder—"

"Leave her be," I cut in sharply, yet I could not help my grin. It spread ear to ear, filled my chest with something exciting and sharp. Something I recognized well.

The rising blood of a chase.

Digestion. Not so literal, after all.

All eyes turned to me as I took the ruined gloves and laid them out on the table.

It was as if bits of the cloth were missing. Whole section, exactly in the shape of fingers whose tips and joints were gnawed out. A bit of the palm.

How strange. How interesting.

How *lovely* that I was right.

"The formula," I said as I plucked one from the table and stripped a glove from my hand, "used the letters D and G. Digestion." I began to pull the ruined glove over my fingers. My palm. "Among various other instructions, it also required aether to imbue it and water to carry it."

"What are you babbling about?" Fanny demanded. "There's no call to put a glove full of holes on your hand."

Yet as my fingers slid into place, I watched them appear within the empty portions. Watched them, yet *felt* the indication of fabric where none showed. "Digestion," I murmured, more now to myself. "As Mr. Pettigrew suggested, it could also be the process by which one element overtakes another. Much the same as the fabric what took on the liquid, bonding both. If it seeps through the body, then won't it do the same?" Worse, to my way of thinking, for the unique properties of a body allowed for a richer consumption through the blood.

"Cherry, really," Fanny said, once more cutting into my thoughts.

I looked up, fingers flexing within the indication of the vanished fabric. "What? Oh." I smiled, distracted and more than a little manic. "Eureka. We are searching for an invisible killer."

"Invisible? Preposterous," Fanny dismissed.

When even Zylphia looked skeptical, I raised my patchworked hand and added, "Oh, not *truly* invisible. It's science, not magic. Zylphia?"

"Miss."

"How long will it take for my costume to be ready?"

"All day," Fanny interjected, deliberately stripping any intent I might have had to go searching for evidence or hunting down my invisible woman.

For I had no more doubts. The dress in Professor Lambkin's office had been my first clue, after all.

Miss Hensworth was dabbling in the alchemical arts. That would make this much harder, but that much more important.

"But I—" I sighed. "Fine. Ready my costume." I stripped off the glove once more.

Yet as I did, I felt what we all heard. A subtle sound, a whisper, but loud as a scream in the silence following my order. *Rip.*

Frowning, I studied the glove. Ran it through my fingers. It gave. Just like that. And what fibers gave, soon crumbled to nothing.

I looked up, my frown turning to sudden concern. "It is wearing down."

"What?"

"It weakens the structure of the fabric," I told them, and spun in agitation. "Perhaps the aether reacts poorly with the long term viability of the material it imbues. Blast! We *must* be at that masquerade. 'Tis life or death, now."

"Cherry," Fanny sighed, and dropped her forehead into her cradling hand.

I left her there, left Mrs. Booth and Zylphia staring in my wake as I hurried up the stairs to begin my own preparations.

Alchemy was not magic. Yet like most scientific endeavors, there were drawbacks to be had. Drawbacks that could build, like a slow poison or a quiet, subtle killer.

I knew this more than most. The drawback to my father's serum had been fatal.

Miss Hensworth might not realize the same.

Chapter Twenty

I t was nearly impossible to retain my focus.

The entirety of King's College had been transformed for the masquerade, turned inside out in a sheer wonderland of surreal decor and unique display. What belonged inside was now outdoors, and what was meant to be outside had gone in.

I had never seen the like.

And clocks, clocks everywhere! So many devices fashioned from so many materials. Guests filed past two large grandfather clocks that I could only assume had cost a small fortune apiece. They tolled out at random increments, skewing my sense of time as I was sure they'd been intended. We passed tables set for tea, shelves filled with books and protected by faux walls attached to nothing at all. The path stones we tread upon were clocks, tiny gears open beneath a pristine plate of glass, numbers lacquered in stark black.

Each gave a different time, each ticked on a different beat.

Over it all, protecting us from the rain falling to the London streets in icy sheets of cold and wet, rose creations in scrollworked metal to resemble pieces of ceiling and dreamlike portions of an abstract house. Telescopes mounted on brass fittings looked out of windows set in walls with no interior.

Desks and bookshelves, parlor furniture, all of it exactly where it shouldn't be.

I did my best not to stare as Fanny and I walked in step with a knot of richly garbed strangers, yet I failed more often than not.

My costume was truly inspired. Madame Troussard had outdone herself. In the guise of a masquerade, gentlemen and ladies can always stretch the bounds of propriety for the favor of surprise and awe. I did both.

Yet there were many who had taken it even farther. I did not see simple sky ship captains or old-fashioned lords and ladies. I saw creatures who stepped from the pages of fantasy; a truly magnificent collection of gowns, coats, hairpieces, masks. The noise, even in the queue, was astonishingly deep; not so much loud as rich and full and vibrant.

My gown was shockingly pink, a paler shade than I usually dared to wear. The sleeves were a diaphanous material that revealed my arms to any who bothered to look, yet whose gathers at the elbow turned them to large puffs of shimmering confection. It was not lace that spilled from the hem but a waterfall of crystals linked together by sturdy net, and they caught the light in a thousand glittering shards.

And clinked like tiny bells with every gesture.

The bodice of the gown was low—much lower than I was usually comfortable with, and I constantly worried for my ability to move, much less my modesty—

yet the same crystal net shaped my décolletage, hugged my throat and made it appear as if I wore crystalline armor. It fastened to a large, ornate brass collar, whose inset cameo did not feature a woman but a single faceted crystal in the shape of a rose.

My corset was tight enough to give my bell-shaped skirt a dramatic flare. The bustle drawn tight at the waist and gathered into a shimmering mix of diaphanous pink and mauve ruffle offered an extreme bit of feminine flirtation, which I rather wryly tolerated. I pitied anyone behind me, for I knew the crystals hanging from the bustle were blinding in the right light.

Yet the split down the front ensured it by no means was a proper skirt. The mauve-ruffled petticoats I wore to give it sway and shape were likewise split, allowing my legs from the thighs to my knee-high tooled boots to be ogled at any viewer's leisure.

Regardless, I was not so bold as to go bare-legged in such vaunted company. Zylphia suggested she might; I was not a sweet, nor looking to be mistaken for one. Instead, I wore trousers beneath the skirt, fitted so well in the same mauve that they rather scandalously clung to each leg before vanishing into the boots.

I looked as if I were a pirate princess in pink and diamonds, rather than Miss St. Croix, the only marginally proper heiress.

I was, much to my surprise, very much not myself.

My mask was not a full one, covering only my eyes and much of my nose. My hair, of course, was easily recognizable, and Zylphia had done a lovely series of curls and loose knots to which the large array of gilded roses could be applied.

I felt weighed down, stuffed into place, and . . .

And remarkably pretty.

Yet I had no weapons, no items which I could use to my advantage. I hunted a murderer bare-handed and alone. Fanny would be no help—lovely as she was in a more subdued creation of smoke and lace, her mask a painted moue and the hood affixed to her bodice covering much of her hair.

Zylphia dared not risk being found sneaking into such an event. And I had no Teddy for even escort.

Somehow, I would have to find Miss Hensworth in this madness without my proper escort becoming the wiser.

I knew she would be here, for the dean was also here. But how would I find her?

Fanny did not speak as we stepped into the ballroom proper. She must have been quite overwhelmed; I could not tell beneath her costumed finery. Yet her hand on my arm tightened as even I was forced to stare.

Trees had been somehow moved inside. The massive ballroom King's College boasted for events such as these had become a garden, with a screen of black night and glittering stars overhead. Pocket watches by the hundreds sparkled in the trees like ornaments, some copper, some gold, some silver or brass.

"Good heavens," Fanny gasped, and I followed her gaze, up into the very heights of the ballroom.

A sky ferry. Lady Rutledge had somehow managed to include a sky ferry into her event, and the dean had allowed it. It hung from supports, a beautiful thing of brass polished to perfection, wooden beams, and a gasbag made of some kind of pale linen shot through with gold. Even as I watched, the flames beneath the bag sparked blue.

As if that weren't surreal enough, I saw men and

women soaring across the ceiling in shimmering gold ribbons. They spun and danced on air and webs, graceful as birds, agile as spiders.

Circus performers.

Lady Rutledge had brought the Menagerie to London proper.

A knot formed in my belly. Hard and tight and anxious.

"Pardon," shouted a man who blundered by me, his voice distorted behind his mask. I saw nothing but black and white, and eyes sparkling from too much drink, perhaps. Or too much heat.

Fashionably late though we were, the event was already a crush.

A masquerade has different rules; ones that are closely mirrored by the Midnight Menagerie below. There are no identities for the evening, no requirements but that the barest forms of propriety be considered. To that end, I escorted Fanny to a likely knot of women wearing costumes slightly more subdued, and waited until she found a friend.

I patted her hand. "I should find the earl," I said, my mouth close to her ear.

She nodded. "Be a good girl, then, and—" She caught my arm. I could all but picture the frown on her stern features. "Do not do anything we will regret, do you hear me?"

"Absolutely not," I assured her, lying through my teeth. Even now, I studied all who passed by me, frittered around me. Many costumes revealed a portion of faces, hands, arms.

I would search for the one that did not.

Digestion. All scientific medicinals took time to reach full potency. Such was indicated by the absorption rate displayed by my glove. It was possible that Miss Hensworth had taken the term literally, for no other method I could envision based on the working formula would work nearly so well. How long had she been drinking the concoction?

Miss Hensworth needed to be stopped.

I left Fanny in good company, threading my way through the crush of people. I heard many conversations, some that told me exactly who spoke. But I also heard so much more, and the sheer anonymity of the event did not make things weigh any less.

At each corner of the ballroom, I found garden hills, covered in flowers and occasionally springing forth another strange little clock. At the top of each hill, a brass cannon. I wondered what it would shoot, if anything.

Glass windmills and beaten silver devices that spun around and around in dizzying patterns dotted the crowd. Over it all, the occasional *whoosh* of the sky ferry's aether engine warming up, and a glint of gold as aerialists danced their airy dance.

I forged my way through a small knot of gentlemen all wearing the same long-nosed mask, and did not pay much attention to the long golden device one held to his mouth until it blared out a sound that rebounded through the already noisy ballroom.

I flinched, spinning around with my shoulders tight, raising a hand to my ear as the cacophony bounced back in a flurry of wild echoes and raucous laughter. The men hooted and hollered, passing the noise-making device to one of their own.

I shook my head as I backed away from the oddly sinister-looking mask each wore.

Started as my back collided with a solid, unyielding warmth.

"I am sorry, I—"

Hands fell to my shoulders. "A dance," came a voice that curled like a velvet promise against my skin.

I stiffened, turned in a frothy confection of pink and mauve, but my masked gentlemen only took my gloved hand in his and led me the few paces to the floor. Without waiting for denial or protest, I found myself expertly inserted into the spiraling, graceful display of iridescent color.

I stared through the awkward confines of my mask at the man who towered above me.

His mask, unlike mine in its glittering pink and pearlescent design, was stark in its simplicity. Solid black, lacking gilt or shine, it covered more than half of his face, leaving only his mouth and square chin free.

His hair was black, queued back into a straight fall past his shoulders, and his costume much less pretentious than even mine. He wore simple black from head to toe, eschewing the proper white shirt, formal tie and gloves for the ebon color.

But his eyes. They met mine without fear or artifice, and I set my jaw as a river of blue flame in brown gleamed like the aether fire above us.

My feet, habitually taking the steps required of the waltz I found myself in, took a misstep. I opened my mouth; his hand splayed across my lower back, pulling me all too closely against his powerful body, and guided our turn across the floor.

My words dried, my tongue suddenly clumsy.

"I was under the perhaps mistaken impression that all ladies in London could dance," Micajah Hawke taunted softly.

My skirts swirled around his legs, an intimate tangle that made it abundantly clear how trousers provided so little barrier between bodies such as ours.

I gritted my teeth. He did not know who I was. He could not.

Zylphia had sworn to it.

I forced my lips into a smile and met his gaze direct. "You have unfortunately found the exception to the rule, if such a rule is to be had." Small talk. Charming conversation.

These were things expected of a lady upon the dance floor.

I would have preferred to take a knee to his most vulnerable flesh and leave him gasping on the floor.

Hawke and I were not friends.

But this lady in pink and crystal had no call to be so rude, and so I swallowed the urge and smiled prettily and counted the beats until I could be free.

"Never fear," he said, his palm pressing all too intimately low on my back. Sweat gathered there. Bloomed across my shoulders, mercifully bare beneath the crystalline net. "You have other talents."

Another misstep; one I caught myself and righted without help. Or, I hoped, revelation of my dismay.

What did he know?

"I'm sure," he added after a moment's study. His gaze was lazy, his smile mirroring that laconic indulgence I so often had seen when he performed for the crowds.

The last I'd been so close to see it, he'd fondled a sweet's breast in a steam-filled room of debauched men and women playacting at Roman bathhouse.

My skin heated.

"You are too bold, sir," I snapped.

He did not let me pull away. His grip tightened, until my chest was pulled against his and I could see each tiny pore where he'd shaved the bristle of a day's work from his strong, swarthy jaw.

Micajah Hawke was temptation given flesh, and he bloody well knew it.

I was better than his simple creatures. I was not his pet.

His mouth lowered to my ear. Relief that he only meant to whisper filled me as he expertly navigated our path through the swish and swirl of beautifully tailored skirts and streamers.

Until his breath touched the sensitive skin there. His chuckle was as dark as his reputation. "I beg a bargain."

I nearly laughed outright, breathless though I remained. The ringmaster of the Menagerie did not beg for anything. "Be careful what you bargain for, sir, for these are not your usual grounds."

"Careful what you taunt me with," he returned in the same soft, nearly inaudible tones. Personal tones; a lover's whisper, a seductive command. "My grounds extend farther than you'd like . . . Miss Black."

My foot caught in his. I lurched, sucked in a breath as I jerked away, but he did not allow it. Skillfully, impossibly expertly, his foot eased from under mine, stepped between my legs and pulled me upright before any could see more than a brush of bodies, a dip of a hand where there needn't have been one.

Clever snake.

"How do you know?" I demanded when I'd once more found the rhythm. "Was it that I recognized you?"

He did not answer me; he rarely bothered. "I come with a bargain," he said again, "and you will do well to hear it."

"What choice have I?" I nearly spat the words from between my teeth. "I am trapped in a waltz that will not end with a man who does not belong here."

"Any more than you belong below," he retorted, a markedly accurate taunt that lanced through me like a knife. Though he held my hand as proper in the dance, his other left my waist to cup my chin. Fingers hard, devilishly handsome features implacable as I knew him best. "Listen to me, Miss Black, and then you may sling your insults from a safe distance."

"As if I require your permission."

His teeth flashed, an even white gleam. "All my pets require my permission." His grip tightened, and I winced beneath the sudden pain of it. "Marry your earl, Miss Black."

I sucked in a breath. "What do you know of it?"

"More than you'd like," came his oh-so-infuriating reply. "Marry him, and I will forgive all debt to the Veil."

"But why?" The words escaped me, torn from me in the midst of the cacophony of the dance, the masquerade, my thoughts.

His offer.

"That is not for you to know," he said, and let my chin go. It ached, even as I wrenched back a step, forced distance between us as was proper.

His smile was lazily lethal. Dark as sin.

The bloody ringmaster always was.

My gaze narrowed. "What is the catch?"

"You give up the life of a collector."

I had expected prevarication. A tease. Perhaps even a price of gold or jewels.

This . . . this command, this order delivered with precise intent, each word clipped, stole my thoughts.

Hawke's smile destroyed what little mind I had left.

The light reflected off his golden skin, turned him

dark as a Gypsy and even more mysterious for it. I stared into eyes cut by the swath of blue, bottomless and unreadable, and could find no answers.

Only the promise, dangling between us.

"Swear it, Miss Black." A command, as aristocratic as any I'd heard above. His fingers curled around the upper portion of my arm, crushing the sugar-spun sleeve of my gown. "You will stay in London above, marry your landed earl, become a countess."

I looked away. "Why?"

"Swear it, or I shall be forced to act against the Northampton family."

That garnered my attention as little else could. "What? Why?"

"You aren't the only toff whose luck fails within the Menagerie," he said, watching me intently. "Many vices come with a price too great for its purchase."

My eyes narrowed. "Lord Piers." When he only inclined his head, my fists clenched into pink tulle. "You wouldn't!"

"I certainly would." This, I believed.

"Why tie my fortunes to his?" I demanded. "Why lose two debts in the space of one event?"

"Marriage is its own price," came his cryptic response, and I gritted my teeth as heat filled my cheeks.

I had no choice. To be free of the Veil. Free of the debt the Menagerie held over me.

Free of Hawke.

And to free Piers from a terrible burden.

"Let me think on it," I said tightly, then snapped when he said nothing, "You ask me to enslave myself to free myself, Hawke. Give me the courtesy of time."

He studied me for a long moment. Took his fill of me, of what he could see beyond the mask shrouding much of my face from his view. The music rose and fell around us; the dancers flitted by. I did not realize we'd stopped until he let me go.

For a long, aching moment, I held his gaze.

He'd saved my life. Wicked as the devil and just as sly, he'd nevertheless come to me when I needed help the most and done what he needed to see me survive it.

Micajah Hawke had been the closest thing to a lover as I'd ever had. Not in spirit, but in flesh, and it meant something that he'd done so.

Was the angel I did not know better than the devil I intimately did?

I opened my mouth; he shook his head once. A silent, imposing command. His fingertips touched my cheek. My mask.

I closed my eyes as they skated, soft as silk, just under the very edge of it.

"You have this night to consider," he whispered, his breath hot and spicy fragrance suddenly thick in my nose. "And a champion," he added wryly, a breath later. "Farewell, Miss St. Croix. Once you capitulate, I will not receive you again."

I started, turned to find a figure in pale gray and blue bearing down on me. His gaze, shrouded by the pearl gray mask he wore, seemed as near to violence as I'd ever seen it.

Earl Compton could not hide behind a mask. No more than Hawke could.

"Are you well?" he demanded as he came to my side. "Did that man put a hand on you?"

That man?

I looked behind me, but Hawke was gone. "No," I murmured. "No, he did not." Not really. " 'Twas only a dance, albeit the sort one expects in a masquerade such as this," I added with a smile I didn't genuinely feel.

"Then if you are feeling gracious," he said, his mustache shifting with his crooked, even somewhat abashed smile, "I would claim a dance."

A dance?

I blinked rapidly, my head clearing as if from a fog. Suddenly, the noise splashed down upon me like a terrible, heavy wave. I clutched at his arm as I staggered.

"Miss St. Croix?"

This time, it was no dark angel's voice in my ear, but that of an alarmed earl. Concern filled it, his fingers tight around my upper arm where moments before another man had held me.

I took a juddering breath. Let it out on a breathless laugh. "I am sorry," I managed, shaking my head. "All is well, I am quite all right. Everything is just so . . ."

His arm slipped around my back, carefully moderated support, and he led me from the ballroom floor. "Frenzied," he supplied. His firm mouth slanted in rueful understanding. "Do you require air?"

Air. A breath of fresh air, cold and lanced by rain as it was, would be welcome. I began to nod, and then hesitated as I spied a tall woman in brilliant violet and copper holding court. Lady Rutledge was impossible to miss, even beneath a powdered wig whose towering curls and structure held a birdcage.

With a live bird within. How . . . surreal.

Lord Compton followed my gaze and could not help a chuckle. The sound loosened a certain anxiety in me.

"There is a clock affixed to the base of that cage," he murmured in my ear. "And a bird that I would swear sings out every three minutes precisely. Did you wish to go see?"

"No, no, there will be time later to . . ." I stared as a figure pushed by us. Garbed all in black and white, with a full-featured mask that glittered.

"Miss St. Croix?" The earl touched my cheek. All but forbidden under normal circumstances.

And shocking enough that I found myself leaning into it. Into him, his taller form and steady figure a comfort against the chaos around us.

His hand, hesitant, crept to my waist.

His eyes met mine through our masks. Yet he said nothing. Neither inquiry nor reassurance.

A prickle of awareness mingled with the heat battering at every inch of my skin. My nose twitched. Faint, but insistent.

I felt too crowded. Too trapped, claustrophobic in the extreme. I needed air.

Yet I didn't dare step away from this oh-so-cautious embrace.

Was this how it could be?

Lady Rutledge's laugh suddenly climbed above that of the others, and I realized—remembered—what I should.

"Too short," I murmured, my eyes widening in rapid realization.

The earl frowned. "I beg your pardon?"

"That guest, in the black and white." I straightened, pulled away with a surge of manic interest. Turning, I began to push my way through the crowd, the dancers. "He lost stature!"

"Miss St. Croix, wait!"

I didn't dare. The man who'd pushed by me in that very same costume had been so much taller. I didn't recall seeing eyes this time.

Mask, gloves, costume.

And a faint, nearly imperceptible trace of lilies.

Chapter Twenty-one

Jt took effort, but I elbowed my way to Lady Rutledge's side. Ignored her ring of sycophants and friends and caught her arm. "Where is the dean?" I demanded.

Gasps ringed me at my interruption, rude as it was.

"Dean Figgins-Coop?" She did not pretend to not know of whom I spoke. "At the beverage table, I believe. Miss St. Croix, you look quite fetching."

I had no time for that, and waved it away with an abrupt hand. "When did you see Miss Hensworth last?"

Beneath her diamond-studded mask and truly inspiring birdcage-decorated wig, Lady Rutledge's mouth pursed. Her beauty mark winked. A diamond inset within it.

Scandalously effective.

I tore my gaze away from the bit of sparkle and met her gaze.

And found it all too serious. "Not since the luncheon some days ago, I'm afraid."

"I need to find her." I turned, gathering my frothy skirts in hand, and added, "Before she finds Figgins-Coop!"

"Do you think—"

I did not allow the lady the chance to finish. Did not allow Compton to catch up with me. Using elbows and shoulders, smiles and apologies, I forced my way across the ballroom. The beverage table would be set up away from the dancing, away from the chaos.

Yet as I ringed the ballroom proper, passing one of the strangely large yet silent cannons, I knew I'd come too late.

A cry set up from the far end of the room. A gasp of horror and dismay that slowly worked its way through the crowd, building strength, building momentum as any hue and cry would.

Whoosh! The sky ferry's engine lit up overhead, casting a blue sheen across the crowd.

"He's dead!"

The cry rose like a banner.

"He's been stabbed!"

I was too late, then.

But not too late to catch the culprit red-handed.

I studied the suddenly shifting crowd, searched its rampant tides as color and chaos melded into one. I saw no black and white figure, but I expected nothing of the sort.

Unfortunately, I did not expect the crowd to surge against me, either. A group of men hurried past me, a shoulder clipped mine and I staggered backward. My booted heel slipped on the grass, tumbled me into the cannon that did not give so much an iota as I collided with its polished surface.

The back of my head introduced itself to the barrel. *Gong!*

What stars there were tripled in my sight.

Yet as I struggled to right myself, my hand slid into a basket of powder so fine, it was like water.

Gold dust.

Of course. The answer came to me as the memories of figures in the fog.

When a quarry was on the run, leave them nowhere to hide.

It did not take a genius to figure out the cannon's purpose, and though my mind had been working as if through wet wool of late, I was still an intelligent being. Within moments, as the guests all but stampeded in the social clash of those who had seen the corpse fall versus those who had no inkling that anything at all had gone amiss, I'd found the mechanism that would trigger the firing array.

I did not bother to aim. The cannon's barrel already pointed up.

I pulled the string and held my breath.

I should have plugged my ears.

Boom! The weapon fired, shooting a comet of gold dust out of its mouth like dragon's fire. The glittering dust ball expanded as it soared, layering a golden fog upon the bemused guests.

Not enough. It wasn't wide enough a net!

But as I started to scramble down the small hill, another controlled explosion of sound thundered across the ballroom. Then again, and finally, a fourth.

My cannon's release must have convinced the other minders that it was time for the display. Luck favored me.

Gold dust shimmered in the air, clung to skin and clothes. I squinted, safe behind the cannon yet already regretting the stuff I knew would get in my nose and throat. It drifted, saturated all it touched.

Just like the damned fog.

And also like the fog, it would reveal my quarry.

I did not have to wait long.

It took effort, but I learned to filter the clothed and bulkier frames of guests now darting this way and that from anything else.

And the *anything else* I spotted came in a lithe figure not so much revealed by the dust as indicated by where the dust *moved*. As when she'd tossed her cloak in the fog below, she'd shed her costume here to do the deed.

"There you are," I whispered, my heart hammering with a fierce joy. Manic anticipation.

I slid down the grassy hill, kicking a clock off its perch in the process, and pushed my way through the crowd. The sylphlike figure had gone for the stair at the back. Fighting the surge of momentum, I caught more than one elbow or shoulder for my troubles.

I would feel these bruises tomorrow.

For now, I was too filled with the chase, the search, the *need* to catch my quarry, and it was to this end that I pulled the most daring maneuver I'd ever committed in full view of Society.

I had to hope they were not watching me. And if they were, that they could not know who waited behind the mask in pink and crystal.

I seized the end of a golden silk ribbon, did not dare check to see if it was occupied at the top. I had to trust that any performer knew to hang on when things went awry. Weighing my options left me with little enough—I grabbed the ribbon hard in both hands, wound it around my wrist and forearm as taught long ago, and ran like the very devil himself was on my heels.

I could not have timed it better. My skirt and bustle, bulky though it was in the back, provided ample freedom to leap to the wall and use the ribbon and my own momentum to keep me in tensile motion. My feet touched the wall, and holding the ribbon tautly in both hands, my weight hanging from the higher, I ran over the masquerade guests' heads.

When I gauged the angle correctly, I leapt, the elation of it loud and familiar in my veins. Once more, I found myself high above my audience.

In that few seconds, a strange thing happened. As if I was me, yet I was also a child once more; as if the ballroom filled with shocked people looked up at me, and yet I swung over the heads of an audience gasping in horror and delight.

It was not the fragrance of too many bodies I smelled, but that of sweat and spice. Of something that reminded me of . . .

Of incense.

I shuddered.

A golden blot vanished into the balcony at the top of the stair, jerked my attention into sharp relief. I swung to the staircase, bypassing the need to fight through the crowd again, and landed halfway up.

I staggered, caught the railing, wrenched myself forward.

Gold grit stung my eyes, coated my skin, but I could not stop to fish the stuff out of my mouth and eyes.

Miss Hensworth was coated in every inch in the stuff. She would be found.

I darted out of the ballroom, following the corridor at the top of the stair. It branched left and right; golden footsteps told me all I needed to know.

"Hortense!" I called, abandoning propriety in favor of speed. "Stop this instant!"

I wouldn't be so lucky. I followed traces of dust, aware I left my own behind me. Hurried past paintings of men all very smart-looking with labels declaring them professors or thinkers or geniuses of old, past the open galleries where this corridor looked down into the ballroom.

The raucous sound of it all faded in and out, like a gramophone whose record had been scored too shallowly in places.

"Hortense," I called again.

"Blast it!" A woman's curse. Anger and vitriol and bitter, *bitter* disappointment.

It came from the end of the hall, where a set of French doors opened beneath a hand I could not entirely see. Only a shimmer of gold warned me of her presence. Not nearly as thick as I'd hoped.

"Stop!" I called. "Hortense, you must hear me out."

I followed her outside, gasped as the October cold snapped the air from my lungs.

If I were this cold, I could not imagine how she felt, nude as she had to be.

I scanned the darkness, only the back-lighting of lanterns from beneath offering anything to see by. It was much darker up here, and the rain sluiced to the terrace, making difficult footing that much more treacherous.

More, it would wash away the dust.

I stepped out onto the veranda. "There's nowhere to hide, Hortense," I warned, as gently as I could. "I want to help you." Rain flattened my sleeves almost immediately. Pounded into the fabric and turned it heavy and unwieldy.

I could not take the time to be cold. Even as a shudder of frozen cognizance began in my spine, I stiffened it.

A rustle to my left. Ivy not yet deadened by winter's grasp sprang into motion. Not rain. A body, a footstep, a hold. I reached out; gold dust turned to liquid and dripped from my fingers.

My eyes strained to see what wasn't there.

"Miss Hensworth," I tried again, "I know what it is you've concocted. 'Tis dangerous. You must let me help you."

"You!" The voice came from somewhere farther down the veranda. Shuddering. Cold? Or anger?

Both, I'd imagine.

"How can you choose to help *them*?" she spat.

"Them?" I inched out into the dark. The rain pierced through my gown, set me to shivering violently.

"Them! *Detective St. Croix*." The moniker all but dripped venom. "Puppet of the same society that keeps women like us on a leash!"

Ah. Rhetoric.

"I'm not here for them," I replied, soft as I could manage. I reached out; nothing but air filtered through my fingers. I heard a slide of something, footstep on stone, all but muted beneath the patter of the precipitation around us. "Miss Hensworth, you must let me help you."

"Help? You are no help to me. Betrothed to an earl, meddlesome bint that you've been!"

I winced, but swallowed my angry retort. "Hortense, the tincture you've been drinking is exceptionally dangerous in large doses. You must believe me."

Silence.

"Please," I pleaded, turning away from the place I was sure she no longer was. But where, now? Look for the rain. Where it fell, and did not fall. "I understand that the digestive qualities allow you to remain all but invisible to the naked eye, but it weakens the—"

"Lies!"

I turned, but too late. A body collided with mine, sent me staggering toward the veranda railing. All the breath left me as my lower back struck the stone balustrade, but I was not alone. Limbs I could not see enfolded me, a body free of clothing to grasp pinned me, breath from a mouth invisible to me wafted over my face.

Too bitter. It smelled wrong.

Sick? No. *Different.*

I grunted a wordless refrain as fingers scrabbled at my throat.

Bless Madame Troussard and her worked brass collar.

As Hortense's grasping fingers failed to find purchase, I found something that seemed like flesh beneath my palms. Grasped whatever it was and wrenched hard.

I received an elbow—a fist?—to my face for my trouble, skewing my mask. Darkness slapped over my eyes; I couldn't see. I flailed, letting go of whatever portion of unclothed anatomy I'd managed.

Blind, grasping, I did the only thing my instincts allowed me to.

I bent, hip gouging against the stone railing, angled my shoulders and *pushed* with all my might. *"Allez, hop!"* I gasped.

Miss Hensworth went flying.

"No!" Her outraged scream came at me from an

angle too sharp to be the direction I'd intended. I struggled to right my mask, panting for breath.

Found myself facing the rain-drenched air beyond the veranda.

My heart dropped like a stone.

"Hortense?" I flung myself at the balustrade, but I saw nothing. Desperate, I patted at the wet rock, hanging half off the railing with my rear quarters curled around it for balance. My skirts dragged at me; I struggled to hang on. I found cold stone, but no chilled flesh. "Hortense! I can't see you, where are you?"

And then I heard it. A low, wild laugh. The kind of laugh I'd heard once before, deep in a tunnel where the sane should not go.

"You will never keep me from it," came the whisper. "I will walk these halls of learning as a free woman. An equal—*no*." The whisper became a bitter sound, a laugh. "Better than them! I deserve this!"

I blanched, reached as far as I could for nothing. Nothing at all.

I could not see what was invisible.

"I am a woman," Hortense rasped. Stone grated. Somewhere to my left? I peered hard.

There! A flicker of droplets where rain did not strike the terrace itself.

And a muted sound beneath. Rock grating. Fingers scrabbling.

I tossed one leg over the balustrade. "Stay where you are, I'm going to—"

"Don't you dare!"

I ignored her, reached until my weakened shoulder screamed with the effort. My fingers found flesh; I grabbed hold, joints popping.

She wrenched at me. "For years I've been forced to endure the scorn from these worthless jackanapes. Placed beneath the boot of men less than myself. I will not go back to nothing!"

"You cannot give up," I countered through my gritted teeth. Rock crumbled as an ornamentation gave way beneath her weight. I cried out as the limb in my grasp pulled, dead weight. The railing grated beneath my leg. "Hortense, you must . . . listen . . ."

"I am *tired* of listening," came the half-screamed words beneath me. Fingers I couldn't see pried at mine. "You should have died below! Why didn't you die?"

I took a deep breath.

Smelled lilies.

The same fragrance I'd caught while trapped in the closet. Organic, sweet, as out of place in this driving force of mania as I was in this sopping pink confection. More of the material gave way like wet tissue, and I jerked as my weight slid to the side.

I winced, muscles burning. "Why?" I demanded. "Why kill the others?"

"They were in my way. All of them, in my way!"

"Even Lambkin?" I demanded. Her limb twisted, slipped. "Hortense, I need your help!"

"Never," she spat, and a grip made of molten steel seized my wrist. I could not see it, only feel the pain of it. See the indentations left by invisible fingers. "You . . . You don't understand! I'd given him everything . . . The position, the knowledge. He filled the tenure that should have been mine and all I ever received was a toss when he wanted it. He laughed at me. Laughed!"

"Hortense—"

"No man will ever laugh at me again!"

And with that ragged scream, as the weight held in my grip thrashed, something cracked. The bone beneath my fingers, I think, although I had no way of being sure. Stone gave way. My wrist popped, sending searing agony up my arm; my fingers loosened as I bit back a cry of pain, even as my other hand curled around the balustrade and clung with all my might.

Hortense Hensworth plummeted to the courtyard below.

Saplings snapped beneath the weight of a woman whose very blood had taken on the qualities of the tincture she'd fed it. I heard the sound of flesh striking earth.

And I screamed in the rain as the same indifferent force of gravity pulled me after her.

"Cherry!"

Fingers locked around my ruined wrist. Another scream, this one made of pure pain, stripped the flesh from my throat. My ribs collided with the anterior stone facing, pushing every last bit of breath I had left from my lungs. "Oomph!"

Rain drove into my eyes, blurred the air above me to a subdued glow of lantern light, yet I heard clear as a bell the genteel curse of a man who'd spent more time with an uncouth navy than the civil company he currently kept.

"Hold on!" Lord Compton ordered, and it *was* an order. I gritted my teeth as fire and gaswork lights popped through my vision. Each press of his finger, each pull twisted my arm until agony was all I could see or feel or breathe.

Until stone scraped at my hips, my legs, and gave way to the banded steel of arms warmer, but no less confining for it.

For a long moment, I shuddered, gasping, my arm aching as I stared over Compton's shoulder and saw nothing. Only a void where the rain could not reach the earth. Nothing at all, in the shape of a body.

The invisible corpse in King's College. The woman who would make her mark on the university after all.

Miss Hensworth had achieved her wish. Even if no one would ever see it.

"Are you hurt?"

My shoulders, already slumped, shook as Earl Compton's effortlessly authoritative tenor cut through my shock. My numb dismay. I was soaked through, the pink confection I wore now a sodden, ruined mass of lumpy cloth and sheer tissue.

My hair clung to my neck and shoulders, half pinned and mostly plastered to my skin, inelegant hanks. My wrist ached, a throbbing pain that warned of deeper damage.

I braced for a lecture, for questions.

One came, but it was not the one I expected. "Miss St. Croix," he said as he guided me away from the ledge that had nearly claimed two tonight, "are you all right? Do you require aid?" Something warm draped across my shoulders.

A coat. His.

I clutched it to me, even as I knew the rain would soak it, too. Drench him, beside me. "I . . ." My breath escaped on a whispered sob. "I think I'd like to go home. I don't feel well."

It was a lie. Sort of.

The earl let me go, but only enough so that he could grip my upper arms and glare down at me. "What possessed you to run off like that?" he demanded, yet it wasn't a sharp sound. An angry sound.

Instead, it bore all the hallmarks of a man who worried. Who'd been . . .

I looked up at him in sudden surprise.

Had he been afraid for me?

He had. Even as the rain coated him in icy rivulets, his hair now as sodden as mine and dripping tendrils into his eyes, his demeanor was not one of anger.

Not, anyway, of true anger. I'd frightened him.

"I . . . I saw the murderer come this way," I managed. "I called, but no one came. So I . . . I . . ."

I tried to collect her.

I closed my teeth around the words trembling between my lips.

His mouth tightened to a hard line.

"Never again," he said, his arm tight around my shoulders. "Do you understand me? *Never* are you to take such matters into your own hands. What possessed you to think you could—!" His question cut off so quickly, it left my ears ringing.

Exhaustion, sorrow, filled me. My head lowered, until my temple came to rest over Lord Compton's chest. His heart beat steadily beneath my ear.

Steady. That was it. He was steady. Always the same, Earl Compton. Even when frightened, when forced out of his formal coat and soaked to the skin, he was the same: stalwart, not stiff as I'd unkindly called him. Balanced. So sure.

His other gloved hand curled around the back of my head, cradling me. As near a gesture of possession as I'd ever allowed.

"Let us find your chaperone," Earl Compton said, bowing his head over mine. Much quieter, now, more in control than I. "It's time for you to return home."

"But what of—"

The fingers at my nape tightened. "I will handle it."

And he would, wouldn't he? Everything in its place.

Just the way it always would be.

"Cornelius—"

He stiffened, and I stepped back suddenly as the rigidity of his body translated to my cold, sluggish mind. His arm tightened; I would not allow the confinement any longer.

As I found balance upon my own two feet, I clutched the warmth of his coat to me and raised my chin to meet his eyes. Pretty eyes, he had. They were appraising, I expected nothing less. Guarded, as if he expected me to do something rash.

Something *else* rash.

Would this qualify? I didn't know. All I could think was that I had reached my quotient of heartache. Perhaps forever.

I cleared my throat. "My lord, it would . . ." The air pulled from my lungs. I fisted my hands into the coat, took a deep breath of the misted rain and said quickly, "It would please me to accept your proposal, sir."

His jaw moved. The golden line of his mustache tilted somewhat as he worked something I could not read through his mind, his expression. Uncertainty, perhaps. Doubt.

"If," I continued, and watched his eyebrows beetle tightly, "you answer for me one question."

"Miss St. Croix, now is hardly the time," he demurred, gesturing to the warmth inside, only ten paces away.

"One question," I pressed stubbornly, all too aware of the icy water dripping into the collar of my borrowed coat. He must be frozen without coat or hat. But I could not give.

I would not, no matter how much my overwrought thoughts begged to let it be.

His lashes flickered. "Ask."

"Why me?" I demanded. "Truthfully, my lord. Why?"

My knees trembled in the intervening silence. Shock, I thought rather clinically. Delayed reaction to nearly taking a tumble, certainly the aftereffects of watching—hearing—a woman die in front of me.

Trepidation, certainly.

The earl turned away from me. "You will think me childish."

"I will not." There could certainly be no comparison to myself, in any regard.

One long-fingered hand, gloveless and pale in the shadows, speared through his rain-flattened curls. "You are many things, Miss St. Croix. Pleasing to the eye, clever, and certainly you are no fortune-seeker."

Dry humor forced a thin line to my lips. It was no smile, but I felt it ease the first hint of warmth into my chilled insides. "Well, you are honest, at least."

He turned, hands clasped behind him in military fashion. Even as the rain slicked across his angled cheek, he looked at me with the kind of forthright precision I imagine he studied his navy men with.

I swallowed hard.

"There is a heart in you that I admire," he said quietly. "A fierce spirit that refuses to break. Despite your ill-conceived attempts at heroism and nonsense, you are the one weakness I will allow myself, no matter what Mother demands. It will be you, Cherry St. Croix, or it will be no other, for I will not tie myself to a simpering maid with neither intellec-

tual wit nor a thirst for life." He gestured passion-
ately. "You will grow to have affection for me, I am
sure of it."

I found myself blinking under this outburst of
honesty, blinking away the rain and the surprise
and the . . .

Pleasure?

Some, I could admit it. Pleasure that for the brief
moment, I found in Earl Cornelius Kerrigan Compton a kindred spirit in the fight against the world
that would take from us our freedoms. Our happi-
ness.

He understood. As only a man could, of course, in
a very limited sense, for the world would not strip
very much from him, but he understood.

"You will study," he told me, offering one hand.
"You will have tutors, the finest there is. You will
outshine every countess England has ever seen,
and you will do my name"—he hesitated, and then,
ever so softly, smiled at me—"and yours," he added
pointedly, "proud."

I would have no choice. To earn the right to be a
woman of intellect and stature, to be as Lady Rutledge, I would have to play by the rules.

Freedom would mean nothing if I lacked the
status to use it.

No man shall ever laugh at me again.

With his name, I could be all but guaranteed.

Slowly, I set my hand in his. My stomach knotted,
a vicious thing of apprehension. "Then I accept," I
whispered.

"Come. Leave everything to me."

"But there will be banns, time—"

"Leave it to me, my future countess," he repeated
firmly. "I will take care of you."

Chapter Twenty-two

The masquerade became the talk of London; the event where the dean of the University of London was murdered by an unknown assailant and a terrible malfunction caused the gold cannons to go off prematurely.

There came no cry, no article or speculation, about a corpse in King's College, nor did I hear of anyone complaining of the smell such an untended thing could instigate.

Whatever happened to Miss Hensworth's altered body, I did not know of it.

To my surprise, I learned nothing of myself in the papers, no gossip of my behavior, recognized or otherwise. Instead, what brain matter was not devoted to the masquerade's endless supply of speculation was turned to the next and final event of the season—an event that would not be open to the public, but whose ramifications would stretch forever into history.

The wedding of Lord Cornelius Kerrigan Compton, Earl Compton and heir to Northampton, to Miss Cherry St. Croix. Heiress. Mad doctor's daughter.

No longer a collector.

I had reformed.

The gossips had taken the news of the Compton's sudden engagement and run mad with it. The sheer amount of speculation now hounding me was enough to paint every mistress and kept woman in London, much less innocent me.

But LAMB, I noticed, had changed their tactics. The marchioness was far too sophisticated to smear her own forthcoming daughter-in-law, no matter her opinion on her son's choice of brides. No, her campaign would be subtler.

The salon's columns these days were filled with deliberations on the perfect wife. The perfect hostess. The perfect, in a word, countess.

That which I would become upon my marriage vows.

"Message noted," I murmured, and put the paper down.

I could not dwell on the fact, the obligations, the *weight* any longer than I had to.

Fanny, simply overjoyed at what she'd always assumed an inevitable thing, kept busy making plans. A gown, flowers, decorations for the event; anything she could possibly stick her meddling fingers in, she did. Lord Compton was nobody's fool— he favored an intimate gathering in his Northampton home and a special license to wed over banns posted for weeks and a large event.

I understood his mother was not pleased by the decisions. I also understood that Compton might understand slightly more of my nature than I had previously credited him. He'd wasted no time in placing an engagement ring on my finger.

I'd never seen the like. Emeralds, richly hued, three set in a tier across my finger. His mother's, he claimed.

The lady must be beside herself.

I allowed Fanny and Mrs. Booth their ignorant bliss and spent the next hour composing a letter. *Dearest Teddy*, I wrote, and stared at the two words in my practiced script for a long time.

What could I say that would not seem as if I took a knife to his back?

I sighed. *I know you will think me foolish, and possibly even mad. Much has happened in the month since you departed for Tollybridge Court.*

I'd always loved the name of his family's rural estate.

The metal nib upon my quill scratched quietly in the parlor as I wrote the words I would never have imagined myself writing, and not in conjunction with the Northampton name.

Marriage. To think that only a month past, I stood in this very parlor and assured dear Teddy that I would not marry.

When I had little more to say that I had not covered in the previous four pages, I finished my letter with a plea.

Have faith, I scribed carefully, *when I tell you that I am doing what I believe is right and correct for myself and my house. You know as well as I the fate of a woman like myself in this, London's own Society. I am well, dear friend, and I am at peace with my decision. Please, do not fret on my account. We will still have our Wednesday debates, this I promise you. Although you may be forced to defend your theories against a countess, now.*

I signed it with my usual cordial address, and made sure Booth would find it to deliver to the post.

"Cherry," Fanny called, "'tis almost time for another fitting!"

Of course it was. Rubbing the back of my neck, I prepared for another lengthy—even endless—

session with the seamstresses who were to perfectly fit Madame Troussard's creation to me.

This marriage was no love match, as the papers claimed, but it was the right choice. My household would be stable, Fanny would be secure for all her days. I could find a harmony with my future husband, I was sure of it.

Love was the kind of vacuous emotional state that turned perfectly reasonable sorts into tragic figures. I had no need of it. I respected the earl, certainly. As a man, as an independent being of thought and reason.

It was enough.

Or so I convinced myself as the day of the wedding approached and I stood in front of the large mirror in the rooms the marchioness had graciously, if coolly, supplied. I rubbed my bruised wrist idly, aware that it ached at intervals and uncertain what to do about it. A splint, perhaps. Or was it too late, now? I should have seen a doctor when the pain was fresh.

Perhaps I would do so after the wedding.

Lady Northampton had not warmed to me. It was a burden I would be forced to carry until I could somehow right the rift between her and the memory of my mother.

A task for another time, I thought, and perhaps more knowledge.

Fanny flitted about me, arranging a fold of my gown just so, tucking a stray curl into place. She hummed cheerily, while Mrs. Booth dabbed at her eyes with a handkerchief and swore she'd never seen anything quite so pretty.

I stared at myself and confessed to the same.

I had never seen anything like the reflection I saw. Never imagined it to be me.

It wasn't.

I did not see Cherry St. Croix in that three-part mirror with its gilded frame and shimmering reflection. Cherry was a girl whose hair was always a little wild. Whose fingers were often stained with the ink of newspapers and periodicals.

Whose eyes often strayed to the books in the room, or the laudanum in its faceted crystal flagon.

This was someone else. Someone poised and polished, someone who had been covered with gold leaf and shined to perfection. Her hair was pinned to within an inch of its life, her gown pristine and perfect in every way. Her cheeks were a little pale, but I could sympathize with this gilt-framed stranger.

Was this what my mother had seen when she looked into the mirror on her wedding day? Had she fretted?

The gown Fanny and Madame Troussard had concocted was white, in the style of Her Majesty at her own wedding. I would have chosen something much less affluent and perhaps a darker color, but as I was to be a countess—a prospect that filled me ever so steadily with a mounting, fiercely guarded terror—it was decided that I would choose the fashion of the Queen over that of more common use.

The bodice was embroidered by gold thread, each stitch hand-sewn by the seamstresses whose faces I had learned to recognize even in my haunted dreams. White lace painted with gold leaf along each scalloped edge clung from neck to wrist, cascaded from my complex chignon with tamed curls arrayed on either side. The same gilt edged the bustle gathered tight at my waist and draped behind me.

I was, to be frank, sick of the stuff. If I never wore gold again, I would consider it a boon beyond measure.

I would not, as a countess, ever be so lucky.

My skirt, in a fashion Madame Troussard swore was just on the horizon—and so I would, rather shrewdly on Fanny's part, be considered the trend-setter for such a thing—remained tight to my thighs, shaping my figure in an hourglass whose base flared from my knees in ruffled white lace and chiffon.

I was white and gold; purity and wealth. I wore no jewelry but simple earbobs of white pearl. My silk stockings were embroidered up the front, and my delicate slippers rose my diminutive stature an inch in height.

Fanny met my gaze in the mirror, her own gown of smoky lavender only forcing a stark contrast between us.

The uncertainty I nursed in my stomach pitted sharply.

"You are beautiful," Fanny said. Tears filled her pale blue eyes. "Truly, I had always hoped to see this day."

"Oh, Fanny." I turned, enfolded her thin figure in my arms. She was taller than I, but she hunched so that we might hug companionably. Familiarly, as a mother and daughter might. Mrs. Booth burst into tears behind us, and I turned to smile upon the woman. "I could not ask for any set of family so kind as you have all been. The house will remain yours," I added firmly. "I'll hear nothing of it, Mrs. Booth."

"Yes, miss." She sniffed, and then added quickly, "My lady. Oh!" Another torrent of tears turned her plump cheeks red, and to my horror, my own eyes prickled in sympathetic warning.

I cast about me, twitching my skirt aside. When I attempted a step, however, I nearly pitched over.

Fanny steadied me. "Tiny steps," she chastised, "tiny or you'll fall."

"Of all the— Who came up with this fashion?" Swallowing the sharper invectives, I forced myself to take smaller steps, searching the suite. "Where is Zylphia?"

"Gone, and this on a day we need her most." Fanny sniffed.

"Gone?"

"She was not in when we prepared to go," Mrs. Booth added. "She'll turn up, I'm sure. Now, your veil."

Mrs. Booth, tucking aside her well-used handkerchief, wrestled the sweeping material of my veil into place. It was a task that required my own hands as well as hers.

A perfunctory knock at the door earned Fanny's attention.

Her gasp warned me before the Marchioness Northampton stepped inside.

As the mother of the groom, her gown was elegant and tasteful. She would command every eye, no matter the bride who claimed the day. It was a fact I simply accepted.

In a pastel orange, reminiscent of the orange blossoms holding the veil in my hair, she certainly commanded *my* attention.

Her cool gaze flicked over Fanny, Mrs. Booth, and dismissed them just as easily. "A moment of your time, Miss St. Croix."

"Granted," I allowed, drawing every ounce of composure I had ever possessed around me now. "What may I do for you, my lady?"

Fanny drifted away, a modicum of privacy. Mrs. Booth busied herself among the many boxes that comprised my trousseau.

"I cannot say that I am delighted by my son's decisions in this matter," came the lady's abrupt and matter-of-fact commencement.

I held my tongue, studying the woman through the patterned lace veil.

"I requested that he wait a full six months, perhaps even a year, and that banns be utilized, yet he has his own mind." The lady approached me, her thin mouth set in a recognizable line.

It bemused me, how like her the earl appeared.

And yet how unlike her he acted, in so many ways.

"I understand," was all I trusted myself to say.

"Do you?" Surprising me, she straightened a fold of my veil, arranged it easily and without fuss. "He has decided to wed you, and privately, with special license. People will talk, yet in this regard, I believe people will talk anyhow."

An olive branch?

I did not frown; it took all I had to refrain. "Your son is of great interest to Society," I said cautiously.

"Yes." The Marchioness Northampton stared at me, unblinking. "He is. Are you prepared for that life, Miss St. Croix?"

No. "I will do everything in my power to make your son proud, my lady," I murmured.

Her eyes narrowed. "My son is the least of your concerns. You will learn, I'm afraid. Let us hope you learn swiftly and with grace." She turned, then. "The ceremony begins shortly. Be ready. I would have this over without consequence."

That frigid— I bit my tongue. "Wait."

Lady Northampton paused, one hand on the door latch.

It was the only welcome I expected to receive. "My mother, my lady. Were you ever friends?"

Her mouth pinched. Then, as she glanced at me, I was surprised to find something like regret shaping her brow, her eyes. "Once. A very long time ago."

"What happened?"

Her jaw firmed, as near a scowl as I'd ever seen on the lady's visage. "A final note, as you are to be my daughter-in-law in a few short hours." I waited, held myself still. "This family will *not* tolerate scandal. Do not disappoint me in this."

The threat inherent in the low, chilly warning was clear enough.

She did not wait for my confirmation, sailing out with as much aplomb as she'd come in.

"Oh, dear," Fanny sighed. She hurried to me, plucked at this fold or that bit of seam. "Never fear, you're a bright, charming girl. She'll come around."

"Hurry, now," Mrs. Booth added seriously. "We can't be late to your own ceremony."

I balked. "Fanny, did you know?"

She did not pretend to misunderstand. "No," she said, and I had no reason to disbelieve her. "Remember, my dove, I was hired some years after your parents died, God rest their souls."

Yes. God rest them.

And keep them well away from me.

Wordless, I turned and strode—"Bloody hell," I hissed as my pace jerked too soon to a halt and I nearly pitched over once more. Reminded, I minced out of the chambers.

As much of a spectacle as the Earl Compton's wedding would have been, it relieved me to no end when he insisted on a private ceremony.

To that end, only sixty some odd guests filled the Northampton home for the event. A much smaller

number than the dinner parties and soirees I would
be expected to host as countess.

I watched it all as if I followed myself, studied
myself and those around me. As if it were a play.

A farce where I would turn to myself, wink and
spout off a flippant soliloquy of chance and circumstance.

It did not happen.

Mrs. Booth faded away, her task as servant done.
I followed my chaperone along the ornately decorated halls, so different from the exotic and foreign
flavoring of my own home. Everything in its place.

Everything touched by gold.

Like me.

The butterflies in my stomach turned to lead.
From lead to shards of glass.

I halted, every limb shaking. This was it. The end
of all things I had imagined I wanted.

Fanny, attuned to her charge on this very important day, stopped. Turned. "Cherry, come along."

I stared through the veiled white haze of my own
vision and could not will myself to take a step.

"Cherry?"

And then a masculine voice, one that shredded
through my haze of doubt and fear. "Cherry!"

I spun. "Teddy!"

"Oh, dear heaven," Fanny sighed, and closed the
distance between us as the Honorable Theodore
Helmsley stepped from a shrouded alcove.

My friend was not the most handsome bachelor in
Society, but his features and rail-thin build lent him
character I found lacking in most of the milquetoast
gentlemen of the elite. His face was comprised of
harsh planes and angles slightly off-center, his nose

more like a hooked blade, his build lanky. A mop of curly brown hair, cut just short enough to salve fashion's demands yet long enough to hint at the curl within, matched his eyes.

He was striking in his formal attire, black tailcoat and white bow tie, starched collar perfect. Yet he looked drawn, and lines I had not noticed before now worked into his brow and beside his mouth.

Ignoring Fanny's scandalized "My lord!" Teddy wrapped his arms around me, veil and gown and all.

Surprised, I returned his embrace warmly. "Teddy, I did not expect you."

"What else was I to do? I departed Tollybridge the instant I received your letter, I only arrived within the hour." He let me go, but his hands remained tight at my shoulders, gaze searching through the veil. "Cherry, are you sure this is what you want?"

"Did you come to attend my wedding," I teased, "or spirit me away on your white charger, Sir Knight?"

But he did not smile at my halfhearted attempt to ease the upset I read clear as day in his eyes. "Tell me this is what you truly want."

"Teddy." I took his hand from my shoulder, clasped it between mine. "You know as well as I the expectations levied upon a woman of my standing."

"Sod your standing!"

"Easily spoken," I replied ruefully, and with no small sting, "by a gentleman whose reputation places him in gaming hells and brothel halls alike with no consequence." I did not couch my words in gentleness.

But it was not anger I saw in his expression. "You are right, of course," he admitted, there a quick flash of the laconic grin I knew so well. "Yet, Cherry, if it were only reputation you worried for, I would have—"

I raised my hand, covered his mouth. "Don't," I warned softly. "Teddy, you are my very dear friend. Have faith that I know what I do."

Even if I, myself, could not.

His shoulders slumped. "Well." A pause, as if he searched for words.

"Cherry, hurry!"

I smiled up at him, my darling Teddy, and assured, "Wednesdays shall continue. I shan't let you off so easy."

"And if that rotter disagrees?"

"He'll be my rotter to disagree with," I replied archly, and let him go. "Go on, take your seat else you'll miss the service."

Like a schoolboy chastised for stepping out of line, he tucked his hands behind him. A smile, more than a touch lopsided and not quite echoed in his eyes, pulled at his lips. With a sketched bow, a shade of a formality, he turned and made his way through the waiting entry. "Mrs. Fortescue, you look enchanting," he murmured, pausing to offer the same formal courtesy.

She sniffed dismissively, but her eyes twinkled as she shooed him along.

It gave me the time I needed to take a deep breath. Hold it.

My nerves would not quell. The shade of white hovering around my vision was not all the lace, I was sure of it. My palms sweated; would they dampen the white gloves I wore? Would everyone see?

I flattened my palm at my corseted waist. "Breathe, Cherry," I said aloud. "Just breathe. There's a girl."

Marry your earl . . .

Because the life he gifted me with his name would be one of peace and provision. Of support and care.

The kind of life I had been born to before my father's madness took it all away.

Oh, God help me. I should have taken some of the laudanum before I left home. I should have smuggled the opium inside my reticule. I could not do this on my own.

My stomach spasmed; tingling sensations vibrated to my fingertips.

"My dove?"

I turned, met Fanny's searching, gentle smile. What would I say?

What could I say that would not make a fool of myself, and the earl to whom I'd committed?

I inclined the heavy weight of my own head.

Taking as deep a breath as my stays allowed, I took my final steps to the garlanded entry, and whispered, *"Allez, hop."*

•

The ceremony became an excruciating torture. Too long. Too solemn.

And then it was over. The earl raised the veil from my face, clearing my vision of the dense fog that had shrouded it for hours. A ring weighed on my finger, a beautifully elegant gold band almost too wide to sit demurely.

His lips touched mine, a chaste kiss. I forgot to breathe.

We walked out without looking right or left, as tradition demanded, yet I was aware of the eyes heavy upon me. My legs trembled.

Do not falter.

Somehow, we made it through the reception. The

cake was cut, the blur of faces around me lost in a sea of tremors and nerves.

Because we would travel immediately after, Fanny took me away after the cake to dress me more appropriately for the journey.

"Where am I going?" I asked as Fanny and Mrs. Booth hurried to attend my dress.

"Nobody knows but the younger Lord Compton," Fanny said sternly, "as is customary of the best man."

"That seems—" I stopped, my gaze pinned upon the vanity I'd used only hours ago to prepare for the ceremony. "What the devil is that?"

Both of the women paused to study the display. Hairbrushes, tongs left and papers singed and discarded. Bits of ribbon.

And a single red rose.

"A gift, it would appear," offered Fanny.

My chest tightened. "So it would seem," was what I managed, when what I truly wanted was to grab the offending flower by its delicate bloom and crush it.

I hadn't seen a rose for nearly a month. What did it mean?

"I understand the young Lord Compton has managed quite the secrecy." Mrs. Booth spoke conspiratorially, her rosy cheeks gleaming, smile wide. "Not even my Mr. Booth knows where you're going. It sounds quite romantic, doesn't it?"

Secrecy. My gaze dragged from the flower, pinned on Fanny with barely concealed distress. "If we don't know where I'm going, what am I to do of my night terrors? I can't—" My sudden panic halted my chaperone, my friend, and she took my hand in hers and squeezed gently.

"Mrs. Booth made certain that all you would need

is packed," she informed me, so seriously that I breathed a touch easier for it. "Hurry, now, mustn't keep them waiting."

And hurry we did. Soon, I found myself outfitted in a lovely new traveling gown of dark brown poplin, bustled and corseted to within an inch of my life, with my hairpins tightened and my gloves in place. A top hat in black sat pertly upon my upswept hair, its gathered net providing a bit of pouf around the band and draped over my features.

Fanny hugged me tightly. "We'll see you soon," she whispered, brushing my cheek with a kiss.

"Toss that," I ordered, a withering glance at the flower.

She only shook her head, rueful resignation. I would forever avoid her complete understanding, I think.

Then I was given no more time. Whisked away in a gondola draped by white silk and garlands, I could not help my surprised laugh as rice and satin slippers sailed after us.

The sound died as the earl—my husband—met my eyes directly for the first time in what seemed like hours.

Too much kneeling. Too many prayers.

Too much demand.

Now Lord Compton, the earl to my newly bestowed countess, sat in the back of the gondola beside me, resplendent in his dark navy morning coat, his striped trousers in charcoal and pale gray gloves. His own top hat was larger than mine, of course, and lent him a stately air.

And oh, he was handsome. With his sandy hair swept aside and his green eyes so forthright upon mine.

I stilled.

The gondolier, a proper sort that I could only assume had come from the earl's own house, kept his focus on the canals we floated along. We were, for all intents and purposes, alone.

Finally.

I swallowed hard. "M-my lord?"

Awkward, as if even he was not sure of the formalities of the moment, he took the hand I fisted against the seat. Smoothed out my fingers and did not comment at how visibly they shook. "It is time," he began slowly, "for you to use my name." A hesitation, the sound of a heartbeat. Mine. Stuttered. "Cherry. My wife."

I sucked in a shaking breath. "I . . . Of course." I licked my dry lips; he studied the gesture. And I was not mistaken when I recognized a certain banked flame lit beneath his so-calm exterior.

He found me attractive as a woman, I recognized that. But would it help? Would it matter?

Relentless, cautious but inarguable, he drew me closer on the seat. His fingers twined with mine. "Must I be injured to hear it from your lips, my lady?"

I did not flinch, though I came close enough that I stiffened. The length of his body against the side of mine was alien. Uncertain. I shook my head, looking away, but no words came.

His gloved fingers cupped my cheek. Not the oft-times cruel grip of Hawke's demand, but gentler. Coaxing. I had no choice but to turn my head until I faced him.

The corners of his mouth tilted. "We are married now," he reminded me, "and away to our honeymoon. There is no need to be quite so formal just yet."

And with no more word than this, no more warning than the glint in his eyes, he leaned down and touched his mouth to mine.

The shudders I'd entertained all day long intensified. A flash of something almost painful seared from the inside out, and I gasped. The fingers at my cheek tightened. Loosened just as fast, and slid instead to my nape.

My eyes closed as my husband's lips brushed over mine. As his mustache tickled the sensitive skin of my upper lip, and I inhaled the breath he exhaled. My mind spiraled.

I was married now.

I would have the rest of my life to learn how to handle the earl who had become my husband.

He did not deepen the kiss, did not plunge his tongue between my lips as I knew a truly passionate kiss would require. Instead, as if he gathered himself, he drew just far enough away that he could lean his forehead against mine.

I licked the warmth of him from my lips. "Where are we to go on our honeymoon?" I asked, my voice a dry rasp.

Again, that faint smile. That twitch of the corners of his mouth, crinkled around his eyes as they opened to meet mine. " 'Tis a secret," he told me.

One that piqued my interest mightily as the fog we drifted across eventually began to rise above the rim.

The earl offered me a small, familiar box.

This time, as I took the beautiful French fog-protectives from its velvet nest, I smiled. "What would you have done had I sent back your gift?" I asked, sounding much more the thing.

His mouth compressed. "I approve that you did not," is all he replied.

I fell silent as I clipped the device to my nose.

Chapter Twenty-three

The gondola touched ground, and the driver stepped off his perch. I raised my eyebrows. "My lord?"

"We must change transport," the earl explained, stepping down the attached ladder and offering me his hand. When I took it, the warmth I saw beneath his stiff formality removed some of the nerves I anticipated.

The fog was thick today, turning the daylight into something resembling evening. We were somewhere past the square, at the point where a gondola would bring more undue attention than not. This deep into the fog-ridden streets, it became a matter of ease, simplicity and safety to acquire a hackney or a horse-drawn affair.

"Is it safe?" I inquired, as if I weren't capable of handling both myself *and* the earl, if it came to it.

We were, as I recalled, not quite mired in any one territory. The gangs wouldn't be so close, but that left footpads or the like.

Even pedestrian traffic seemed all but nonexistent.

The perfect place for an ambush.

My mind wandered to a single red rose on my vanity, and I straightened, studying the fog with a caution bred of too many years spent within it.

"I can stay until the carriage arrives," offered the driver, an average-appearing sort with blond hair and earnest brown eyes. His livery was much fancier than anything commonly found below.

Likely as much a target as we were.

"Thank you, Laurence, I'm sure the next transport shall be arriving soon." Dismissed by the earl, who perhaps shared my view of the man's monetary appeal, Laurence bobbed his acquiescence and climbed back into his gondola.

I watched him leave with some trepidation.

Then started in surprise as warm arms wrapped around me from behind. I looked down at the earl's embrace, turned so that I could read his features. They were still so set.

So cautious.

Was it me? Was it that I was not welcoming?

I rested my fingertips on his chest; he tensed. The look in his eye suggested I'd done right by it. "Are we perfectly safe?"

"I've brought a pistol, just in case." Admiration for the man grew. "Fret not, Countess. 'Until death do us part,' recall? I will protect you until my last breath, as befits a countess."

I could not help my grin. "And how long until then, my lord?"

"So eager to be rid of your husband already?" His fingers laced around me, a cage by which I would be held for the duration of our vows.

My breath hitched. My throat closed.

And a whistle filtered tunelessly through the fog.

I blinked rapidly. "Of course not," I demurred. "How else am I to lay claim to your library of books?" Yet my gaze strayed to the fog swirling and roiling around us, coal-ridden black and streaked in yellow from the struggling gas lamps.

That whistle . . . A red rose, and now a whistle from somewhere beyond.

My heart clamored. *It couldn't be.*

I pulled away from the earl, shaking out my traveling skirts as excuse. Yet I studied the street beside us as it vanished into the pea souper claiming the sound.

A whistle in the dark.

Fear drove me to take a step to the curb.

"Cherry?"

"Just looking at the view," I lied. My eyes raked across what little there was to see. Buildings lost in the shroud, the whole of the street eaten by it. My heart shuddered in my chest.

There.

A shape. A shadow! A man's figure, hat pulled low, coat collar turned up high.

He was back.

Worse, he knew where I was. Where the earl was.

The silhouette I studied turned, hesitated and looked over his shoulder. And that whistle, that damnable whistle!

A challenge. The murderer Zylphia and her fellow sweets called the sweet tooth for his killing of several of them *challenged me*. The murderer of my father.

The collector I'd thought gone in the weeks of silence.

Not gone at all.

This would not stand.

"I shall return," I said over my shoulder, and darted into the fog.

"Cherry!" The earl's call lashed after me, surprise, anger. I ignored it, forging through the mist with only the French spectacles to protect me.

I could handle the collector. I *was* a collector. Armed or otherwise, I knew how to track a man, and I would hunt this one down.

Hunt him, and then take from him my pound of flesh!

The whistle drew me deeper into the district, teasing, taunting; he knew what it did to me. The memory, shrouded in the vague sort of oblivion that comes with opium use, still haunted my dreams.

I would not allow him to haunt me.

"Cease your running," I called. The fog shifted, revealing a lamppost flickering mightily against the damp. I spun. "Come out!"

A whistle in the dark . . . A tuneless thing, a lazy drift of sound.

I hiked up my skirts as a shadow darted just out of sight, lowered my head and sprinted like mad for my quarry.

Perhaps he did not expect a frontal attack. Perhaps he had not realized how close I was in the drift.

Perhaps I was meant to catch him.

All of these things collided in my brain as I leapt at the narrow back fleeing from me. We fell to the street in a tangle of limbs and curses, and seizing my opportunity—sucking a breath through the pain of elbows and knees jammed against damp cobble—I wrenched off the low-pulled bowler hat.

"Don't 'urt me!" begged a voice too young to be more than fifteen, perhaps less. On the brink of becoming a man, it cracked in terror.

I scrambled off him. "Where is he?" I demanded, already convinced this was not my true quarry.

The youth scrabbled backward on all fours, like an awkward animal. "I dunno," he pleaded, "ye gotta believe me, miss!"

I took a step forward, fists clenched. *"Where?"*

"'E just paid me to put on that bleedin' 'at and whistle!"

Blast! I spun, searching for any signs. Had he watched, laughing? Had he sprinted after me, a merry jester with the upper hand?

No.

A gunshot echoed across the smoke-filled streets.

My heart stopped. Time ceased to move. In that fraction of a moment, I understood.

"Cornelius," I breathed, and ran. Somehow, perhaps the years I'd spent combing much of the city, my feet knew the direction my brain could not fathom. Every step screamed in my head; every second an eternity of torture.

I ran harder, faster than I had ever run, in or out of a skirt, and it wasn't fast enough.

The collector had let me chase his decoy in the dark.

I stumbled out of an alley shortcut, caught myself against the brick facing and sucked in a raw breath at the sight that greeted me.

Two figures, long of form, wrapped in great-coats against the chill. They leaned against each other, two silhouettes merged into one. The guttering lamp overhead painted each in flickering light and shadow; I saw only a hat pulled low. A top hat knocked free, shading sandy hair in depths of gold.

"Cornelius!" I screamed.

One figure separated from the other.

One clung to the lamppost behind him.

The first turned to me. I saw nothing, only shoulders and a gesture impossible to read in the faux night. But I could not misapprehend the words. "Weep for the widowed bride," he spat, a masculine taunt that ripped my scream from the air and hammered it to a death of swallowed echoes.

"What the—" Another man's voice, terse and baffled. And then, three strode from the fog—workingmen, factory laborers gauging from coal-stained skin and clothing. All three stilled.

And then one broke into a run. "Hey! Hey, you!"

The other two hurried to the fallen earl; I had no breath for further words. No thought for safety. I raced across the street, my lungs ready to burst from the constricting stays, and could not follow when the silhouette faded into the dark.

The earl slumped to the damp sidewalk beneath him. His skin, ghastly pale in the sickly light, gleamed wetly. The men bent over him, I shoved one aside.

"Oi, lady, you can't—"

"He's my husband!" Oh, God. *Oh, God!* I fell to my knees, gloved hands hovering over his shoulders, his head, his waist. "Are you hurt? Are you all right? Cornelius!"

His breath guttered in his chest. Grimly, hastily, I tore at his coat buttons. Flinched when his features constricted in agony, his staggered breath choked. His gaze clouded with it.

"Cor," whispered the heavyset one. "Get the doctor, mate. Hurry!" His friend darted into the fog.

"Please," I sobbed, tears thick in my throat. Burning my eyes. "Please, don't—oh, God." My gloves came away crimson, obscenely bright against the tan fabric. So much of it, warm on my skin; too wet, too much. "No, no, this isn't—I never—!"

A hand touched my shoulder. "Dr. Lattimer'll be right along. Lives on this street."

Not soon enough. The earl's legs shifted as if he struggled to stand. It wouldn't help. As I covered the gaping wounds in his chest, as I pushed hard and moaned with his ragged, garbled sound of pain, I knew it wouldn't matter.

"Please!" I screamed. "Hurry!"

"Jesus have mercy."

"Ch-Cherry," he whispered. Blood flecked his lips.

The tears ran hot and blinding as I lowered my forehead to his. "Don't die," I ordered. Begged. "Cornelius Kerrigan Compton, you *will not die on me.*"

A quirk at the corner of his mouth. A drop of blood, a series of bubbles blown on his uneven exhale. One hand encircled my nape. Too heavy.

But if he meant to say anything, if he meant to tell me anything at all, he could not.

A lung, I thought hysterically. The knife wounds had gone deep. Two, three. They spilled blood in a growing pool, soaked into my skirt, my hands.

The ground beneath us.

The knife, nearly a straight razor but for the point and hilt, not a yard from us.

Rage carried each blow. Terrible, black fury. Why? For God's sake, *why?*

Footsteps pounded on the street.

"This way," yelled my sympathetic witness.

Too late. All too late. I sobbed as Earl Compton's gaze drifted from mine. Clouded.

"Out of the way," blustered a new voice, old but not worn.

Hands grabbed my shoulders. Voices lifted. The fog wafted across it all.

Surrounded by strangers, everything ended.

I did not recall losing consciousness.

I sat in my bed and did not look up when Fanny stepped inside. I had been sitting up for an eternity; I did not eat the food they laid for me. I did not touch the tea.

I stared into the darkened room of my boudoir, lavender and rose dulled to gray and brown, and I said nothing of the pain ravaging me from the inside. Of the voices clamoring for my attention.

Of the accusations weighed upon my soul.

Until death do us part. For all my bravado and claimed skill, how quickly I had allowed that condition to come to pass.

Fanny tiptoed around me. Mrs. Booth whispered even when she thought I was asleep.

It had been . . . some days, perhaps, since my lord husband passed on. The doctor, bless his soul, could do nothing for him.

I could do nothing.

"Come, now, my dove," crooned my chaperone—now simply my friend, as I was a widow with no need for a chaperone.

A widow who'd seen her husband dead before the honeymoon had even started.

I knew the talk. I did not hear it, I did not have to. I spoke it aloud. I whispered it to myself in the darkness and the night. I did not rise from my bed, and I did not leave it but to tend to my business.

And even that I did as if from a distance. A shell, shocked beyond all reason. Beyond understanding.

I could not even reach myself.

Was this what the ghost of my mother had seen as my father toiled all those years? The ruined shell of her widower husband, mindlessly working to restore what was his.

Yet I did not work to restore anything. There was nothing *to* restore. There was only vengeance. A man to unmask; a murderer to hunt, like the mangy beast he was.

Weep for the widowed bride.

I did not look at Fanny. I did not smile. I did not do anything with the tea she placed in my hands, cradled in my lap.

I stared into the dusty shadows and saw them painted crimson. Heard the death rattle of a man who could not even say his final words.

My doing. I had left him for the collector to find. I had sprinted from his side with vengeance in my heart, pride riding me for insults delivered.

I'd as good as killed the man who'd sworn to protect me until his last breath.

How little he knew.

Fanny took the tea from my unresponsive fingers and placed it on my nightstand. Gone, the bottle of laudanum—packed in the luggage Lord Piers had delivered to the HMS *Ophelia*. My belongings had not been retrieved yet, waiting to be rescued from its sad and tragic little misadventure that ended so abruptly before it had begun.

My lord husband had remembered my fascination with the Queen's own flagship. He'd remembered the conversation so long ago, when first we'd met.

He'd booked passage on the sky ship's maiden voyage. Just us and the crew.

I could not cry. I had no tears to shed.

Only a fierce, boiling anger, numbing all it burned away.

"How is she?" Mrs. Booth's whisper. Always, a whisper.

"The same, poor thing," Fanny replied.

Tearfully, Mrs. Booth sniffed. "The marchioness is threatening litigation—"

"*Sod* the marchioness," Fanny hissed.

I did not smile.

Booth's uneven tread outside my door. "I've written to the master," he said, quiet as his polished baritone allowed. "I expect a reply any—" *Click*.

Now they were only mumbles through my door. Concerned, worried, frightened.

Sad.

I felt none of these things.

I did not move for another hour, at least. Perhaps longer. The shadows shifted subtly with the day.

Murderer.

Silently, I leaned over, jammed my hand beneath the mattress. The small, wax-wrapped bundle came easily to my grasp. Zylphia had brought it to me sometime in the past day. Perhaps to coax something of a response from me.

I sat up once more, looked down at the palm-size parcel.

Weep for the widowed bride.

Not today. Perhaps not ever. I unwrapped the waxen paper, looked down at the small selection of gummy opium tar.

My laudanum had been packed.

But I did not want laudanum now.

Murderer!

Quietly, wordlessly, I took a small square of the resin and placed it on my tongue.

The bitter taste seared through ice, burned through the dead husk that was all I'd become.

I grimaced; the first expression I'd managed for days.

The juices mingled now with my saliva. Tricked down my throat in tingling currents of warmth.

And then I swallowed.

Opium tar would relieve the shock, my scientist's brain assured me. And when the shock wore off, it would deaden the pain.

And when the pain was no longer so great that I could not breathe, then it would be time to stoke the fires of fury and collect a murderer.

No matter the cost.

Chapter Twenty-four

Blood splattered across a cheek pale as fine china and as dainty as the same. Crimson streaks left tracks where his pleading tears had not dried. "Please!" he begged, "I don't know nothin'!"

Sweet Tom Billings had sometimes worked for me on occasion, but mostly he worked for the hand with the right coin. Beneath his femininely delicate features lived a mind as cunning as a rat's, with every bit the instinct to survive and none of the animal's more delicate sensibilities. Sewage or carnage, coin was coin, and Sweet Tom would no sooner turn a nose at one than go hungry for the other.

Which did not explain why he dared brave the collectors' sanctum. We were not known for our tolerance of outsiders, and I was in *no* mood to play.

To that end, I held him now, pinned against the wall beside the collectors' bounties, my knuckles raw and aching. I didn't mind the pain of bones ground against flesh. It was something more real than the soul-deep promise of something a thousand times less civilized hovering in the back of my thoughts. Waiting.

Hungry.

Opium dulled the beast. Just enough that I could think through the bloody film saturating my mind. My fist tightened in Sweet Tom's collar, my other held threateningly back, elbow cocked. "Don't nose me about, Sweet Tom," I hissed. "You're no collector. Or have you cast an eye up in the world?"

He cringed, pushing up high on his toes as he could, his hat trod under my own boot and his scarf tangled up in the collar I clenched. His head wobbled, shoulders desperately flattened against the damp brick as if seeking a way through the pitted stone and away from me. Whatever mask shaped my face, it paled the boy's own, until the whites of his eyes shone yellow-tinged in the lamplight from his turned over lantern.

When I'd come to the collectors' station, I hadn't expected to find anyone mulling over the bounties posted. I certainly would never have expected a noncollector, especially Sweet Tom.

If he'd gone collector, I'd eat his scarf.

"Answer me!"

"Was sorted out!" he squeaked as his scarf tightened dangerously about his skinny throat. His eyes, always pretty in a way that put me in mind of a cat's, were slowly going lopsided beneath the shiner I'd given. "Paid right good to come by, find a notice. That's all!"

"And you're one who can read," I finished for him. "What notice?"

"Anything what demands a toppin'." A murder, then.

I bared my teeth at him. "For who?" I saw it on his

features before he even opened his mouth to deny me. I thrust my face into his, smelled the copper tang of the blood leaking from his nose, an acrid trace of wine and a whiff of something both spicy and sharp. My eyes narrowed. *"Vin Mariani."*

His fingers scrabbled into the wall behind him.

I glowered from underneath the brim of my cap. The brand of coca wine was one of those much beloved by Her Majesty and Pope Leo XIII, and too expensive to be found on the breath of guttersnipes of any stripe. "Where did you receive the coin, Sweet Tom?"

"What?" He laughed, a mawkish thing that showed at least three blackened teeth and a sickly yellow tinge to his gums. "No, that's not—"

Crack. My hand stung with the impact, but the heavy cloud of opium enfolding me soothed it away just as quick.

"Some bloke!" he screeched, thrashing now in my grip. His knee collided with mine, sending a dulled rush of pain and awareness to the part of my mind still aware of things. A quiet part. One I silenced mercilessly.

"Who?" I demanded. "A name, Sweet Tom, and I'll let you limp off to a dollymop's mercies."

Fat tears rolled out of the frightened man's eyes. The fingers wrapped around my wrist bit, but Sweet Tom was no scrapper, and well he and I both knew it. "He never gave no name, you got to believe me!"

I gritted my teeth. "What'd he look like?"

"Hat and coat and a real quiet voice," my reluctant informant revealed. "But it were real dark! He said he needed a clever eye and quick hand and more's the coin for silence." Each word stoked that eager hunger within me, and I stared at him for a long moment, tracing the trickle of blood leaking from his left nostril.

When his eyebrows twisted together, a wince shaping his face as he drew his head back far from me as the wall and my grip allowed, I realized that I was smiling up into Sweet Tom's terrified face.

I didn't ease the expression. I wanted to laugh outright, but muffled it to ask, "How long?"

"Eh?"

I gave him a shake, the kind street mongrels the world over learned quickly to interpret. "How long have you been fetching bounties for him?"

"Just started!" He swallowed hard enough that I felt the bob of his throat against my knuckles; heard the sound it made as he forced his dry throat to cooperate. "Please, miss, I'm just a gonoph, don't know nothin'."

My smiled widened. "That's where you're wrong, Sweet Tom. Do you have plans to meet this benefactor of yours again?"

"No, miss. I just pick up the notes what look right and leave 'em where he wants."

"Where?"

"Whitechapel Station," he told me, and even as he spoke, the image of the fog-filled rail yard rose like a specter in front of me. Whitechapel, the Ripper's own haunt and prime ground for the collector I hunted. "Just by the first gate, there's an old postbox what don't get used none."

"When were you to deliver?" I asked, sweet for all I hadn't let him go.

I was sure he recognized that fact. Smart lad, he said nothing about it. "Midnight," he whispered. "Stroke of it by the bell."

My cheeks ached from the width of my smile.

"Good," I assured him, although I'm positive the menace by which the word slipped from me did nothing of the sort. "You're a good sort, Sweet Tom. Do be wandering, now. If I learn you're lying, I'll find you soon enough."

"But—" A sickly sheen coated his sallow skin. "But if I don't fetch his notes, he'll kill me!"

"You think?" I let him go, straightening his scarf and patched fustian jacket as tenderly as his own mother might, if she'd ever cared. "Then keep low, mate, and if you're lucky, neither him nor the collectors will find you."

The smile he summoned looked ill, but he wasted no breath arguing. Hurrying from the hallowed grounds—which I was rather more certain he'd never attempt to trod upon again—he left a drifting wake of coal-stuffed yellow in his path.

My own smile faded as if it'd never been.

The bounties posted were the usual sorts, though a bit scarce. They'd pick up again before Christmas, they always did. Not much Yuletide spirit to go around when coin was the concern.

I'd already found nothing of interest. Nothing, at least, of interest specifically to me.

I sought a different quarry tonight.

Whitechapel Station, then? I wondered why there. As I snuffed Sweet Tom's lost lantern and adjusted the protective seam of my fog-prevention goggles around my eyes, I ran the facts as I'd learned them through my head. A bloke rich enough to pay a man like Sweet Tom enough to afford the coca wine he'd always been a lush for, one who looked for murder and assassination dispatches over the rest.

It was possible that I could be dealing with one of the London above collectors, but none ever engaged in more than a simple shaking of the merchant tree, or so I'd heard. To think of any of the three Society collectors as murderers was to laugh outright.

I knew all three lordlings, at least in passing. One had offered for my hand in desperate bid for wealth, two pretended I didn't exist. I could send any one of them pissing his drawers with a calculated word and minimal effort.

None would dare risk so much as a scrape, much less life or limb, on a dispatch request. And certainly none would dare murder an earl. No, I knew who'd done that; I still shuddered if I so much as fancied the whisper of a whistle in the gloom.

A part of me hoped he followed me now.

A part of me craved blood, just as surely as he'd spilled it in my lap.

I fished in my jacket pocket, fingers wrapping around the small wedge of wax paper I'd stuffed there before I left. I'd forgotten my respirator, but I'd pocketed the tar ball.

That should have bothered me.

Yet, rather than dwell on it, just before I stepped into the dark street, I unwrapped the sticky resin from its protective covering, bit a corner and grimaced at the first acrid taste of it on my tongue.

I would find this man, this monster. I would start with Sweet Tom's mysterious benefactor.

God help anyone in my way.

Which seemed likely, as I crossed out of the collectors' station and picked my way to Whitechapel. It took time, more than I liked but less than I expected. Not a soul crossed my path, not working girl nor footpad. Not even the shadow of those who spent their evenings trolling the streets for coin or company.

I floated as formless as the devil-fog that carried me adrift upon it. The opium I'd swallowed turned every sound into a symphony of the night. Where I did not see shadows, I heard voices. Where they lifted, they seemed like a hosanna. I felt uplifted and righteous; I felt guided and sublime.

I was neither Cherry St. Croix nor Miss Black, but a woman on a path of virtue and justice.

Opium has always done so much for me. This was simply another step taken, another benefit to a habit that had comforted me through the long nights and difficult times. And yet, as I continued to nibble corners off the tar ball, I failed to understand what would be made all the clearer soon enough: that there would, in time, be a price.

My sanity had already begun to pay.

The Westminster bell rang the eleven o'clock warning just as I arrived at the rail yard. It took no time at all to locate the postbox Sweet Tom had indicated, and even less time to find a place in the shadows from whence I could watch. For the next hour, I sat in the cold and damp and inhaled the bitter fog, succored myself with a bit of the Chinese tar when the cold proved too strong, and entertained myself with all the ways I would enact my revenge upon the soon-to-be-surprised collector when he came.

As Big Ben's sonorous chime tolled the midnight hour, I did not give up.

As my skin turned damp and my body began to shiver, I watched the postbox with its crooked, sad little numbers and started now and again when a particularly dense weft of fog rolled past. My fingers twitched from within the gloves I'd pulled on, the index finger of one gnawed off because it'd given me something to do, and allowed for easier access to the paper in my pocket.

My heart pounded in slow, rhythmic assurance that I, at least, was still where I expected to be, but slowly the fog thickened. Slowly, the tar shrank, little by little, until my tongue burned and my vision was beginning to blur from the hours as they passed. The one o'clock bell, and then two more.

Pain spiked through my temples; when had I started gritting my teeth?

By the three o'clock bell, my legs had gone numb, and my heart followed suit. I stared blankly into the yellow-black fog, my working lens highlighting the postbox in a corona that I wasn't positive actually existed, but who was I to worry? I could see it perfectly. Waiting. Undisturbed. Unapproached.

I should move. Return home, but I waited.

What was there for me to find above? A house swathed in black crepe. Fanny watching me with such sorrow in her eyes.

A dead husband.

So I stayed. Long after the rain had started and I was soaked to the flesh, long after the five o'clock bells chimed and the fog began to lighten as a cold wind ghosted through.

I stayed and watched an empty, lonely postbox, because I knew what it was like to feel the same.

Sometime between one breath and the next, lost in the opium mist swaddling me, I fell asleep.

" 'Ey! 'Ey, what about me pay?"

I startled awake at the shrill demand, found one foot in the air and pitched over. I had a brief glimpse of the yawning void between the gangplank of the

Scarlet Philosopher and the dock it berthed beside before I collided with the dock facing. The air slammed out of me, knocking any words I'd intended right out of my head.

"'Ere, now," bellowed the captain, hurrying across the gangplank. Three large men closed the gap within seconds, their faces a blur as I struggled to stand. "You all righ', then?"

"Yes!" I gasped, meaning anything but. The docks swirled around me; the men leered, though when I squinted, I was sure I saw only concern and, rightfully so, anger.

"Be careful, lad!" one barked, angry at the scare, I imagine, and the wasted time.

"You sure?" said the captain, grabbing my arm. Did I sway? I must have. He frowned at me, his fleshy jowls wobbling. "Need me t' whistle down some 'ackney?"

"Gondola," I whispered, and shrugged off his hand. I locked my knees with force of will alone, squinted to find myself atop the docks where I usually alighted after a night below.

How did I get here?

The men stalked off, cursing, while Captain Abercott grunted. "You didn't pay me nuffin'," he accused. "Cough up."

"'Course." My throat felt dry and swollen. My mind numb, sluggish. I patted my pockets, found the empty bit of wax paper and a bit of lint. I frowned at it, certain there'd been tar left over only a few hours prior.

I must have looked utterly pathetic, because for the first time in our acquaintance—possible even in his miserable life—Captain Abercott showed mercy. He took his hands from his rotund hips and sighed a blustery, less-than-gracious sigh. "Get on, then. Guess y'pay well 'nuff fer a spot or two. But no more!" he barked, the effect somewhat ruined by the tufted fringe poking out from around his jaunty sailor's cap.

I blinked. "I . . . Right. On, then."

"Barmy," I heard as I turned my back on the mysterious sky ferry I didn't remember taking.

Barmy. Crazy, he meant, and perhaps rightfully so. The last I'd known, I'd been studying a postbox. How did I arrive at the *Scarlet Philosopher*?

And what time was it?

Late enough, I realized, that stumbling home on the walkways would net more attention than not. It took a great deal of effort, and my head began to ache fiercely, but I managed to find my way home to Chelsea, and the Cheyne Walk house festooned in the black crepe of mourning.

I walked as if I'd never left the fog below, found my way through the familiar steps by sheer habit more than attention. I was sure I looked a fright: a street boy from below capped by dirt and soot, likely looking as if I'd more than enough of the hair of the dog even this early. Yet as I approached through the hedgerows, I heard no hue and cry, saw no sign of Fanny waiting.

Was it possible that it was still early enough that she had not checked upon me in my mourning bed?

The gray light and chill air wasn't enough to tell me what time it was, and I'd not thought to bring my pocket watch. A first, for I never left home without.

The ladder I'd left from my window was still in evidence. I darted through the yard, ready to seize the knotted rungs and begin my climb, exhausted though I was.

"This is uncivilized!"

Fanny's words. Her voice, tight and shrill; icy as I'd ever heard her.

And outside?

I stilled, glancing left to right. There were no bodies in sight, no ghosts even. I could not blame my hearing on opium dreams today.

"Be that as it may," came a voice I didn't recognize, "it is all perfectly legitimate."

"Legitimate," spat my once-chaperone. " 'Tis ungodly, that's what it is! Turning us out without so much as a warning. You have no right!"

Turning us out?

It took me too long, but I realized the voice came from around the house. I should have climbed the ladder, dressed myself in appropriate garb for a morning's repast interrupted, and gone to see what the fuss was about, but I didn't. Too much effort. Instead, I trailed across the browning grass, past the windows I marked as the sitting room, the kitchens, and to the corner where I flattened myself against the siding and strained to hear.

"I assure you," intoned the snooty, educated voice I decided then and there I didn't like, "all is perfectly legal and proper. This residence belongs now to the Marquess and Marchioness Northampton to dispose of as they see fit. My lady's orders are quite concise—"

"Orders!" Fanny's impassioned repetition flew in the face of every propriety she'd ever hammered into me. "This home belongs to Miss St. Croix, and no other."

"Upon whose marriage to the late earl, God rest him—"

I closed my eyes.

"—ensured that all of her estates now belong to his heirs. To wit, my Lord and Lady Northampton. She may stay in residence, as is expected of a lady in mourning, but you, Mrs. Fortescue, and all staff are hereby dismissed."

"But what of her well-being?"

Yes. What *of* my well-being? I leaned around the corner, hugged it to study the tableau arrayed in front of the once-fashionable Cheyne Walk residence. Oh, if only society could see us now. The Mad St. Croix's daughter, spying on her staff and once-chaperone as they faced down a *perfectly legal* magistrate.

The man squaring off against the very indignant Fanny was dressed as every bureaucratic, pompous official I'd ever met. His tailor was topnotch, certainly, but the colors he chose clashed rather garishly in reds and brilliant yellows. Fanny, in black as befitting a house of mourning, stood in front of Booth, who was very stiff in his shared indignation. Tucked behind his shoulder clung Mrs. Booth, already tearfully expecting the worst.

An empty cart waited behind the officious mouthpiece of the marchioness, surrounded by four men wearing the Northampton livery.

"My Lady Northampton will see that Her Ladyship, the countess, receive one servant in her time of mourning," came the nasal intonation. "She will be well cared for as is expected. Once mourning is adjourned, all living arrangements shall be revisited, with a dower house already set aside in the country for her use." His beaklike nose lifted into the air. "Now, if you'll excuse me—"

I rested my forehead against the siding, squeezed my eyes shut. My throat continued to ache, a vicious burning sinking deeper into my chest with every word. Clever, vicious woman. By all rights, she had the legal authority to do exactly this. With my estate now belonging to the earl's family, it would be thought nothing at all untoward if I vanished from Society for upward of a year.

And then retired, the mournful widow, to a reclusive country estate somewhere. Packed away, like a meddlesome object, or a dowager long past her prime.

I would not be easily forgiven for my lord husband's death.

Fair enough. I would not easily forgive myself.

"Mr. Ashmore will require his things," Fanny snapped. "Not all inside is yours to claim."

"All of Mr. Oliver Ashmore's things shall be accounted for." I could hear the pandering smile in every word, even if I didn't see it. "Truly, you would not wish the countess to be bothered with such a task in her grief?"

There was a short, charged silence.

"All servants who leave quietly," wheedled the man whose tone suggested he was in control and knew it, "will receive excellent letters of recommendation from the marchioness."

"We are not hers to let go," Booth said, so solemnly that was left of my heart shattered into a thousand pieces at my feet. The ache intensified, until I found myself swallowing often and licking my lips.

I needed something to take the strain off. A bit of laudanum.

A touch more opium.

Fanny sighed. "Then we are only guests, and she is free to turn us out. Step aside, Booth. Mrs. Booth, collect your things."

"But what of my lady?" demanded Booth, his dear voice now a whisper of pain inside my head.

How easily Lady Northampton had worked this all out. The marchioness's mercy.

I would have none, myself.

I squeezed my eyes shut tighter as Fanny said softly, "I will wake her and explain. Mr. Ashmore has been summoned, my dear Mrs. Booth, fret not."

The door opened. I heard the hinges creak ever so slightly, heard Booth's *step-thunk* as he crossed the threshold.

"Good," sniffed the mouthpiece of the woman I was coming to loathe almost as much, I was certain, as she loathed me. "Prepare to load the cart. You! Boy!"

I started at the shrill command, raised my head from the siding and stared at the beady eyes pinned to me.

My fists clenched.

"Don't just stand there," the magistrate demanded. "Fetch any of your other . . ." His lips twisted. "Staff," was the best he could garner, "and help load the cart."

My jaw shifted. "Sir," I managed through the lump in my throat. I stepped back into the fragile safety of the yard behind the house, looked up as I crossed under my own window.

I saw no motion, no movement. Had Fanny garnered the courage to wake me?

To explain that my home was no longer my own, that I would be deprived of my family and friends? Of my own beloved staff.

My breath caught in my chest. With feet like lead, I turned to the hedges, pushed through them.

My things remained behind. My books, my father's items, my mother's journal. My respirator.

As did Fanny, Booth and his wife.

The home I'd known for seven years, the closest I had ever come to something of my own.

Yet I would not be a prisoner.

The pain inside my skin became something very real. Hurting, limping now and hunched around myself, I pushed on.

No matter what it cost me, no matter what I would give up, I *would not* be a prisoner. Not until I'd found the murderer; not until I'd forced him to beg for his life, the way I'd begged for the earl's.

I had leads to follow. A quarry to chase down. I'd begin with Sweet Tom and assure myself that he had not lied to me, and then I would follow every clue, every path, every last trail until I located the sweet tooth, the murderer.

I had no more choices left. With an ache in my chest and my throat burning as if on fire, with my head throbbing steadily in time with every footstep, I made my way once more to the docks and awaited the return of the *Scarlet Philosopher.*

In all of London, above or below, there was but one place that would take me now.

For better or for worse, I would become the Karakash Veil's collector. Their pet. Miss Black, fallen so far. Desperate for sanctuary, desperate for . . . Simply *desperate.*

Hawke, of all people, would understand. Yet as I stared down, down, ever so far down into the depths of gloomy London below the drift, I wondered: What would be the price of that understanding?

What wouldn't I pay to exact my retribution?

THE DARK MISSION NOVELS BY
KARINA COOPER

BLOOD OF THE WICKED
978-0-06-204685-7

An independent witch living off the grid, Jessie Leigh has spent her life running, trying to blend in amidst the rebuilt New Seattle. Forced into a twisting web of half-truths and lies, Silas Smith, a soldier of the Holy Order, must stay close to Jessie, the most sensuous woman he has ever seen, and follow her to the witch he has to kill: her brother.

LURE OF THE WICKED
978-0-06-204690-1

Naomi West is an agent of the Holy Order, trained to hunt the guilty and render justice. But when she's placed undercover in the gilded cage that is Timeless, New Seattle's premier spa and resort, Naomi has to go up against owner Phinneas Clarke. Phin is the most seductive man Naomi has ever met—and he may be hiding a killer.

ALL THINGS WICKED
978-0-06-204693-2

Juliet Carpenter thought of the coven as a family, but when she falls for a man who betrays them all, she's left alone and desperately searching for a reason why. When Juliet finds Caleb Leigh a year later, her need for vengeance clashes with the hunger still burning between them.

At Avon Books, we know your passion for romance—once you finish one of our novels, you find yourself wanting more.

May we tempt you with . . .

- **Excerpts** from our upcoming releases.

- Entertaining **extras**, including authors' personal photo albums and book lists.

- Behind-the-scenes **scoop** on your favorite characters and series.

- **Sweepstakes** for the chance to win free books, romantic getaways, and other fun prizes.

- Writing **tips** from our authors and editors.

- **Blog** with our authors and find out why they love to write romance.

- **Exclusive content** that's not contained within the pages of our novels.

Join us at
www.avonbooks.com

AVON

An Imprint of HarperCollins*Publishers*
www.avonromance.com